Meg Henderson

was born in Glasgow, spending part of her childhood in Drumchapel, on the outskirts of Clydebank. She is a journalist and the author of *Finding Peggy*, a memoir of her Glasgow childhood, and the novel *The Holy City*.

From the reviews of *The Holy City*:

'*The Holy City* is a novel about growing up in the close-knit blue-collar community of Clydeside from the Twenties through to the present day. Meg Henderson has pieced together an enormous jigsaw of memories to create a vision reminiscent of a Stanley Spencer painting. The overall effect is of being at your auntie's, of listening to an enthusiastic storyteller, of the fascination of taking a microscope to seemingly ordinary lives, seemingly mundane situations and bringing them into dramatic focus.'

Scotland on Sunday

'An enchanting tale of a remarkable woman from Clydebank, whose sometimes heartbreaking, sometimes hilarious but always mesmerising memories of the wartime blitz on her beloved town stay sharp half a century later, giving her the strength and the courage to meet everything that life throws at her.' *Scotsman*

'A hard-hitting but hilarious novel.' *Clydebank Post*

'This marvellous debut is packed with characters whose grittiness and passion transcends poverty and tragedy.' *Options*

'A hugely absorbing story. Henderson brings the horror and pain of these wartime experiences vividly to life with vigorous humour, common-sense wisdom and vitality.' *Observer*

'Meg Henderson mingles fact and fiction to moving effect – her account of the Blitz on Clydebank and its aftermath is harrowing.'

The Times

BLOODY MARY

Meg Henderson

Flamingo
An Imprint of HarperCollins*Publishers*

Flamingo
An imprint of HarperCollins*Publishers*
77–85 Fulham Palace Road,
Hammersmith, London w6 8jb

www.**fire**and**water**.com

Published by Flamingo 2000
9 8 7 6 5 4 3 2 1

First published in Great Britain by
Flamingo 1999

The Author and Publisher are grateful to the Glasgow Museums:
The People's Palace for permission to reproduce the photographs
on pages 328 and 329; and to the *Glasgow Herald* for permission
to reproduce the photographs on pages 330 and 331.

Photograph of author © Scotsman Publications Limited

ISBN 0 00 655027 4

Set in Bembo

Printed and bound in Great Britain by
Clays Ltd, St Ives plc

ACKNOWLEDGEMENTS

Acknowledgements are always difficult, because putting a book together can be like working on a committee. The whole picture builds up so gradually that it's often hard to say which bits of information came from where. You mention something you've been told to someone else and they come up with another bit to add on. When the whole thing eventually comes together, hopefully you can't see the joins, but you also can't remember exactly where the component parts came from. And, inevitably, there are some people who are convinced that they recognize members of their own families among the characters and write pompous, self-righteous letters, demanding the withdrawal of the book forthwith, over the 'obvious' references to Uncle Fred or whoever, even though Uncle Fred and I have never made each other's acquaintance. I'm told this is a compliment, but it's really a damned nuisance, so anyone out there who recognizes a relative within these pages, please don't write to me. I warn you now that my Granny's Irish Curse is dusted down and ready for action, and it never misses.

There are others, too, whose little human foibles have been utilized, but who shrink from the limelight. Like Bunty, whose interesting reaction to the slightest drop of the demon drink is well known to everyone in her small community, but not to the world at large, and that's how she'd rather keep it. For my part, I wish she'd step forward and take a bow for coming up with something more entertaining than the usual boozy, tearful rendition of 'My Granny's Hielan' Hame'. My good friend Joe Docherty, on the other hand, an indestructible Bankie now happily settled in Auckland, New Zealand, is no shrinking violet. Joe is a man of fiercesome intelligence who was born in an era when work, not education, was considered good enough for the working classes. Now in retirement in Takapuna, he haunts the libraries educating and entertaining himself, and he is a constant source of many a good tale, some of which crop up in this book while others will be kept for another time. Joe's life is a perpetual learning curve, and one day I must write a book about Ancient Egypt to use up all the knowledge his most recent efforts have uncovered.

There are others, though, who have provided more factual information: Craig Shaw, formerly ADO with Strathclyde Fire Brigade; Professor David Walker and Bill Craig, Deputy Chief Registrar at Martha Street Registry Office, Glasgow, who both gave me information about marriages in Scotland's pre-Registry Office days; and John Carmichael of Media nan Eilean for his advice on the Gaelic language. Marylka Banasiak of *The Scotsman*, cat-lover and good friend, donated both her name and advice on matters Polish, and my other pal Harry Dunlop, curator of the St Mungo Museum, as ever gave me his time and his boundless knowledge of Glasgow, providing straight factual information on the city's past, interwoven with his usual mixture of hilarious anecdotes and opinions, much of it, alas, too scurrilous to use! And Sylvia Jamieson, theatre administrator at the Ramshorn Kirk, who went out of her way to get me whatever bizarre information I asked for, including persuading someone to climb the steeple for the cause, Roddy MacKenzie, Assistant Archivist at Strathclyde University, and Winnie Tyrrell of the Burrell Collection, who both spent time seeking out photos for me. Thanks also to Eric McKenzie, latterly of Barnardo's, for kindly allowing me to use his extensive knowledge of what passed for local authority childcare in days gone by.

And almost lastly, the thread running through this book is, I hope recognizable as the influence of Dr A. Cameron MacDonald, to whom this book is dedicated. He has been the Cam, beloved – and I have used that word in its truest sense – of generations of medics in Glasgow because that is what he has been. Cam it was who instilled caring into the caring professionals who were fortunate enough to come within his radius, and our patients in turn benefitted from what we learned from him. He taught us to look beyond the textbooks and the technology and to see our patients and ourselves as human beings, and never to be afraid of our instincts and emotions, and he did so with great humour. I first encountered Cam when I was eighteen years old, and out of all the medics I worked with, the good, the bad and the infamous, it is still Cam who stands head and shoulders above them all.

And finally, my thanks to all the Glaswegians I have met along the way, who, to my delight, constantly prove that however impersonal modern relationships become, at heart Glaswegians remain the same. To prove this I offer the following entirely factual account of one day in the life of an author doing research. Familiarity, I have found, doesn't so much breed contempt as ignorance. For instance, though I was born a stone's throw from George Square and spent much of my childhood playing in and around that area, I realized I had never really looked at the statues. Oh, I could describe them, tell you which one was most likely to be adorned with a traffic cone, but I had no idea who they were. So one day, after doing a spot of shopping, I set off for the square, carrier bags in one hand, notebook and pen in the other. Within seconds I had my first companion, asking 'Whit ye daein', hen?' Now I know better than to claim to be a writer; writers are Jackie Collins, not some wee wifie with carrier bags, so I replied that I was engaged on 'a project'.

By this time several citizens were looking over my shoulder as I wrote, and following me from one stone worthy to another. 'She's writin' doon the names o' the statues,' one informed the other, and in no time a growing crowd was busily engaged on what had started out as a solitary quest. I tried discreetly muttering 'Bugger off!' and 'I've changed my mind', but they were oblivious to insult, they were enjoying themselves. There were frequent, good-natured cries of 'Did you know *he* was here?' and 'My God! Ah never knew Rabbie was there tae, by the way!' 'Christ! Ah wouldnae've believed auld Walter Scott was oan tappa that big yin in the middle!' Soon we had become a convention, and though I was only strictly interested in the statues bordering one side of the square, I was dragged off to record fascinating stone personages elsewhere, everywhere. And all the time they were telling each other stories from their childhoods, all starting with the immortal line, 'Ah mind when Ah was a wean . . .', tales their mothers had told them, things their grannies swore were true. As I left they were still there, a little band of Glaswegians touring the square, trading discoveries and memories, each one a stranger to the others until some wifie working on 'a project' arrived with a couple of carrier bags, notebook and pen.

These days people mind their own business and think it better to avoid eye contact with strangers, far less conversation, and I had thought that must apply to Glasgow too by now. But I was wrong; Glaswegians, it seems, are still Glaswegians after all, and concepts like privacy are not part of their make-up. And there's no escaping their interest or their contributions to situations that have nothing whatever to do with them. Glaswegians themselves already know this, but to people from Edinburgh and other even more foreign parts who may not, I offer this advice: take a deep breath and just go with the flow, it's far easier on the nerves – by the way.

For Dr A. Cameron MacDonald,
the beloved Cam to generations of Glasgow medics,
guru, colleague and above all, friend.

1

On Eilean Òg, an island off the north-west coast of Scotland, Betty Craig sat by the porch window of her son's home in the shadow of Beinn Alasdair, watching the newly arrived swallows swoop over the fields in pursuit of insects. Every autumn when they left she wondered if she would still be here the following spring when they came back again, and every year she was surprised when she was. They arrived gradually, first a few, then soon the whole lot, flying down the glen in that glorious way that only swallows knew, as though they flew for the joy of the thing and not just because they had to. Back to Beinn Alasdair they came, to mate, lay eggs, raise their young and then return to Africa. Once, a pair had constructed a nest in the coalhouse outside; a tiny thing it was, built of mud and twigs, and she had brought in the coal herself rather than let the children do it until the birds had successfully reared their brood. And even after they'd gone, all through the following winter the abandoned nest had remained attached to the wall of the coalhouse, so that every time you saw the tiny mud cup you could picture them skimming over the fields again in the sun, even though the ground was hard with frost.

It was how she had counted time when she was a child, not by weeks and months, seasons and years, but by the arrival and departure of the swallows. It seemed to Betty that she had spent her entire life waiting, counting time by the swallows, without being entirely sure why, or indeed what she was waiting for. But it couldn't be long now, there couldn't be too many more swallow migrations to count. Around her the family was clearing up after yet another 'surprise' birthday party. Yesterday she had been seventy-nine, and today she was eighty years old; it was surprising how much difference that made. And still there was that sense of waiting. She knew fine when it had started. It was during a time she couldn't clearly remember, a time when everything was vague and blurred, and there were only feelings rather than memories.

She had come to Eilean Òg some time in the 1920s, when she was around the age of four or five, maybe even six; no one had kept note. But the vague, blurred time pre-dated that. People said the old remembered long ago better than yesterday, but she knew there had once been a time when she could recall more than she could now, she was aware of having forgotten things and people she wished now she could remember. Often she had sat as she did now, with a tiny scrap of a memory, trying to link it to other scraps to make a whole, to remember what she once knew. It didn't work, though; her half-remembrances would slip away through the corridors of her mind before she could catch them. It was like trying to hold on to a fast-moving burn as it rushed to the sea before your eyes.

There was a feeling, an atmosphere, that she associated with a female presence, though she couldn't say why. Not a particular woman, she couldn't picture a woman, but there had been someone there, and she felt that someone had been female. Then she'd vanished, but the feeling of her once being there remained, still did sometimes. Sometimes when you were warm in your bed, when you wakened early and knew you could lie there for a while longer, cosy, safe and snug, it was that kind of feeling. Then there was a time of being anxious, of being not so much alone as without someone, a cold time. And there was the boat, she remembered being on the boat for a long, long time with a man who wore a black coat and hat. There were four other children on the boat too, three boys older than herself and a younger girl, children she didn't know any better than the man; she knew that even before she understood why they were all travelling together. They weren't part of the feelings she had of the time when the woman had been there, they didn't belong together. The people around them on the boat were speaking strangely, she didn't know what it was at the time, only that she didn't understand what they were saying. Alec, the eldest of the three boys, whispered that he thought they were Germans, but one foreigner was as good or bad as another as far as she had been concerned.

She looked around the cottage at her family. It was times like this she tried to work it all out, when she looked at them, children, grandchildren, great-grandchildren, all of them stretching forwards, but no one backwards or sideways. There were no parents, sisters, brothers, aunts, uncles or cousins in her life, it was as if her existence related to no one until she had married, as though she had only become a person then. And that was true when you thought about it, though it shouldn't bother her after all these years. But it did, it always had. If the vague blur that she remembered from before hadn't been there maybe it wouldn't have bothered her, but the fact that it was there meant she had existed in another time and somewhere else, that she was a person before Eilean Òg.

When they had come off the boat all those years ago they were tired and cold, and there was no light anywhere; she had never seen blackness like it. Though Eilean Òg was one of the bigger islands off the Scottish mainland, with over 3000 inhabitants, it didn't have electricity for a long time. Someone had taken her and the other girl, Martha, and put them on a bus, and when they arrived where they were going it was just as black. They couldn't see where they were walking, so they held hands, each hoping that the other wouldn't fall and bring them both down. Then they were taken to a kind of wooden shed where there were two beds. Martha was younger than her, and she cried throughout that first night; Betty just waited.

No one explained anything, they had no idea where they were, why, or how long they were expected to stay. The next day Martha stayed behind and Betty was taken to a tiny school where everyone spoke the way the people on the boat had.

She couldn't understand what they were saying, but she quickly felt that she was not welcome here, that she was not one of them. Back wherever she had come from, she had gone for a short time to a big school with a sea of children wherever you looked, and for the first time she realized she had felt one of them, because now she knew what it was to be an outsider. In time she came to understand that she was a 'boarded-out', that she was indeed an outsider and would remain so all of her life. No matter how long she lived on Eilean Òg she would never be completely accepted, and she wasn't sure if she wanted to be anyway. Deep inside herself she held on to the conviction that she belonged somewhere else, wherever that warm, safe feeling had been, that one day she would go back there. She never did, of course, but whenever the islanders treated her badly she clung to her conviction that she wasn't one of them, nor did she want to be. She belonged somewhere else, some-where better.

The 'boarded-outs' were destitute or orphaned children from the poorest areas of Glasgow, shipped out to whoever would take them in the Highlands and Islands from 1770 to the 1970s. There was a story that a man would set out from Glasgow heading north in a car crammed with children, and at every house he came to he would ask if they wanted a child. When every child had been taken he returned to Glasgow for another cargo of helpless humanity. There was no vetting; anyone who was prepared to take a child could have one, or two, or three. Some people made 'boarded-outs' their main source of income, because Glasgow Corporation paid a fee for every child to what was called the carer. That made Betty laugh. Some children did indeed find good, caring people to live with, but no one bothered whether they did or not, and many did not. They were lifted from one life and deposited into another with no explanation from anyone, least of all the Glasgow Corporation officials who organized it, because it was thought to be 'better' for them.

Many had simply been slaves. Throughout their childhood

4

Betty and Martha had worked on Fearann Ban, White Farm, doing back-breaking work more suited to men than children, and they had slept in a shed. In the mornings they would be woken early and sent to work in the fields before school, and on the way back they wouldn't dare take their time or stop to play, because there was more work to be done in the fields or with the animals. And if there was a moment's pause, when the harvest was in, or the beasts were fed and milked, and they thought they could draw breath, Mistress Campbell proved them wrong. Mistress Campbell, the lady of the house, had been an incomer too. She had come to the island as a school-teacher, and while she was still admiring the scenery, before the realities of island life sank in, she had married Jim Campbell, the biggest landowner. In the early days she had seen herself as the bringer of culture and sophistication to Eilean Òg, an ambition that the islanders quickly frustrated. So while Mistress Campbell came to terms with the harshness of her new life, or didn't, her husband drank and chased women, both without losing any status in the eyes of the God-fearing islanders. They knew he had been like that all his days, as had his father before him, and as would the sons that came after him, all born to island women while his wife produced three daughters. That he was an arrogant, disreputable, coarse individual there was no doubt, but he was a native and he had money. As far as the islanders were concerned his wealth alone qualified him to sit on God's right hand, and being a native islander absolved all sins.

Over the years Mistress Campbell became a bitter, humiliated woman, who looked down on the island and its inhabitants and took her anger out on anyone she considered her inferior, which included the entire island. She refused to learn the language or become a farmer's wife, busying herself in trying to keep beautiful and stylish, in a desperate kind of way. Once, when she was young and still had high hopes of life she must have been a bonnie woman, Betty thought. But in truth the passage of time had nothing to do with the awful, demoralized look in her sad blue eyes; it was all down to her isolation on Eilean Òg, even if it had been voluntary. The poor woman had probably expected to lead a happy life as the lady of the manor, respected and admired by the simple people she had agreed to live among, but what she didn't know was that an outsider was always an outsider on Eilean Òg. Maybe that was why she tried so hard to stay young, refusing to give up on her looks; maybe she still hoped acceptance and happiness would happen this year, or next. In time, though, she had acquired a defeated air, her features trying and failing to remain taut and pretty, despite layers of perfectly applied make-up, and her blonde locks looking more and more false and out of kilter with her once-attractive face. Mistress Campbell spent her life arranging bridge parties and playing golf with a few similarly bored, resentful, rich, women friends, trying not to acknowledge that everyone on the island knew what her life was really like, or that they laughingly called her '*A' bhean uasal*' – Her Ladyship. Looking back, it had almost been possible to feel sorry for her. Almost, but not quite. Her Ladyship could always be relied upon to find something to do for the two little girls she was supposed to care for. Betty and Martha had calluses on their knees from hours spent kneeling on the wet, filthy farm courtyard, scraping grass from between the cobbles with a nail for instance, because Her Ladyship could abide neither grass nor sloth.

Betty used to wonder why the three Campbell girls who lived in the big house didn't work in the fields too, why it was only her and Martha, but she gradually absorbed the social structure; they were only slaves, the Campbell girls were the daughters of the slave owners. Fearann Ban was the biggest farm on the island, and there the boarded-outs worked unpaid, indeed were paid for. Betty used to laugh wryly when she thought back at how the boarded-outs were probably the first form of farm subsidy. And it didn't matter that she and Martha were only children, because they were better off there than where they had come from, or so they were frequently informed down the years. The two alien children ate together in the cold scullery while the Campbells ate in the warm kitchen. The

6

family ate real food, while the two little girls were served scraps. 'They had the chicken,' Betty would tell her own children many years later, 'we had the bones and the skin of the chicken.' When the man in the black hat and coat came back once or twice a year to see how they were doing, he told Betty and Martha that they were very lucky to have two meals a day, and a good, kind lady like Mistress Campbell to look after them. They were children all alone in a foreign land, how were they supposed to reply to that? So they didn't. They simply accepted their lot, but deep inside Betty the conviction that this was wrong, that she was due better, persisted.

At school the teachers and the island children laughed at the boarded-outs. Children everywhere could be cruel, of course, that was what the native islanders said these days when you mentioned it, but the children only repeated insults they heard the adults express in their homes, that was how Betty saw it. She knew they were being insulted long before she knew what was being said, but Martha had a year or so before she started school to pick up the Gaelic language, so although she faced the same taunts, she at least understood them from the start. It didn't help, of course, that Glasgow Corporation sent clothes parcels twice a year to the boarded-outs, clothes that never quite fitted either the children or their situation, so that their differences were even more apparent and easy to laugh at. Even where children were placed with decent people, and there were many, the 'them and us' mentality persisted for generations. After the Second World War, when a monument was being put up in memory of the fallen from the island, the native islanders refused to allow the names of the boarded-outs to be carved on the stone too, even those who had lived and worked there since the age of two or three. Yet you saw those same islanders going to and from church every Sunday, with their pious expressions and their devotion to the Bible. And perhaps more to the point, you also saw the ministers, and the ministers saw you and the way you lived, yet they did and said nothing. Good Christian people every one!

Betty had lived on Eilean Òg for over seventy years, she had family were there, all the family she knew about, anyhow. And as visitors never tired of saying, it was a beautiful place, full of gently sloping hillsides, dramatic mountain ridges, romantic glens, and silvery sands leading down to an azure sea. There was nowhere quite like Eilean Òg; it was acknowledged as the jewel in the crown of Scottish islands. Even if rain fell more often than the sun shone, they would say, look what they got in return, all that lush greenery, and the high waterfalls gracing every glen, falling like liquid crystal. The islanders were so lucky to live in such a beautiful spot, well away from the noise and pollution of the city. Well, visitors could fantasize about Eilean Òg all they wanted to, but given her time over again, given a free choice, Betty would not have wanted to live there. From her very earliest days on the island, she would stand looking out across the sea to the mainland in the far, far distance, and if the night was especially clear and crisp she might catch a glimpse of the bright, twinkling, shimmering lights gleaming on the horizon. She didn't know where those lights were, or what that place was like, but she wished she could be there all the same. There should, she thought, be a higher court somewhere where appeals could be heard, and if she ever found it she would plead that there had been a mistake. She would say that this was not the life she had been intended to live, or the place she was meant to live it in, and she would request another lifetime somewhere, anywhere else, in compensation.

The days and nights of working in the fields had robbed her not only of her childhood, but of her education; learning wasn't easy when you were so tired you fell asleep at your desk and were then wakened to face the tawse for doing it. Hard labour and poor nourishment had a bad effect on young bodies too, which was why she ached so much that it became a part of who she was very early. But some were worse off, the ones who had to collect kelp from the shore while the tide was out, to put on the fields as fertilizer, for instance. Working for years in wet conditions, shovelling wet kelp, had crippled many boarded-outs; you saw them hobbling about painfully on sticks or in their wheelchairs these days, and had to turn away to hide the tears of pity, and anger too.

But Betty had been fortunate, even if the word did make her smile. While Donnie Fraser, the youngest of the boys on the boat with her that day, had gone to live at the other end of the island, the others, Alec Craig and his wee brother Will, were taken in by Ishbel and Murdo Young at Fearann Creag Ruadh, Red Rock Farm. Ishbel and Murdo had no children and had worked their small farm together all of their married life, tending to the milk cows, planting, sowing and reaping the fields, but they were getting too old to manage alone, and from the start they had regarded Alec and Will as their sons. They were the other side of boarding-out, good, caring people, and they looked after Alec and Will well and fed them better. Red Rock was a few miles from White Farm but Betty met the Craig boys at the island school every day, Alec four years older than her, and Will, a shy lad as red-haired as Alec was dark, ages with herself. The three children had the shared experiences of travelling together on the boat, as well as being laughed at in school in the strange language they didn't understand, and that bond between them never weakened.

Hunger was ever present in Betty's life in those days, her thoughts were always of what she wished she could eat, and Alec would bring food from the croft when he could. They would hunker down in a corner of the schoolyard at playtimes and he would give Betty whatever was left over from the night before, or whatever he had been given for a playpiece. Years later, when she told Ishbel Young of those days, the old woman had tears in her eyes. There had been no need for Alec to sneak food out of the croft; had Ishbel known how Betty and Martha had been treated by Her Ladyship she would've fed them herself. But Alec and Betty were just children then, children who had learned early that they had to rely on themselves and each other. They had no control over what the adults would do next, so they couldn't take any chances, not even where the kindly

Youngs were concerned. In the kitchen at Red Rock Ishbel and Murdo made sure there was always plenty of food, in fact there was too much, but they say giving food is a form of affection, and the Youngs were very fond of their boys. Not that they didn't have to work on the land and with the beasts as well, but they weren't slaves, they were members of the family. Alec and Will had love, that was the crucial factor, the factor entirely missing from her own childhood on the island, though she sensed that it had not always been the case. In her years at White Farm, though, there was never any love.

2

When the boarded-outs reached the age of sixteen they were usually taken back to Glasgow, after spending years in as different a culture as anyone could imagine. It wasn't the one they had chosen, but it was the one they knew, and for many the upheaval and transplanting back into cities they didn't know was as traumatic as being boarded-out all those years before. The same thing would've happened to Alec, but the Youngs had started paying him a wage as a means of keeping him with them at Red Rock. Will was never farmer material, though. All through his years on Eilean Òg he had escaped to the sea whenever he could, doing anything that would get him on to a boat. Once he had done his chores on the farm you would find him down at the harbour, helping the fishermen unload their catches, repairing nets, or messing about in the tiny sailing dinghy old Murdo had helped him salvage and rebuild. It had always been his avowed intention to join the Merchant Service as soon as he could, and when he turned sixteen he did just that, rather than be sent back to Glasgow. The Merchant Service was a traditional occupation for the men of the Western Isles, it was either that, the fishing or the land, and few ships on the seven seas were without at least one Scottish islander on the crew.

The Youngs could see that Alec and Betty were close, so when she became sixteen, a few months after Will's departure, they took her in and gave her a home too. A year later Martha was sent from White Farm back to Glasgow and never heard of again. Betty often wondered what had become of her, but she understood why Martha had never been in touch again, why doing your damnedest to forget about Eilean Òg might be the best way of coping with it at all.

The Youngs were the best people she ever knew, and by the time Betty went to live at Red Rock they had more than earned their retirement and Alec was gradually taking over the running of the place. He and Murdo built an extension on to the main croft where the old couple could live, helping out when they felt like it, but ever careful not to interfere in what they saw as Alec's farm. The extension was whitewashed and the outside door and windows painted a bright red to match the main steading, and outside a rowan tree was planted, to ward off evil spirits. The roof was constructed of sheets of galvanized, corrugated iron, because tiles had to be imported from the mainland and were expensive, but the plan was that some day it would be replaced with tiles. There were roofs just like it all over the Highlands and Islands, waiting for better days that never came, the corrugated iron gone orange and perforated with rust over the years. But Red Rock wasn't one of them, Alec and Betty saw to that.

When Alec and Betty married in 1936 Red Rock officially became theirs. She had been eighteen years old, and how she loved passing White Farm and Her Ladyship, with her nose in the air. She was Mistress Craig now, a married woman with her own farm instead of a slave, and she enjoyed treating Her Ladyship with all the contempt she had earned. It was inevitable that she and Alec would marry, and she was convinced that they would've ended up together anyway, even if they had met in Glasgow by chance. He was a good man, she couldn't have done better, and she wouldn't have anyway. Boarded-outs didn't marry islanders, they were tainted and considered not good enough, and so if they stayed where they had been delivered to, they married their own kind. And that suited Betty; she had no love for the islanders anyway and no wish to be one of them. She didn't belong, and she took pride in that.

Before they could get married Betty and Alec had to find their birth certificates, which meant a visit to Glasgow, the first time either of them had been off the island since arriving on that cold, dark night long ago. It was early April, the quietest time on the farm apart from winter, but in winter there would be more gales to disrupt the boat sailings. Everything was organized and double-checked. The crops had been planted with harvest time still three months away, enough peats had been cut and stacked to dry, and more than would be needed placed by the back door so that Murdo and Ishbel wouldn't have far to walk and carry. For the two or three days they would be away the old folk would see to the milk cows, feed and water Elsie and Daisy the horses, and keep an eye on the place. Alec had arranged for the milk tanker driver to call into the farm, so that Murdo wouldn't have to take the full churns to the top of the road. They had thought of everything, but still, they were anxious not to be away for longer than necessary.

In 1936 the boat called at the island only three times a week, and it took four hours to reach Oban, which seemed incredibly big and sophisticated to them. Having no distinct memories of their earliest days, everything they saw seemed to be a 'first'. They stayed in lodgings in Oban that night, and on the Thursday morning boarded the train from Oban to Glasgow, the first train either of them recalled seeing apart from in newspapers, a big black, LMS engine, pulling maroon-coloured carriages for another four long hours. They arrived at Buchanan Street Station and walked out into the noise and bustle of the big city, into a land where there were pavements on both sides of every road, where the roads were wide and had tramcars running in both directions along the middle, and buses, lorries, cars, horses and carts and street lights, and more people than they had ever seen. There was so much movement and noise that it was hard to take in even a bit of it at a time, because all your senses were being assaulted with so many foreign sights and sounds at once, and everything moved so fast. And the people were dressed in what on the island would've been regarded as Sunday best, though it was only Thursday, wearing hats and gloves as though that was what they always wore. And they talked differently too. Out of defiance Betty had always made a point of thinking in English and speaking it as often as she could, but she now realized that either the Glaswegians had acquired an accent or her English had, because she had to strain to understand them as much as they strained to understand her. But it was the noise more than anything that she noticed, so loud that she had to force her voice to be heard above it, and her ears to hear.

Eventually they found their way to the Registrar's Office in Martha Street, then discovered that they had gone the long way round, meandering up and down unfamiliar streets when they could have walked straight there from the station in minutes. Inside the office they gave the clerk behind the counter what they knew of their beginnings, that they had been born in the city, their names and dates of birth. Then the certificates were produced, and in the space where it said 'Father' was written 'Unknown' on both. It had cost them five shillings each to find out that they were bastards. So that, Betty thought, was why she had been shipped off to Eilean Òg as a slave. Alec seemed unconcerned about his discovery, it was what he had always assumed anyway, but for Betty it changed everything. She would not have any island minister smirking at them, congratulating himself on being right all along, using something of which they were blameless to justify the way the boarded-outs had been treated. She would, she decided, be married in Glasgow or not at all. They approached the clerk behind the counter once again and asked the procedure for marrying in the city. There was only one way, he said. They would have to put up their banns and remain in Glasgow for three weeks, then marry in a church. But they couldn't stay in the city for three weeks, they explained; old Murdo was looking after the farm, and at his age he couldn't manage for more than the few days they would be away. Besides, they had nowhere to stay and though they had saved every penny they could afford for nearly two years to make this trip, they would never have enough to live on for three long weeks in the city. The clerk looked around and then beckoned them closer. There was, he said, lowering his voice, another way. He took a piece of paper and wrote down the name and address of a solicitor in Argyle Street, then quietly slipped it into Alec's hand.

In Scotland in 1936 there was no legal alternative to a religious marriage, but a blind eye was turned to irregular marriages. A couple could walk into any solicitor's office and ask to make a declaration of marriage in front of two witnesses, and then the solicitor would take them before a sheriff, to 'confess' that they had entered into an irregular marriage. The sheriff would 'fine' them three shillings and issue a warrant, which they then took to the Registrar, who would register the marriage, thus making it legal. There were no banns, no three-week wait and no minister involved, and the practice was so widespread that for some solicitors it was their main source of income. Those who couldn't afford the fee for their marriage certificates had them retained by the solicitor, to be redeemed when they could pay, and in decades to come, when solicitors went out of business, their safes were often found to contain roll after roll of ancient, unpaid-for certificates.

It was to one of these solicitors that the clerk sent Alec and Betty, no doubt receiving a small consideration from the solicitor for sending business his way. Eventually irregular marriages were so common that the authorities decided there had to be some means of controlling the business, and so civil marriages in register offices became legal in 1940. Civil ceremonies had already existed for some seventy years in England, but the churches had a stronger grip in Scotland than south of the Border, and their influence took longer to overcome.

In Argyle Street Betty and Alec went into the first jewellers' shop they came to, trying to give the impression that this was the very one they had in mind all along, and bought a narrow, gold, wedding band, engraved with an orange blossom pattern. Their determinedly casual air evaporated when they didn't know the difference between nine- and eighteen-carat gold, and the salesman, recognizing an easy mark when he saw it, sold them the more expensive eighteen carat. Then they set off for the address of the solicitor on the piece of paper Alec had been given, all the while worrying that the clerk had been teasing a couple of teuchters, and wondering if they would be arrested and sent to jail the moment they opened their mouths. Instead they were asked to wait for ten minutes, then ushered into the presence of the solicitor whose name was on the piece of paper in Alec's hand, a rotund little man wearing striped trousers, a black jacket, a waistcoat with a gold fob watch, a white shirt with an impossibly stiff-looking collar, and on his feet, grey spats. Two witnesses wandered in as though they did this every day, which indeed they did, and watched as Alec and Betty self-consciously declared that there was no lawful bar to their marriage. The ring with the orange blossom pattern was slipped on to Betty's finger, the witnesses disappeared back to work, and in one swift movement the little man in spats quickly ushered them outside and along the street to the nearby sheriff court. There they were 'fined' three shillings by a sheriff who didn't even bother to glance up at them, and within minutes they were back outside. The rotund solicitor relieved them of a further five shillings, handed them a piece of paper and sent them back to Martha Street, where the same clerk issued a marriage certificate. And that was all there was to it. They had come to Glasgow for their birth certificates in order to arrange a wedding at some later date, and within two hours they were man and wife. Outside in Martha Street the two young people stood looking at each other and laughing nervously, Betty twisting the ring on her finger. And all this time later she still smiled at that memory, though in the sixty years and more since she first wore her wedding ring, a working life at Red Rock had long since worn away the orange blossom, leaving a plain gold band on her finger.

Afterwards Mr and Mrs Craig had wandered towards the city centre, not sure what to do next or where to go, and because they were unsure of their sense of direction and unused to the place, they found that they were walking in small circles and ending up back at the same spot, which made them laugh at themselves. They had been warned that Glasgow was a dangerous place, so they concentrated on being alert, and not looking like over-awed country cousins. But that was difficult, because they so obviously were and, try as they did, they couldn't stop staring. They walked about the city, making great efforts to look as though they knew exactly where they were going. Just past George Square they spotted a tobacconist's shop on the corner. The street sign high above the shop door said St Vincent Place. The air inside was heavy with the mingling aromas of tobacco and the predatory looks of the salesmen, but Alec was determined to take back some pipe tobacco for old Murdo Young. Bravely he approached a salesman who advised him to buy two ounces of Sobranie, and they left, not quite sure if they'd been conned. On the other side of the street stood tall, impressive buildings, two of white stone and one in the middle, of red sandstone. They marvelled at the carvings and the height and beauty of them, wondering what kind of people were inside and what they could be doing. If this was where they worked, what, they mused, could their houses be like? Then they turned left down Buchanan Street, struggling to keep their excitement in check at walking along legendary streets that few on the island would ever see, and trying to memorize every detail, because questions would be asked when they returned, especially by the other Glaswegian boarded-outs. So that Ishbel wouldn't feel left out they stopped at a grand shop, where Betty bought two handkerchiefs, with flowers embroidered in one corner and framed by a little edging of cotton lace. They were arranged in a box, gold at the bottom, clear plastic at the top so that the fancy detail of the handkerchiefs could be admired. Ishbel would, she knew, never use them, but she would keep them where she could see them and show them off to visitors.

It had been an odd wedding-day, but she was glad it had happened as it had, she decided. In Glasgow, far away from Eilean Òg, so none of the islanders could dance at her wedding even if they wanted to – and they always wanted to, she thought darkly, if drink was involved. Like all the boarded-outs she had always been inferior in their eyes, but by not following their marriage traditions *she* had rejected *them*, and when she and Alec returned as newly-weds the islanders would know this and be in no doubt about how she felt towards them. When they got back they would have a ceilidh with Murdo and Ishbel and invite the other boarded-outs. It hadn't been the wedding they would've planned, to be sure, and their one regret was that Alec's brother Will hadn't been there to act as best man. But Will was on some ocean on the other side of the world most of the time anyway. Apart from that, looking back it was a perfect wedding-day, the finest they could have had.

They couldn't return to the island till Friday so they found cheap lodgings, and though they had both the ring and the certificate to prove they were man and wife, they still expected someone to burst in and tell them they had no right to be in the same bed. Next day they took the long journey back to Eilean Òg, and since then they had left it again only once or twice more, for visits to Oban when finances allowed, but never again to Glasgow.

They belonged to Glasgow because it was the city of their birth, but they knew that they didn't belong in it. They had spent most of their lives on the island and were used to island ways, if not island mentalities; to her dying day Betty would never accept the attitudes and petty prejudices of the islanders. A rage simmered there and coloured the rest of her life, that people with less decency and humanity than Glasgow bastards should look down on parentless children and think themselves above them. To be sure then they didn't belong to or in Eilean Òg either, they only lived there. The truth was that they didn't belong anywhere, they were misfits with no roots, condemned to exist somewhere they didn't want to be, because there was nowhere else. And though that didn't bother Alec, gentle, easy-going Alec, it bothered Betty deeply and always would.

As they walked around the city during their unplanned wedding trip, in Betty's mind the questions and turmoil had whirled. She still didn't know who she was, and it still mattered. It was

1936, she had come out of her childhood slavery better than most boarded-outs, and here she was about to start a new life with the good man who was smiling shyly by her side, as they walked along arm-in-arm. Alec was her future so she should be able to put the past behind her, a past she didn't know and one that anyway obviously had no use for her. There shouldn't be a cloud in her sky, her new life with Alec should be enough for her, she knew that. But God forgive her for the ungrateful bitch that she was, it wasn't enough. Sitting in the porch at Red Rock, the remnants of her eightieth birthday party being cleared up behind her, she adjusted her gaze from the swallows outside to her reflection in the window in front. She looked at the white-haired cailleach staring back at her. She was a very old woman now, and it still mattered. It did matter.

3

It was raining again. Well, of course it was raining. If there was one thing you could count on in February in Glasgow it was that your parade would be rained upon, even if in Helen Kowalski nee Davidson's case it was her hair-do. As she had left the office in St Vincent Place two hours before, to keep her appointment with Rita Rusk in West Nile Street, she had still been asking 'the big question', even after what seemed like a lifetime of debate, discussion and musing. To tint or not to tint, and if to tint, what colour? She just wanted a change, that was all, it had nothing to do with those stray grey hairs. They were unfair at her age, to be sure, but she wasn't one of those vain females who tried to pretend she was younger than her years, her fifty years very soon in fact. There, she had said it, and the world hadn't stopped turning, not a thunderbolt in sight. Mind you, if as part of her transformation, as a by-product, so to speak, those unfair grey hairs got covered too, well so much the better. If you said it often enough, she decided, it almost sounded plausible.

She had left the car in the overpriced multi-storey car park in Mitchell Lane. One of these days she was going to challenge someone about that. £1.80 per hour was extortionate, but it was the car park nearest to the office, and as her droll daughter Marylka remarked, because of the price you rubbed bumpers with a better class of poser there, you fair drowned in Mercs, Porsches and BMWs with personalized number plates. Marylka always laughed when Helen got annoyed at being ripped off. 'If you've got it,' she'd say, 'what's wrong with laying a bit of it around?' And it wasn't as if she had the classic excuse of having come from a poor background where every penny counted; on the contrary, long before she was born her grandfather, Old Hector Davidson, had made sure no one in the family would ever be short of a bob. But still, she hated being cheated, being treated as a soft touch. If she wanted to give money to anyone or any cause, she would do it, but she objected to the assumption that she should let it be taken from her just because she was a Davidson, and everyone in Glasgow knew the Davidsons had it to give.

When she left the office the snow of the last few days was melting quietly in the sunlight, but now that she had emerged freshly tinted and coiffed, the God of Getting Even with Mean Rich Bitches had pulled a fast one. As she climbed into the taxi the wind was concentrating on every strand, opening up pathways where the rain followed gleefully. She caught sight of herself in the taxi's rear mirror. 'Oh God!' she thought. 'It's too light! What have I let them do to me?' When the taxi reached the office she dashed out and into the old building, hoping she wouldn't meet anyone she knew. If she did they would look at her and smile, but when they got to their offices they would say 'Saw Helen Davidson in the lift. She's joined the Desperate Old Women's Blonde Club!'

As she went into her office her longtime secretary Annie looked up.

'What do you think?' Helen asked, as though she'd had a major nose job in the last couple of hours.

'It's nice,' Annie said. 'It suits you.'

'Suits me? What do you mean?'

Annie laughed. 'I mean it suits you, it's a flattering hair-style!'

'You're not just being nice because the colour looks different?'

'Is it? I never noticed.'

'Och, of course you noticed! It's too light, isn't it? I didn't want it this light, from brown to platinum for God's sake! It's a mess, isn't it? Mutton dressed as lamb!'

'Helen, it's nowhere near platinum! Stop exaggerating! It's

fine,' Annie protested. 'Better than fine, lovely. I wouldn't have noticed it was a different colour if you hadn't mentioned it. Nobody would notice, it looks like you with a new hair-do, that's all.'

'I don't look as though I've joined the Desperate Old Women's Blonde Club then?'

'The what?'

'You know, those old birds you see with so many facelifts their ears meet at the back of their heads, and hair that's ten shades blonder than nature could manage?'

Annie started laughing again. 'You'd think you were eighty this year instead of fifty, Helen! Behave yourself, your hair's gorgeous, *naturally* gorgeous! You're talking as if they'd made you a real brassy blonde with dark roots. You won't be mistaken for a working girl from Blythswood Square, don't worry!'

'You're sure?'

'I'm *sure*!'

'Right. Fine. OK. Any messages?'

'A couple on your desk. The one from Rabbie sounds important, but then Rabbie always does, doesn't he?'

Poor old – young – Robert Burns, the family's esteemed solicitor, there couldn't be a day of his life went by without someone thinking they were the first to call him Rabbie. He had once made the mistake of letting this slip when Annie was around, and from then onwards he was Rob to everyone else, but Rabbie to Annie for annoyance's sake.

'Did he say what it was about?' Helen asked. She knew what it was about, what she wanted from Annie was an alternative, but Annie shook her head.

'I did ask in case it was something I could help him with,' she said innocently, 'but he went that frosty way he does.'

'I think that's because you keep calling him Rabbie.'

'I know,' Annie sighed. 'The poor craitur doesn't have his sorrows to seek, does he? I don't know how he stands it, boring bugger!' She looked up at Helen and grinned. 'You go in and I'll get you a coffee. Buzz when you want me to get the great man on the phone for you. I hope you've tipped off Marylka about the incipient, insipid candidate for her hand by the way?'

'Annie, Rob's not after Marylka, that's all in your mind!'

'He is! Fate worse than spinsterhood it would be too!'

'Never mind your flights of fancy –'

'Fancy? Sure, who'd fancy him? That's the point!'

'– are you sure about the hair?'

Annie lifted a telephone directory and pretended to take aim with it.

'OK, OK, I'm going!'

Rob wanted to speak to her about Auntie Mary's will, she knew that, or rather the letter Mary had left for Helen with the will. Trust Auntie Mary to leave her in this position! The trouble was that three years on she still didn't know what to do about it. The old woman's estate had taken this long to wind up, so that had provided a breathing space. Now something would have to be done, but why had Auntie Mary decided she was the one to do it? Why hadn't she left this can of worms to Young Hector to unravel instead? She knew why, of course; Young Hector was Helen's father, so who knew better than her? He was a nice man, a quiet, almost sad man; Young Hector had been defeated long ago by his own father, Old Hector. Helen suspected that he had been a sensitive character all his life, which naturally made Old Hector think of him as a weakling; everyone knew that her grandfather had battled all his days to make his son what he regarded as strong. In doing so he had all but extinguished the gentle soul the boy had been, so that there was nothing very much left there now.

Young Hector was no businessman, indeed it looked sometimes as though he was deliberately trying to destroy everything his father had created. The joke in Glasgow business circles had been that the Davidsons had gone from rags to riches and back again in one generation, until Helen had largely taken over the running of the family firm and put it back on a course Old Hector would have been proud of. This left her father with as much to do as he wanted, which wasn't that much. These days he seemed to wander aimlessly, doing this and that not very enthusiastically, passing time till he was carted off by the under-taking wing of the family empire, and laid to rest beside all the other Davidsons in the crypt in the Necropolis. Sometimes she wished she could do or say something that might help him live the life he had wanted, but in her heart she knew it was too late. And anyway, the sad truth was that she didn't really know him well enough. She, like her father, had been produced to keep the family line and its business going. Young Hector had done his duty, even if he had failed to provide that all-important grandson for Old Hector. There was no more closeness between her father and herself than there had been between her father and his; they were simply business assets. So Mary had been right to leave this task to her, because she too knew that Young Hector wasn't particularly imaginative; he wouldn't understand something like this.

She thought for a minute then buzzed her secretary. 'Annie, could you get hold of Marylka at the hospital, please? I've a feeling she's Receiving Physician today. If she is, tell the switch-board that it's a personal call, and leave a message asking her to call me. I'll be at home tonight.' Marylka would know what to do, she decided. How she had produced this logical, practical child she had no idea; those genes must have been donated by her father, along with the Slavic cheekbones. She should have discussed this with Marylka before now, but the girl was always so busy and so tired. Sometimes she wondered if she would have been better off in the business than being a doctor, but she didn't wonder seriously. Marylka was her one triumph, Marylka had escaped and done her own thing, the mark of Old Hector hadn't blighted her daughter's life as he had Young Hector's and her own.

The phone rang.

'Helen, you were right,' Annie said. 'Marylka's Receiving Physician today, so I've left the message with the switchboard.

I said it wasn't urgent, you just wanted to discuss something with her. Is that OK?'

'Fine, Annie.' Helen looked at her watch. Quarter to three. 'Annie, I'll return a few of these calls then sneak off early and do some shopping. Could you try Rob first, please?'

The phone went through the regulation clicks and bleeps, then Annie came back on. 'He'll be busy with clients till five, Helen.'

'Oh, well. Look, tell his secretary that I'll be in touch tomorrow, after I've discussed the situation with Marylka.'

She put the phone down. 'Mary,' she thought wryly, 'Bloody Mary indeed! If ever anyone was well named it was her, and here she is, still causing all this hassle, even from the grave.' And in her mind she heard Auntie Mary chuckling with mischief.

Mary was Helen's great-aunt, her grandfather's younger sister, and if you listened to Old Hector she was 'the thorn in my flesh'. He said it as though everyone had two arms, two legs and one thorn in their flesh; it just so happened that his thorn was his sister Mary, who was close enough not to be ignored. He called her 'Bloody Mary' with more of a touch of disapproval and exasperation than dark humour; Old Hector was a demon businessman, but he never was big on humour. And yet, looking at the angelic old lady, no outsider would have believed him. That, Helen Kowalski, nee Davidson, used to say with a smile, was where Auntie Mary had him beaten every time and she knew it; an expert in the art of psychological warfare, Mary.

Auntie Mary was Helen's childhood, that was the only way she could put it; childhood was Mary and Mary was childhood. When she let her mind wander back to those seemingly carefree days of endless sunshine that probably never existed, Mary was there, Mary *was* that sunshine. A tiny, graceful woman – no, *lady*; Mary was a lady all of her life – always dressed in the black of her post-Victorian childhood, from the polished toes that peeked out from under her ankle-length, high-buttoned coat, to the shiny, black straw hat perched on top of her snow-white hair. The hat supported a liberal covering of brightly coloured artificial fruit; Helen would laugh quietly at the memory, the Carmen Miranda of Duke Street. Helen used to wonder if she had a standing order for the exact same outfit. Somewhere in a Glasgow store – a Davidson store, of course – there stood a wardrobe filled with Auntie Mary outfits, and whenever she needed a new one it would appear, complete, at her door. She loved the old woman's rebellious streak and the fact that she never, ever, gave in to Old Hector; she had even outlived him by five years. It was a fear that haunted him even before he had gone, and Helen remembered one particular conversation between them that had started half-jokingly, but ended in a strange tenseness. What stuck in her mind was that it ended on a hint of something dark, something secret, an impression she had picked up on more than once after that first time, probably because she had been alerted to it. They were in the sitting room of the big house, Old Hector and his sister arguing with each other across the fireplace as they sipped their tea, a scene that was commonplace.

'My reputation·will be destroyed if she outlives me. She'll be badmouthing me the minute I'm gone!' Old Hector complained.

'Reputation? Phaw! What's the difference?' Mary replied. 'I badmouth you now, and I don't think death will change a miserable old teuchter like you for the better, do you?'

'I wouldn't worry,' Helen said, joining in with the banter, 'the Davidsons live so long we'll need silver bullets to make sure you've really gone, Grandpa.'

'Silver bullets are for vampires!' Old Hector replied.

'I know, Grandpa!' Helen laughed.

'Aye, that's you all right!' Mary chuckled. 'A blood-sucking old bat!'

'And don't you think I don't know where the girl gets her smart mouth and her lack of respect from!' Hector shouted at his sister.

'Och, be quiet, you miserable old teuchter. Respect is for them that earns it, not them that can only buy it!'

'And don't call me a teuchter!'

'Where were you born?' Mary asked quietly.

'I've lived in Glasgow for more years than –'

'Where were you born, Hector Davidson?'

'You know fine well that I was born in Oban, but –'

'Thank you,' she smiled smugly. 'So I'm not a liar after all. You *are* a miserable, blood-sucking, old teuchter! Whereas I,' she continued, directing those bright eyes at him, 'was born in Weaver Street in the Calton, and I'm proud of it!'

'You only say that because you think it annoys me,' Old Hector spat at her. 'But it doesn't! If you're happy to be scruff, then I'm happy for you.'

'Scruff, am I? You'd do better to watch your own smart mouth, Hector,' Mary replied icily. 'You just remember there are things I know that prove who's scruff in this family, things you don't want me to tell whether you're dead or alive!'

'What things?' Helen asked, but the atmosphere had changed in the blink of an eye.

'Just things,' Mary replied, and turning that fierce gaze once again on her now silent brother, she said pointedly: 'He knows what things.'

When she had a child of her own Helen had called her after her old aunt; Marylka was a Polish name, but it was still Mary, and a sleekit stab at Old Hector. Auntie Mary was a subversive, she thought fondly, and made all the more so by her looks, but it was Mary's eyes that she remembered: bright blue, twinkling eyes that showed every emotion. Mary was a lady in the best sense of the word, a lady of grace and impeccable manners, no matter what coarse circumstances or individuals she met, but you always knew what she was really feeling because her eyes betrayed her best intentions. The eyes, she always thought, of a closet romantic whose true nature was only revealed with a look.

Mary had lived on the top floor of a tenement at the corner of Duke Street and Sydney Street, in the east end of Glasgow, since the days when the area was considered upmarket, and she stayed there out of defiance, long after Old Hector had made enough to house her in the south side compound that he gradually added to as the family grew, a home more suitable for a Davidson. She had moved into the tenement on her marriage at the age of eighteen to Captain Ferrier of the Merchant Marine, who was no more than a name to Helen, a shadowy figure rarely mentioned. When Mary gave birth to Millie after eighteen months of marriage, it was instantly obvious that the child was 'not right', and Captain Ferrier had taken to the high seas, never to be heard of again. The family version was that he was a rat who had deserted his young wife, leaving her to care for his mentally handicapped child – and let there be no mistake, the child was *his*; there was nothing of that sort on the Davidson side. Whatever rogue gene had made the child 'not right' was obviously a weakness from the Ferrier side. Mary talked of him only once, when a five-year-old Helen had asked what Millie's daddy had been like. Mary, as she always did, thought for a moment before replying. 'He had a moustache,' she said. The words were spoken with quiet decorum, but the look in her eyes said something else, something deep and dark, and Helen remembered staring at every mustachioed gent she encountered for a long time afterwards, wondering 'Is he Captain Ferrier?' And thereafter Mary's words became Helen's secret putdown; anyone she didn't like 'had a moustache', even if he didn't, or if 'he' was a 'she'.

So as far back as she could remember, Helen had the feeling that Mary wasn't exactly distraught at the disappearance of her husband of barely more than a year. She had often thought of herself in the same position, ironic, really, when she thought of her own experiences lying up ahead in wait for her to inhabit them. Wouldn't she have scoured the earth trying to find him? Wouldn't she have been distracted with grief, or at least seem to miss him? But Mary did neither, or perhaps that was simply

Helen's perception because the event had happened, and was done and dusted, long before she was born. There had only been Mary and Millie; Captain Ferrier was never part of their life together. But still, over the years there were times when Helen wondered aloud about him, wondered why he had gone and what had become of him, this man with a moustache she had never met or seen a picture of; she had never even heard his Christian name come to that. She wondered if maybe the family had been right. Millie's handicap may well have come from the Ferrier side, and perhaps his guilt, his anguish about that, had made him take off into the blue – or perhaps he was indeed a rat, just as they said.

But then Helen had her own reasons for turning the disappearance of Captain Ferrier over in her mind, even if in her case she knew what had become of her own absent husband. Jan Kowalski had left Helen and gone to Australia when Marylka was barely three years old. He was a young Polish academic who had fled Warsaw as Russia's iron grip tightened, and he was studying at Glasgow University when he met Helen. He was good at getting out when the going got tough, Marylka used to say. So young and so cynical; was that her nature, Helen would wonder, or had she done that to her only child? Old Hector had fought hard against her marriage to Jan; he had had higher things in mind for the heiress to his fortune. But Helen was twenty-four and she had taken the precaution of not taking precautions; she was pregnant. 'There was no way Old Hector could have a bastard in the family,' Marylka used to say with a wry grin. 'One was enough. Him.' So Hector had accepted the situation, on the outside at least. After all, Helen could be carrying a son, and if not she was still young, and next time round he'd make sure the right sire had been selected – once this foreign interloper was out of the way, and he would make sure of that.

Jan Kowalski was a means of escape; deep down Helen knew right from the start that she was using him. She had married in an attempt to get away from the family, and he had provided a different identity as well as a different life. If it had worked out, well, that would simply have been a bonus. But being an outsider he had no idea how tenacious and destructive the Davidson connection could be, and eventually he had given Helen the choice of breaking the family stranglehold and going with him, or staying in Glasgow, alone with their child, and Helen's rebellion couldn't stretch quite that far. There was also a theory, floated by Auntie Mary, that Old Hector had paid Kowalski off and purchased a divorce, thereby ensuring that Helen, her future child-bearing prospects and his money, remained within his control. By that time he had come to terms with the awful fact that Young Hector would never provide him with a grandson. Helen would inherit the business and the money, and he didn't want any of it going outside the family, and hopefully she would have a son by that time. 'He did the same with me, even if no money changed hands,' Mary said. 'I was married off at eighteen in case I went to the bad and gave him a showing up that affected his ambitions. And once I had a child with no man and no money, Hector had me trapped.'

Just like Captain Ferrier, Jan Kowalski made no attempt to contact Helen and their daughter again, nor they him, though they knew where he was. Whenever his name was mentioned Marylka would say curtly that she neither knew nor cared what had caused him to leave, nor what had become of him. Whether her father had taken Old Hector's shilling or not, he had deserted them; in her eyes he wasn't a real man, and one sperm fulfilling its biological function didn't make him her father in any meaningful sense. He had nothing to offer her that she wanted. Anyway, she couldn't remember him, and thought of him only when Helen brought him up; either way she considered him as big a coward as Captain Ferrier.

To make matters even on the missing husbands score, Old Hector had his own theory about his sister's desertion by the seafarer, one he repeated in times of Mary-induced stress, that no normal man could be blamed for running away from his sister. She was a beauty in her youth, no doubt about that, and she was family, he would say, so who would know better than him what a trial she could be, and was, all her life? Anyway, Mary and Millie managed perfectly well without the absent mariner, giving no impression of missing him, and there was the family money to keep them from poverty. Old Hector, for all he was driven to distraction by 'Bloody Mary', made sure she and her child wanted for nothing. That was his trap.

But there again, who knew what happened when Mary was alone in her bed at night and what tears she might have shed when no one could see or hear? Who knew indeed what facts Mary had kept to herself that might have explained the mystery of Captain Ferrier's disappearance? When she was a child, Helen would say, she accepted the only picture of Mary that the old lady presented, but as she grew up she realized that there must have been more than she saw, more than she or anyone else was intended to see. Mary was surely a woman like any other, with the same emotions, hopes and dreams; who knew what hurts and secret sorrows she hid behind that carefully crafted facade?

4

Mary and Millie were a familiar sight in the centre of Glasgow, the tiny, genteel, black-clad matron and the six-foot Millie, never apart and always 'up to something', as Old Hector used to say. They would wander the streets, Mary with a book of some sort, rummaging around parts of the city Old Hector thought she shouldn't know about, far less visit, discovering the history then insisting on sharing it with everyone else. And Millie was always by her side, towering over her – the height must have come from Captain Ferrier's side too. Millie was always beautifully dressed in pastel colours, her mother's unconscious acknowledgement of the child who never grew up, and she wore gloves and a tiny hat with a band of artificial flowers that ran from ear to ear across her huge head. She must have had that same hat and matching gloves in every pastel shade, and she was never without a small, pink Bakelite box, whimsically shaped like a beehive, that hung over her arm from a strap. From the beehive ran a thin line of wool, linking it to her latest mystery under construction on two thick knitting needles, and as Mary made yet another discovery about the origins of Glasgow, Millie knitted. All through the years Millie had been knitting, no finished article ever appeared; it was the act of knitting that mattered, not the final creation. Helen used to tell a story of when she was very little. She had looked at the long piece of work hanging from the needles, and innocently asked Millie if she was knitting a cardigan. 'No!' Millie replied loudly, pulling a face that suggested the question was offensive as well as stupid. 'A scarf, well?' Helen had persisted. Millie turned away from her sourly and continued knitting in furious silence. 'Socks? 'Cos if it's socks you have to turn for the heel —' Millie's huge head suddenly came down level with her own small one. 'Mind your own business!' she shouted. 'Cheeky bizzum!' and returned to her knitting.

Millie was not noted for her good humour. It was as if the world and its inhabitants were a curious burden to her that she kept at arm's length by being grumpy, and she undoubtedly had reason for doing so. The world was not a welcoming or accepting place even in the nineties for anyone who did not conform to what was regarded as the norm. Inside the family she was protected, but the world outside that Millie had to brave every day in the 1940s and 1950s must have been considerably less sensitive. It had taken Helen some time to become aware of it; Millie was after all just Millie, part of her family and therefore unexceptional. Indeed if Old Hector assumed everyone had a thorn in their flesh, it was his granddaughter's natural belief that everyone had a Millie too. There was a story repeated so often that it almost fell apart with distress, of how Helen had asked a friend at school which of her family was handicapped. The child had replied that none of them was handicapped, and Helen had put her hand on the child's arm in sympathy and asked 'Why not?'

Gradually Helen had been included in Mary's excursions into Glasgow, something Old Hector allowed only because at that time he hadn't given up hope of having a grandson, and girls weren't of too much importance to Old Hector. One day, as Mary, Millie and Helen were returning to Duke Street, a crowd of boys spotted the incongruous little trio. 'Daft Millie!' they shouted. 'Here comes Millie the Daftie!' It had apparently been the worst shock of Helen's young life, coming suddenly face to face with a side of Mary and Millie's life she had never had any reason to suspect existed. Mary totally ignored the sniggers and abuse and engaged in polite conversation until they were safely upstairs, and once there she made no reference to what had happened, then, or ever. But Millie was upset and confused by a scenario that she obviously faced frequently, and once safely inside the house Mary reached up to her enormous, persecuted daughter and embraced her. It was an oddly comic, yet heart-rending scene, that Helen carried in her mind for ever and described frequently, stopping to bite her lip at the pity of it. The memory was so often recounted that Marylka almost felt she had witnessed it too. Tiny Auntie Mary on tiptoe reaching up to comfort her hurt child, while the child stooped down to be comforted. For Helen, that day was the start of her suspicion that carefree, endlessly sunny days were perhaps an illusion. And just how, she had wondered over and over again, could Mary explain to the innocent Millie that the ignorant people who taunted her were not worth bothering about? Millie was a child all of her life, and children have a very good grasp of what is fair and what is not. They also know that mothers are there to defend them, to protect them from unfairness. Any child being openly persecuted would expect their mother to step in and stop it, to banish the persecutors and send them off chastened, with a flea in their ear. Mary did the right thing, the sensible thing in ignoring Millie's tormentors, of that there was no doubt. But did Millie ever under-stand that, or did she feel as let down by her mother as she had been by mother nature? And of course it made matters worse that Mary had small, delicate features and a dainty demeanour, whereas mother nature had made Millie not only handicapped, but of a size and plainness that ensured she had no hiding place; poor Millie was a very obvious target.

Despite her lack of mental agility she had instincts, though, and like any wounded creature she sensed that the best means of defence was to attack first. So she had become used to treating any word spoken to her as hostile, and she shot down every approach, just in case. Her guard only came down if you gave her wool. The best, the only present you could give Millie was a skein of wool, a long, many-layered loop that had to be wound into a ball by hand. Only then would you see her eyes light up, and an oddly touching smile crease those broad, unbecoming features, almost rendering them pretty. Even when she was too young to understand why, that smile caused a sharp pain some-where inside Helen, as if an invisible hand had reached deep within her and twisted her soul for a fleeting second. Millie would instantly abandon her current work in progress and press someone into holding the skein open across stretched arms, so that she could convert the wool into a more manageable ball. Being on the skein end was a laborious task. The wool rubbed against the inside of the thumbs as it unwound, so that you ended up almost with two tiny friction burns on the soft skin between the thumb and first finger, and your arms grew increasingly tired, until you found yourself swaying from side to side, in an effort to speed up the process of winding the ball. You learned very early that there was no real way of refusing Millie this service. Once the operation had been completed she would remove the top of the little bee-hive, insert the ball, replace the top, then pull the wool through a hole at the front, to be incorporated into whatever it was she was knitting.

When she was a child Helen used to worry about Millie, that there was nothing she could do for her, until she saw the joy in her eyes at another skein of wool, and thereafter she would look around for yarns of exotic colours and textures to offer as gifts. Sometimes Millie would take the proffered gift with an air that suggested that she was far too busy to stop knitting, and anyway, she really had more than enough wool, but she would take it for your sake, as long as you were aware of the fact. But once it was in her hands she couldn't keep up the pretence and her face would beam with happiness and excitement. Once, when Helen was knitting a hat for her doll, she had experimented with different colours. Two stitches in blue, four in white, another two in blue, and much to her surprise and delight she looked up to find Millie watching her intently, entranced at what she was doing. There the two of them sat, at Mary's big, polished table by the window, high above Duke Street, the small girl teaching the huge, but much more childlike Millie the subtleties of creating patterns with colour, Helen desperately trying to preserve the moment by keeping to the rule that Millie was really doing her a favour. Thinking back, that moment had given her more joy than almost anything she had ever achieved in the rest of her life, either in the family business or in her personal life, apart from Marylka that was. She often smiled wryly at that thought. 'You see the kind of mother you have?' she would laugh not quite convincingly to her daughter. 'I peaked at the age of eight!'

And these days there were yarns that had never been thought of when Millie was still busily knitting, wools with silver threads, sequins and shiny, contrasting strands and textures, all of them in ready-made balls. And long after both Mary and Millie lay together in the family crypt, the sight of those fancy yarns could bring tears to Helen's eyes. 'Imagine the smile on Millie's face if you gave her that!' she would say. 'She would've been so happy to have it.' It was so sad and unfair that Millie's life had consisted of so little; nature and fate had cruelly mistreated her. Apart from everything else, her size had made her slightly intimidating, especially in a city and in an era of very small people, and the irony was that there was nothing in her to frighten anyone. All her days she had been an outsider, an odd, crotchety, unattractive creature. But she had been a simple soul with a blameless heart, and somehow a cheated one too.

The Davidsons had come to Glasgow from Oban in Argyll, on the west coast of Scotland, towards the end of the 1800s. As far as anyone had been bothered to find out, Old Hector's father had earned a reasonable living as a draper there, though both he and his wife Elizabeth had come from farming stock. What had prompted him to uproot Beth and their young family was lost somewhere in the distance, but the traditional west coast fishing industry was in decline at that time, and it was likely that no one had the money to buy his wares. Like many before and since, he hoped for better prospects in the city, and when the family arrived in Glasgow he found a cramped home in Weaver Street for them and immediately set himself up in a one-man business. Every morning he would set out from the room and kitchen in Calton with his suitcase full of drapery, odds and ends and basic household goods, knocking on doors trying to interest housewives in the contents, and every night he would come back and carefully count the coins he had made. He had a vision of the future and plans to make his family rich, and if in the meantime that meant they barely scraped by, then so be it. Old Hector and his brothers, John and Albert, were all born in Oban, and after the family settled in Glasgow Lizzie was born, then finally Mary. To the end of her life Mary would disparagingly refer to her brother as 'a miserable teuchter', because it drove him insane, 'teuchter' in Glasgow meaning a particularly stupid Highlander.

As soon as the children could walk they were pressed into the family 'business', an experience that would affect them all in different ways, though probably none as profoundly as Hector, who was the eldest. He was at heart a country boy, raised in a small community, used to knowing and trusting everyone he met, and he hated tramping around the slums of Glasgow, being accosted by drunks and attacked by hard people the likes of whom he had never encountered at home. Those early experiences in Glasgow made him the man he would become, a man scared and disgusted by poverty and determined to climb as far from it as he could.

Whether that first Hector did the right thing by his family is a question no one can ever answer. It was immaterial whether his dreams of a better future justified the harshness and empty bellies of a foreign city that his children grew used to. That was what they got, and only their own efforts would change what they got in the future. He made sure that the boys were as educated as he could afford, and for that, constant hunger was the price he chose to pay, but his family paid too, including the uneducated girls, and they had no choice in the matter. It seemed that as soon as he got some money together he would spend it not on the basic needs of his wife and children, but on something else for the empire that lived in his mind's eye, for the future. The highlight of his achievement was the lease of a small grocery shop in Parliamentary Road, off Castle Street, that would open all day, selling whatever people wanted in whatever amounts they could pay for. Not that the first Hector lived to see it. On the day that his son and namesake put down the deposit on the premises the old man lay dying of cancer of the throat in the house in Weaver Street, and on the day of his funeral the rites were carried out without his eldest child, because he had a business to run.

Throughout his life Old Hector Davidson would recount this tale as a demonstration of his tenacity and determination to succeed; he didn't see it as an affront to his father, but rather as a tribute. His father would've understood and approved, he said, he would've been proud that he had put the security of the family before sentiment. And later, when he was a rich man, he had his father's body, and also his mother's, exhumed from the Calton Burial Ground in Bridgeton and re-interred in a splendid family crypt in the Necropolis. He had more than done his duty by his father.

Every time he told the story, which he did often, he would look at his small granddaughter for admiration, but Helen never knew whether she felt it. She in turn would look at Auntie Mary, who would sit with her lips pursed, not looking at her brother till he finished his tale, before turning the full gaze of those eyes on him. She didn't have to say a word, it was all there in her silent look, and Old Hector saw it, heard it, and felt the thorn dig deeper into his flesh. Once, when she was about ten years old, Helen was taking tea in the Duke Street house after one of her excursions with Mary and Millie, and she asked the old lady if she thought her grandfather had done the right thing.

'Who knows?' the old lady replied diplomatically.

'You don't think he did, do you, Auntie Mary?'

Mary considered her reply for a few moments, as though this was the first time she had ever turned the matter over in her mind.

'Maybe he did,' she said finally. 'The thing you have to understand, Helen, is that your grandfather is a miserable old teuchter. He doesn't like it when I call him that, but he knows I'm right. But it was that miserable old teuchter who built the business up and made the money that keeps us all. He uses it to control us too, but that's another matter, and when you're older we will talk of that too. But what I say, Helen, as you ask, is that he should not be proud of selling pats of butter as his father was lowered into his grave, he should feel the worst sort of pain about it. He should feel maybe that he had to make the choice he did, but it was a terrible choice and it should have bothered him and made him angry all his days. That's what I think, and the miserable old teuchter knows that too, because I've told him often enough.' Then she beamed a smile of kindness and love at her great-niece and offered her a rock cake. Beside them Millie kept knitting.

Mary's function in her brother's life had been as his conscience. Whatever deals he did, however successful he became, that sharp twinge of pain reminded him of where he had come from, and even though he didn't want to remember, Mary ensured that he did. Mary was the embodiment of that old Glasgow leveller, 'Ah kent his faither.'

Old Hector was a distinguished figure, not tall, because men of his generation lacked the diet to make them grow, but he had a pugnacious air that made him seem bigger than he was, made him memorable even decades after his death. And there was that glorious full head of steel-grey hair, by the time Helen was born in 1948 at least, when he would have been fifty-eight years old, and blue eyes like Auntie Mary's, but with the mercurial facility for registering emotion missing, or perhaps suppressed. Even when he smiled it never quite reached his eyes. As his fame grew Mary would look at his photo in the newspapers, either marking some business success or handing over a donation to some worthy cause – which in reality was business too, and she would sniff and say quietly 'Mmm, I see he's wearing his picture smile. I think it's the only one he has anyway.' But to Helen there *was* an expression in his eyes, if not of joy then of an honest emotion at any rate. It was so obvious to her even when she was a child that she assumed everyone saw it, so she never thought to mention it. It was fear; fear was the dominant strand in Old Hector's character, it was in his eyes and in every aspect of his life.

But to outsiders he was an impressive man, always beautifully and expensively dressed in the finest clothes, that he somehow wore as though freshly donned only minutes before, and he carried that insistence on perfection till the end of his days. Old Hector was the kind of man who only felt comfortable in the presence of other rich men wearing equally expensive clothes. Everything he possessed had to be of the very best quality or he felt that he was slipping back into the days he didn't want to remember but couldn't forget, the days he felt chasing him and catching up, no matter how successful and wealthy he became. He wore a heavy gold pocket watch on a thick chain, a diamond tie-pin, and on his left hand a pinkie ring, with a large, oval ruby in a claw setting. His cufflinks and his cigar case were heavy gold too, bearing the Davidson clan crest and specially made to his instructions in London. His feelings of inferiority made him prefer the London mark, signalling that he was so rich, so important, that his own country had nothing to offer that would adequately reflect his elevated position. Old Hector's insecurity would always outstrip his achievements, no matter how high his empire and his stock rose.

Helen would go through many stages of feeling about her grandfather as she grew up, from childish adoration all the way to loathing and hatred and back again several times, a range of feelings she suspected he had about himself. He could be arrogant beyond belief, ostentatious, manipulative, insensitive and sometimes vulgar in his pursuit of wealth and position, but it wasn't really to impress others. He didn't really care what others thought – apart from Mary, of course – he was impressing himself, reassuring himself that he had made it out of the Calton, that perhaps the Calton had never really existed except in his nightmares.

Those days of knocking on doors had shaped his brothers' lives too. Neither John nor Albert wanted anything to do with the family business when their father died, which at that time only consisted of the shop in Parliamentary Road. John went into merchant banking, starting as a clerk and working his way on to the board with typical Davidson application and drive over the years, and Albert departed for New York and went into shipping. When she was small, Helen had assumed that they were both looking for Captain Ferrier; after all he was in the Merchant Marine and John and Albert sounded like they had connections with both, or so it seemed to her. She spent a long time expecting the imminent arrival of the reprobate with the moustache, but she was never to meet either him or Albert, who obviously preferred to delete his early years; his life started when he landed in America. John was a cold, serious character she saw in the distance at family functions, talking to her grandfather about money, the favourite subject of both men. Apart from Mary, the only other Davidson was their sister Lizzie, who had been a nurse in France during the First World War and had died at the age of twenty-six. Helen never asked what had happened to her, she simply accepted the fact that people often died young in those times.

The Calton days had marked the men of the family in one way, it seemed, and the women in another. The men felt revulsion and turned away from it, while the women had somehow faced it and somehow deliberately embraced it. Great Britain was at that time the richest nation on earth, yet people lived in squalor all their lives and high infant mortality was the norm, with most families losing several children. Lizzie had been so affected by the disease and sickness in Glasgow at the turn of the century that she had become a nurse as a result. This was against Old Hector's wishes, but as she was a female what she did didn't matter very much, as long as she didn't bring any shame upon the family that might affect business. And what Old Hector regarded as 'the bad old days' held no horrors for Mary either. She loved Glasgow and related easily and naturally to ordinary people. She spent her entire life delving into the history of the city, gleefully digging up the past, Helen said, quicker than old Hector could bury it, and perhaps because he wanted to. It was Mary's self-imposed duty to pass on the kind of details that her upwardly mobile brother did not want passed on, the kind that all children find fascinating.

'Lizzie was a good lass,' Mary would always say, her eyes glistening. 'She was my big sister and she was the best. One day, Helen, I'll tell you all about Lizzie. She was called Elizabeth after my mother. My mother was always called Beth; she was a saint of a woman. Her and my father, their people were farmers in Argyll you know, but my father wanted better for his family than toiling on the land. Your grandfather talks about him and sometimes he mentions my mother, but he never talks about Lizzie.' Mary would stop, the silence stretching, before saying in an odd voice that Helen never forgot, 'And he has his reasons.'

'What reasons?' Helen would ask.

'Oh, his own,' Mary replied. 'One day you'll know and you'll be able to judge, but not now, you're too young.'

'And what happened to Granny?' The word came uneasily from her lips, because it implied a certain intimacy with someone she had never known and could barely envisage.

'She nursed my father in the Calton house till he died,' she said. 'Then three months later so did she. It seems she had TB all the time she was nursing him, and when her work was done she died too. Or maybe it was a broken heart.' The old lady smiled sadly. 'There's precious little love in this family, Helen, but theirs was a real love story.'

She produced a photo Helen had seen often, a postcard-sized, sepia-tinted portrait of a woman wearing a long skirt with a bustle and a high-necked blouse. It was obviously taken long before the flight to Glasgow, in the more affluent Oban days.

'That was my Mammy when she was sixteen,' Mary said. 'Wasn't she a beauty?'

Helen took the studio-posed photo, as she had many times in the past, and stared at the serious, shy-looking young woman standing to the side of a chintz-covered chair, her hand resting on the back. She had a strong face and hair pinned up in a bun, no beauty at all till you looked at her eyes. They were Mary's eyes, with the same gentle expression in them that Mary's had now, looking at her mother's photo.

'Aye,' Helen said, deliberately using a word her grandfather considered to be slang, and that Mary loved to use when talking to him. 'Granny was a beauty, Auntie Mary.'

Over the years Old Hector added to his business, buying shops and property and moving the family to ever bigger, ever more exclusive addresses in his determination to get as far away from the early days as he could. He engaged a chauffeur to drive him to and from his impressive offices in St Vincent Place, where only the most moneyed entrepreneurs could afford to base their businesses. The chauffeur's name was Stewart, and Helen had clear memories of the years he drove her grandfather in what in time became his vintage Rolls. When Stewart finally died his son took over, and later drove for Young Hector, Helen's father. It was only then she discovered that the man she had called Stewart all her life was in fact Mr Stewart, that it hadn't been his Christian name. He had been in Old Hector's employ for over forty years and he had never once been called by his Christian name, if anyone knew it. Her grandfather had bought and paid for a servant in uniform with one name, but Stewart – Mr Stewart – had a wife and family, and away from his driving duties he had a life, though until his son took over from him in the employment of the Davidsons, no one had thought of him as anything but the one-dimensional character in the front of the Rolls.

It was an odd thing growing up and finding that life wasn't what you thought it was. By degrees it came into sharper focus, and you began the painful discovery that the people you loved weren't quite who you thought they were, and their clay feet became so gigantic and out of proportion that you wondered how you could have missed them in the first place.

5

There was something deliciously naughty about slipping out of the office early. She had hardly done anything all day, apart from the hair of course, and she wasn't sure if she could live with that yet. The squally wind had died down, taking the rain with it, as she looked left and right at the traffic. She knew the sequence of the lights. The traffic coming from George Square stopped, then the cars coming round the corner from Queen Street got their chance, before the wee green man crossing, or Jimmy Johnstone as he was known in Glasgow in honour of a certain Celtic FC player, gave pedestrians right of way. But Glaswegians were the worst jay-walkers in the world, they had this laid-back attitude to traffic, as if it didn't matter to them that they could be hurt or killed; that was the driver's problem. And Helen was no different; she had spent too many years on jaunts with Auntie Mary and Millie to give in gracefully to traffic. In the split second between the red light at the Square and the green light sending the traffic round from Queen Street, every Glaswegian regarded it as his and her absolute duty to run across and dice with death. They would fix the traffic with an arrogant glare, almost daring it to do its worst, then stroll on without a backward glance; it was how Glaswegians were. But this time Helen was too late, she had missed that fraction-of-a-second window and was forced to wait for Jimmy Johnstone after all.

On the other side of the road, on the corner of Queen Street and St Vincent Place, used to stand Murray Frame the tobacconist's; it was the Alliance and Leicester now. For some unfathomable reason, when they took the place over they tore out the entire interior of the old shop, only to rebuild it exactly the same in every detail to the one they had torn out. Once it had been *the* tobacconist's in Glasgow, and Old Hector would make his grand entrance every day to buy his expensive Romeo and Juliet Cuban cigars. When she was a child she sometimes visited the office with Auntie Mary and Millie, if the old lady had a bone to pick with her brother, and she often did. Anxious to get her out of earshot in case she heard some truth he didn't want her to hear, Old Hector would send Helen to collect his cigars instead; she had thought it such an honour too. It had been illegal to give children tobacco, but she was Old Hector's granddaughter so the normal rules didn't apply. She'd dash back upstairs to the office, panting, cigars in hand. In those days she thought the lift was too slow and only for old folk, and now she was one of those old folk. Standing beside her grandfather's big leather chair she would put the package on the old roll-top desk he used, and still deep in hostilities with Bloody Mary he would reach out and pat Helen's head without looking at her. The old desk now stood in the corner of what was now her office, still smelling of Old Hector's cigars. Marylka thought she was being sentimental of course, said she should burn the damn thing. Helen smiled; Marylka could be so funny. 'Look at it lurking there,' she'd say, nudging the old desk with her toe. 'Glowering and sending out malevolent vibes to the world. It's like being haunted by an evil demon, and by choice too.' But somehow Helen couldn't bring herself to get rid of it.

Just then she looked along to the Square and changed her mind about shopping in Buchanan Street, and when Jimmy lit up she turned and headed in the opposite direction instead. Thanks to the devious stunt she had pulled over her will Auntie Mary was on her mind, churning up memories that perhaps Helen shouldn't have forgotten in the first place. How long was it since she had taken that route? Years, she realized, years and years. Yet it had always been her favourite, so full of things to see and stories told by an animated Bloody Mary. She walked along the side of George Square, past statues she had known all her life; Auntie Mary was a stern tutor who demanded total recall and she must still know every statue in Glasgow. First was James Watt then, separated by a patch of garden, Rabbie Burns and Thomas Campbell at the back, with Lieutenant General Sir John Moore and Field Marshal Lord Clyde in front. After another piece of garden she came to the two enormous stone lions guarding the war memorial in front of the City Chambers, and finally Thomas Graham. James Watt and Thomas Graham were both seated, and naturally she had asked why. 'Because,' explained Mary, 'they're too old to stand about all the time, so they're allowed to sit down.' She smiled; it made perfect sense even now.

In these less respectful days the statues as often as not had traffic cones put on their heads faster than the authorities could remove them, but in her day the stone lions were the main focus of mischievous attention, and children were forever trying to sit on top of them for the joy of being chased off by the park keeper who looked after the Square and its bedded gardens. Of course the children weren't to know that the man in the black peaked cap had very probably served in at least one of the wars himself, and that to him the memorial meant something it didn't to them. She hadn't thought of it herself when she was a child, though no matter how she had pleaded with her, Auntie Mary would never allow her to try her luck against the park keeper. And now she knew why, she thought wryly.

There was a story that a shelter had been built underneath the City Chambers, behind the memorial, to save the elected members from air raids during the Second World War, while the ordinary people took their chances in Anderson shelters and huge, communal, surface shelters built in their back courts. Local government was too important, it would go on it seemed, even if there were no citizens left alive to govern. And in case a Nazi bomb should score a direct hit and demolish the civic building on top of the self-appointed elite, a secret tunnel was said to run under the road from the shelter, coming out at the two lions. Helen had no idea if any of it was true, nor did she wish to know, but she believed it anyway, because of Mary's slant on the debate. Auntie Mary didn't like councillors, she had watched enough of them queue up to be seen, or better still, photographed, shaking the hand of her brother, Old Hector. 'It's not his character they respect either,' she would say sniffily. 'It's his money and his power, regardless of how he came by either.' It was Mary's opinion that the shelter and the tunnel therefore did exist, but not to save the councillors. 'If the Germans had invaded,' she would explain with relish, 'we would've shown them the tunnel, so that they'd have run down and got those creatures first!'

To the side of the City Chambers she walked along Cochrane Street, turning right down John Street, then left into Ingram Street itself. It stood out in her childhood, a bright tapestry of memories woven around this area. It seemed odd that day after day, year after year, she had gone to the office no more than a few hundred yards from Ingram Street, and yet she hadn't thought of walking this way before. Ghosts, she thought, more ghosts than she could bear. And not just of people either, but of happy days spent with Auntie Mary and Millie, days so clear and sharp in her mind that they brought tears to her eyes as she walked along now, hearing voices and seeing scenes now gone for ever. 'Silly cow!' she chided herself, blowing her nose and looking round to make sure no one was watching her. 'If Marylka could see you now you'd never hear the end of it!'

What made it all the more poignant was that the buildings and the layout of the street had remained much the same, even if they were put to other uses these days. She crossed the road quickly and made her way to where the Fruit Market had been. The entire block had once been taken up by the market, noisy, bustling streets full of people side-stepping squashed fruit on the pavements and piles of horse dung on the cobbled streets, all combining to produce that characteristic rich aroma of humanity, slightly off fruit and the dung. Horses and carts were the main means of transport then, all of them piled precariously high with fruit and vegetables from all over the world, with the carters stopping at the door of each import company and carrying the heavy boxes on their backs inside for inspection. When she was about five years old she had gone through a phase of being frightened of the horses, she had never been able to explain why. It was something to do with the sheer size of the animals, but more especially it was the odd glimpse she got of their eyes behind the blinkers, fitted to block out the busy movements around them to stop them bolting. All the horses were allowed to see was the road directly in front of them, but they turned their heads constantly, trying to see more, snorting and neighing, and seen from a child's perspective there was a disturbing terror in those huge eyes. Not that the blinkers always worked. Sometimes a horse would take off through the crowded streets, scattering boxes of fruit that the local children scrambled to collect. All you could do was press yourself tightly against the metal and wood shutters that served as walls, and hope that one of the carters would be able to catch the animal quickly and calm it down again. Maybe that was what scared her, she thought, the feeling that the horses could suddenly bolt and no one would know when or why, and the noise of the shoes on their huge hoofs, scraping and pawing the cobbles. But she got to the point where she was unable to pass them even from the safety of the pavement. She would feel the panic rising the nearer she got, then she would simply stop and refuse to go on. And it didn't help when well-meaning people tried to reassure her by holding her up to stroke a horse, it only brought her that much closer to those terrified eyes, and the enormous head tossing blindly about. She wasn't afraid of the horses themselves anyway, other people didn't seem to understand that, but of the awful, suffering look in their eyes that no one else seemed aware of.

Gradually the fear had subsided for no more reason than it had first appeared, though the memory of it remained for the rest of her life. It was a family joke that Helen remembered only people's eyes. Ask her what someone looked like and she would describe the shape and colour of their eyes and the expression in them, though often she might barely recall their name. 'If you ever get mugged by a stark naked thug wearing just a stocking over his face,' Marylka would say, 'you'd be able to describe his eyes in detail, but nothing else.' And Helen had laughed, but she had to admit that it was probably true. Maybe, she thought suddenly, that was why she had noticed the expression in Old Hector's eyes, and had been surprised when no one else seemed to; because of the Fruit Market horses she had become sensitive to eyes. God, that would give Old Hector something to think about, a common horse, not even a thoroughbred!

She had been about five years old when her mother left Young Hector and went to live in South Africa, so the psychiatrists would probably say she had been projecting her anxiety over the separation in another direction, hiding her confusion about her parents' situation behind one she had concocted for just that reason. But what did they know? They sat there making up reasons for everything that ailed mankind, keeping themselves in a job that no one could prove was worthless, even though they knew it in their souls. She remembered no anxiety about her mother leaving; her mother had rarely been there at any time. As long as Auntie Mary was there she felt safe, and Auntie Mary always was.

She would come out of Laurel Bank, her posh West End school where rich girls went to pass their time before marrying rich boys, and more often than not the two familiar figures would be waiting for her. The only time she had ever been in trouble at school was when another green-uniformed pupil had caught sight of Auntie Mary and Millie and laughed. To Helen the tiny woman jumping up and down to catch her attention, and the huge one forever knitting by her side didn't seem odd. She had grown up with them, they were her family, but after the incident when the boys in Duke Street had laughed at 'Daft Millie', her sensitivity had been heightened and she no longer let any remark pass. So she had turned instinctively and let the laughing girl have her schoolbag across the nose, and suddenly there was blood everywhere. She didn't even feel sorry, having a talent for Art she remembered thinking 'Red looks awful with lime green'; that was all. And when she was soundly reprimanded by the Head Mistress she refused to explain why the incident had happened, so it was decided that it had all been an unfortunate accident. Violence only happened after all in the lower orders, it simply wasn't part of their culture. 'It wasn't an accident,' Helen declared defiantly. 'I meant to hit her. She knows why.' But even in the fifties it was not the done thing for a nicely-brought-up gel to admit to laughing at a 'daftie', so the victim kept quiet and the matter was just as quietly forgotten. Looking back she would laugh to herself though; Mary and Millie did look odd together, but belovedly odd, not funny odd, and she still didn't regret her accuracy with the schoolbag.

Once freed from school the city was theirs to investigate, and she remembered their visits to Harry, who ran Drysdale's Fruit Importers in the market. Auntie Mary knew everyone, though Helen was sure her friends had no idea of her connections, not at the time and not afterwards. She loved the gentle way they treated the old lady, like the way Harry placed a fresh piece of hessian from a bag of carrots across an upturned box for her to sit on. Mary would sit down graciously as though sitting on the finest Chippendale chair, ask politely after Harry's wife and family and admire the photos he produced with pride. His office was whatever slatted wooden crate he had around, festooned with pieces of paper with orders and messages written on them, and on top of another, higher box was a framed postcard-sized photo of Harry and his wife, Irene, after their wedding in the Barony Church in Castle Street.

The photo was sepia-tinted, showing a young, darkly handsome and somewhat slimmer Harry in uniform, and his bride wearing a sumptuous wedding dress and veil with a long train. By that time Helen had become aware of the divide between rich and poor people, and she knew which side of that divide Harry and Irene lived on. Auntie Mary had told her of the poverty of her own childhood, and she had explained that some people were still poor. Even though Harry had a job, if his children needed shoes or clothes, and growing children always did, he would probably have to save up to buy them, she said, or pay over the odds for a Provident check, a piece of paper with a fixed value which could only be used in certain shops. The other way was to join the list of an agent who dealt with various warehouses, and by paying whatever commission he wanted, the cost of the goods could be paid off weekly, just like a Provy check. Either way, whatever was bought was overpriced and of inferior quality, and though they knew they were being cheated, it was the only means poor people had of keeping their children clothed. It wasn't like in her house, Mary said, where whatever Helen needed simply appeared whenever she needed it. For people like Harry she knew life was still a struggle, so she had always been tempted to ask how then the bride's family could have afforded such a gown. But she never did, because that would have been bad manners, and bad manners were not tolerated in anyone, regardless of their station in life. 'Good manners,' Auntie Mary would say with quiet but firm dignity, 'cost nothing. Always treat people as you would wish to be treated yourself.' And Mary always did, with the exception of Old Hector of course, he was due no such courtesy because he showed it to no one else. But Harry, she remembered, didn't once comment on the fact that she was wearing the uniform of a school where the yearly fees would have been at least double his annual salary. Harry was a gentleman who accepted her as Mary's niece, and who treated her with kindness. When she mentioned this to Auntie Mary she was told this was because Harry had breeding, and that had nothing to do with money. 'Look at Old Hector,' Mary would say with a dismissive sniff. 'No matter how much money he spends he'll never be a gentleman. Breeding can't be bought.'

When it had been established that Harry's wife was happy and healthy, and his children thriving and doing well at school, Mary would then ask about business, which was his chance to bring out whatever fruit had just arrived from foreign parts. What Helen, a post-war child, didn't realize at the time of course, was that fruit was still a luxury, even years after the war had ended. And there, in the presence of Auntie Mary and Millie, she had been privileged to sample the produce of countries she knew only from her geography books. Bananas were prizes, as were what Harry called blood oranges, and even though the name had been changed to a more acceptable ruby oranges in later years, Helen still couldn't bring herself to eat one. There, surrounded by boxes of fruit and steeped in that distinctive over-ripe smell that permeated the entire Fruit Market area, she had tasted fresh figs for the first time, and coconuts, and pineapples and pears, as Harry stood at her side, waiting anxiously for her opinion. They would share a cup of tea, and as he and Mary discussed the events of the day, Helen would wander through the storehouse examining the boxes stored floor to ceiling, putting her in touching distance with the universe.

When they left Drysdale's, carrying brown paper bags filled with apples, oranges and whatever else was in season and available, they would walk further along to the Central Division Fire Station, where yet another cup of tea was accepted with grace by Mary, without the slightest hint that she had just finished one with Harry. Behind the red sandstone front of the station with its huge arches where the engines stood, not just shining, but gleaming, equipped and ready to spring into action at the next call-out, there were blocks of flats, four storeys high, on three sides. The flats were separated from the fire station by a large washing green, and the front doors led on to an open walkway, with metal railings around the edges, creating a communal balcony on each floor. There in their own compound the firemen lived with their families, and it seemed to Helen that it must be the best feeling in the world for children to be living there, to be able to say their fathers were firemen. To leave your schoolmates on the way home and go into the fire houses must make them the proudest, the luckiest of children, or so she had once thought.

Helen remembered the sensation in her throat when they visited the station, which always smelt of polish, the choking, nervous excitement that any moment the alarm might sound and the powerful engines would go off, bells ringing, lights flashing, swaying through the traffic to save lives. And inside were firemen that she, Helen Davidson, actually knew by name and to talk to. They were heroes in every sense of the word she could find; she adored firemen. She loved their cheerfulness and their seemingly unconscious bravery. Marylka had listened to this all through her childhood, had witnessed the tears of emotion in Helen's eyes as she talked of the Central Division men she had known, and their children she had played with. Being of a more down-to-earth bent, Marylka would laugh, shake her head and say 'What are we to do with you, Mum? Despite everything you're still a hopeless romantic!' And Helen used to think 'Maybe not despite everything, may be because of it.'

It was sad to look at the station now. Oh, it was beautifully kept, efficiently looked after, but for the workplace of those fine men to be a restaurant, and the former homes of heroes to be lived in by people who had no connection with them but simply had enough money to spend on swish, refurbished, Merchant City flats. Well, it just wasn't right somehow. It was good that the buildings had been kept standing instead of Glasgow's usual solution, to rip them down, but still, it offended her in a way she couldn't explain. Those ghosts again she expected, and there were plenty in the old station. The Cheapside Fire in 1960 had added a few more of them.

The area around Anderston, near the River Clyde, housed lots of warehouses in its cramped, congested streets, and the bonded warehouse in Cheapside Street contained over a million gallons of whisky and rum. When it went on fire, because of the narrow streets the firemen faced great difficulties in fighting the blaze, which could be seen lighting up the skyline from eight miles away. Then the volatile contents of the place exploded, bringing the building down on top of the firemen. Five men from the Salvage Corps died, and fourteen firemen, seven from the Central Division station in Ingram Street. That night and into the next morning, seven families in those houses behind the arches waited in vain for their men to come home. She knew the faces of those wives and families, they, like their lost men, were real people to her, and she had often tried to imagine what that terrible time must have been like, but it was too painful to dwell on. It was said that most of the families of men killed in fires moved out of Fire Brigade houses as soon as possible. They couldn't bear to be around a routine and lifestyle they were no longer part of, and Helen could understand that. Imagine, she thought, hearing the alarm go off and watching the engines going out, and thinking of the last time, when your man or your father had gone out too and never come back. And once she had so envied those children.

There was nowhere else she could go next but the Ramshorn Kirk, across the road and back along on the other side, almost opposite where Harry ran Drysdale's. It was really called St David's Church, but everyone knew it as the Ramshorn, the Firemen's Church. Following the Cheapside Fire, engraved for ever in the hearts and minds of Glaswegians, this was where part of the funeral service had been held. She remembered watching the coffins being carried by other firemen, and going up the stairs into the Kirk, holding tightly to Auntie Mary's hand. The old lady had only cried twice that Helen could remember, and one of those times was at the firemen's funerals. She called them 'braw chiels', a phrase she had doubtless heard from her Highland mother, and poor Millie had been so confused and upset by it all that she had to be taken over to Drysdale's to sit on one of Harry's boxes, where she knitted even more furiously than usual. It was only then Helen had understood that those needles, and the endless works of many colours and shapes hanging from them, were Millie's shield. They protected her from a reality she wasn't part of and therefore found threatening. We all have our shields, she thought, some more effective than others.

Both the Firemen's Church and the Fruit Market were theatres now. She had heard that the bell had been removed from the Kirk steeple and taken who knew where, but she hadn't tried to find out for sure because she didn't want to hear that it was true. Oh, the sound of the bell on that awful day! It still broke your heart just remembering it. Now, on the site of that sad funeral service for the bravest of men, and on the very spot where Harry had offered her tastes of the orient, where Mary had sipped tea with him and listened to his family news, plays and comedies were performed instead. Would anyone remember how it had been, she wondered, would they remember the people who had lived, worked and died here? Was there somebody taking notes so that it wouldn't be forgotten? Closing her eyes she could still smell the polish of the fire station mixed with the scent of the flowers for the Cheapside firemen. And that familiar market aroma was so easy to recall, the noise of the horses' hoofs on the cobbles, and the clang of the fire engines as they left to fight another fire. It was all still there, just below the surface, all you had to do was to want to look hard enough.

The final funeral service for the firemen was held in Glasgow Cathedral, then they were buried in the nearby Necropolis, not far from the Davidson crypt, and as a child she felt proud, honoured by that. But she never felt right going back to the fire station afterwards. The men who worked there, the replacements for those who had died, were still heroes, but it wasn't the same any longer; her mind had been opened up to the reality behind their heroism. So she would look at them and wonder if they would be next, and she would look at their families, and wonder what had become of the ones who had fled to where fire bells were no longer a way of life, but a sad reminder of the day that had changed their lives for ever.

And just past the Ramshorn Kirk and cemetery was a curious paving stone, edged in gold metal and with the initials 'RF' and 'AF'. Under that stone lay the coffins containing the mortal remains of brothers Robert and Andrew Foulis. She stood on top of it now, repeating in her mind the question she had asked Auntie Mary. 'Why would anyone be buried under the pavement?'

Mary had smiled gleefully, her eyes shining. 'See if you can guess.'

Helen stared at her blankly.

'Look at the church and the cemetery.'

Helen shrugged, still nothing.

'Well, the church used to stand in the middle of the cemetery.'

'So did they move the church as well then?' Helen asked incredulously.

Mary clapped her black-lace gloved hands and laughed. 'No, that's not it! The cemetery used to be bigger and the church was in the middle. Then the pavement and the road were built over part of it, so now the church stands on the pavement. These two men were buried in the cemetery, exactly there. Only, because they were considered important, which means rich, the the spot was marked.'

'So are there other people under here too?' Helen asked, looking around where they stood.

Mary nodded. 'But they weren't as important as the Foulis brothers, so nobody bothers about them of course!'

'What did they do that was important?'

'Well, they were printers, and Robert started an Academy of Art in the University in the High Street, even if it did eventually fail,' Mary replied. 'So that's why they're remembered. Only not too many know about it, they just walk over them and probably never notice the paving stone. I think that's called justice, don't you?'

Helen had a secret sympathy for the artistically inclined Robert Foulis; they had both experienced the collapse of similar dreams. She had wanted to study art after leaving Laurel Bank, but her plan, like his, had also failed. Not that she had fought for it; she had barely mentioned it because she knew there was no point. By that time her fate was more or less sealed, even if she did have one last dash for freedom in marrying the hapless Jan Kowalski. No one ever won against Old Hector, and though she had staged one or two rebellions in her life, they were minor events. Her marriage was a good example. Instead of Art School she had joined the family business, and it had been just as much of a shock to her that she had an aptitude for it as it had been to the Glasgow business mafia. They had regarded her as 'just a lassie', and more to the point, 'Young Hector's lassie', and as he had lacked the necesssary chip off the old block, it was likely that she would too. Sometimes she shuddered at the thought of perhaps sharing something of Old Hector's character, but her mother's family had been successful in business too, so she decided to take comfort in that connection instead. Not that there was much to choose when you thought about it. Her parents' marriage had been an alliance of riches, a means for both families of protecting what they had from gold diggers. 'It was a bit like the debate on nuclear weapons,' she had laughingly explained to Marylka. 'If both sides had the cash that was supposed to bring security!'

6

Old Hector had packaged his son in much the same way as he had packaged himself. There were frequent photo calls to mark events in his son and heir's life, producing images of the young man that haunted those who knew him. Young Hector standing by a sleek sports car, denoting his jet-set lifestyle. Young Hector on the ski slopes, accompanied by a host of famous faces. Young Hector coming out of a Monte Carlo casino, with several society beauties vying for his attentions. His image was carefully crafted to show a confident, sophisticated man about town, a man about the world, surrounded by beautiful people, accepted by those who mattered. Auntie Mary would look at the photos and shake her head. 'Look at the poor laddie,' she would say sadly. 'Hector's made him into a puppet, and how he enjoys pulling the strings.'

But there were times when the press photographers weren't invited, when the playboy had to be removed from the top spots, times when his father had to use his money to hide the boy away. Young Hector couldn't be the man his father wanted him to be, he couldn't be Old Hector Mark II, and if his mother, the beautiful, aristocratic Christine had known, she would have realized that she had won in the end. She had produced for her crass, vulgar husband a son who was quite beautiful and photogenic, but unhappy in the limelight and uncomfortable with people, a son who couldn't cope with his father's demands that he be an exact replica of himself. Sojourns in various private nursing homes were at least as frequent as the photos of Young Hector as a life and soul of the party playboy, but the Davidson money bought public silence, though rumours were rife in business circles.

The drinking binges were less a display of alcoholism than an attempt to escape being who he wasn't, and didn't want to be. And he was a failure at drinking himself to death as well as everything else; he couldn't drink enough to make himself a spectacular drunk and just ended up being sick instead. When the drink didn't work he became depressed, and his guilt at failing in his father's eyes compounded that. In looks as in nature he favoured his mother, a tall, slim lad with finely chiselled, handsome features, fair hair and a pained expression in his soft brown eyes. His personality would have been more suited to Christine's genteel lifestyle, but his mother had no interest in him because he was a Davidson. Throughout his childhood she had appeared for official events, but even then she ignored the child; he grew up in his father's house, in the care of nannies who were always overseen and overruled by his father. If he hadn't been Old Hector's heir Mary would have taken him over, but he was the all-important son the business needed, so he had become his father's prisoner from the day he was born. And Old Hector knew only one way, force, and every time the boy buckled under that force his father increased it next time, 'to make a man of him, to toughen him up'. It broke him, of course, but Old Hector probably wouldn't have known the difference.

In time Young Hector was married off in a blaze of publicity to an heiress, the daughter and only child of a fellow tycoon. If the citizens of Scotland didn't spend their money in a Davidson store, a service provided by a Davidson subsidiary, or on a Davidson property, they spent it in some arm of the Crawford empire, and now the only children of both families had been married off to each other, thereby uniting two fortunes. But at least neither of the newly-weds was under any illusion; they were both fully aware that the romance existed only in the newspaper headlines and the newsreels. Sheila Crawford knew that after producing a pedigree heir both she and Young Hector would be free to live as they wished, as long as they were discreet and word didn't reach the ears of the public. That after all might affect the sales figures of both empires.

Now what Young Hector needed more than anything was someone who loved him, someone who could teach him how to love, but personal happiness was not a recognized element of a successful business. Successful business brought personal happiness, that was how Old Hector saw it, so that was how it was and had to be for everyone.

And Sheila played her part well, no tantrums, no problems, and even if she had produced a daughter first time round, she knew that a son would have to be produced next time. Only something awful happened, or wonderful, depending on your point of view. One day Sheila's car broke down in Great Western Road and an RAC man answered her call. A month later they had taken off together for South Africa; Sheila Davidson nee Crawford, who had been brought up to do her duty by the family money, had found true love over a broken fan belt. The scandal was the talk of the business community, but Old Hector controlled the press of the day, which anyway wasn't anywhere near as intrusive or salacious as the tabloids of today, so the story was safely contained. And if Young Hector felt anything it was envy. He and his wife had never loved each other and never pretended to, except for the official photos, but they came from similar prisons and they did like each other, and he wished her well. But Sheila and her RAC man were proof that happiness was out there somewhere, that it was possible to find the end of the rainbow, and he wished he could find it too. The only child of the marriage, Helen, stayed with the Davidsons, that was part of the deal, and the subsequent divorce had been quietly pain free, in that each side kept their own money; it was more of a de-merger than a divorce.

For Helen, the long summer school holidays were spent in Cape Town with people she didn't know, until she was eventually excused from the obligation. Old Hector still had hopes of his son remarrying and producing a son, so Bloody Mary was allowed access to Helen because, as a girl, she didn't matter. Helen grew up with Auntie Mary and Millie and when she was away from them she missed them and became miserable. Gradually Cape Town, her mother and the brood of half-brothers that soon arrived — a bitter pill for her former father-in-law to swallow — became part of the same distant memory. Photos and Christmas cards were exchanged out of courtesy, and when Sheila and her RAC man came back for visits they would meet for slightly awkward lunches between people who thought they should meet, but had little in common. Young Hector never married again, but by the time her grandfather accepted the situation, Helen belonged irrevocably to Bloody Mary. Helen had been saved.

Helen looked up; she had forgotten about the time and the winter afternoon had suddenly grown dark. Just up the road in the High Street was the site of that first University, where Robert Foulis's failed Academy of Art had been, but when Helen was touring these parts with Auntie Mary and Millie it was a railway goods yard. They would stand watching the little red and yellow workhorse lorries with their triangular-shaped cabs, moving trailers of mysterious cargoes from one place to another, for all the world like ants scuttling back and forth. The University had been pulled down in the eighteenth century and relocated to Gilmorehill in the West End. Auntie Mary had explained that only rich boys went to university, and the area around the High Street and the Calton was thought too poor, run-down and drink-sodden for them to frequent. When Helen grew up she discovered that the objections hadn't been to the poverty and the drunkenness so much as the poverty-stricken, drunken prostitutes around the area. A higher, presumably sober and altogether more acceptable class of prostitute was seemingly to be found in the more affluent West End, but Auntie Mary had been too much of a lady to say such a thing to her innocent niece. The original arches and a fine staircase from the old High Street site were transported to Gilmorehill, and if there was any justice, Helen mused, the ghosts of the Calton prostitutes might have sneaked in there with them.

Further up, where High Street became Castle Street, was the

Barony Church where Harry and Irene had been married, now taken over by Strathclyde University's Student Union, and across from it the site where Duke Street Prison had stood. It housed women when Helen was a child, and she used to look at the high, high walls, and think about the women inside and wonder what they had done to land them in such a place. And what of their families, what would become of them? Even now that it had long gone, there were still graves inside of those hanged in the prison, but they were unmarked and of course, untended. On the same side was the St Mungo Museum of Religious Life. The Dali painting she hated, *Christ of St John on the Cross*, had been moved there from the art galleries at Kelvingrove; she had closed her eyes when she came to it during the grand pre-opening tour. The building was new, but it had been designed to look old, so that it blended in with the historic buildings around it. They had had to shuffle David Livingstone's statue along a bit to build it there, so he was still exploring pastures new in a way. In her mind's eye, though, there was no new old building, in her memory it was all just as it had been and the museum merely an illusion.

She looked at her watch. Past five o'clock; she had no time to go up there now, Marylka would expect her to be at home around 6 p.m. and she needed to talk to her about this Bloody Mary thing. She would have to halt her tour down memory lane, collect her car from the Mitchell Lane extortionists and start off home, but she was glad she had strolled down at least part of the way. Just yards beyond the Barony Church was the Calton, and across from it the Necropolis, where Auntie Mary and Millie both lay; a major regret that, even if they were in the company of those 'braw chiels'. If she had been more in control at the time she would have thought of somewhere more appropriate, but she had been consumed with grief, even though the old lady had lived to ninety-five. She had let the family machine take over, and Mary had been put in an expensive coffin and dispatched in a boringly conventional manner. She felt she had betrayed her. Mary should have gone in style, in a manner more fitting to a lifetime rebel and thorn in Old Hector's flesh, but there she was, lying alongside him in the family crypt. 'Never mind, Mum,' Marylka had said comfortingly. 'Hopefully she'll still be giving him hell!' 'Yes, but he knows where she is now,' Helen replied. 'That was what he always wanted. He hated it when she was out of his sight, because he didn't know what she was up to.'

But she was with Millie, so maybe the crypt was where she needed to be. 'Poor Millie,' she thought, her eyes filling with tears again. 'Millie the Daftie! God, what a shock that was!' Mary had gone to wake her one morning in the house in Duke Street and found her dead in bed. Cardiomyopathy, the doctors had decided; her heart had supported that large frame for over forty years without anyone knowing how weak the muscle was, and one night her heart had simply stopped. People said things like 'At least she felt no pain,' but they didn't know the pain of those taunts and sniggers, for the crime of being 'different'. They said 'It's all for the best,' which really meant 'She's never been right in the head, so her life isn't worth as much. It's a blessing for everyone that she's gone.' But they were wrong there too. Loving Millie didn't depend on her having a high IQ, she was loved for herself, and Helen remembered the anger she felt at those assumptions. Millie had been short-changed all through her difficult, unfair life and then she had died young, yet somehow no one else seemed to see the tragedy or feel angry about that. They thought it was 'all for the best', and dismissed Millie as though she didn't matter.

Helen had been fifteen when Millie died. Maybe the rebellious teenage years had something to do with the anger she felt, but she didn't think so, because recalling that awful event made her even angrier today. She remembered Auntie Mary's inconsolable grief at the loss of her blighted daughter, and she raged for the old lady at the insensitivity of those who told her in effect that Millie had just been a nuisance, and she was better off without her. But she had tended her large child all those years, looked after her, cared for her and loved her.

Whether or not Millie was an intellectual was of no consequence, she was there, she was theirs, and she was loved. Now that she was gone, she was missed sorely, and the old lady was bereft.

It had taken Helen a long time to get over Millie's death, if indeed she ever did. Inside a drawer in her office desk she kept a small, Bakelite beehive with a plastic strap, and inside that was a shapeless piece of knitting with many colours, textures and dropped stitches. Every now and again she would take Millie's shield out, look at it and remember, then she'd get angry all over again about the unfairness of poor Millie's life. If anyone ever came across it in her desk they wouldn't have a clue what it was and they would probably throw it out. One of these days she would have to put it somewhere safe, just in case. Helen blew her nose again, and called herself all sorts of silly, sentimental idiots. 'If Marylka saw you now,' she started to say to herself, but then she shook her head. 'No,' she whispered. 'Marylka would understand about Millie.'

She hadn't reached as far as the Calton this time, but in a few weeks' time it would be the anniversary of Auntie Mary's death, and she and Marylka always took flowers to the Necropolis, so she'd spend more time looking around the old haunts then. It suddenly struck her that Millie always shared Auntie Mary's flowers, she never had her own. Why was that? Because they were never apart maybe, but still, she should have flowers on her special dates too, Auntie Mary would like her to do that for her daughter. She rummaged in her bag and brought out a pen and a used envelope. 'Flowers for Millie too,' she wrote, then placed the pen and envelope back in the bag.

She thought of all the countries in the world she had seen since those days with Auntie Mary and Millie, or rather the hotels and airports she had seen. This area of her home town was where her happiest memories were, though; this is where she felt she belonged. Somewhere here the child she was, the happy child she was, still skipped along Ingram Street and all the others leading from it; happiness like that couldn't just evaporate because you'd grown up. She stopped outside Hutcheson's Hall at the corner of John Street, looked back along Ingram Street and smiled. The ghosts were alive after all, every one still there if you wanted them to be.

7

Eilean Òg wasn't where Alec and Betty Craig would've chosen to live, but Red Rock Farm had been good to them all the same. Though the work was hard and relentless, Alec and Betty had a happy marriage with few cross words, probably, as she often thought with a smile, because Alec was so easy-going that he was impossible to argue with. Her own temper, she knew, was quicker, but she often wondered how much of that was due to her inability to leave the past where it belonged. Still, though the old questions about who she was and where she should be remained stubbornly in the back of her mind, nagging at her despite her best intentions not to hear them, the arrival of their son in 1937 was a happy time. It was the first birth at Red Rock since old Murdo had been born there himself, so it seemed appropriate therefore to name the child after the old man. Murdo and Ishbel were as good and as proud as any grandparents could be, and given the sparseness of the boy's family they would be his only grandparents anyway.

The local doctor, Dr Sandy Adams, was that cliché, the man who doubled as vet and doctor, and he openly admitted that given the choice he would rather have been the vet. Dr Sandy, a dour little man with eyes set too close together, wire-rimmed spectacles and Homburg hat, looked like the Wee Free adherent that he was. He loved animals, but hated people, and more than anything else he detested delivering babies, so he had made a rule of his own to eliminate as many island births as possible. Sandy Adams had decided that any woman under the height of five foot two should be sent to hospital in Oban to deliver her child, which because of the erratic, weather-dependent boat service, often meant in effect spending weeks away from home. The women didn't like it; they had families to look after and work to do, and anyway, they saw no sense in it. And as most women at that time were under five feet two tall, Dr Adams's edict encompassed almost every female on the island. But the women fought back by not calling him till they were in the late stages of labour, so that there was no time in those pre-helicopter days to get to the mainland in time for the birth. How many mothers and babies died as a result no one would ever know, because there were undoubtedly some complications that should have been dealt with in hospital, with as modern equipment as existed then. But when her time came Betty did the same as the others, and was safely delivered of young Murdo Craig at home a year after her marriage.

He was a strapping lad, young Murdo, a boy of huge character, and she often wondered where that could have come from. Ishbel and Murdo were of course devoted to him, and when the boy was barely a toddler he would follow his grandfather around, wearing one of the old man's waistcoats trailing on the ground behind him, chewing on one of his pipes. And always that enormous personality, that cheerful assumption that there was nothing he could not do. At the age of three he had armed himself with a stick and gone into the field to bring the beasts into the byre for milking, just as he had seen the adults do many, many times. When inevitably one nudged him to the ground he had been mortally insulted. As far as young Murdo was concerned there was no reason why he couldn't do any of the work on the farm, and neither size nor age had any bearing on the matter. He sobbed in his mother's arms with rage and shame as the muck was cleaned off his backside, as the adults tried to hide their laughter for fear of making his indignity all the worse. Not that his encounter with the cows put him off, nothing ever put Murdo off what he thought he could do, and as a result there was little he could not.

He was, from the first, a farm boy, as though working on the land had been in his blood for generations, and indeed neither of his parents was in a position to disprove this. He was an honest boy too, sometimes brutally and loudly honest, but no one could ever accuse him of being two-faced. And always that huge grin on his face, even when someone objected to his plain speaking, and that amazing, infuriating sometimes, inability to take offence, even when someone was trying their hardest to give it. He held no grudges because something in him couldn't see a bad turn in the first place, yet all through his life he had a motto which he repeated with gusto in that strong, loud voice to anyone who asked, 'Get the buggers before they get you!' That, Betty always thought, was her influence, something her son had taken in at the breast, a reflection of her attitude towards the islanders she lived among but wasn't one of, and certainly didn't want to be, but Murdo delivered it with more good humour than she ever could. Even so, he had a reputation for not allowing anyone to – how was it people put it these days? – to mess, that was it; no one ever messed with Murdo Craig and his.

Now that she was a cailleach herself, an old woman, Betty lived in the extension Alec and Murdo had built on to the Red Rock steading for Ishbel and Murdo, both long gone, as was Alec himself these last fifteen years. The roof was tiled now and the rowan tree tall and strong, but she could still close her eyes and see her son, aged six or seven, sitting up the tree, throwing stones on the corrugated roof, so that Granny Ishbel had to come out to him and complain about the racket. The wee old woman would dance about under the tree waving her arms about, remonstrating with him, shouting Gaelic threats at him from the ground, calling him all sorts of rascals, before finally enticing him down with the sugary butter tablet that she had made for him while he was at school anyhow. He would put on one of Grandpa Murdo's waistcoats and spend time with her, eating tablet, drinking milk and listening to her stories of the old days. It was a game the two of them played, but even so, Betty was glad that the tile roof had been put on before she moved in, when young Murdo and his wife took over at Red

Rock. She was far from sure that she would've treated her own grandchildren as fondly as Granny Ishbel had treated Murdo.

He was always in trouble at school too, her Murdo; he spoke his mind and knew no tact and the teachers didn't like that, especially from the son of boarded-outs. Not that Murdo cared about their censure, he took their punishments without malice but without regard either, secure in the knowledge that he was right and they were wrong. And the truth was that Betty never scolded him when she thought he was right; she encouraged him to stand up for himself, to speak and think for himself. Another child might have been crushed by the disapproval, but somehow Murdo never was, he had such strength of character and resilience, and such a sense of what was right and wrong. But where had it come from, she often wondered, as she wondered about so many things. To be sure she had encouraged his honesty, but it came in the first place from his own spirit, there was no doubt about that, she hadn't pushed a shy child into showing a bravado that wasn't natural to him. And that tall, robust frame, who did he take that from? Alec had been tall and slim, a good-looking, dark-haired man but not one who stood out in a crowd by looks or personality, nor did he ever want to. Alec was content with his lot, happy with his family, his life and his work, a gentle, good-natured man. Yet here was this big, blue-eyed laddie, with that glorious mane of black hair, not handsome, she always knew, but impossible to ignore. He didn't need to be handsome, he had such magnetism, it was almost as though whatever rules governed attractiveness didn't really apply to Murdo. But he could be hell to live with; she was his mother, but she knew Murdo could be wearing. He had no moods. There was only one way to be: loud, open, forever cheerful, till you could kill him sometimes. When he was a teenager she would get so tired of his constant talking and eternal cheerfulness that she would push him out of the Red Rock kitchen. 'Go away! Give me peace!' she'd shout. 'Find somebody else to annoy!' And he'd laugh even louder then put his muscular arms around her waist, pick her up and put her down outside in the yard, locking the door behind her. 'How far's too far?' she would demand of him. 'Och, down by the shore at the south end of the island,' he would reply with mock seriousness, then that big grin would split his face again.

How Catriona had managed being married to Murdo was a mystery, because she was nobody's fool herself, yet there were no genuine battles between them. Watching them together, Betty saw how her tiny daughter-in-law coped with day-in, day-out Murdo, and she did have her own ways. Murdo was a great man for starting something then getting other people involved, like the annual whitewashing of the steading, for instance. There would be no discussion of when it might be convenient to start; Murdo would just appear with the various brushes, the ladders and the bags of whitewash, and everyone else had to join in, as he walked around, supervising. 'Missed a bit there, Catriona,' he would comment loudly. 'That'll no' do ye know!' Then after pointing out various other imperfections and examples of sloppy workmanship, he would walk back to his own, unsupervised patch. Watching this performance one year Betty worked out how Catriona kept sane. Catriona was up a ladder, and whatever advice and direction Murdo gave she ignored completely, but there came a moment when she had had enough, not that there was any explosion of temper, or even an announcement. Without a word Catriona dismantled the ladder, put her brush back in the bucket of whitewash and disappeared into the kitchen.

'Is that you puttin' the kettle on, Catriona?' Murdo asked brightly.

Silence.

He walked to the kitchen door and peered in. 'Aye,' he said, 'she's got the kettle on, the tea'll be oot in a minute.'

Time passed, and then Catriona entered the porch that Murdo had built on to the front of the house, picked up a book and settled herself into her chair, a cup of tea and a few biscuits within reach. Murdo, still stirring the whitewash, wandered over to the porch, puzzled, and bellowed through the glass 'Whit ye daein'?'

'Ah'm readin' a book Murdo, whit does it look like?' Catriona replied amiably.

'But we're no' finished!' Murdo laughed.

'Oh, *Ah'm* finished, Murdo,' Catriona replied without looking up from her book. Then reaching for her cup she glanced up at him through the window of the porch. 'Besides, you know how tae dae it better than anybody else. Ye can bloody well get oan wi' it.'

'Women!' Murdo muttered, wandering off again, still grinning. 'Ye canny say anythin' tae them ye know!'

But it didn't dent his mood, or his supervisory skills, and he continued to oversee everyone else's efforts till the job was done. It was the right, the only way anyone could cope with non-stop Murdo, Betty reflected, to physically withdraw from him from time to time, but maybe only a wife could get away with that, everyone else had to put up with him.

8

Helen collected her car at the Mitchell Lane car park, drove down the tight, twisting, exit lane and paid her 'ransom' at the kiosk. 'Ten quid for seven hours!' she muttered, 'Ridiculous! Sheer bloody daylight robbery! If Old Hector had put his money into car parks we wouldn't need to work at all!' Then she laughed at herself. Long before she was born Old Hector had the family's financial position well secured, but he couldn't rest there. It was as if every time he pulled off some big deal he thought he had made it, but shortly the gloss would wear off, making it seem mediocre to him, and so he had to aim higher, achieve something bigger next time. Maybe somewhere in his mind he thought the day would come when he could relax and enjoy the fruits of his labours, but the truth was he never could and never did. Auntie Mary had been right; he was indeed a miserable old teuchter. After he achieved all there was to achieve in business and there were more shops, stores and property carrying the Davidson name than made sense, he looked in another direction. Wealth wasn't enough, he needed position and respect, and as money made in trade was looked down on by Glasgow's more established society, the acceptance of the Davidsons into the upper echelons became desperately desirable to him.

When he was twenty-nine years old he had wooed and wed Christine, the daughter of a Perthshire distillery owner with aristocratic connections. She was a woman of breeding and refinement as well as beauty, a willowy blonde with huge soft brown eyes. No one in the family ever understood what she had seen in Hector, though her attraction for him was obvious.

The lovely Christine brought a foothold in the higher ranks of society that Hector craved. Christine was a trophy, an achievement, paraded to boost his standing rather than his happiness. Christine, like everything and everyone else, was business. What he brought to her family was the Davidson money; aristocratic connections did not always translate into an excess of pounds, shillings and pence.

It was his sister's opinion that Christine must have imbibed too much of her family's fine old malt whisky before she accepted Hector's proposal, and furthermore, that she had only married him at the behest of her own grasping old father. But even Mary admitted that at first there did seem to be some sort of spark between them, the natural result perhaps of a meeting between two very different people from even more different backgrounds. If that was true, though, the initial spark must have flared briefly and died quickly. Maybe Christine thought she was marrying an exciting young man; after all, everyone was talking about him then, but what she got was a construction Hector had carefully crafted of who he wanted to be, or rather, who his ambitions needed him to be. A generation on he would package his son in exactly the same manner, with even more disastrous results, because his son was a different, more sensitive and vulnerable person than Old Hector could ever have understood. Whatever impression he gave as a young suitor, the truth was that Hector's enthusiasm consisted only of an obsession with business, money and position. He was undoubtedly different from the huntin', shootin' and fishin' males Christine had encountered, but it was part of Hector's tragedy that there was a lot less to him than met the eye.

Whatever the reason, the lovely Christine came to regard him as common and vulgar and soon despised him. She bore him one son, Helen's father, and if the rumours were true, thereafter the boudoir door was firmly closed against him. Whenever they talked of the family Marylka would say drily that they were all damned. Once upon a time, she said, a Highland faerie woman had put a curse on the family, and no good would come to them. Helen would laugh, but it might just be true; certainly from Old Hector onwards the curse had been watertight. As long as Christine appeared at his side when needed to keep up the appearance of a happy family, Hector seemed content to go along with the arrangement, but his wife's loathing for him was almost palpable. She regarded their son as his alone, as the price she had been obliged to pay, and she took little interest in Young Hector, or the rest of the Davidsons.

All of this came to Helen by a sort of osmosis; no one ever explained her grandmother's lack of contact, or her indifference when circumstances temporarily demanded it. It was how things had always been, it was normal to her, and as a child she just absorbed the various undercurrents somehow. There were parties and receptions at the gracious, and increasingly palatial, South Side home of Mr & Mrs Hector Davidson and their family, all of them smiling for the ever present newspaper photographers as they snapped away. But if fear was in Hector's eyes in those snaps, there was something even more heartbreaking in Christine's. There was an indelible image in Helen's memory of those sad, almost bitter, brown eyes that the very earliest pictures had captured full of sparkling brightness. She had seen those sad, bitter brown eyes somewhere else too, whenever she looked at her father.

In those later photos Christine looked as though she was counting the seconds till the performance ended so that she could get away from this life and these people, who were her family too, if only by marriage. And once the event was over she would instantly leave for her parents' home in Perthshire, free once again. Unsurprisingly, the remains of Christine Davidson were never to rest in the family crypt. She had hated them all in life, and when death finally came she would lie with her own family in Perth, and Old Hector raised no objections. Hector had put on a show of grief every bit as seamless as Christine's performances of family harmony, then both families were free of each other thereafter. It was chilling when you looked back on it.

Sitting at the traffic lights that February evening, Helen wondered again, as she often did, which had come first. Did Hector completely devote himself to his business and his money because his marriage was non-existent and his wife hated him, or was it the other way round? Marylka's opinion was that Helen was far too sentimental about Old Hector, that he was every bit as bad as Auntie Mary said, and that Christine had been a virgin sacrificed on the altar of male ambition. And judging by the letter Auntie Mary had left behind after her death Marylka was more right than she knew. She smiled to herself. After she'd shared this with her daughter life would be full of 'Didn't I tell you?' and smug grins. All those hints Mary had dropped, all those threats about what she knew, and she did know after all. She thought back to Old Hector's death. He had lived to see a hundred, probably trying to outlive Mary and save his reputation, and when the end came he had said 'Tell Mary I'm sorry.'

'What do you think he meant by that?' Helen had asked the old lady.

'Oh, I know what he meant,' Mary said quietly, the gentlest of smiles on her lips.

'What then?'

'Things,' Mary said. 'Just things. You'll know in time, Helen.'

And at the funeral, as Old Hector was laid to rest in the family crypt Mary, by then ninety years old and slightly unsteady on her legs, held on to her niece's arm for support and remarked: 'He wants it all to die with him, but it won't.' Then she had spent a few moments beside where Millie lay, and before they left the Necropolis she had insisted on visiting the last resting place of the firemen who had died in the Cheapside Fire. 'Poor laddies,' she murmured, 'braw chiels every one, and them so young!'

But as they left Helen's mind had still been on Old Hector.

'Auntie Mary, what did Grandpa want to die with him? What did he do?'

Mary laughed wryly. 'What did he do? Where do you want

me to start, lass? One day I'll tell you, I promise. You're not supposed to speak ill of the dead, especially while you're burying them, I imagine, but you already know that he wasn't altogether a good man. He did plenty of wrong in his time, and saying "Sorry" at the end couldn't put right his main sin. I know them all too, maybe I'm the only one who does.'

But instead of telling what she knew, the old lady had written down Old Hector's misdemeanours in a time bomb designed to go off underneath Helen once Bloody Mary herself had safely shuffled off this mortal coil. At first Helen had been shocked, then she had been angry – what was the point after all these years? Finally she had laughed. What else would you expect from Bloody Mary?

9

At the far end of St Vincent Street the traffic was forced to zig-zag through a pointless one-way system. And oh, God, she was in the wrong lane. Nothing for it, she'd have to turn right towards Charing Cross; she hated those people who thought lanes were optional and ended up driving across you or pushing their way in. Driving was no pleasure these days; if it wasn't for her memories of Mr Stewart, her grandfather's chauffeur, she would get someone to drive her to and from work. Just thinking of how impersonally he had been regarded made her face blush crimson with shame for Old Hector. No, she could never have a chauffeur.

Occasionally it had been suggested that she leave Glasgow and take up residence in London, so that she could keep an eye on that branch of the business, and sometimes she thought it might be good to get away from the constant recognition, and the way she was regarded as somehow not quite a human being. She couldn't be, after all, she was a Davidson, so she had to be different. But if nothing else, the traffic in London set her mind firmly against the idea, and there were other considerations. Like the way Londoners never looked you in the eye, for instance. Their self-imposed isolation was unnerving. Glasgow felt like home, even if you had to fight for the feeling sometimes, and there was the odd bizarre happening that proved the point. Once, hurrying out of the office on her way home, she had been accosted by a small boy about ten years old, carrying a dog of extremely mixed parentage. The dog's face had a look of embarrassment and confusion, as though it wasn't quite sure how it had come to be in this undignified position, with its paws hanging forlornly over the boy's right shoulder and its rear end supported by a pair of grubby human hands, but it wasn't entirely sure how to get out of the situation. If it had been human the look in its eyes would have read 'Please don't let any of my friends see me like this.' The boy inclined the dog in Helen's direction.

'Dae ye waant a wee dug, Missus?' he asked.

Taken aback by the approach Helen struggled to preserve her decorum. 'No,' she enunciated very precisely. 'I do not want a wee dug, thank you!'

'But Missus, it's loast!' wheedled the boy.

'I don't care!' Helen said, wondering how she had wandered into this scenario. 'It's not my dug, why would I want it?'

'But Missus, it's a wee ginger dug!' the boy explained.

'I don't care if it's bumbee tartan!' Helen exclaimed. 'I do not want a wee dug! Is that all right?'

'OK, well,' said the boy amiably, and wandered off to offer the small lost ginger dog to someone else.

When she told the tale to Marylka, Helen's eyes streamed with tears of laughter. '"Dae ye waant a wee dug?"' she kept repeating and bursting into helpless giggles again. Marylka, sceptical as ever, wondered if the boy had offered to *sell* the dog, or perhaps touched her for a donation.

'No, it wasn't a scam,' Helen replied. 'It was just Glasgow. It couldn't have happened anywhere but Glasgow. That's why I don't think I could move away. I mean where else can you think of where you'd get an offer like that out of the blue?'

Marylka shook her head. 'Just because a snotty-nosed kid asked you if you wanted a dog?'

'No! It wasn't just a dog, it was "a wee loast ginger dug!"' Helen explained and immediately sank back on the couch into another burst of helpless laughter.

Marylka smiled as she watched Helen dabbing at her eyes and she shook her head again. 'You're a deeply sad person, Mother,' she said. 'D'you know that?'

And for some reason that had made Helen laugh even more.

Maybe, Helen thought, you had to have spent time in the streets of Glasgow to appreciate the story, to get the best out of it. Maybe you had to have grown up with Auntie Mary, Millie and their cast of thousands to see the humour. Just thinking of the 'wee loast ginger dug' as she sat in the traffic had her giggling again and searching through her bag for a hankie.

Past the Mitchell Library on her left. Her class had been taken there once by a teacher, and much to her acute embarrassment she discovered that a file existed charting the rise of the Davidsons. It was the first time she became aware that her family, rightly or wrongly, occupied a certain position in the life and history of Glasgow, that they were not just like everyone else. And judging by the reactions of her schoolmates it was the first they knew of it too. Helen had felt exposed somehow. You got used to it over the years, this being stared at, being treated not quite the same as other people. At first it had been difficult telling those who wanted to know you for yourself from the others, who wanted to know you for who your family was, but gradually you grew another layer of skin to cover the one that insisted on blushing, you managed to put on a veneer. At least she had enabled Marylka to escape that; very few would see a connection between Dr Marylka Kowalski and the Davidsons, and the only ones who did were in the inner circle anyway. Like Rob Burns, who was heading for a fall if Annie was right. Rob's father and grandfather had been the Davidsons' solicitors from the very earliest days of Old Hector's empire building. Rob and Marylka had known each other all their lives. Annie was forever trying to get her to warn Marylka, and Helen always argued that, like everything else her secretary used against Rob, it was all in her mind, though she was far from sure herself. Every time Rob's name came up she and Annie rowed about him and his supposed intentions towards Marylka, and Annie never gave an inch.

'It's nonsense, Annie! You never give him a chance, you suspect Rob of everything. You'd do anything to wrong-foot him!'

'Huh, like he needs help! I'm telling you!' Annie protested. 'He sees himself as the obvious choice. He thinks he's family already. If he gets a foot in the door I'll be the first one out.'

'He's not that vindictive. Anyway, you bring it on yourself. You deliberately set out to annoy him.'

'I mean,' said Annie with heavy emphasis, 'I would leave the moment he arrived, he wouldn't get the chance to sack me! He fancies his chances in more ways than one, he's after your job, anybody can see that. And he's not good enough for Marylka.'

'She'd eat him for breakfast anyway. Marylka's not stupid.'

'Aye, well, I'm only saying you should prepare to repel that particular boarder, that's all.' She shuddered theatrically. 'God, what a thought! What age is he anyway?'

'Mid, late twenties?' Helen mused.

'Going on seventy-five,' Annie said. 'I've never met such a dry, lifeless, humourless individual in my life!'

'Och, he's not that bad,' Helen laughed. Then she thought for a moment. 'Mind you,' she said, 'he isn't the liveliest I've met either. Not exactly full of the joys, and he was like that as a child too. A serious lad, a natural solicitor.'

'A dry, boring, lifeless, humourless craitur!' Annie repeated, stressing every word. 'Just make sure Marylka doesn't mistake that for deep and possibly interesting, that's all!'

But there was little chance of that, little chance of Marylka being interested in anyone. She hadn't known one male in her life who could be classified as reliable or strong, and Helen felt she had contributed to that. She had been as much to blame for Jan Kowalski's leaving as he had, because she knew she shouldn't have married him in the first place. And the least she could have done for her daughter after the marriage had ended was to re-marry, to give the child a father, but the truth was that there had been no one. Helen had put all her energies into retrieving the business from Young Hector's best efforts to wreck it, and into raising Marylka. There had been the odd blip on the romantic horizon, but the only men she met were connected with the business world, and she spent too much time with them during working hours to be attracted to them outside. She had dreams of course, that someone not unlike Humphrey Bogart might come into her life and take her away from all this, but no one had. She had a thing about old Humphrey since she was a child. Dear God, he was actually from the generation before that, but a thing knows no barriers of time. That was something else a time machine would sort out, even if she had to fight Lauren Bacall for Humphrey's favours. Marylka thought it was terribly witty to call him 'Humph the Dumph' for some reason, probably because Helen hated it, though she tried to pretend it didn't bother her. Anyhow, the decent contenders, even if they weren't up to Humphrey's standard, were, she suspected, intimidated by the Davidson name and all that went with it, and now she had been on her own too long to defer to any man. Even if old Humphrey arrived tomorrow, she might have to think about it. But it seemed that Marylka had grown up cynical, determined to be her own person, as though she had ruled out marriage from an early age.

'Just because I made a mess of it doesn't mean there aren't some very decent men out there,' Helen would say.

'I'm sure there are, Mother,' Marylka would reply, 'and they can stay out there. Who needs the hassle?'

'But why should it be a hassle? You could meet someone tomorrow and fall madly in love.'

'I'll let you know if I do, OK?'

'All I'm saying,' said Helen, 'is that you shouldn't have your mind so set against it, that's all.'

'Right. Anything you say. Look.'

Helen looked at her daughter, who had her eyes crossed and her mouth hanging open.

'My mind is so wide open it's a void. Happy now?'

Helen laughed, but she still worried that she'd put Marylka off men for life, and on the other hand she suspected that underneath that logical, independent, cynical exterior might lurk a desperate romantic like Auntie Mary. Mary had sacrificed her life to care for Millie, and Helen too, but Marylka had only her work. What if she should suddenly come across some charismatic male who knew how to handle women, and having no first-hand experience of dealing with men, she was bowled over by a bounder with nothing more than a strong personality? Maybe even dry, boring Rob Burns would be better than that, she thought. Then she thought again. 'No, Annie's right. She'd be better on her own than bored out of her mind with Rob.'

Eventually she was on Dumbarton Road, with Kelvin Hall on the left. The Schoolboys' and Girls' Exhibitions she'd been to in there over the years. There was a Spitfire plane there one year, and a long line of children waiting to sit in it, her included. She remembered thinking how tiny it was, and yet the pilots had been heroes, and everyone knew that heroes were tall, dark and handsome like Gregory Peck, or in Alan Ladd's case, small, fair and handsome, if you liked the type, and standing on a box in Hollywood to make him look heroic. But they were only boys, those RAF pilots, and not much older than she was when she was queuing up to sit in the cramped cockpit of the little plane.

On the right stood the Art Galleries, where she had famously been sick when the school art teacher had taken the class to see that Dali painting she hated. Why pick on one? She hated all of them. These days there was a watch with the worst one of all on the dial; *The Persistence of Memory*, the old Spanish oddity had named it, with clocks dripping off surfaces. She smiled; Marylka was always threatening to buy the watch for her birthday. Behind the Art Galleries stood Glasgow University, the West End one, where morally pure students attended, devoid of drunkenness and debauchery presumably, and a little further on in Dumbarton Road was the Western Infirmary, where Marylka would be hard at work this very moment. It used to have a long driveway leading upwards to a rather distinguished and solid Victorian building. Passing it at night when it was all lit up, it had looked for all the world like a huge liner, like one of the Queens, grounded on a sandbank. Appropriate in a way, because the Western had been built with money from the Clydebank shipyard owners in whose yards the Queens had been built. But these days all you could see from the road was this awful modern box that had been grafted on to the front. No doubt it was designed to be practical, to make working on the human body easier, she thought, but it did nothing for the eye, and considerably less for the human soul.

The road seemed to go on for ever; she should have taken a shorter route to Anniesland. She often went a different way to distract her thoughts from the moment when she would arrive at the junction. Marylka was right; she should go up Maryhill Road and through Bearsden Cross, missing Anniesland out all together, but she hated giving in. It was like the horses' eyes; you just persevered until you had conquered the fear. All the same, she knew she would breathe a sigh of relief once she had safely negotiated her way on to Bearsden Road again, as she did every night. Turn right into Crow Road, and then before she knew it she was at Anniesland Cross, but about six traffic light sequences away from the junction. To keep her company she pushed a Goons tape into the cassette player; what an absolute gift that someone from the BBC should have hit on the idea of putting the Goons on tape. At each change of lights she moved forward, that much nearer to journey's end. She removed the tape and searched out the one with the 'Ying Tong' song, then dropped it on the floor. She unclipped her seat belt, leaned forward, picked up the tape and pushed it into the cassette slot. Just then she realized she could make this sequence of the traffic lights. She quickly put the car in gear and moved into the familiar but confusing conjunction of roads that was Anniesland Cross.

Suddenly the familiar voices of Neddy Seagoon, Bluebottle, Eccles and Bloodnok merged with the sound of screaming brakes and a bone-crunching thud. There was the noise of glass breaking and horns sounding never-endingly. Finally there was another terrible thudding crunch. The silence lasted a long, long time, until she heard voices above and around her, discussions going on that she couldn't understand or take part in. That was all she felt, this encapsulating silence and a vague confusion, though neither bothered her unduly. Oh, and there was a feeling in her chest like trapped wind. She floated somewhere, idly wondering if she had any Asilone antacid tablets in her bag. She often got indigestion after some official function, though she couldn't offhand recall having been at one recently. Marylka said Asilone tablets were the best, and Marylka after all should know. A medical education, she thought, was a wonderful thing. Somewhere in the back of her mind she wondered what was going on, where she was, and what the voices were talking about. She made a half-hearted attempt to move, for no other reason than to signal that she was there, and a voice told her sternly to keep still, that the Fire Brigade was on the way. Helen was cheered by that. She had no idea why the Fire Brigade was on the way or why this should stop her moving, but she was content to go along with it. She liked firemen.

In the distance she heard sirens wailing and idly wondered why, then a face appeared under a policeman's hat. It was true what they said about policemen getting younger, she thought; she smiled to the policeman and to herself. He was saying something to her, leaning in close to her face and saying something about the Fire Brigade again. She nodded and smiled. She still didn't understand why the attendance of the Fire Brigade kept being announced, but she liked firemen, they were always welcome. Somewhere near by a mobile phone rang. 'Bloody thing! Might as well be electronically tagged!' she muttered, or thought she did. 'But they still haven't come up with my time machine, have they?'

'What did she say?' said a voice.

'What's wrong with your ears?' she thought. She repeated what she had said, or thought she did.

'Something about the time,' said another voice.

'Don't worry about the time,' the boy policeman enunciated slowly beside her. 'They'll be here soon.'

'Get your ears tested!' she said.

'Aye,' said the boy policeman. 'They'll be here. Soon. Just hold on.'

She gave up then, and seemed to retreat to a place that wasn't really anywhere, but when she came back again there were two firemen above her, in earnest discussion with lots of other people. It suddenly dawned on her that whatever the hold-up was she would be late home, and Marylka might be trying to get through to her on the phone.

'Marylka,' she said.

'What's that ye're sayin' lass?' asked a fireman.

She smiled at him. Nice eyes. She liked firemen.

'Whit did she say?' he asked.

'Somethin' about Mary Ah think,' said another voice.

'God Almighty!' she thought, 'Has the entire world lost its hearing?' 'MARYLKA!' she tried to shout.

'Monica? Somethin' aboot her car mibbe?' someone suggested.

'Don't worry, lass,' said the lovely fireman with the nice eyes again. 'The ambulance will be here in a minute an' we'll soon have ye oota there.'

She nodded, but she didn't understand any of it.

'We'll havtae cut ye oot, there'll be a lotta noise, but don't let that bother ye.'

She nodded again. Whatever was going on it was all right, because the firemen were here. Nothing bad could happen. She nodded and smiled, aware that she was wandering off again, watching the nice fireman's face fade. 'I'll tell him all about Auntie Mary's "braw chiels" in Ingram Street when I come back,' she thought hazily. But this time she didn't come back.

'Too late,' said a paramedic. 'Just cut her oot boys an' we'll get her certified.'

'There's nothin' we can dae then? Ye're sure?' asked the fireman.

'Nothin'. The chest injuries are massive, seat belt or no'.

Bloody things. Was she wearin' a seat belt d'ye know? Did somebody mibbe unclip it?'

'Dunno,' said the fireman. 'We didnae, Ah know that, but ye know whit these eedjits are like. They watch *Casualty* on TV an' suddenly every joiner an' road sweeper is doin' open heart surgery on the pavement. Could be somebody unclipped her, thinkin' they were doin' the right thing like.'

'Christ aye, Ah know whit ye mean. They're a' obsessed wi' cars catchin' fire for some reason, think they havtae drag people oota wrecks before they burn, it's the first thing on the agenda. No' that it matters,' said the paramedic wearily. 'Sometimes Ah think seat belts cause merr sufferin' in these cases. Sometimes if they're no' wearin' wan they'd be killed instantly, insteada hingin' oan for an hour an' dyin' anyway. Know whit Ah mean? Looks a nice woman tae. Daft sayin' that intit? Like only the ugly or the no' nice should die. But ye say it anyway.'

'No' very auld either,' said the fireman helplessly. 'Ah hate it when ye canny dae anythin'.'

'Aye, me tae, son,' replied the paramedic, 'but there ye go. It wasnae anybody's fault, even if ye'd got her oot earlier, her internal injuries were too serious.'

'Look, lads,' the boy policeman interrupted, 'any chance we can speed this up noo that we're no' dealin' wi' a casualty any longer? We needtae get the traffic movin'.'

'Aye, gie us a minute here Mac,' said the fireman angrily. 'It's likely somebody's wife, somebody's mother we're dealin' wi' here, no' a stray dug!'

'Ah'm jist sayin',' said the policeman guiltily.

'Aye, well, then,' muttered the fireman. 'Dae ye want us tae get a bulldozer an' jist shove her oota the way like? We're daein' whit we can as fast as we can, an' it'll take as long as it takes. The traffic can just wait tae we're finished. An' you tae come tae that. A'right?'

The young policeman moved away. Tempers got frayed when you lost one, and besides, the days when the firemen, and the ambulance crews for that matter, saw the police as their friends and equals were long gone. Once they were mates, they worked alongside each other at incidents and so there was a kindred spirit between them. But during the Fire Brigade dispute in the 1980s, when the Thatcher government used the police as political muscle, they leaned on their old comrades during marches and on the picket lines, and it had never been forgotten. Relationships were broken then and had never recovered. The firemen were civil to them, but the automatic friendship between all three emergency services had gone for good; they no longer regarded the police as one of them. They had a point, the young policeman knew, the animosity that had replaced the camaraderie was well-founded, so you tried not to antagonize them too much. All the same, when the firemen went back to the station to wait for their next call-out, the police would still be working on this case. Someone would have to retrieve the personal effects from the wreck once the body had been removed. And then the next of kin would have to be informed.

10

When war was declared against Germany in 1939, Murdo was only two years old and another child was on the way. Alec Craig had been exempted from military service because his work on the farm on Eilean Òg was considered essential. With the long tradition of island men going to sea though, many, like his brother Will, found themselves in the peculiar position of being both civilians and serving on the front line. With the entire country either in the services or engaged in the war effort in some capacity, the government commandeered merchant ships and brought them under the control of the Admiralty. Everything the country needed, raw materials, food and armaments, would have to be brought in by sea, with the German U-boats and fighter planes waiting to attack. The Merchant Service now became the Merchant Navy, serving under the Red Ensign, or as the men called it 'the Red Duster'. Cargo ships arranged into convoys would cross the oceans of the world, with ships of the Royal Navy providing whatever protection they could throughout the war. With the fall of France and Italy's entry into the war on the German side in the summer of 1940, pressure on the Merchant Navy was increased, and without them the British Government would've been forced to accept a peace settlement as humiliating as the one imposed by the Germans on France. So Will, who had joined the Merchant Service because he loved the sea, now found himself serving in the Merchant Navy, facing torpedoes, gunfire, and the imminent threat of being sunk, to help stave off defeat by Germany.

In the autumn of 1939 Betty gave birth to a daughter. She called the baby Alison, because she liked the name, and Ishbel after her grandmother. In no time at all, though, Murdo had shortened that mouthful to Alibel, and so it had remained from that day on. A year later saw the arrival of a second son. Betty had planned to call him Gavin, but a few weeks before his birth, in October 1940, they were informed that Will's ship had been sunk and he was 'missing in action', and so the child was named in his honour. During wartime, listing men as 'missing', even though they were known to be dead, was a common practice and it would be a long time before the Craigs knew how and where Will had died. The close-knit sea-faring community had its own means of communication, and it was a returning seaman who had served with Will who later filled in the details.

At the beginning of the war the level of preparedness at sea as well as everywhere else was very low. The principle of protected convoys was established, but the actual protection wasn't, and until July 1940 the Merchant Navy convoys were only provided with escorts as far as 150 miles west of Ireland. Beyond that they could only put their trust in luck, or whatever God they might believe in. It wasn't until 1943 that Merchant Navy convoys were escorted throughout their dangerous journeys, where fighter planes lurked on high, U-boats waited beneath the sea and fast E-boats, designed for night raids and able to operate on the choppiest water, stalked the surface. And such protection as they had in 1940 was further reduced by the German successes in the Low Countries and France. When it seemed likely they would invade Britain at any moment, Churchill ordered the Royal Navy to form 'flotillas in the narrow seas', on guard against the expected German assault, leaving the convoys even more under-protected.

From August to December 1940 became what the German Navy called '*Die glückliche Zeit*', the happy time, when they inflicted the heaviest sea losses of the war. On 2 June of that year, Will had been on the 1800-ton steamer *Paris*, sailing in convoy down the Channel, when it was attacked by a German plane. The *Paris* was first machine-gunned, then a bomb pierced the port side. A second bomb blew out the ship's starboard side, causing a fifteen-degree list, and in an attack lasting less than twenty seconds the *Paris* went down. But the crew, including Will, took to the boats and were quickly picked up by the convoy escort, and by all accounts the Glaswegian from Eilean Òg was in boyish high spirits and ready for more. After the loss of the *Paris* he was posted temporarily to the 11,000-ton *City of Benares*, sailing from Liverpool on 13 September with 400 passengers on board. One hundred of them were children being evacuated for the duration of the war across the Atlantic, under the Children's Overseas Resettlement Scheme.

Five days out from Liverpool and still unescorted, the *City of Benares* was torpedoed in the darkness by *U-48*, 600 miles from land. The passengers found themselves shipwrecked and struggling against a gale, and 300 of them died in the rough seas. Will had been injured but managed to steer a lifeboat full of children for more than twenty hours, before they were picked up by a destroyer, with those who had died after the sinking floating in the water inside the lifeboat. Shortly after they were rescued Will died of his injuries and was later buried at sea. And after the war it emerged that many survivors of enemy attacks at sea owed their lives to lads from the Western Isles who, like Will, had grown up with boats and whose skills had been passed down through countless seagoing generations. Apart from individual accounts of their bravery and skill from those who lived to tell the tale though, the contributions of Merchant seamen went largely unrecognized by the authorities. Even their pay stopped the minute their ships were hit, and as they were still adrift on some cold ocean, trying to save lives, their own and others too.

All sorts of reasons were given for sending official telegrams listing men known to be dead as 'missing in action', but whatever the truth, it brought an added cruelty to families like the Craigs. At the end of the war one of Will's friends, a fellow crewman on the *City of Benares*, had kindly made the long journey to the island to tell Alec and Betty what had happened to Will. It was, he said, the boy's last wish before slipping into unconsciousness. He had witnessed Will's burial at sea, and if he hadn't contacted them they would not have known what had become of him. With no official confirmation of death the task of claiming a pension was made that much harder for those left behind, but no amount of money could ever justify leaving a family with false hope, however slender. They would gladly have forgone the highest pension just to know, to truly know the truth. That chink of light, of false hope, cruelly created by the bureaucrats was never completely extinguished in Alec's heart, even though his head knew better. Not that he doubted Will's crewmate, but deep inside and for the rest of his life, Alec clung to the illogical hope that as they hadn't been told officially that he was dead, maybe, just maybe there was a chance that it was all a mistake. Perhaps somewhere, against all the odds, Will was safe and one day he'd come home.

By a quirk of fate the new Will Craig was the only one of Alec and Betty's children to have red hair, just like the late uncle he would never see. Will's death at the age of twenty-two was the biggest blow they had suffered, and Alec was creased by the loss of the younger brother he had looked after all his life. Alec was everyone's protector, and even though he had the might of the German military machine against him, he still felt deep down that he had failed to look after his wee brother. And the fact that, as they kept saying themselves, it was a blow shared with countless families across the world at that time didn't help when it was your own. It was as well that Will had been buried at sea, though, because Betty knew she could not have listened to any minister trying to thank God for his sad, blighted young life, without saying what she thought. Being a boarded-out Will's name was not automatically included on the island monument to the fallen. The Craigs didn't give a moment's consideration to requesting it, partly, Betty knew, because Alec still hadn't given up hope of seeing Will again, but mainly because Will Craig *wasn't* an islander. Like Alec and Betty he was a Glaswegian, and Betty, defiant as ever, regarded it an honour not to have him included on the stone. His memory was carved for ever in the hearts of those who loved him, and that was enough. They knew what they could do with their stone. Alec rarely spoke of his brother, and when others did he became even more silent than usual, sinking deeper into his own thoughts and grief. The dinghy he had played in as a boy was brought to lie in the barn at Red Rock, because Alec couldn't bear to get rid of it. And there it stayed, landbound, for many years, as poignant a reminder of Will as any photograph.

Often, though, Betty would look out to sea and think of him, that little red-headed laddie with such a passion for boats all his short life. When he was down at the sea he lost all track of time, and many's the time they'd had to go looking for him and chase him home for his tea. Now he was lying for ever at the bottom of the ocean, far away from home, and he would never come back again. It was a strange thing having no body to bury, it was like unfinished business. Often over the years she would look at Alec, aware that he was thinking of Will, and still waiting, hoping against hope for the sight of him coming along the road to Red Rock, even later than usual.

Both Alibel and Will immediately came under the fiefdom of Murdo, and so it had continued all their lives. Alibel became a nurse at the local hospital, and Will a schoolteacher. Murdo, as everyone had always known he would, took over at Red Rock, though he had already taken it over in every meaningful sense the day he had let out his first yell. They were all good children, she had no complaints about any of them. They were all very different, though, the younger two were more placid, like Alec, and where Murdo's personality had come from was anybody's guess. Will adored him, yet he was always a lad with hidden depths, strong, quiet, but with a firm sense of himself. She would watch him watching Murdo and shaking his head at his older brother's excesses, catching her eye and smiling affectionately, a silent message passing between them, 'Whit can ye dae wi' him?' She was glad to have a schoolteacher in the family, it did her heart good to think of *her* son passing on wisdom and learning to the children of native islanders, teaching them that all people were equal. The school where she and the other boarded-outs had suffered so many unhappy indignities and cruelties had been pulled down long ago and a new, modern one put up on the site, but she could still see it in her memory and feel the hurts inflicted there, too many and too deep to ever forget, and if she was honest, to forgive either.

It was when she had had her own children that she had felt angriest, and it had surprised her. She had thought, hoped, that having her own family would be a kind of balm that would banish all the questions and resentments from her mind. But it was only then that she truly understood what she had missed herself. The natural affection between mother and child, that bond of belonging, the kisses and cuddles when they were hurt, the shared joys and sadnesses, the love. That's what had been stolen from her, and it made her angry, bitter and sad in equal measure. No one had the right to deprive a child of all that was normal in childhood. Many years later, one of the islanders tried to defend the treatment of the boarded-outs when it was written about in a newspaper. 'There was no cruelty involved,' she had said. 'They were well looked after. Most people in those days had hard lives and all the children in the family worked on the land.' Well, some were well cared for to be sure, but even those who were fed and clothed had been deprived of their families and childhoods, their freedom and their lives. Donnie Fraser, the boy who had come over on the boat with herself, Martha, Alec and Will, had spent all his life on the farm he had been delivered to as a small, frightened child, where he slept in the barn, like the other livestock. When he reached sixteen the farmer had paid him a nominal wage, anxious to keep the cheapest form of labour he had ever had. All through Donnie's able years he had been hired out to work on other farms, as though he was a horse or a piece of machinery. He never married, never had a life, because he didn't know how to, ending his days in the local hospital a sick old man, because there was nowhere else for him to go. Long after Dr Sandy had gone, another doctor, an incomer, had asked to see a member of the family Donnie had been boarded-out to. Donnie had, said the young doctor, laboured many years for her family; didn't she consider that perhaps she owed him something, if not kindness, then at least a duty of responsibility in his frail old age? She had replied 'He's not family. He was only a worker. He's nothing to do with me.' Alibel had been on duty at the hospital that day, and she had described how Donnie had clung to the woman's hand. They had grown up alongside each other, she was the nearest thing to a relative he had ever known, and the tears had streamed down the old man's face as she denied him then turned and left. No, there was no cruelty involved, but there are many ways of kicking a dog so that the wounds don't show.

Meanwhile their island had been used as a deep-water anchorage, and because of the hills, glens and lochs, as a training ground for Commandos. It used to strike her as ironic that while so many other people's sons were in her own backyard, the island boys were in someone else's. For the children it was an exciting time, of course, and every tide washed up treasures, bits of uniforms, ammunition, semaphore flags, everything you could think of, from the huge ships anchored in the bay. In that really bad winter, with the snow up to the upstairs windows, Murdo and Will had once climbed out and waved a set of flags about. Just then there came a 'Whoop-whoop' from a destroyer in the bay, the boom was lifted, and part of the assembled fleet sailed off. It was coincidence, of course, but both boys were convinced that their 'message' had caused the fleet to leave port. Will hid for days, waiting for the MPs to come and get him. Murdo just laughed.

To keep the Commandos amused the village hall showed films, which was a bonus for the children too. A chair was placed at the door, and as the Commandos came in they would throw their daggers like darts into the wooden seat, collecting them again when the evening's entertainment was over. They were a tough, mostly city-bred lot, their bodies honed to the peak of physical fitness, their minds ready for action. It was hardly surprising that sometimes the boredom would get to them, and they would steal bikes and rampage through farmland and fields till the MPs managed to round them up again. Fighting often broke out too between the international crews of the warships, as boredom united with national pride, all of it adding to the enjoyment of the local children, who stood watching and cheering on their own particular champions. It was an era when children could talk to strangers, and the men were far from home, far from their own families, so a mutual affection existed between the servicemen and the island children. In a time of strict security and secrecy, the children knew every ship by name, and could recite the names of the officers faster and more accurately than they could the four times table.

The children accepted the situation; military hardware and training runs were part of their lives. Landing craft would suddenly rush out of the sea towards the windows of the local school, and as heavily camouflaged men dashed out, armed to the teeth, and headed for the nearest cover, the children would scarcely bother to look up. After school the boys would search the shoreline for ammunition to play with, often bringing their live treasures home. For decades after the war long-buried ammunition was regularly dug up in various parts of the island, and bits of planes surfaced from time to time too, planes that hadn't quite made it on to waiting aircraft-carrier decks.

And there were accidents too that were kept secret from the rest of the country for thirty or fifty years, that islanders had watched happen. Like the time when a plane came in to land on its carrier, only the deck hadn't been raised, and the plane had plunged into the open bowels of the carrier, exploding in a huge fireball, killing who knew how many men. And that other time, when a U-boat had got through the boom and hit a destroyer before being detected and chased out to sea again. All those boys, she used to think, some mother's sons, killed in a foreign place and their families wouldn't be told for years and years what had happened to them, or even where they lay. The bodies that had been recovered were buried in the local cemetery. They stood out so sorely among the family graves with their personal inscriptions, a little group of white, uniform, military headstones, and under each one lay a boy. It broke your heart to look at them, so young and so far from home, with no one to remember and lay a flower on their graves. It was hardly surprising that she always felt a kind of affinity with them, a kind of longing to have their families know where they were so that they could be re-united. Perhaps that was why when she visited Ishbel and Murdo, and in time her own Alec in the cemetery, she brought flowers for those lost boys too. She could never pass that sad little row of young lives cut short, all of them, like her, condemned to remain for ever in a place they didn't choose, where they didn't belong and shouldn't be.

11

The trick was to distance yourself from the proceedings in any way you could, Marylka had decided. Didn't matter what you thought about, or how disrespectful, in fact the more disrespectful the better. It took your mind off the fact that you were standing inside Maryhill Crematorium as the early February snow finished thawing in the drizzle outside, and that your mother was lying in that box at the front. Wrong; think of something else. *Fast.* The coffin was covered with a tatty-looking purple velvet cloth; 'That proves none of this is real,' she thought wryly. 'My mother would have taken that thing home first and given it a damn good washing before she'd let them drape it over her!' Too near the bone, Marylka; get off this train of thought and concentrate on something else. Think about Andy, yes, that should take up a few minutes.

Despite her best intentions, as the cortege started out she had briefly glanced at the hearse and was surprised to see Andy driving it. Andy was one of the Western Infirmary's regular paramedics, and instalments of his double act with his ambulance partner, Mad Mick, were part of the hospital's folklore. Every now and again Andy got fed up and went off to work at something else for a while, before donning the green overall once again and taking his place behind the ambulance steering wheel, Mad Mick at his side. This must be one of his rebellious phases, but how bizarre, how wonderful, to find him driving her mother; it was like finding a friend in a strange, frightening country.

Thinking about Andy was far better at any rate than listening to the minister droning on. Not that his contribution was in danger of making her cry, though she might faint from boredom. It was all pretty far removed from her mother, but best not to dwell on his pious errors or you would start correcting them and think about what she is – was – really like. She really would have to get her head round using the past tense. But not yet; take a deep breath, raise your mind, look at it all from a different angle and just get through it.

She thought of all those relatives she routinely broke sad news to at the hospital. From the safety of her white coat, stethoscope casually draped around her neck in the best TV hospital soaps tradition, she sent them off on tragic journeys that ended just like this. She had never thought about it before, but this must be what happened at the conclusion of each uncomfortable little interview, once you had breathed a sigh of relief that it was over and watched them depart, disappearing from your life for ever, leaving you feeling slightly guilty.

Some of them just left without a word, weighed down with silent grief and numbed by shock, and if you were honest, those were the ones you preferred, while others burst into loud tears or wept quietly, so that you felt even more inadequate. There was that one awful occasion when she had told a woman her husband had died. The woman had walked into the room a wife and emerged a few sad words later a widow, and young Dr Kowalski had watched her leave, seemingly completely composed. Ten minutes later, as the ward round was assembling for the daily ritual humiliation of the houseman, Sister Woods from the medical unit downstairs, Crusher Woods that all departing housemen warned their replacements not to cross, had arrived in a state of barely controlled rage, looking for young Dr Kowalski. The new widow had got as far as the floor below when the tragedy of her new status had sunk in, and she had then collapsed in the arms of the passing Sister. 'Christ!' thought Marylka desperately. 'It had to be Beryl Woods! There is no God!'

She was out of her depth and embarrassed by the fact, so taking the road signposted 'For the Stupid', she retreated behind the dignity she hoped had been bestowed by the MB, ChB newly installed after her name. 'It's not my problem, Sister,' she replied, in a tone of cool authority that would have fooled eight out of ten nurses. 'Her husband was my patient. I can't be expected to take on the entire family!' But this was Crusher Woods, who regularly ate consultants never mind lowly housemen like Kowalski, who pronounced 'Doctor' with a kind of distaste, as though it were a term of deepest insult, and who then reacted by almost putting Marylka in a head-lock. 'Bloody doctors!' she shouted, to the considerable enjoyment of the rest of the medical team. 'You take no responsibility for anything! Bloody tin-pot Gods every one of you! You think you can destroy people's lives and then wash your hands of them. If you're as incapable of basic humanity as you seem, Doctor, get one of the nurses to help that poor woman – *now*!' Then she gave young Dr Kowalski a look that indicated she was marked down for life in Sister Woods's little black book, and returned to her own ward. Watching her go Marylka thought of her fellow houseman, Mark Galbraith, the unfortunate soul who had ended up, through no fault of his own, on Sister Woods's ward. Mark ran himself ragged working all the time; maybe there was a connection.

'Don't worry, Marylka,' her Senior House Officer grinned smugly. A year ago he had been doing Marylka's job, so he was now twelve glorious months removed from being scum. 'Crusher obviously took a shine to you. If she had been really angry we'd be lifting you off the floor with a fish slice. But I shouldn't make any plans for later, just in case.'

'Yes, thanks, Doctor,' she smiled back sweetly, 'and I was so grateful for the way you stood up for me there.'

'Do I look stupid? Try to see it as a learning curve. Tell yourself that one day you'll look back on your first run-in with Beryl Woods and smile. Try to –'

'Oh, shut up,' Marylka replied, walking away and trying to ignore the ward round sniggering behind her.

★ ★ ★

In her heart she knew Beryl Woods was right, but the trouble was that no one gave you any training in dealing with emotions while you were in medical school, and once you were out there in the wards you had no time to learn, no time to do anything beyond the supreme achievement of staying awake. But the older hands could reach the level Beryl Woods clearly inhabited, where you could cope with someone else's grief in a humane, sympathetic manner, while still staying detached. Once you got sucked into their emotions you were lost, that's what everyone said, and she was sure they were right. Yet there you were, sharing intimate, defining moments in the lives of total strangers you would never see again. She remembered the only lecture that even touched on it, given by an old chap smoking a pipe, Dr Alasdair MacKay, known affectionately as Ali to generations of medics. He was the calmest consultant she'd ever seen, very laid back and approachable, a physician naturally, not a surgeon. He worked in another medical unit in the Western; she saw him in the distance sometimes, watching everyone and everything around him and smiling in his gentle, amused way. 'Be careful how you explain these things,' he had told them that day, between puffs, the smoke from his pipe spiralling around the huge lecture room. In between his pronouncements he would stop and peer at the listening students, a friendly, gentle smile playing across all his features, not just his mouth. 'Be assured that the relatives will remember you, your words, your demeanour, and possibly even what you wore, long years after you have forgotten they even exist.' He stopped again and gazed at them in silence before continuing. 'It has to be said that the medical profession doesn't like emotions, and if you tell my esteemed colleagues that I talked to you of feelings they will tell you I am a heretic, or at the very least barking mad.' He gave a quiet little chuckle. 'This is a game they play. I am placed here before you today as the nutter in the woodpile, as an example of what not to turn into.' He chuckled again, puffed on his pipe and stared silently but amiably at the bemused students before him, as they stared back at him. It had almost felt like hypnosis, and he was right; the rest of the medical fraternity regarded Ali with affection, as well-intentioned but wrong, kindly but demented. To many he was the sort of daft old boy students should be exposed to just once, so that they would recognize danger in the future; he was a form of immunization against the disease of empathy with other human life forms.

Marylka couldn't get Ali out of her mind, though. Every other lecturer dealt in facts, but he had seemed like an oasis of calm reason amid all the thrusting ambition and technology. Maybe she had a weakness for white-haired, blue-eyed subversives, maybe it was just her contrary nature, but the longer she was on the wards the more sense his words seemed to make. Yet like all the rest she followed the conditioning, the traditional procedure for passing on sad news. You said simply that you were very sorry, but their relative had died, then you gave them a quick explanation and tried to get them to sign a post mortem consent before they had time to gather their thoughts and refuse; the Pathology Department had to be kept gainfully employed after all. After a few moments you stood up, expressing your sympathy once again in the same time-honoured, emotionless manner, giving them their cue to go, and finally you hustled them out of the door.

After that you hopefully never met them again; even the handing over of the death certificate and the double-signed cremation form could be handled by someone less involved. It was only if the interview had been especially horrendous that they sometimes lingered obstinately in your mind for a little while longer, making you scared that you had been infected by the Ali immunization and might be turning into a nutter yourself. A few days later, when they were going through the burial rites of the patient you had failed, you had forgotten all about them. By that time you had doubtless failed someone else, and were in the process of failing God knows how many more.

Marylka looked around the crematorium chapel at the

assembled company and smiled wryly. Mostly business acquaint-ances, and the detritus of the long-lived Davidson clan. Usually long-lived, she corrected herself; there were one or two excep-tions, the lady lying in the box for instance. Wrong again. Quick, there's a plane overhead, concentrate on where it might be going. Think about the people, why they might be travelling. Take yourself out of this raw performance. You only have to be here, you don't have to take part; it has nothing to do with her or what she means – meant – to you. She heard a muffled noise and looked sideways. Her grandfather, the latest and last in a long line of Hector Davidsons, and father of the deceased, was losing his battle to keep his grief under control. She caught the minister's eye and silently drew a finger across her throat. He had been saying nothing of importance anyway, only waffling on about Helen Davidson Kowalski's contributions to charity, the Arts, etc., but Marylka almost smiled as he suddenly stopped mid-oration, his eyes wide. He hesitated for a second as she maintained stern eye-contact with him, then he reached forward to press the button on the console in front of him. Some hymn or other droned out to cover the sound of the hydraulics system, as the coffin began to move downwards, towards the conveyor belt bearing it to the waiting furnace.

Earlier, when he had tried to discuss the funeral service with the deceased's daughter, the minister had been shocked at Marylka's indifferent attitude, and she in turn had been shocked that he thought any of this mattered. She had discovered that the less she accepted what was happening the better she coped. So those who did accept it and, worse still, took the process forward threatened her self-control and thus became her enemies. In the days following her mother's death she had perfected the art of getting them before they got her. From a distance she watched herself and concluded it must be an anger response, but whatever it was, it was carrying her through the unthinkable and unbearable, for the moment at least. She sus-pected that her mother would have been appalled by her behaviour, 'But she's not here, is she?' she thought, inexplicably angry at Helen. 'That's the problem. So I'll handle this any damn way I want!'

'Who cares what kind of service you have?' she had asked the minister. 'Do whatever you want, get up and do a soft-shoe shuffle for all I care, for all my mother cares either come to that. Just get it over with. We don't want a feature-length drama.'

'But your mother wasn't just anyone,' he had pointed out, with that kindly, understanding, sanctimonious smile they must give out with theology degrees.

'Good heavens!' she said. 'If you'll pardon the pun. Are you saying that we are not all equal in the sight of God after all, then?'

'I mean,' he said, the kindly smile looking somewhat weaker, 'there will be a big attendance, from that point of view this will not be an ordinary funeral service.'

'Well, let them all get up and do a soft-shoe shuffle, then,' Marylka responded. 'If you're determined to turn it into a circus anyway, I suppose we may as well have the three ring variety.'

He tried again. 'I thought we might make this a celebration, an occasion for joy and thanksgiving for your mother's life.'

'Oh yes, very good, the "silver lining" approach!' Marylka responded very quietly and calmly. 'She didn't quite reach fifty, but she *was* a Davidson, she had lots of cash, so let's be thankful!'

The minister opened his mouth to speak but nothing came out.

'Perhaps,' Marylka continued, 'she did something awful in a previous life, and she's been made to atone in this one. No, no, that won't work; the Church of Scotland doesn't go in much for reincarnation, does it? Oh, well, I'm afraid it's back to the drawing board, Minister, see if you can't think up some other useless platitude!'

The minister reflected that grief affected everyone differently, and decided it might be better to arrange the service himself without further distressing young Dr Kowalski.

The only strong decision she had made was that Helen

Kowalski should be cremated; there would be no lying in the Davidson crypt for her, rotting away with the rest of the clan. Afterwards she would think of somewhere suitable to scatter the ashes. The minister tried to question that one too, advised perhaps consulting her grandfather.

'Look, the only reason I'm here at all and just about prepared to put up with this theatrical event, is because of my grandfather. If it were left to me this would be an entirely private occasion with only immediate family and no service of any kind,' she said coldly. 'And may I remind you that my grandfather is seventy-eight years old and he has just lost his only child. I am the next of kin, go near him to question any of my decisions and I would be most unhappy. In fact, if you disapprove of my arrangements, or lack of them, Minister, you are quite free to stand down and let someone else take over.'

The minister decided he had never met anyone who exhibited grief in quite this way, but it did the trick, and thereafter he gave up with his helpful hints. Marylka smiled to herself. There was no way he was going to let anyone else preside over an event like this one. It was a Davidson do, it would be covered by all parts of the media at home and, because of the business interests abroad, it would most probably be reported overseas too. Miss out on getting a new frock and looking pious in front of that audience? Like Hell he would! As she turned to leave she said 'Thank you for your time, Minister, it was a pleasure doing business with you.'

The minister merely smiled in response, his look suggesting perhaps that the pleasure had been all hers.

'Pillock!' she thought, 'Hasn't got the guts to call a member of the Davidsons a charmless brat. He'd take any amount of abuse rather than risk losing the leading role in this farce!'

The strange thing was that from the start it had all been like watching it happen to someone else. She had been Receiving Physician, a grand title which meant that for a twenty-four-hour spell she saw every medical case in the Western Infirmary's catchment area. Misleading too; she had already been on duty for forty-eight hours straight when the two PCs asked to talk to her. It happened frequently; people were always being found unconscious and carted off to the nearest hospital by passing police officers. Inquiries had, as they said, to be made, and always when you could least spare the time. But it wasn't business this time, it was personal. The policewoman did all the talking. Was she the daughter of Mrs Helen Kowalski, nee Davidson? Yes, she was. Then the young policewoman was sorry to tell her that her mother had been fatally injured in a car crash in Great Western Road some hours ago.

From that moment on she became detached in a curious way. She even began making mental notes. God, the policewoman was good at this; it was like a demonstration on how to deliver bad news without the recipient dissolving in a shrieking mass in front of you. She wished she had listened when the policewoman told her her name. She was a pretty girl with hazel eyes, and a ponytail of fair hair caught up with a black stretchy elastic band at the back of the unflattering police hat that made them all look identical. Mid twenties, she'd say, just like herself, but considerably healthier looking; she looked as though she slept regularly. She was listening to the words the young policewoman was saying, yet she was keeping them at bay. The thought kept repeating itself that it was like watching from the sidelines as someone else went through this torturous, yet oddly familiar experience. 'Is this what they call an out of body experience?' she thought frivolously. She had already decided that if she didn't take this seriously then it wasn't true. The policewoman's right upper canine tooth was slightly crooked, she noticed, and she had a blue plaster over a wound on the third finger of her right hand, the kind of plaster chefs wear so that they can see it if it comes off in the food. It was stained where blood had seeped through and dried; she must give the girl a fresh dressing once this was over. Irish Catholic background, judging by the gold Claddagh ring on her cut finger, Marylka thought. She wondered what had caused the wound.

'What happened to your finger?' She wasn't sure if she had actually said it aloud.

The young policewoman looked nonplussed for a moment. 'Sorry?' she said.

Marylka tried to laugh, tried to appear carefree, but her throat was dry, so she coughed and repeated the question. 'Your finger,' she said, indicating the blue plaster. 'I was wondering what happened to it?'

'Oh, that. It's nothing, a wee dog snapped at it. He was lost; we were trying to catch him. It's nothing, honestly.' She put the hand with the plaster behind her back as punishment for intruding on the moment, but Marylka wouldn't let it go, she needed the distraction. She almost asked if the lost dog had been ginger and felt her mouth beginning to twitch at the corners. 'My God!' she thought. 'Welcome to the land of hysteria, you idiot!' She turned her attention to the policewoman's finger again.

'Have you had a tetanus recently?' she asked.

'No, no I don't think so,' the girl replied uncertainly.

'Well you should have one while you're here. I'll call A & E and arrange it before you go.'

The policewoman nodded, but the colour spreading across her cheeks betrayed her confusion over where this conversation was going. Instantly Marylka felt ashamed of herself and her delaying tactics. Part of her wanted to live in this scenario for ever rather than face the next step, but another part wondered furiously what the hell she thought she was doing. Putting the girl off her stride like this wasn't fair, what she had to do was bad enough. The least she could do was play her allotted role in the customary manner and let the policewoman get out of this awful situation as quickly as seemed decent.

She suddenly realized that Ali MacKay, the well-known heretic from her student days, had indeed told no lies. She was memorizing this young girl, almost as though her looks mattered more than what she was saying. 'Are you sure?' she heard herself ask. How many times had she been asked that herself by shocked relatives? So *that* was why they asked, because it was the only thing that came to mind, not because they didn't believe you. It was a way of buying time, of holding off searing reality for a few precious seconds longer. And did they all feel this sudden urge to be sick as well, she wondered? And this same need to be told the smallest details without being able to take them in? She was listening to every word, but somehow each one slipped away before her memory could store it. Something about driving home to Bearsden from the office in St Vincent Place in the city centre, and making a mistake at the Anniesland Junction. Her mother had always hated that junction.

'The traffic comes at you from every direction,' she grumbled.
   'Well why don't you take the other route up Maryhill Road instead?' Marylka suggested. 'Or better still, get a chauffeur like your ostentatious forebears!'
   'No, I refuse!' Helen laughed. 'I won't be intimidated by it, I'll do what I always do, just follow the others and get across into Bearsden Road on a wing and a prayer!'

Well, they had both failed her this time, and facing her fears hadn't worked out too well either, come to that. She had apparently driven across too late, on the last blink of the amber light, been hit by one car, somersaulted, and then been hit by another coming from the other direction. Maybe her dislike of the junction had been some sort of premonition then. Marylka tried to concentrate, but it was so unreal, it felt like a nightmare; that cliché at least was spot on. Someone's hands grasped her arms above the elbows, trying to make her sit down but she resisted, suspecting that she might not be able to stand again if she did. Her legs were trembling with the instinct to run, to get as far away as possible to some place where this wasn't happening. It wasn't true, it was all nonsense. She knew for a fact that her mother was safely at home. Helen had left a message for her with the switchboard earlier, but when she'd called the office she had been on the phone.

★   ★   ★

'It's nothing urgent, Marylka,' Annie had said. 'Just call her when you can, that's what she said. She's nipping off to do some shopping before she heads home. You could always try her on the mobile of course!' Annie chuckled. They both knew Helen's suspicions that her mobile phone was a tracking device, ensuring she could never be free. As long as she carried it she could always be 'got at', and every time it rang she gave that lecture to whoever was on the other end.

'I don't really think so, Annie, thanks for the suggestion, though!' Marylka laughed. 'Tell her I'll phone her later at home. I've got patients piled up to the ceiling, but hopefully it'll slacken off later, fingers crossed anyway.'

'OK, Marylka, I'll pass it on. Isn't this weather horrible? The snow always looks so nice, but when it starts to thaw and gets all wet and slushy like this, yuk!'

'I know what you mean,' Marylka said politely. She hadn't been out of the hospital for days, she had no idea what was happening or what the weather was like, in that big wide world outside, where ordinary people lived. 'I'll have to go now Annie, these folk have no consideration, all getting sick at the same time. 'Bye!'

Later, when there had been a lull between patients, she called the house in Bearsden; lulls came rarely on Receiving Days and if things hotted up later she might not have chance to call. When there was no reply she risked Helen's wrath and tried the mobile phone. She was almost relieved when there was no reply again; arguing with Helen about the merits and short-comings of technology was a thankless and hopeless task after all. 'She probably threw it out of the car window at the first ring anyway!' she thought, and smiled at the image of Helen driving off in a rage, leaving the still ringing phone lying in the gutter.

She knew Helen would still address the empty car on the subject though, then she'd put on one of her 'Goons' tapes. Her mother had grown up in the 1950s, listening to the Goons on the radio in Auntie Mary's house. Her great joy as she drove along was to join in with Milligan, Sellers and Secombe at the top of her voice as they sang the famous 'Ying Tong Tiddlc-i-Po' song. A Patron of the Arts she might be, but even a black and white photo of Spike Milligan could reduce her to tears of helpless laughter. Marylka smiled and shook her head at the thought, and immediately her pager sounded with news of yet another patient. The lull was over.

She went over the earlier conversation with Annie. It occurred to her that if she'd hung on till Helen had finished the call she was on, or if she'd asked her to call straight back, then Helen might have left the office later and missed that sequence of lights at Anniesland. And those two cars . . . No, that wouldn't do, she decided firmly; thinking like that makes it real, and it isn't. It must be someone else, and she immediately felt desperately sorry for the family of whoever it really was who had been cut from the wreckage of the car by firemen some hours ago, and pronounced dead at the scene. 'My mother always loved firemen,' she thought. She shook her head to stop the picture that was trying to paint itself into her mind and her memory. Later she'd phone Helen at home and they'd laugh about it in a relieved way. 'What a shock!' she'd say. 'As if being Receiving Physician isn't bad enough without your own mother getting in on the act! They really thought it was you.' And Helen would laugh back and say 'Well, only the good die young.' She remembered her saying that once; where, when was that?

12

She took it in by as many degrees as she was prepared to accept. First of all she had sneaked off like a child doing something naughty and phoned her mother's home, but there was no answer. She should be there by now, she would be there by now, unless, well, unless something had happened. Well, if you intended running away it was as well to know how far you needed to retreat to find a safe vantage point. She needed to be near enough to see and keep tabs on what was happening, yet too far away to be seen and forced to participate. Then identifying Helen's body advanced the process considerably. She looked so peaceful. Everyone said that about the dead and Marylka had always been puzzled; she thought they simply looked dead. But she was wrong and they were right. She could hazard a guess about the horrors concealed under the carefully positioned sheet, and one day perhaps she would. But for the moment, looking at the only features visible, it had to be said that her mother looked peaceful. Her habitual expression had relaxed, that mixture of resignation and slight resentment was gone, at being a Davidson, Marylka had always thought. Instead there was this incredibly peaceful person who looked, and yet didn't look, like her mother.

Suddenly she noticed that Helen's hair was lighter than she remembered. She had this picture of her mother in her mind from years ago that somehow hadn't altered, and Helen's hair had always been dark brown. In recent years, with the gradual appearance of grey strands, the women's magazines had been consulted. Should she deal with it herself, or could her hair-dresser be trusted not to spread the false rumour that she had grey hair? 'So you're planning to disguise yourself, put on the dark glasses then sidle up to someone in Boots the Chemist, with a hair colourant craftily concealed about your person, are you?' Marylka smiled. 'If you're caught and interrogated I suppose you can always say it's for a friend.'

Helen drew her a look then ignored her. 'Says here,' she read from one of her magazines, 'that as your hair loses colour, you lose pigment from your face too.' She looked up. 'Not fair is it?' She returned to her magazine. 'So you're supposed to cover the grey – in my case the very premature grey – with lighter shades, not your natural colour, as you get older. *Older? Older?* I'm maturing, not getting older!'

Yet Marylka had never noticed it, had never changed the mental picture she had of her mother, until now, when she saw those newly dressed, light brown locks resting on the pillow. 'Maybe she's just had it done,' she thought. 'How would I know? I haven't seen her in weeks.' The stab of guilt was like a knife. She hadn't wanted her grandfather to see his daughter, but now she realized that it was OK. The lads in the morgue had done a good job, a favour for one of their own, and apart from a couple of tiny bruises there was nothing obviously grotesque to haunt his dreams for however long he had left, if he ever dreamt, that was. It was abnormal enough that he had outlived his only child, but there was nothing she could do to protect him from that one.

The thought of funeral arrangements was unbearable, it was like a kind of torture. Her grandfather had suggested getting one of the family's army of assistants to take care of it, but Marylka had refused, it was her job. The whole death thing had once included rituals that had survived for generations, rituals there were good reasons for. In more enlightened times attending to the details personally helped families adjust to their loss, but these days death was held at arm's length, passed on to strangers and sanitized of all beneficial emotion. It had been taken over by the funeral business, and a big business it had become. When Auntie Mary died three years ago, Helen had been angry that there was nothing of Mary in the whole performance. A lady who had lived for more than ninety action- and emotion-packed years, had been safely and neatly packaged inside a tiny box lined with pink satin. In Mary's day the family would have taken charge of laying the body out, of washing it and dressing it; it was the last kindness that could be performed, and it was done with tenderness and care. White sheets would have been placed over the windows, as a public announcement of a death within the family and the community. Seeing the sign, neighbours and even strangers, would pass the bereaved home in hushed, silent respect, and their children wouldn't play outside for the same reason. No one had to ask for these courtesies, they were done instinctively because everyone knew what it was to lose a loved one, and living so closely they identified with each other.

Mary had told both Helen and Marylka about how poor families lived in those days, and how they had coped with the ordinary tragedies of everyday life. As a girl she had helped lay out both her parents. She remembered polishing her father's best shoes till they shone, and scraped together a few farthings to buy a hankie for his top pocket, first embroidering it with his initials. Though still very young, she and her older sister Lizzie had washed their mother, combed her hair, dressed her in freshly washed and pressed best clothes, then put pennies on her eyes. That was back in the days when the Davidsons had no money, before they could afford not to deal with their grief, before anyone could afford it. But these days everyone either could or forced themselves to afford it, and the duties of burying the dead were performed by paid strangers who had no reason to carry them out with any feeling or even respect. Marylka had often found herself squirming in the morgue as bodies were handled in the most impersonal way. The assistants didn't mean it, it was how those who worked there were able to tolerate it day in, day out; hardening themselves to what they saw and what they did made it possible to bear. Once she had watched two porters collect a newly dead patient from a bed in the ward, and place the body in the metal container used to transport them to the morgue. In the tradition of hospital black humour it was known as 'the bread bin'. All the screens in the ward were closed so that the patients wouldn't be distressed by the sight of 'the bread bin', but a silence would fall, because they all knew what was happening out of their sight anyway. Marylka saw one of the porters heave the still warm body into the metal container. 'That's someone's mother, you know!' she had chided him, and he replied with a grin: 'It's not yours, why should you care?' But now it was, and she did.

The undertaking business that would take care of Helen's funeral arrangements was an arm of the empire, of course. There was nothing quite like a Davidson send-off; it was said in upper-class circles that you wouldn't be admitted to Heaven unless you'd been done by Davidsons. When Marylka arrived at the discreetly morbid office she was outwardly calm, glib even, but inside she was dreading the next hour, so it helped slightly to discover that Mr Raymond Andrews, the man himself, was a seriously odd caricature of an undertaker. 'I bet he calls himself a "Mortician",' she thought, and almost laughed out loud when he did. He was a small man, though he seemed set in a permanently bowed position, so it was difficult to tell, and he had a long face suffused with grovelling duty and veneration. 'It's a mask,' she decided. 'He must take it off when he goes home and put it in a drawer. The Uriah Heep model, if I'm not mistaken.' Every hair on his head was perfectly in place. 'Mortician chic; grey tinged brown,' she thought, and he had the longest earlobes she had ever seen. As he conveyed her to his inner sanctum he glided silently from her left side to her right and back again, so that she kept losing him for a moment while he completed each manœuvre, smiling deferentially as he went, his huge, fleshy earlobes bobbing about with a will of their own. If she had to see an undertaker, she thought, this was exactly the kind she needed to see.

But still it was wearing work. There was choosing the perfect coffin from all the other coffins, and the expectation was that given Helen's elevated position in society, only the best, the most expensive, top-of-the-range coffins would be considered. And would Madam be wearing her own clothes 'for her last journey', or one of the little man's very finest, à la mode shrouds? And socks? Gloves? And Dr Kowalski would of course require a hairdresser and a make-up artist to attend to the deceased. Stated, not asked. Marylka looked at Uriah as though he had just escaped from the local funny farm, and had to stifle the urge to ask if he was still taking his medication.

'Relatives do prefer to see the deceased in the best of condition,' he explained, in a soft, concerned, reassuring voice, in response to Marylka's bemused expression. She continued to stare at him, so he tried again. 'Our make-up artists can achieve wonderful results, you know,' he said earnestly. 'They can make the deceased appear almost life-like.'

It was like something from a 'Carry On' film. Any moment now Kenneth Williams would pop up and shout 'Frying tonight!'

'But she's *dead*!' Marylka said, trying to stem the hysterical laughter that was burbling up from her throat towards her mouth. 'I mean, isn't that why we're having this discussion? Or have I missed something? The second coming perhaps, another Lazarus trick?'

He cleared his throat and began to suspect that, just like the minister, he might be on to a loser here. 'And do you have any preference about presentation?' he asked, glossing over his unease.

'You're planning to give her some sort of posthumous award, are you?' she asked coolly.

'Well, it's very popular in America these days to arrange the deceased with a slight smile, or with the head slightly to the side,' said the little man encouragingly. 'It's sheer artistry. It looks more natural, and gives the impression that the deceased is only asleep.'

'Must come as a helluva shock when they waken up six feet under, don't you think so? Look Mr, um, Andrews.' She had been about to say 'Heep', and had only just stopped herself. 'In fact I've been mulling this over for the last couple of days. We'll have no viewing, the coffin will be closed. And I've decided that my mother will be cremated, so give her the cheapest box you can find, and leave the plastic handles on. My mother might not have been stuck for a bob, but she couldn't abide waste or being ripped off. She and I would be very displeased to discover the handles being used afterwards on someone else's coffin.'

She was delighted with his expression of amazement, hurt and shock.

'And as for clothes,' she continued. 'I'll send in some outfit or other. It'll be from one of the designer collections so it will work out considerably cheaper and in better taste than any of your shrouds.' Then, as she got up to go she thought of another barb. 'And Mr Andrews, we don't want to see the firm's name anywhere, on the hearse, the cars, or held up on a placard. My mother always thought it was terribly tacky to use the dead for advertising purposes, in fact she had been meaning to have a word with someone to put an end to it. Perhaps you'd see to that. Good day.'

So the whole, awful thing had been got over with, she was pleased to note, maximum offence caused to those who knew how to make a similar amount of money out of bereaved families. Marylka felt massive relief at continuing to keep it all at a distance where she could handle it. The reckoning would come, she knew that, but some time when the world wasn't watching, some other time. Then the next thing she felt was annoyance. Everyone she knew would know who she was, she realized, the Davidson stamp would be on her for ever now, as if Old Hector, the family patriarch, had reached out from his fancy crypt and grabbed her as his own. She had a mental picture of him smiling triumphantly and saying 'Gotcha! I always get what I want in the end.'

When Receiving Day started she was Dr Marylka Kowalski, a faceless, 25-year-old houseman nearing the end of her eighteen-month sentence, the lowest form of medical life, like all the others in the Western. Now her mother's death was splashed over the newspapers and TV, enabling the Davidsons to lasso her and drag her kicking and screaming into the corral, regardless of the name she hid behind. Despite her brief marriage, Glasgow had always known Helen as Helen Davidson, so it was understandable that in reports of her sudden death the newspapers still described her as 'granddaughter of Hector Davidson Senior'. Marylka Kowalski, however, had always been safely anonymous, but now she would forever be Old Hector's great-granddaughter, it would run through the rest of her life like the lettering in a stick of rock. Every member of the family was defined by their relationship to him, she alone had escaped. Till now. She looked at her picture in every daily newspaper and grimaced 'Bugger!' she thought, 'Bugger, bugger!'

When the service ended she went in search of Andy, and found him leaning against a headstone having a quick smoke.

'Hi, Andy!'

'Christ, ye gave me a fright there!' he said, dramatically placing his hand over his heart. 'Whit you doin' here, Doctor? Ah know ye don't like giein' up, but is this no' takin' it a bit far like?'

'I'm at a funeral, saw you driving the hearse. This another one of your huffs with the ambulance service?'

'Ye could say,' he grinned sheepishly, stubbing his cigarette out on the headstone. 'Went tae an RTA the other week, blood an' guts a' ower the place, bones sticking oot, ye know, the usual, an' when Ah opened the emergency chest know how many bandages Ah find? Wan! Wan bloody bandage!' He shook his head, still enraged. 'It's no' right, is it?'

Marylka shook her head too.

'Ah said tae that daft bugger Mad Mick "Whit am Ah supposed tae dae wi' wan bandage?" an' he says, "Ye can put it

roond your mooth for a start, we've a' heard it afore." So Ah
laid intae him, the polis hadtae separate us. So Ah said tae masel'
"Time for another wee rest, Andrew, gie up savin' lives for a
while an' go an' dae somethin' worthwhile instead."'

'The two of you actually had a set-to in the middle of the
incident?' Marylka laughed.

'Och aye, it happens. Mick's an eedjit that doesnae know
he's an eedjit, an' that's the worst kind. Sometimes the only
thing ye can dae is hit him he's that stupid. He acts the fool a'
the time an' then when ye're at an incident he stays bloody
calm and reasonable!'

'Isn't that one of his best points?' Marylka laughed.

'Aye, but it's no' normal is it?' Andy stuck his hands in his
pockets and wandered about, nudging the odd headstone with
his toe. 'He's a . . . a . . . a bloody robot, that's whit he is!
Everybody that hastae work wi' him when Ah go away says
when Ah go back "Thank Christ ye're back, Andy, he's no'
right in the heid, you're the only wan that can work wi' him."'

'And you punch him!'

'Aye, well, Mick needs a good doin' noo an' again,' Andy
grinned. 'An' Ah'll tell ye somethin' else aboot him, even when
ye hit him it doesnae leave a mark. Ye should get up close if
ye can stand it and have a look, Mad Mick's no' normal!' He
lit another cigarette.

'But you're not long back are you? What was it made you
quit the last time?'

'It was that big accident in Argyle Street when the bus ran
intae that shop. Remember it? Well we had this woman trapped
by the leg an' the whole place threatenin' tae come doon oan
us if we didnae get oot smartish like. So Ah opens the emergency
chest that time and there's nae saw! Can ye imagine it? We're
havin' tae take aff her leg tae get her oot, an' there's nae bloody
saw! Wanna the firemen hadtae gie us his, Ah was that embarrassed! An' ye know whit they firemen can be like.'

Marylka shook her head slightly; she didn't want to think
about firemen. Andy caught her expression and misunderstood.

'Oh aye, Ah know!' he said. 'Salt o' the earth an' a' that, an' right sarcastic swines intae the bargain! Especially that John the Baptist.'

'John the Baptist?'

'Aye, John Docherty. He was at a fire in a Baptist Chapel an' he fell in the baptismal pool. Him bein' a good Catholic boy that was him double-dipped so tae speak, an' efter that he was called John the Baptist. An' a right smartarse he is tae, every time he claps eyes on me it's "Don't forget your bandage noo Andy boy!" or "Ah never 'saw' ye there!" Hings oota the fire engine windae just tae shout that! Wanna these days he'll fa' oot on his napper, an' Ah'll say "Sorry John, still havnae got a bandage for ye, mibbe a saw wid dae?"' He chuckled to himself at the thought. 'Anyhow, Ah gied it up for a coupla months efter that tae, then Ah went back for a while, an' noo Ah'm doin' this.'

'And do you like this better?' Marylka asked.

'Well at least the buggers don't answer ye back,' he grinned. 'They jist lie there an' keep quiet. No' had wan that's slapped me oan the ear yet, so ye might say they're pleasanter company deid! Ah'm doin' a fancy funeral the day, some rich bint killed in a car smash the other night. But ye know me, Ah'm a mug, Ah aye go back. Besides, naebody but me can stand workin' wi' Mad Mick. Ah bet whoever's been put oan wi' him will be near chokin' the daft sod tae death by noo.' He looked up at the mourners coming out of the chapel. 'That's ma well-heeled lot comin' oot noo,' he said. 'It's like a bloody production line in these places. Whit funeral were ye at? Wis it a friend, hen?'

'My mother, Andy, that rich bint who died in that car smash the other night!'

Andy looked aghast. 'Oh, hen, Ah'm sorry! Me an' ma big mooth! Baith bloody big feet in again, uptae the oxters! Christ, Ah'm helluva sorry, hen!'

'No, no, it's OK, Andy,' she laughed. 'But do you never read the papers nor watch the news on TV?'

'Only if there's somethin' aboot the 'Gers,' he replied with a grin. 'The rest is a' aboot politicians an' they're a' liars. Doesnae matter which party they come frae, they can only tell lies, an' that just gets me angry. So noo Ah never bother wi' anythin' but the fitba'.'

'Oh, well, my mother had no connection with Ibrox, so you weren't to know then. Anyway, you've no idea how good it is to see a friendly face in all this.'

'Lookin' at that shower Ah see whit ye mean,' he said, watching the august assembly settling into their limos. 'They don't look a laugh a minute, no' exactly the life an' soul – Christ, hen, Ah've done it again! Ah didnae mean –'

'Relax, Andy,' she smiled. 'You've done my mother more service than most of those free-loaders ever did. I just wanted to thank you.'

She had been about to invite him to the reception afterwards, but she realized it wouldn't be fair. As far as she knew there would be no Rangers players there, so Andy would probably have felt out of place; a bit like herself in fact, though for different reasons. Later she asked her grandfather to have a few hundred pounds put in an envelope, which she then gave to Uriah Heep. 'Give that to Andy the hearse driver from my grandfather,' she said. 'Make sure he knows it's not from me, it's from Young Hector, and don't open the envelope and take a cut. I know how much is there and Andy's a friend of mine, I'll ask him later to make sure he got it all. OK?'

13

Going back to work was a double-edged sword. The first reason for returning as soon as possible was for the sake of whoever had covered for her over the last three days, and whether there was a good reason for her absence or not, and regardless of their inherent good nature, her fellow housemen were too tired trying to keep up with their own workload to be more than temporarily understanding about taking on someone else's. And the other reason, possibly the best one, was that she needed to get back into a normal routine. One day, she knew, she would have to face the reality of Helen's death, but at that particular moment she couldn't. Being at work, business as usual, would keep her mind occupied to the point of total exhaustion till she felt ready to cope with what had to be coped with. Struggling with the hospital routine and the demands of the patients, and more importantly, the consultants, she would have no time to think, no time to dwell on the 'ifs' and 'maybes'; it would be a support system for denial for as long as she needed it.

But still, going back meant facing people who would see her as a whole different person. She would be a Davidson in their eyes now rather than Dr Marylka Kowalski, and she had no idea exactly who would be affected by that or in what way. In effect she had decided to cope with life bit by bit; her only luxury was being able to choose which bit and when, and the hospital was first. She was apprehensive, but there was no alternative; she had to grit her teeth and get over this first hurdle, and whatever was going to happen would happen. It was simply a case, she decided, of taking a deep breath, head up, back straight and getting the show on the road. But still, it was easier said than done all the same.

It was one of those tricks of fate that the first person she met was Mad Mick, Andy's paramedic on and off partner, not the first individual anyone would chose to meet, even in normal circumstances. Mad Mick stood over six feet tall and he was the thinnest man anyone ever recalled seeing alive, 'a hauf-blin' skeleton wi' feet. If he wasnae wearin' his green overalls there'd be nothin' tae keep him up,' being Andy's usual and very accurate description, and though Mick's glasses might have corrected his sight, they couldn't disguise his obvious squint. He wore what was left of his hair in a severe short-back-and-sides style that probably hadn't changed since his father's day, let alone Mick's, and all in all he looked like a more than usually deranged train-spotter. He had an equal opportunities personality, he came at everyone in the same manner, like a sledgehammer. If you happened upon him it came at you whether you could take it or not.

'Here she is. Ma wee doll!' he shouted, ensuring that every eye was turned upon Marylka as she tried to walk quietly and unnoticed into the hospital. Maybe Andy's opinion that Mick 'needs a good doin' noo an' again' had more to commend it than she had previously suspected. 'This is the lassie Ah'm gonny marry! Whit's your name again Darlin'?' The others around the ambulance radio control centre chuckled quietly instead of the usual raucous laughter, unsure, she realized, how to treat her, now that she wasn't who they had thought she was. Mick turned to address the assembled ranks of whoever happened to be about, patients, porters, his fellow paramedics, and the populace at large. 'We have kept oor love secret long enough,' he announced gravely, throwing his long, skinny arms wide for emphasis. He looked like an out-of-control windmill. 'We are noo aboot tae pledge oor troth, though no' in front of yoose lot. An' Darling,' he said to Marylka, in a mock whisper that he thought sounded like the tones of an upper-class playboy, 'if you'll just leave the keys of the Roller wi' me, Ah'll pick up the fish suppers on the way hame the night!' He gave a deep bow as she passed and blew extravagant kisses in her wake.

'Bog off, Mick,' she said, and was relieved to hear everyone laughing in a more normal way. Maybe meeting Mad Mick was the best thing after all, it had at least broken the ice.

'Don't be fooled by that!' Mick once again addressed his audience, spinning in a circle, arms going in every direction, making sure his explanation missed no one within earshot. 'She's just annoyed because last time Ah went tae the chippie Ah forgot the pickled onions! I forgive ye dearest, see ye later at the penthoose!' he called after her.

'Could've been worse, I suppose,' Marylka smiled to herself. 'The first person I met could have been someone sensitive, or even sensible.'

She retrieved her white coat from her room, then informed her two wards and the switchboard that she was back.

'Who's been covering for me?' she asked the operator.

'Doctor Galbraith from the floor below,' came the reply. 'He has your pager.'

'Oh, it would be Mark!' she sighed. 'How many other pagers is he looking after as well?'

'You've said it,' replied the operator. 'At a rough count I'd say he's got four more in his pocket. The guy's a pushover.'

She went in search of Mark Galbraith; it had to be Mark, of course it had, she thought. Mark covered for everyone. He missed every party because he said he couldn't spare the time, and he took the pagers of the others so that they could go; the others played on it to some extent too, it had to be said. 'Those bloody voices keep running around my head,' he would say, 'telling me to get on with it.' They were all slaves to the consultants, though, there wasn't a day went by without a bawl-ing-out from one of them, and not because it was always deserved either, but on principle more than anything. On top of that Mark had Beryl Woods as one of his ward sisters; how unlucky could one bloke get? Marylka could never make up her mind if he was less efficient than the rest of the housemen and so had to constantly run to keep up, or if he simply drove himself too hard. He was sitting at the desk in his duty room, a long, thin chap with mousy hair and glasses, poring over a pile of case-notes. He looked tired, she thought, but then they all looked tired, it was part of their normal condition. Mark looked up and stared at her blankly for a moment, his mind still lost in blood, urine and X-ray results, then he smiled wearily.

'I should've known it would be you, Mark,' Marylka said. 'You really should put your foot down when they put pressure on you to cover for someone else, you know.'

'I didn't mind, Marylka, you'd do the same for me,' he said. 'And besides, it didn't matter.' He nodded towards the case-notes he was working on. 'I wasn't going anywhere, I had to be here for my own lot anyway.'

As he handed her back her pager she looked at his pockets, laden down with the pagers of other doctors who would be either asleep or indulging in a trip outside the hospital, trying to remember what normal people did. 'You know, you must do at least double the work the rest of us do, Mark. If you don't learn to say "NO" occasionally you'll fold up!'

'I don't have the time to fold up!' he laughed. 'I can hear them even in my sleep, "Galbraith you are a slacker!" "If you don't buck up, you're out!" "You're a loser, you're going nowhere!"'

'Yeah,' Marylka sighed in sympathy, 'it's almost as though they were never housemen themselves the way they go on. They don't want you to succeed, at times it's almost as though they're doing their damnedest to make sure you don't. And you have the delicious Beryl to deal with!'

'Oh, you've met her, have you?' he grinned. 'Quite a woman, don't you think?'

'She ripped me into shreds in front of a ward round. God, but she goes for the jugular, doesn't she?'

'Every time!' Mark replied. 'And she never misses!'

'She certainly didn't miss me, I can tell you. You'd have to be made of Teflon to survive her. Listen, Mark, I'm grateful that you covered for me and I hope my little flock hasn't been too much trouble. Have I missed anything?'

He gave her a rundown of everyone in her care, their conditions and the criticisms of their individual consultants about work not done, test results either not back or not showing what had been expected, the progress or lack of it by each patient – the whole sorry catalogue the fault of the houseman – and a quick update on hospital gossip. 'There's more gossip,' he added mysteriously, 'but it can wait till I'm in a fit state to do it justice in the telling.' He studiously ignored her own situation until she was leaving. 'Oh, Marylka, sorry about your mother,' he said kindly. 'You may as well be warned that there will be a good few marriage proposals coming your way. We were fighting over who should get first crack at it in the residency last night in fact. I'm not sure, but I think I won!'

'Too late,' she said. 'Mad Mick's already proposed.'

'Oh, damn, I wanted to get in first! But what have I, what have any of us to offer against the charms of Mad Mick?' He gave her a tired grin then turned quite serious and said in a sympathetic tone, 'Best of luck, Marylka. I don't suppose this can be easy for you, what with all the, you know. But bear with it, it can only get easier, you'll survive.'

She caught her breath and held it as she walked to the door. For some reason his intimate tone and honest sympathy had almost managed to pierce the barrier she had erected, as the young policewoman with the crooked tooth was still breaking the news, three short days ago. She was shocked by how easily it had so nearly been done and for a split second all her resolve almost vanished. If she was liable to break down at the first few kind words, what chance had she?

'At least,' Mark continued, 'that's my reading of the situation from my extensive knowledge of human psychology. There again, I know as much about that as I do about medicine, so don't listen to me!'

At the door she turned to thank him again, but by that time his head was once more bent over the mountain of case-notes on his desk, in an attempt to stop the voices yelling at him tomorrow.

Next morning the ward round assembled in the duty room with no more or less than the usual ceremony, though there were a few extra inquisitive glances in her direction, she thought, or maybe she just imagined it. The round of the female ward went without a hitch, all the women remembering their lines and behaving with quiet decorum, according the consultants the God-like status they required. As they left each bed, though, the occupant would beam a smile of kindly sympathy in Marylka's direction, which she correctly read as 'Sorry aboot your Mammy, hen.' The sisterhood knew instinctively that for a woman to lose her mother meant living with a void that could never, would never be filled. Men after all found substitutes in their wives, so losing their mothers affected them less. As the old saying went, 'Your son's your son till he finds a wife, but your daughter's your daughter the rest of her life.'

Then the crowd of doctors made their stately progress from bed to bed of the male ward, the ward Sister pushing the little trolley carrying the patients' case-notes before them. Every ward had its own etiquette. Some Sisters regarded it as a mark of their authority to push the trolley, some would have been insulted if you had expected it. The trick was in remembering which was which, because ward Sisters took such offences seriously and never forgot an insult. Your entire career could be blighted by one well-intentioned slip-up, innocently committed in a moment of near-comatose exhaustion. And luckily the male patients were equally well versed in ward round behaviour, which was akin to the entrance of the Gods, aka the consultants in charge of their care, and most lay silently, hands folded on the wrinkle-free counterpanes of their perfectly and precisely arranged beds. Not a flower was out of place, not a newspaper on show to offend the eyes of the consultants; according them their due respect almost demanded that the beating of hearts be stilled while they held court.

Professor Stein was in his usual mode, loftily put-upon, a martyr to his calling but determined to be good-natured about it, while making sure everyone noticed his suffering at the hands of lesser mortals. This consisted of demanding everything instantly, if not sooner, finding fault with every word, thought or action, and the performance was accompanied by many heavy, sad, loud sighs, that someone of his obvious genius and worth should be treated thus. A routine ECG tracing done the day before on Danny Morrison, the forty-something chest pain in Bed 4, hadn't come back from Cardiology, so the Prof demanded that another be done immediately. And *no*, he did *not* simply want yesterday's, he wanted a fresh one done *now*, to show those Cardiology people who was boss. The Cardiology people would naturally blame the person phoning with the 'urgent' request that they both knew wasn't, i.e. the houseman, Dr Kowalski, and next time they were in a position to do her a favour they would decide not to. It was all swings and roundabouts. The round was at the top of the ward, and about to work down the other side and out to freedom when the singing started.

'What on earth is that?' demanded Professor Stein, in a shocked tone that suggested he had never heard a voice raised in song before.

'It's Mr Morrison, Sir,' Marylka responded.

'Well what is Mr Morrison *doing*, Doctor?'

'He's singing, Sir. "Please Release Me", if I'm not mistaken. It usually is when he's having an ECG done.'

The rest of the team on the ward round sniggered quietly; there was nothing quite as enjoyable as a comic interlude at the expense of the houseman. Prof Stein removed his half-moon spectacles and stared in disbelief at the lowest minion present.

'Did you say "Please Release Me", Doctor Kowalski?' he demanded.

'Yes, Sir. Mr Morrison was a child of the 1960s, and I believe that song was popular then. I think it was sung by someone called Engelbert Humperdinck. He's still going strong in Las

Vegas, so Mr Morrison tells me. He's a big hit with ladies of a certain age. They throw their knickers at him to show their devotion, apparently.'

'I don't care about the whereabouts of Mr Humperdinck, or the current status of his audience, or indeed what they do with their nether garments, Doctor Kowalski. I don't want to book him for the next consultants' Dinner, you know,' said the Prof. 'I just want to know why Mr Morrison is singing *at all?*'

'Well, as soon as the technicians put the electrodes on his ankles and wrists to record an ECG, he thinks it's appropriate to sing "Please Release Me", Sir. He always does it.'

'Well, he will *not* do so during my ward round! Kindly go now and instruct him to desist.'

Marylka was about to inform the Prof that telling Mr Morrison to desist would in all probability do no good, but the Prof was putting on a performance for the ward round every bit as much as Mr Morrison was for his fellow patients, and she was but a prop in both productions. She walked down to Mr Morrison's bed and pulled back the screens.

'Hi, Fiona,' she said to the technician nervously. 'Thanks for coming up so quickly, and I'm sorry –'

'It's OK, Marylka,' she said. She indicated with her head towards the top of the ward, 'We all know what he's like!'

Marylka turned to the patient who was still warbling away. 'Danny, will you for God's sake shut up! I'm getting hell from the Professor up there.'

Danny Morrison stopped briefly. 'Canny dae it, hen, sorry,' he said. 'Wid if Ah could, but Ah canny.' He then carried on where he had left off. 'To live a lie would be a sin, so release me and let me love again.' His rendition was that typically Glaswegian bar-room demolition job that made every song, good or bad, sound uniformly terrible, and up close the racket was even worse than from the top of the ward. Danny had a truly awful voice, there was no getting away from it, which indeed was the main problem.

'Why can't you shut up just till the ward round's finished?'

Danny gave her a look of annoyance at being interrupted once again. 'It's these wires an' things,' he said, indicating the ECG machine and its accoutrements.

'Stop movin', you, or else!' said the exasperated technician, four feet ten of coiled threat, disguised under long, luxuriously shiny, brown hair, flawless skin and large, grey-green eyes, and with an attitude that could only be described as gallus. It wasn't for nothing that the Cardiac Technicians were known as the ECG Dollies.

'Move again, ya big chancer,' Fiona informed Danny Morrison, 'an' ye'll be singin' falsetto!' That was the other thing. Because they tended to come from the same background as the patients, unlike the doctors, the Dollies were effortlessly bilingual. They spoke to their working-class patients in Glaswegian and to the more limited doctors in English, a skill that came in handy when translation was needed. Fiona tore off a long strip of paper from the machine, the tracing of Danny's heartbeat rendered unreadable by his hand signals.

'Sorry, hen!' he said to her contritely, then he turned again to Marylka. 'Look hen, Ah know for a fact that if Ah don't sing, this gadget here will explode and me wi' it. It's a known fact o' physics, or electronics, or somethin', whichever is the greater. An' Ah'm no' goin' up in smoke for naebody.'

'Daft big sod!' Fiona muttered. 'Don't try talkin' logic to him, it's a waste of time. You'd be better doin' a brain scan, see if there's wan in there. Guess where ma money is?' The remark was intended less for Marylka than for Danny, who contrived out of courtesy not to hear her.

'Well can you sing quietly, Danny? Surely it would have the same effect if you sang it quietly? That would be a good compromise, wouldn't it?'

'Whit?' he said, sitting up, shocked to the core.

'Shit!' Fiona exploded. She ripped off more paper, crumpled it up, stopped the machine and stood against it, her arms folded and her right leg posed across the left at an angle, the toes pointing to the floor to indicate she meant business. 'I'm no' doin' this while you two negotiate!' she said. 'If you want this done now, for Christ's sake just let him sing any way he wants for another couple of minutes and let me finish, or else slap him across the kisser. How's *that* for a compromise?'

Danny drew her a look that said he would not stoop to providing a response, then he addressed Marylka as if talking to a child.

'Look, hen,' he explained patiently. 'Ye canny sing "Please Release Me" any way but full belt. It'd be an insult tae the great Engelbert! See?'

'But the Professor is complaining, Danny, he's sent me to make you shut up. I'll get hell if you don't,' Marylka said as pathetically as she could, playing to whatever chivalry might lurk in the heart of Engelbert's admirer.

'The swine!' Danny said aghast. 'Imagine takin' it oot oan a wee lassie! Tell the miserable auld bastard frae me tae bugger aff an' bile his heid!' And with that he started singing again.

'Christ,' Fiona muttered, her head once more bent over the machine, 'that's all we need, Mingin' Morrison as Young Lochinvar!'

As Marylka made the long journey back up the ward to where the round had ground to a halt, with Danny still singing in the background as evidence of her failure, every white coat, every smirk, was turned towards her.

'Well, Doctor?' said the Professor. 'You don't seem to have done what I asked. Did you tell Mr Morrison what I said?'

'Yes, Sir.'

'And what did he reply?'

'The long or the short version, Sir?'

'The short should be sufficient, I think.' A pained expression played across his august features as he looked at his watch, implying that he had urgent business elsewhere, and it was entirely the fault of the houseman that he was being kept from it. 'Either a game of golf or a private patient,' Marylka thought savagely, and suddenly she had had enough of this.

'Bugger off, Sir,' she said.

There was a sudden intake of breath, followed by a stunned silence. 'Or to be precise, Sir,' Marylka continued, 'what he actually said was "Tell the miserable auld, um, Professor, tae bugger aff an' bile his heid."'

The ward round stood in their stunned silence, waiting for the Prof's response. Eventually he turned to the ward Sister and in a calm and dismissive tone he said 'Throw him out, Sister!'

'Very good, Professor,' she replied, with no intention of carrying out the order; it was the Prof's standard tactical withdrawal with, he hoped, his dignity intact. If every patient who offended the Prof in some way was thrown out there wouldn't be an occupied bed in either ward.

'And, Doctor Kowalski,' he said, looking down his nose with theatrical disapproval. 'You really should have dealt with the situation better than that. I hold you entirely responsible for my ward round being disrupted in this totally unacceptable manner. In future I will not stand for the presence of technicians in my wards during rounds, is that clear? I know we all have work to do, but they can at least have the courtesy to confine theirs to times outwith ward rounds. That is when *we* are doing *our* work, and I think you might just agree that *our* work, and *my* time especially, is more important than that of any technician. These people only serve us, there are times when they have to be reminded of that fact. Kindly inform them of my instructions.'

'Yes, Sir,' Marylka muttered, silently adding 'And then I'll slash my wrists.' In the background Danny was still singing.

No favours there, so maybe not everyone had read the papers then. But there again, Professor Stein was probably a bad example, he was too stupid to base any judgement on, and even if he had read the papers, the discovery of her elevation into the ranks of the rich Davidsons would only have served to deepen his own well-documented insecurity. The day's events proved that she had made the right decision to return to work as soon as she did, though, the world the hospital inhabited was so weird that it barely connected to reality; it was the perfect place to hide from life. Normally that was a valid criticism, but for now it was a plus, and just the therapy she needed.

After the round had dispersed and the ward was once again blessedly free of both Gods and God-awful singing, the technician presented Marylka with Danny Morrison's finally completed tracing. Like most of the technicians, Fiona was an educated working-class lassie and her roots still shone a bright and unashamed Red, something the mainly middle- and upper-class housemen warned their successors about at the changeover every six months. It was also said, though, that when she was in the mood, and in the company of friends, Fiona did a mean and memorable impersonation of Marlene Dietrich singing 'Falling in love again'. And the technicians were known to be in the mood often; it had to be said that they enjoyed life and freely admitted to imbibing the odd noggin. They tended to stay in the job for years, and even when they moved on, those who replaced them seemed to have come from the same mould, as though somewhere out there was a caste appointed by birth to become ECG Dollies. It was almost as if they were all related, or cloned from the same irreverent source. There was that occasion, enshrined in hospital lore, when they had gone on a night out and encountered the Greek singer Nana Mouskouri's backing group. The bemused Greeks were brought back to the Coronary Care Unit, which the Dollies regarded as their home territory and, accompanied by the group on bouzoukis, they performed the dance from *Zorba the Greek* in the early hours of the morning, until a posse of nurses managed to evict them. The nurses said the erratic tracings across the patient monitors showed stress, but the Dollies reckoned it was a sign of enjoyment, and the Dollies usually had a sixth sense where heart disease was concerned.

Fiona looked at the tracing and grinned. 'What did Stein say?' she asked. 'Doctors are Gods, technicians are vermin, I don't want to see them even when I ask for them?'

'Something like that.'

'Don't worry, he's said it before. We have our own little ways of gettin' even. Every time he wants one of our machines for a private patient we give him an old belter hangin' in bits. And we have our dreams. One day, when he has his heart attack, we'll be there!'

'You're sure he'll have one?'

'Positive, we've made offerin's at the technicians' shrine.'

'Where's that?' Marylka grinned, 'The Rubaiyat Bar?'

'Sometimes the Aragon in Byres Road,' Fiona replied with mock seriousness. 'We don't always fall into the first pub we see y'know. Ah can remember times when we've got as far as the Griffin in Bath Street, so there!' She returned to future plans for Prof Stein's demise. 'His first chest discomfort will strike as his eyes fall on that old machine again, because each time he sees it it's slightly worse than the time before. Or we only give him three limb electrodes instead of four, an' one of them has an intermittent fault, or the paper's nearly runnin' out an' we don't put a spare roll in. When he brings it back next day an' complains we say he must have broken or lost whatever it was. He almost goes up in flames sometimes, it can be really hard keepin' a straight face, especially when you can hear the rest of them chucklin' in the background. He'll crack one of these days!'

'You vicious buggers!' Marylka laughed. 'No wonder we get advised never to cross you lot! "Keep in with the ECG Dollies, they run a Communist Collective in that department," that's what I was told.'

'Yes, well, we do take a political stance somewhere to the Left,' Fiona grinned. 'We have this belief that the NHS should be for the people, as it once was, so in medical eyes that makes us card-carryin' Trotskyites. Anyhow, serves Stein right, and the rest as well, they have no business taking NHS equipment to use on private patients, but they all get away with it. Not that any of them can work our machines anyway,' she chuckled, 'an' Stein's no different, the man's as cack-handed as he is cack-headed.'

'Now if you carry on in that vein I'll have to report you for religious bigotry,' Marylka said. 'The Prof reckons everyone who doesn't like him is an anti-semite, you know.'

'Yeah, Ah know, an' that's anti-semitic in its own right. It implies that there is somethin' about Jews that is inherently unlikeable. Ah have this theory,' she assumed an Austrian accent, 'that his name used to be Goldstein or Bernstein, an' he changed it to sound less Jewish. Now not only is that ideologically unsound,' she gave another little chuckle, 'but it doesn't take into account the fact that Ah lust after Jeff Goldblum's large, delectable, Jewish body. Any funny cracks about the gorgeous an' sainted Jeff bein' six foot six, an' me bein',' she gave a dignified cough, 'on the petite side, an' you can cope with big Morrison on your own in future. Besides, it's no' true anyhow, the only reason we all hate Stein is because he's such a horrible big bastard.'

Marylka started to laugh. 'I see you have much knowledge of the man!'

'Well you lot only see each set of Gods for six months or so, then you move on to another set somewhere else; we're stuck here with them. When Ah was young an' innocent –'

'There was such a time, then?' Marylka interrupted.

Fiona ignored her and continued. 'Ah was so impressed by Stein, you know. There he was every year, joinin' in the Christmas Day celebrations with his wife an' weans, an' him Jewish. Ah used to think "How admirable! How ecumenical!" Ah mean we don't join in at Hanukah, do we? But it's got nothin' to do with that. The only reason he turns up every year is to make sure he doesnae miss anythin', an' that nob'dy stabs him in the back when he's no' around, if you see what Ah mean.'

'A reasonable precaution, don't you think?'

'Doesnae stop the rest of his medical brethren at any other time, does it? No, he just believes there should be no show without Punch, that's all.' She pulled out Danny's ECG tracing and looked at it again, scanning each section.

'Anything on it?' Marylka asked. Though the technicians did it with ease, decoding an ECG tracing was a skill acquired over many moons and it did you no good to pretend you had picked it up in a trice. The ECG Dollies were a powerful bunch, they could get you out of trouble if you had forgotten to order a test, or to ask for a diagnosis, if they liked you, that was. At cardiac arrests, where their experience outstripped anyone else's, they could guide you in the right direction without making it too obvious, but once again, only if they liked you. If they didn't, if you had been foolish enough to have made them your enemies, they could make your life hell. They had, as Fiona had said, ways of getting even.

'Well, say something,' Marylka said. 'Anything there?'

'Nothin', but . . .'

'Oh God, what does "But" mean? I think we're about to throw him out, and not just because of his singing. Every test we've done is negative, the consensus is that his chest pain is probably anxiety.'

'Aye,' Fiona said unconvincingly, 'probably. But first you'd have to convince me the big mug's capable of anxiety! It's just, well, nothin' really . . .'

'Christ, don't do this to me, Fiona!'

'It's nothin', honest. Just a feelin'.'

'A feeling?'

Fiona laughed. 'Ah don't know, Ah just have this feelin' about him, that's all. Stein would look down from Olympus an' say "I think we are in the realms of feminine intuition. Har har har." What Ah was goin' to say was Ah'll leave the good machine out for you tonight, just in case, an' make sure you keep it chained to your wrist at all times!'

'You're terrifying me!' Marylka said. 'What do you think's going to happen? And if something does, can you please arrange for it to happen during the day, when the Dollies are on duty?'

'Ah'm no' sayin' anythin' will happen, but in case it does, you'll have the good machine. An' don't lose it, sell it, or let anybody from another unit take it, or else, OK?'

14

Once inside the duty room Marylka took out Danny Morrison's notes and read through them again. Aged forty-five, history of chest pain. Every test performed showed nothing and the only reason they had kept him for two weeks was his family history. His father had died at forty, and all his uncles around the same age, all from heart disease. Maybe that was all it was, maybe the chest pain came from Danny's expectation of dying young from a heart attack. And even if it hadn't happened this time it was odds on that it would happen some time in the future. As Dr Ian Paton, the Cardiologist wag, had remarked when he looked at the notes, 'The correct treatment for this patient is perfectly clear. His grandfather should've been castrated.' Well, the technician would've been aware of all that too, Marylka thought, so 'just in case' was probably Fiona's reaction to Danny's family history. Yes, that was it . . . at least she hoped so.

She decided to seek out Ian Paton again later, and see what he thought, once she had cleared her feet and completed all the extra tests, the necessary as well as the blatantly nonsensical that Professor Stein and his colleagues had ordered. It was a known fact that Professorial units did more tests than others, not because they needed to be done, but because they were there, and it somehow enhanced the standing of the consultants in their own eyes if they ordered more than anyone else, more than each other. It was competition rather than patient care, an exercise in 'mine's bigger than yours', and it generated reams of useless, worthless paper that the houseman had to somehow keep track of. No one had told her about this, Marylka would muse bitterly, spending hours putting pieces of paper into the right case-notes, when she could've been, should've been, catching up on her sleep. She had wanted to be a doctor, and it was such a wonderful achievement to be one of the bright elite and therefore selected for a Professorial unit, where only the academic cream worked. But in reality she had ended up as an office junior, shuffling bits of paper around, an office junior with a sleep obsession. And sleep was on her mind when her pager went off.

'Marylka, it's me, Annie.'

She didn't want to hear whatever it was Annie had to say. Her mother's secretary came from that other world that she wasn't ready to face yet.

'Marylka?'

'I'm here, Annie.'

'Marylka, I'm sorry to bother you with this, I know you're busy but I'm going through Helen's desk. There are things, personal things. You know, diaries, letters, that kind of thing. I'm not sure whether to go through them or whether you'd rather do it yourself.'

'No, Annie, I wouldn't,' Marylka said, then she collected herself. 'I mean, I would Annie, but I can't leave the patients. It would mean getting someone else to cover for me, you see, and everyone's in the same boat.'

'I understand, Marylka, I know you're busy. Would you rather I left this till you can do it yourself?'

Marylka felt a surge of panic; she was being forced into a corner. 'No, it's all right,' she said, hoping her voice sounded calmer than she felt. 'I know this has to be done, but you're family too, Annie, you've been around as long as I can remember. If anyone should go through the personal stuff, you should.'

There was a silence at the end of the phone that she sensed was Annie breaking down. 'Please don't do this!' she thought as the silence extended. But she knew it wasn't fair to offload this on to Annie; it was her responsibility to her mother, not her secretary's. She swallowed and then assumed a bright tone.

'On second thoughts, Annie,' she said, 'just deal with the business papers. I know that can't wait, and when I have time I'll go through her personal stuff. OK?'

'Yes, that's fine, Marylka,' Annie said huskily. 'If you're sure. I didn't want to do anything without consulting you first. I'm sorry, I know I'm not much help, but I just don't know how we'll get through this. I keep expecting her to walk in, I —' Annie's voice broke.

'We will get through it, Annie,' Marylka said in her best doctor's voice. 'It'll take time, but we will. I'll have to go now, Annie, but I'll be in touch as soon as I can.'

In the background she heard Annie blowing her nose. 'Of course, I understand. Your mother was so proud of you, you know.'

When she hung up the phone she stood for a moment collecting herself, pushing the emotion back into its box. She was all right while she was working, she was fine as long as no one mentioned it. She hadn't seen her grandfather in the week since the funeral for that very reason. Young Hector was as much of an enigma to Marylka as he had been to her mother, neither of them ever felt that she knew him, yet he had been upset at the funeral. She couldn't handle that any more than she could handle Annie or a search through Helen's personal effects, but it would have to be done some time all the same.

She forgot about Danny Morrison. Or rather he was put on the endless list of things to be done that she kept in her mind, each one ultra urgent. He only reached the top when one of the nurses dashed into the duty room next day shouting 'Cardiac arrest, Daniel Morrison, Bed 4!'

'Oh, God!' muttered Marylka, 'He couldn't even do the decent thing and wait till I'd seen Paton, could he?'

Then the well-oiled wheels of chaos swung into action, with the important players, the Cardiologists, the ECG Dollies, the duty anaesthetist, the porters with the emergency equipment, and whichever poor sod of a houseman happened to be medical receiving officer of the day, being summoned by special pager. Fiona arrived minus her usual Scholl sandals, which were impossible to run in. You always knew there had been a cardiac arrest somewhere if you came across an abandoned pair of Scholl sandals. They were simply picked up and returned to the Cardiology Department by the finder.

'You!' Marylka accused Fiona, drawing up a syringe of bicarbonate to inject into the hastily set-up intravenous drip in Danny's arm. 'This is all your fault y'know! If you hadn't had one of your premonitions this wouldn't have happened. You hexed him!'

'Oh, stop complainin'! Ah arranged it during the day for you, what more do you want?' Fiona replied calmly, attaching the lifeless Danny to a monitor and immediately scanning the tracing. 'VF,' she said to Ian Paton, greased the defibrillator paddles with conducting gel and handed them to him. Just then a voice was heard at the ward door and the Senior Registrar, Graham Spencer, ran in and took the paddles from Paton. 'Oh, God,' muttered Fiona, 'might as well give up now! Nothing personal, Danny son, but your goose is cooked now he's arrived.'

Spencer was Paton's senior in the Cardiac Team, but he was a well-known idiot and disaster merchant. His nickname throughout the Glasgow medical fraternity was 'Colonel Spencer of the First Foot-in-Mouth'. If it could be managed Dr Spencer was never called to emergencies, because with his appearance the patient's chances took an immediate downturn. At a time when smooth-running efficiency and co-operation were needed, Spencer panicked. He shouted, fell over people, disconnected equipment and generally caused mayhem when they had no more than four minutes to stop the patient suffering irreversible brain damage. In fact there was a theory that he had at some time suffered a cardiac arrest himself at which he had been the senior doctor in attendance; it was the only way to explain his blatant brainlessness.

'Right,' he called out, 'I'll handle this!' He took the defibrillator paddles from Ian Paton and yelled 'Stand back! Everyone stand back! No touching, no contact!' As he was ensuring that his colleagues were thus safe from electrocution, he omitted to do the same for himself, and Danny's lifeless arm was lying against Spencer's thigh. Several people tried to tell him, but he yelled them down. Marylka hadn't seen Spencer in action before, but like everyone else she had heard the stories, which until now she thought had to be exaggerated. It was like a Laurel and Hardy film. When the defibrillator button was pushed Danny's body writhed and jumped, in response to the jolt of electricity intended to restore his heart rhythm to something near normal, and his arm then conducted the shock to Spencer, who in turn leapt in the air with a scream.

'Did you see that?' he screeched.

'Did that just happen?' Marylka whispered.

'Yeah, bugger it!' muttered Fiona. 'He's still alive!'

Paton retrieved the paddles and proceeded to shock Danny again, as Spencer ran around telling everyone what had happened, then he got his feet entangled in the numerous cables and fell to the floor.

'Thank God for that,' an anonymous voice spoke for them all.

'Leave him where he is, he's less trouble there and at least the patient has a chance!' And as Spencer lay trapped by the ankles yelling for assistance, the others got on with trying to resuscitate Engelbert's biggest fan.

After another jolt of electricity the jagged tracing on the monitor screen settled into a straight line, which was worse in a way because it meant there was no activity at all; random activity was better than none. Adrenalin was injected and they waited, the seconds ticking by, before a single heartbeat danced across the screen, then another, and another, till a decent rhythm was established. But that simply meant there was electrical activity in the heart, it didn't mean the heart was beating in response, till someone felt a pulse in Danny's groin and gave the thumbs up.

And once Danny had been brought back to the land of the living he came back at a gallop. 'He's fighting the tube already!' smiled Dr Duffy the anaesthetist, but before they knew it Danny was physically fighting them all. Behind the drama around the bed Spencer was struggling to extricate himself from the cables tightly binding his ankles, while the patient was punching and kicking out at his saviours.

'I know what it is,' said Dr Duffy. 'He's fighting us because we're holding on to him, it's an entirely natural reaction when you think about it. If we let go he'll calm down. On a count of three then. One, two, three!'

They all let go of various bits of Danny's anatomy, whereupon he almost stood bolt upright.

'As you were!' said Dr Duffy diplomatically, and hands again grabbed Danny and tried to hold him down on the bed. Just then Professor Stein entered, leading several Board members around his little domain to impress them with the smooth-running efficiency. He pulled apart the screens round Bed 4 and asked 'So what's going on here?' as though it were a pre-arranged practice run.

'Oh, nothing much,' Ian Paton replied, calmly smiling up at the great man himself. 'We're just holding down a cardiac arrest here. And how are things with yourself then, Prof?'

The Prof turned without a word, and ushered his guests out of the ward, leaving the struggling medics to their task.

'Can you ever remember anything like this before?' Paton asked laughing.

'Which thing?' Fiona asked. 'Spencer lyin' there screamin' like a stuck pig, or us gettin' beat up by a cardiac arrest?'

'Either?'

'Well, aye an' naw really!' Everybody laughed.

'Look, we're going to have to do something,' Paton said, as Danny landed a hefty punch at his ribs. 'Otherwise he'll kill us all! Any ideas?'

'Let me try,' Fiona said, and kneeling down beside Danny's

left ear she addressed him in Glaswegian. 'Listen ya big mug!' she bellowed. 'If ye don't lie still we're gonny get yer mother in here tae gub ye wan! Ye've had a wee blackoot,' she said, 'but ye're OK, an' if ye don't stop thumpin' us ye won't live to hear Engelbert again. Lie still, Danny, d'ye hear me?'

'Please don't take ma heart oot!' Danny pleaded.

'Whit the hell are ye goin' on aboot?' Fiona demanded. 'Why would we take yer heart oot?'

'Tae gie tae somebody else!' Danny wailed. 'Ah don't want ye tae transplant ma heart intae somebody else, Ah need it!'

'Away ye go ya big clown!' Fiona scoffed. 'Whit poor sod would be daft enough tae want *your* heart, Morrison? Who dae ye know that's in that bad a state? Noo lie still, we're tryin' to help ye, but wan merr kick an' Ah'll kick back. Understand?'

Danny gradually relaxed and those who had been wrestling with him slowly released their grasp and began rubbing at their wounds.

'Right,' Fiona said to him, 'we're movin' ye tae another ward where we can keep an eye oan ye. Don't move tae we tell ye, OK?'

Danny nodded behind his oxygen mask.

'An' Morrison,' she said. 'Noo that ye're as sensible as ye're ever likely to be, wan other thing. Ye'll be hooked up wi' ECG leads tae a monitor for a coupla days. They'll be oan yer chest, no' yer arms an' legs. So nae bloody singin', an' that's an order!'

'Ye're a helluva hard wee bugger!' Danny whispered.

'Ye'd better believe it, sunshine!'

Then from behind there came a cry. 'Why will nobody help me out of these cables?'

'We're a bit busy right now, Doctor Spencer,' Ian Paton replied, helping to manoeuvre the bed with the now becalmed Danny on board out of the ward and along the corridor to the Coronary Care Unit, 'we'll come back for you when we have a minute. Don't go away now!'

'Aye,' sniggered Fiona, 'see you next week some time!'

★   ★   ★

Later, in the duty room, Marylka and Fiona were having a coffee and reviewing the day's events.

'Is Spencer always like that?' Marylka asked.

'No,' Fiona replied, 'this was a good day. Sometimes he gets near enough to the patient to do some damage. We'll have to try an' remember how we got him trapped this time, maybe we can do it again.'

'Everybody tells Spencer stories,' said Marylka, 'but does nobody realize how dangerous he is?'

'Yup. But it's impossible to get rid of a bad doctor. You have joined a very safe profession, Doctor, as long as you don't do somethin' indecent with the rubber plant in the corner nothin' will ever happen to you. You know that, sure. We've tried everythin'. We've helped umpteen pagers to get lost, we've put so many down the bog that they're now recognized as a newly-discovered aquatic species. They used to say salmon comin' back to the Clyde was a sign that the river was cleaner, now they talk about Spencer's pagers appearin' instead!'

'And didn't he notice this sabotage?'

''Course he did! Even Spencer can recognize a soggy pager! The Chief called me in one day an' said "You lot are doing this, don't deny it, I can spot one of your plots from a mile away." So the next cardiac arrest we had in a surgical ward we called him as well. You know what the surgeons are like, they didn't know the Chief hadn't seen an arrest since nineteen-canteen, an' he was that flattered at being asked for that he just toddled along. And Spencer was in fine form, injected a nurse with adrenalin, broke a bottle of bicarb, pulled a drip out; the patient died, of course. Afterwards the Chief pulled me aside. "Is it always like that?" he asked. "Pretty much," I said. "Well, don't let that bastard near me when my time comes!" he said. "That's all very well, Chief," I said, "you can stipulate that the bastard gets kept away from you, but what about the patients?"'

'And what did he say?'

'He said "To hell with the patients, look after number one every time."'

Marylka laughed. 'It's not really funny though, is it?'

'Well no' funny ha-ha anyway, but it's funny just the same I suppose!'

Marylka's pager sounded again. 'Oh, God! You couldn't put this one down the bog as well could you?' she asked, reaching for the phone.

'It's WPC Williams here, Doctor,' said a young female voice. 'I saw you a few days ago. About your mother. Remember?'

'Crooked tooth, plaster on finger,' Marylka reminded herself silently. 'Yes, I remember. What can I do for you? How's your finger, by the way?' Play for time.

'My finger? Oh, um, fine thanks.'

'You got that tetanus like I told you then?' Another minute or so saved.

'Oh, yes, I did, thanks.'

'Can't be too careful in our line of work,' she said, hoping she sounded ultra-professional. From the corner chair she heard Fiona snorting into her coffee mug.

'It's about your mother's personal effects, Doctor,' WPC Williams continued. 'The things she had in the car. Her handbag, tapes and things, you know.'

'I know,' Marylka thought. 'The Goons, probably.' She blinked hard.

'I'll drop them off at the hospital if you like, save you collecting them. I know how busy you are.'

Marylka tried to staunch the panic for the second time in a few hours. They were closing in on her. Why couldn't they leave her alone?

'No, tell you what, WPC,' she said calmly. 'Would it be too much trouble to drop them off at the family solicitor's in St Vincent Street instead? R & R Burns, say I asked for them to be given to Mr Burns Junior, I'll phone him to let him know to expect them. It'll be easier going through them with her other personal effects when I have time.'

'That's fine, Doctor Kowalski, I'll do that. 'Bye.'

* * *

She sat in her chair, deep in trying not to think, but the thoughts kept pushing into her mind anyway. Helen, who came from a long-lived, stubbornly healthy family, hadn't had a chance. One hit and that was it. Yet there was Danny Morrison with his family history of heart disease, brought back to life against the odds. And even with by-pass surgery, in all probability he wouldn't last too many more years. One unhealthy life had been saved, one healthy one snuffed out. None of it made any sense.

'You OK?' Fiona asked, getting up and heading for the door.

'Yeah, just things, y'know.'

'Aye,' Fiona said quietly, 'Mammies is terrible things. From the minute you're conceived all your efforts go into gettin' away from them, but the minute they go you'd do anythin' to have them back.'

'Yours as well?' Marylka asked.

Fiona shook her head. 'No; no' yet,' she replied darkly. 'Ah'm workin' on it, though. Ah've left her in every supermarket in Glasgow, every Marks and Sparks in Scotland; she always finds her way back. Sometimes a couple of days can pass an' just as Ah think Ah'm safe Ah hear those unforgettable words, an' Ah know Ah've failed again.' She changed her voice to a shrill screech. '"Hiv ye still no' goat yersel' a man yit? When am Ah gonny be a granny?" No, she's still there, but as Ah say, Ah'm workin' on it!'

15

It was a typical Sunday at Red Rock. Even though Alibel and Will were long married with homes and families of their own, they always came back to Red Rock every weekend, partly, she suspected, because now that she was into her eighties they didn't know how much longer she would be there for them to visit. Alec had been gone these fifteen years; he hadn't lived to see their grandchildren married and the arrival of great-grandchildren. She took no joy in outliving her husband. The family were good to her of course, they knew that she missed Alec, but not how much; she was lonely now in a deep way that she couldn't explain to anyone. No matter how close you were to your children, there was a bond, a closeness between husband and wife that grew from the inside out. It was almost a spiritual thing, and when that was broken nothing could fill the void. They had shared so much, her and Alec, they were so much part of each other, and even with him gone that feeling still existed, like some poor, lost creature, wandering about looking for the place where it used to live, and still felt that it belonged.

His sudden death had knocked her off course more than anything in her entire life, and it had shocked the rest of the family too. He had gone just like that, on an ordinary day, sitting by the fireside of the home they had shared since Murdo and Catriona had taken over the full-time running of the farm, the extension that had been built for the elderly Youngs all those years ago. One moment he was sitting across the hearth from her, sipping his tea and reading snippets to her out of the local paper. The funny thing was that he hated other people reading things out to him, so whenever he did so the family would exchange little amused glances. Then there was a silence, and when she looked up he was dead. It had happened in less than the blink of the eye. A heart attack, the doctor said, though there hadn't been time to get him to hospital, there had been no time even to say goodbye. At times she thought the suddenness of his going was no bad thing, though, as long as he hadn't felt any pain and didn't know he was going, perhaps it had been a blessing, for him at any rate. It was certainly better than spending weeks or months in a hospital bed, slowly wasting away; she knew Alec would've hated being in hospital. He was a family man; life for him was being surrounded by his own. He couldn't have taken being among strangers, no matter how kindly, waiting every day for visiting time. His going the way he did had focused their minds, though, and she was aware that they had suddenly realized that they could lose her too any day now; she knew it too.

Alibel and her husband, Lachie, had just left Red Rock. They were expecting their daughter and her family up from Glasgow for a visit. They were coming off the next boat and Alibel was excited about seeing them again and had nagged Lachie away earlier than need be. Glasgow wasn't the end of the earth, but you missed seeing them every day. Mind you, it didn't help any that Murdo had forced that sherry on her, he knew what she was like. He was everywhere, getting in everyone's way, advising, supervising and getting shouted at. Whatever was going on, Murdo knew about it or how to do it better than anyone else; he'd always been the same. She had watched him all his life, getting on people's nerves, reducing the nicest individuals to screaming rages, and he neither took offence nor saw any link between their irritation and himself or his behaviour. He would listen to the most detailed abuse being screamed inches from his face, and then shake his head, a bemused, tolerant smile on his face, wondering what was wrong with people these days. As often as not it was that unasked tolerance, after he'd exhausted everyone else's, that in fact finally tipped most people over.

She watched him from inside his porch, his pride and joy, the throne from which he surveyed his empire. Every night when he had finished work at Red Rock he showered, dressed and then took up his position in the porch. There he would read the newspapers, discuss the day's events, give advice that was rarely needed and never wanted, and espy whoever was approaching Red Rock. This was his castle, he had a right to know first who would appear over the drawbridge.

He and Catriona had two children; first a son, Neil, then a daughter, Seona. Seona was married to a fisherman and they had provided Betty with three great-grandchildren, but she had to admit it, her grandson Neil was the light of her life. You shouldn't have favourites, she knew that, but Neil was hers. When he was young he was a fine boy, and now that he was a man of almost thirty he was just as fine. He was a combination of the best features of both families, tall, well built, handsome too, with clear blue eyes and a thick mop of auburn hair, and despite having Murdo as his father he was good-natured and easy-going. Nothing troubled her Neil, he was his own man and he did what he wanted with his life, letting the curiosity of others slide off him with a smile as self-effacing as his father's was infuriating. Murdo, being Murdo, was anxious that his son should marry and produce children; that for Murdo was what life was for, creating a family. But Neil was in no hurry. 'Ye're no' wanna they funny fellas that likes men are ye?' Murdo would demand sensitively of his son, and Neil would grin quietly and reply, 'Funny ye should say that, Da. Ah'll be bringin' Tarquin tae meet ye any day now.' Murdo would shake his head; he never got any change out of Neil. He was unused to anyone who didn't take offence and scream at him, or run in the opposite direction, but simply smiled.

And right from the start the boy never had any interest in the farm either. If he had any particular leaning it was towards the sea, like his great-uncle Will. When he had been a wee lad he had asked Grandpa Alec for the sad old dinghy that lay in the barn. To Neil, who had never known Will, it was just a dinghy going to waste, but to Alec of course it was so much more, and Betty had waited for a terse refusal. But Neil was such an appealing child, bright and pleasant, and after a moment's thought Alec had not only given his permission, but offered to help make the little craft seaworthy once again. They had worked on it together, restoring Will's treasure, and it had done more to heal the wounds of Will's death than time ever could. On the day they launched it back into the water from the same shore that Will loved, Alec had watched his grandson sitting proudly in the dinghy and said quietly to Betty 'He has a look of him, don't ye think?' And he did, too; though his hair wasn't the same red as Will's, there was more than a hint of it, a little burnished halo where the sun touched his profile as he sailed around the bay, getting his bearings and learning about the sea.

'Christ, Ah don't know,' Murdo had said, watching his son on the water, 'but Ah doubt the auld man woulda let me have that boat.'

'There's a world o' difference between you an' Neil,' Betty had replied. 'Neil has a nice nature!'

Murdo just wandered off smiling, surprised yet again at how so many people went through life tetchy, just glad that he wasn't one of them and was so good-natured himself.

'Aw, for God's sake!' she heard Murdo muttering at yelling pitch in the kitchen. 'No' again! Catriona! Catriona! Ye'll need-tae phone Lachie! Catriona! Catriona! D'ye hear me?'

'Will ye shut up!' Catriona shouted back at him, the phone already in her hand. 'Or so help me, Murdo Craig, ye'll get this phone about your ears!'

'Ah'm only sayin', Catriona,' he protested, retreating to the porch and sitting down beside Betty. 'Can Ah no' even say?'

'It's already bein' dealt wi' Murdo!' Catriona shouted at him. 'Mammy,' she pleaded with Betty, 'will ye take a hauda him an' keep him there?' She turned to the phone again. 'There's no answer. They only left minutes ago, they've probably no' got home yet.'

'What is it?' Betty asked. 'Alibel again?'

'Aye, Alibel again,' boomed Murdo. 'An' if Ah had my way —'

'*Murdo!*' Catriona shouted at him, covering her ears with her hands in despair. 'We've a' heard it! Keep it tae yerself!'

The Craigs had known Lachie all his life, he and his brother had gone to school with Murdo, Alibel and Will. His family had worked Culag, the next farm along from Red Rock, but Lachie was the second son and when his father died his older brother had sold the farm from under him. So Lachie took the job as the island ambulanceman, which brought him into closer contact with Alibel at the hospital. They had been married for more than twenty years, and the only thing that annoyed Alibel was how happy it had made Murdo. Lachie and Murdo had been the greatest of friends since childhood, soul mates almost, and they adored each other's company. Both were natural men of the soil, and having worked on the land long before tractors were common, they had a love of Clydesdale horses. Long after the time of the horses had passed Murdo had kept his two, the descendants of Daisy and Elsie who had worked the land with Alec when he was a youngster.

Betty remembered the harvest times of years ago, when there was no time to stop and come back to the house, and Murdo would go down to the field with a lemonade bottle of tea, wrapped in a sock to keep it warm for Alec and old Murdo. Another generation on she had watched Neil taking tea and sandwiches to the same fields for his father and grandfather too, only the vacuum flask had taken over from the bottle in a sock. And another generation on from Neil harvest time had all but been taken over by outside contractors, with their own teams of workers and combine harvesters, travelling the country from farm to farm, doing the work for farmers. It made sound economic sense to pay contractors, rather than keep your own expensive combine harvester in working order for only a few days' work every year. It was the same with sheep shearing; few farmers these days would know where to start, because traditional shearing had been taken over by teams of professional shearers. It was called progress, she mused, but she wasn't at all sure it could be called farming any longer. Not that the professionals got away with just doing the job, taking the money and leaving of course, not with Murdo around. He was always there, telling them where they were going wrong, advising them to do things his way, and though they tended to smile and get on with their work, she knew from experience that this wasn't necessarily easy on the nerves.

The rest of the family teased Murdo for being sentimental about his horses, any tactic was legitimate in getting one up on him after all, and he always defended himself by making use of the economic argument too. Horses, he insisted, made better economic sense than tractors. If pushed he would also say that you could talk to a horse, it was company, and you could get it to do your bidding if you knew how to treat it, but what could you do when a tractor broke down, except kick it? Lachie understood this, he too had been a horse man, and he and Murdo were still to the fore every year in the heavy horse competitions. Few could match their ploughing with a couple of horses, and as time went on there would be fewer still. And it had to be said that there was something noble almost about watching man and horse working together. Horses were a lot of work and their welfare came before everything else. They had to be fed and watered before you thought of taking a bite yourself, and settled down for the night first too, regardless of how tired you were by the toils of the day. They had to be combed, brushed, their huge hairy feet shod and cared for, and they had to know you could deal with them too. It was an ability you either did or didn't have, and the horses knew instantly who didn't. They would try it on, leaning their huge weight and bulk on a stranger, finding out who they could push about and those, like Murdo, who just pushed back and told them off, firmly but gently. You could forgive Murdo a lot when you'd seen him with the Clydesdales; even as a young boy he'd had that closeness, that affinity with them. Though he'd die rather than admit it, he controlled them with an affection that went both ways. Maybe she was just getting sentimental in her old age, but she did understand Murdo's point that the companionship of man and tractor was just not the same. There were some things she would never admit out loud, and agreeing with Murdo was one of them, even when she did.

It was one of the things that city folk wouldn't understand, and the irony was that they were the very ones who made decisions about island life. For instance, whoever made these decisions on the mainland had decreed that only one ambulanceman was required, islanders presumably having the happy facility of never needing to be carried into an ambulance, regardless of how ill they were, or even if they were unconscious. Lachie was strong from having spent his life on the farm and working with horses; he was a small, well-muscled man, but even he needed help in carrying a patient on a stretcher. Murdo had therefore appointed himself unpaid ambulanceman, a position that suited all concerned because a second pair of hands was obviously needed. Except that being Murdo he took it several stages further, of course, and promoted himself to doctor. As they carried patients into the cottage hospital, Murdo would advise the medical and nursing staff on the patient's chances as he saw them. 'Don't bother hurryin',' he'd pronounce, as the patient lay listening. 'This yin's no' gonny make it. Mark my words, he'll be in the wooden box within a coupla hours.' His predictions and prognoses were always of the gloomy variety, regardless of the patient's symptoms; broken bones, appendicitis, a gashed leg, they were all the same to Murdo, all were pronounced not only incurable, but leading to imminent death. As a result the nurses at the hospital, his sister included, had renamed him Dr Kildare or, to be precise, 'Dr Bloody Kildare', and he was regularly, and for no reason that he understood, banned from the premises. He always came back, though, with no grudges held, at least not on Murdo's part, because no matter how hard Lachie tried, a lone ambulanceman simply wasn't a practical arrangement. Besides, no one but Murdo would have been prepared to take on the work unpaid, apart from the glory, turning out at any hour of the day or night with his brother-in-law. Murdo liked being a medic and he liked being with Lachie, and what was more, Lachie liked being with Murdo. He reminded you of one of those wee fish that lived among stinging anemones without being affected by the venom. Indeed Murdo's only criticism of the otherwise perfect Lachie was that he would not obey him when it came to Alibel, and the present difficulty was an example of why he should. Something, he thought, and something drastic at that, had to be done about his sister.

'Aye, she's done it again!' Murdo announced loudly to Betty. 'We were supposed to be havin' a wee hot chip in a minute.'

He meant lunch; all meals were to Murdo 'a wee hot chip', regardless of what they were comprised of, just as every flower, from a lupin to a rose, was 'a nice lily'.

'So what's she taken this time?' Betty enquired.

'The roast oota the oven, a bag o' onions an' the hotplates off the cooker!' Murdo replied loudly.

'Aye, well it's your own fault, Murdo. Ye know better than to gie her drink,' Betty reminded him. 'And anyway, ye'll get it a' back. There's nae need tae set up road blocks or anythin'.'

'That's no' the point!' Murdo yelled. 'It's no' normal is it? Ah've been sayin' for years that she needs treatment, haven't Ah? She's a nuisance tae people an' she needs tae be put somewhere! Haven't Ah always said that?'

'Aye Murdo, ye have. You of a' people!' Betty replied.

Murdo ignored his mother's jibe. 'It was only a wee sherry! Just as well Ah didnae gie her a dab o' the Vino Collapso!' he said. Vino Collapso was the name given locally to the potent beer Murdo brewed himself, which was said to be guaranteed to blow your head off at the first sip. It rarely had any effect on Murdo, it wouldn't have dared. 'Noo,' he continued, 'naebody can say Alibel's normal when a wee daft sherry can dae that tae her, can they?'

*   *   *

Alibel had the misfortune to have no head for drink. She wasn't a drunk, or maybe she was, but no one ever saw her get that far. The merest sniff of alcohol and Alibel was tipsy, genteelly, discreetly tipsy, but tipsy all the same. 'She just has tae lick a wine gum,' as her vociferous brother put it, and she became someone else, an irrational, indiscriminate thief. She would spend hours agonizing over whether she should imbibe 'a wee daft sherry', anxiously debating the matter with herself. 'Maybe Ah will . . . No, ye know whit happened last time . . . But it's only the wan . . . No, I shouldnae . . . Well this time Ah'll be careful.' And it always ended the same way; she stole things.

Once she was discovered in a neighbour's garden after a small libation hours earlier, cutting every cabbage out of the ground and stuffing them into a pillowcase. In her time she'd gone home from ceilidhs with lamps, books, framed photos, teapots, toilet rolls, shoes and anything else that had caught her eye, and next morning the owners would either turn up at her door to retrieve their property, or phone and ask Lachie to return it next time he was passing. And Alibel was always full of remorse, she could never remember where she had collected the strange accumulation of items from, or why she had taken them in the first place. In fact she wouldn't have believed she had taken them if there had been any other logical explanation, and if she hadn't been seen by various impeccable witnesses purloining whatever it was. Alibel's thievery was so well known that no one apart from her brother ever took offence, but according to Murdo, who went through life causing mayhem for everyone, his sister needed to be locked up, and so he had loudly advised Lachie for years. As Murdo was once again justifying the unlimited incarceration of his sister the phone rang and he pounced on it.

'Aye, that's right, Lachie, a nice big bitta roast beef,' he said into the receiver. 'Only hauf bloody cooked tae, she's whipped it oota the oven. An' see if she's got a bag o' onions there as well. Whit else is missin' Catriona?' he yelled. 'Oh, aye, she's away wi' the hotplates frae the cooker tae Lachie, God knows where she puts it a'.' He listened to Lachie's side of the conversation. 'Aye, but Lachie, Ah've been tellin' ye for years, there's somethin' up wi' her. It's no' normal noo is it? Ye'll needtae have her put away, ye owe it tae yersel'.'

Behind him Catriona and Betty exchanged looks, then Catriona wrestled the phone from Murdo's grasp.

'Listen, Lachie, ye know better than tae take any notice o' Superman here,' she said. 'But can ye just run ower wi' his tea, or life won't be worth livin'? The only thing that shuts him up is fillin' his face. Aye, cheerio, Lachie son.' She replaced the receiver. 'An' will you stop makin' such a fuss?' she demanded of Murdo. 'That's your sister ye're aye tryin' tae have committed, ye know, an' she's a damn sight merr normal than you are!'

'*Me? Me?*' Murdo demanded, cut to the quick. 'Since when dae Ah go aboot stealin' folk's tea?'

'Ye steal oor peace o' mind, Murdo!' Catriona shouted at him. 'Have ye ever heard o' the sound o' silence?'

'Aye, but whit has –'

'Then practise it for God's sake! Your mammy's ower eighty, she needs a bitta quiet at her age, an' peace frae your opinions an' yer nonsense! Noo sit doon an' shut up!'

Murdo appealed to the assembled company of relatives, none of whom had turned a hair at what was an ordinary and common occurrence at Craig family gatherings. 'Noo how did Ah come tae be the wan in the wrong here?' he demanded, his voice full of innocent disbelief.

'*Murdo!*' Catriona hissed menacingly from the kitchen.

'Well Ah don't know,' Murdo muttered, sitting down in his porch, once again bemused at the weird ways of the world and other human beings. 'Seems tae me that the world's a daft place right enuff when a man canny state the obvious in his ain hoose!'

'*Murdo!* This is your last warnin'! No' another word!' Catriona shouted, racing out of the kitchen again, a soup ladle in her hand.

As Murdo fell silent, in her chair beside her big son Betty smiled to herself. Catriona was a tiny, gentle speck of a woman, and

Murdo was a big, broad, loud bruiser, but by God she could handle him better than anybody else ever could. Herself included. Neil was sitting by the fire, watching and listening with enjoyment, then he got up and went into the porch. Earlier he had been out at his lobster pots, but now he had changed and was wearing his post office uniform. When the boat came in he would collect the mail and take it to the sorting office, and once it was sorted into different areas he'd go out on his run to deliver it in the morning, one of his many jobs around the island. He was a good lad, nothing was too much trouble for him. Before he left with the mail he'd call at the chemist's and pick up any prescriptions for delivery, and he'd call in at the cottages around the island, making sure the old ones were all right too, getting peat in for one, carrying the milk for another. The difference was, as she often pointed out, and always to native islanders, that her Neil did it out of good nature, whereas unpaid fetching and carrying had been what the boarded-outs were for. Somehow she could never accept her own family as native islanders, though she knew they were, she didn't want them to be like all the rest. She only hoped that once she'd gone they wouldn't forget that people like her had been forced labour. She wanted them to remember too that they were a cut above the islanders, not the same as them, and certainly not beneath them, even if the people of Eilean Òg thought they were.

She looked up at the sky. Autumn was almost on them and it was nearly time for the swallows to leave for another year. They were already restless, gathering in little groups and taking to the air for a while. Soon the small groups would merge into one big one and they'd be off again. Somehow you didn't notice them going, you just looked up one day and they'd be gone. Where would she be when they came back next spring, she wondered?

16

A few weeks after her mother's funeral, Marylka swung her car past Glasgow Cathedral and then stopped on the new, updated cobbles, wondering what to do next. It was her day off and she had done what she set out to do. Now she had time on her hands and on her mind, time she didn't really want, because she didn't want to think. Since Helen's death she had used two main tactics to avoid thinking about it; first, she had worked hard at being offensive to everyone who accepted the situation, and second, her work at the hospital left her too exhausted to dwell on what had happened. On days off, rare though those were, she felt reality creeping up on her, so she had to fill the time in some way that kept it at bay. She was aware of living in a dreamlike state, as though she had wandered into someone else's life, a life that was similar enough to hers to make the mistake understandable, and so she was obliged to remain within it till someone noticed the error. It was as if at some point the director of this life she had stumbled into would interrupt and say 'You shouldn't be here,' and let her go back to her own existence. On one level she refused to think about her mother's death, yet on another, a part of her was already re-assessing Helen, in the way that sometimes you don't really see the detail in someone close to you till they have moved away. She would suddenly find innocuous conversations she had had with Helen popping into her mind from nowhere. Her instinct was to quickly think about something else, but as time was passing she noticed that before she could do so, her mind would start to examine them minutely, for what she had no idea. She sensed from this that somewhere up ahead the two levels would meet, and that was when she would have to come to terms with life as it really was, but she wasn't in any hurry.

She looked around at the Calton, her gaze resting on the religious museum that Helen had never been quite sure she approved of. 'I mean,' she'd say earnestly, 'old is old and new is new, right?' It stood across the road from what had been the old red sandstone Barony Church. What was it she should remember about the Barony? Oh yes, that was it. Harry, from the old Fruit Market in Ingram Street, had been married there. She had never known Harry, but thanks to Helen's stories she felt as though she would've recognized him in the street. The first fig her mother ever tasted was in Harry's 'office', sitting on a wooden box beside Auntie Mary and Millie. Every time she saw a fig Helen would recount that tale, even if you groaned and begged her not to. She realized with a start that she would never hear that story again, would never hear any of them again. She felt a double sense of panic welling up inside her. She couldn't bear to think of her mother in the past tense, but at the same time she knew all those old stories were now irrevocably in the past, and she wasn't sure how many, or how much of them, she could remember. Helen had been recounting them all her life, Helen would always be there to go over them again, at least that was how it had seemed, a reasonable assumption when your mother was young and healthy. Only now, no matter how hard she tried to keep the thought at bay, she wasn't there and wouldn't be ever again. What if she couldn't remember Helen's stories properly, now there was no way of hearing them again? What if those stories had gone for ever because she had assumed that life would never change? She swallowed hard and looked around for a diversion to lock her mind on to. It crept up on you, this feeling of panic. There you would be, perfectly composed, on top of things, congratulating yourself on how well you were doing, then suddenly your eyes were swimming as you fought back the tears; not just tears, but sometimes great gasping sobs too. And you never saw it coming, that was the frightening thing, you never really knew when and where the panic would overwhelm you. She wasn't used to this either. Helen had cried easily from sadness and joy. She cried when she laughed, watched films, listened to music, everything made her cry, but Marylka was always composed, always logical and practical, everyone knew that. It made you wonder if you knew yourself at all, and if you weren't who you thought you were, well then, who were you?

She settled her mind on the Barony Church. It was now the social club of Strathclyde University's students, which, if her own student days were anything to go by, meant somewhere for them to get drunk. Marylka smiled; Helen used to sniff disapprovingly at the thought of students imbibing in the Barony, very much in the manner of Auntie Mary, though she was sure Helen wasn't aware of that. But even with the major and minor changes, the area was still the Calton as her family would have known it, including those who preferred not to. This was where it had all started; if she had roots in this city they lay here. In every direction there was a link with the Davidsons, starting with the tiny slum house in Weaver Street, one of the warren of little streets that had stood behind Glasgow's oldest house, Provand's Lordship. The Calton was a famous part of Glasgow, an area steeped in history. The houses had once been inhabited by handloom weavers and other workers from the cotton factories, and in 1787 the workers had gone on strike in protest at cuts in their wages. In the riots that followed, the 39th Regiment of the Dorset Militia was ordered to fire on the strikers; three of the strikers were killed instantly and another three died later. It was typical of Glasgow that the city was still singing a song about it more than two hundred years later. Marylka smiled; the incident had been the subject of one of Auntie Mary's lessons on old Glasgow, and if pushed she could still sing a few lines of the song.

If the ghosts of the Calton Weavers haunted Calton they would pass those of the Davidsons on the way; their footsteps too must echo through these streets, ingrained for ever in these stones. Strange that they should have come so far in any direction you chose to examine, yet all but one of them now lay just across the road in the Necropolis, barely a stone's throw from the poverty they started in, but still worlds away.

She looked at herself in the rear-view mirror and wondered at how normal she looked, given the utter turmoil she felt inside. A slightly tired-looking female in her twenties stared back at her, medium-length brown hair in a non-style, swept behind her ears to take it off an unspectacular face, even with the high cheekbones that Helen always envied; brown eyes in need of sleep. She looked like a woman who was too busy, or who couldn't be bothered, to make an effort. She recognized in her eyes a feeling that had become a way of life for her mother, a vague discontent, natural in the circumstances she supposed, it was early days in bereavement terms. And they were both bereaved, Marylka for her mother, and her mother for the life she should have had, a life of her own. When she'd looked at Helen she'd sensed it, felt it almost. In her own case it was the events of the last few weeks coupled with the exhaustion of the last months as a houseman. But for her mother, she felt, it had been part of a growing preoccupation with the past and a hunger to escape from the present. She had talked increasingly of when life had been better, when she still had hope for the future, perhaps. Sometimes Marylka would ask if anything was troubling Helen, and the reply, always with a good-natured smile, was 'Life. Have you got an answer?' A means of going back and enjoying past happiness over again, or changing unhappy events, that's what she wanted, and Marylka knew exactly where this conversation always led, no matter how hard she tried to divert it.

'All this technology that no one really wants controlling every aspect of our lives,' Helen would complain. 'And as for whoever invented the mobile phone!'

'Oh, God!' Marylka would wail. 'Please, not the time machine diatribe again! You can't negotiate Anniesland Cross and you want to take on journeys through time and space!'

'Well, if I had a time machine I wouldn't have to drive

through Anniesland Cross, would I?' Helen would demand. 'I could just press a button and escape the traffic lights instantly!'

Well, she had escaped now all right, and unless Marylka was very wrong, she wouldn't be coming back. She felt another wave of panic at that thought, the still unacceptable thought of never again seeing her mother, and she closed her eyes to let it wash over and recede. Not now, please. Not now.

Marylka had been to the family crypt at the Necropolis behind the Royal Infirmary. Strange juxta-position, she had always thought, imagining desperately ill patients recovering enough to look out of their ward windows, and finding themselves gazing directly on to thousands of graves. It would be enough to give anyone a relapse, even if they *were* upmarket graves. Fleetingly she wondered if the fatality rate might be higher on that side of the hospital than on the one looking on to Castle Street. Now *there* was a research project for some enterprising, academically inclined medic who didn't want to soil his hands touching real patients, one that would no doubt finance a good few years of gracious living without producing anything of value, just like all the other research projects.

She had taken flowers to Auntie Mary on what would have been the old lady's birthday, as she and her mother also had each year on the anniversary of the old lady's death at the age of ninety-five, in 1995. A curious ritual and one she couldn't explain to anyone else, had they asked, because she found it difficult to understand herself. Especially when they hadn't performed the flower ceremony for any of the others buried there, the ones Marylka had refused to allow Helen to join. She had taken flowers to Auntie Mary because her mother had, that was it, she supposed, and she'd go on doing so for that same reason; it had meant something to Helen. Every male in her mother's family lay there together, though fewer of the females, she noted wryly. Every Hector Davidson who had ever been, in Glasgow at least, her great-great-grandfather, great-grandfather, and presumably her grandfather would lie beside them too when his time came. After him there would be no more Hector

Davidsons, because the line had run out. And good riddance too, she thought. It was part of the family curse. Once, at a christening party generations ago, some slighted Highland faerie woman had stood before them and told them what would become of them. They would have money, possessions and position, but no marriage would survive, and the male line would one day falter, leaving everything in the hands of strangers. Well, if it hadn't happened quite like that it should have.

The flowers she had brought for Auntie Mary were for Millie too, that was understood somehow; when you thought of Auntie Mary you automatically included her daughter Millie anyway. There was a little stab of guilt at that. Poor Millie, Millie the Daftie. 'Only the good die young,' that was what Helen always said when she talked of Millie; she'd never quite got over her life, never mind her death. Well, if flowers were on offer Millie should at least have her own; she'd check up on that. It went into her mental notebook: flowers for Millie. She looked around at the square she was in. Behind her was Glasgow Cathedral, crawling with tourists, and on her right, above the side entrance of the Royal Infirmary, the one the consultants used, was a statue of Queen Victoria, to whom the Infirmary was dedicated. To the left was a collection of civic worthies frozen in time and stone. Once Helen's knowledge of every statue in Glasgow, and her insistence on Marylka knowing them too used to annoy her. Now she was desperate not to forget them. She closed her eyes and went over the list, James Lumsden, Francis Henderson, and in the middle stood a curiously unfinished little stone commemorating the thirteenth-century site of the Bishop's House. Auntie Mary said it was originally intended to put a statue of Saint Mungo on top of the stone, but the local councillors decided it would be too Papish, and so the stone had stood, uncrowned, ever since. She remembered Auntie Mary clapping her black-lace gloved hands with delight when she told you these little snippets. She got such a kick out of finding these things out and just knowing.

Who was next? David Livingstone and the museum, and at the back, probably hiding, as indeed he should, stood Lord Overtoun, whose chromium factories had left behind massive contamination in Glasgow. Acres of land in Rutherglen were unsafe because of dear old Lord Overtoun's efforts, including the very site where Rutherglen Maternity Hospital had been built. Yet there he was, honoured by his friends and the city, even if he only lurked in the background. See, Mum, I do remember. The phone rang.

'Marylka, it's Annie.'

She closed her eyes; she knew what Annie wanted and it was the last thing *she* wanted, but how long could she keep putting it off?

'I'm sorry to bother you, love,' said Annie gently.

Marylka felt doubly guilty; she had used every excuse she could come up with these last few weeks to evade Annie, knowing that it wasn't fair, and now Annie was almost apologizing to her.

She sighed deeply, then replied in a cheerful, carefree voice. 'It's OK, Annie,' she said. 'For once I've got nothing to do.'

'Well, Young Hector was wondering if you had time for a word with him, and Rabbie has been looking for you again.' There was a slight pause. 'And if you want to get Helen's office cleared, we could do it together, if you've got time.'

Marylka smiled. 'My own grandfather,' she thought, 'and he can't even call me himself, he has to get Annie to do it. If that doesn't say it all about this bizarre family!'

'Is Young Hector there now, Annie?'

'He's in his office, but you know your grandfather, he might not be there long.'

'Well, ask him – no, *tell* him I'm on my way, not to leave. Do you know what it's about, Annie?'

Annie laughed. 'No idea, Marylka. And what do I tell Rabbie?'

'I'll be in touch. Tell him that. Talking to Rob isn't something you want to do if you're in any way under par, he could bore me into a coma on my best day.'

The red sandstone Davidson building was sandwiched between two spectacularly white ones in St Vincent Place. On the fourth floor, above the big clock, were two high windows, each with its own stepped gable, like a frilly surround, giving the impression of a pair of cuckoo clocks sitting side by side. She grinned at the thought; the comparison was very apt considering whose offices lay behind the windows. The one on the left as you looked up had been Old Hector's office, with his heir apparent, Young Hector, occupying the one on the right. When the old tyrant died it had been assumed that his son would step into both his father's shoes and 'the chief office', his domain. There was no difference in size between the two rooms, but wherever the old man was had to be superior in some way. But Young Hector chose not to move; he had given the top cat's lair to Helen instead. He had a real problem following his father; while everyone else regarded Old Hector with open suspicion, and in Mary's case, open hostility, his son revered him. Lord, I am not worthy to take his office, follow in his footsteps, or in any way seem to regard him as human; the man is a god. Even after his death, he was still a god, Young Hector's vision of his father never made it into the past tense.

Young Hector's office always made Marylka think of an army officer's quarters. It was sparsely, if expensively, furnished and decorated, with models and paintings of boats around the walls, interspersed with a ghastly collection of photos of Old Hector. 'Maybe,' Marylka thought, 'he keeps a set of darts, or a loaded water pistol, in his right-hand drawer, and while no one's looking he uses those pictures for target practice.' The thought of Young Hector gleefully taking aim at the old goat when no one was about was an attractive one, but realistically she doubted it. The office was unnaturally neat and tidy, it had an unused look about it, probably because it was. Young Hector spent just enough time here to be briefed by Helen on what was happening in the business. This gave the illusion that he was in charge, that he was running the place, though everyone knew, and was grateful, that he was not. The rest of the time he was said to be 'travelling', giving the impression that he was engaged on some unspecified business. Thus his involvement within the firm was kept to an acceptable minimum, and Young Hector's dignity, on the surface at any rate, remained intact.

Sitting across the desk from her grandfather waiting for the interview to begin, Marylka wondered, as she had many times, if his outward adoration of his father was a cover, a desperate suppression of his real rage and hatred. One day, she suspected, something deep within that sad, sophisticated facade would give, and Young Hector would scream out all the years of anger and humiliation that were his father's legacy. He looked so good, so tall and handsome; even at nearly eighty he was a class act. He wore clothes with an understated elegance, in fact he wore his wealth the way Old Hector would've wanted to, but was incapable of doing himself. She looked again at the photos of the two Hectors together on all sorts of occasions, and smiled at the contrast. There stood the little gargoyle, over-dressed, showing as much gold as he could, trying desperately to embody his notion of a wealthy man, and beside him stood this tall, good-looking chap with class oozing out of every pore. 'Beauty and the beast,' she thought.

'Grandfather,' she said, 'why do you keep all these photos of the old reprobate on show?'

Young Hector smiled. 'Marylka, the fact is that he was a legend in the business life of this city, of the country in fact, whatever you may think of him. In fact I've often wondered why he was never knighted; lesser men in commerce were and I'm sure he would've wanted to be called "Sir".'

'Yes,' said Marylka acidly, 'and he certainly would've known the right palms to grease. It's curious right enough, he bought everything and everyone else after all.'

'I know you don't necessarily agree, Marylka,' he said, 'but your great-grandfather *was* a great man.'

'No he *wasn't*. You see, that's my point. He caused such pain within the family, and yet you keep up this hero-worship thing. He ruined every life he touched, yours included. Grandfather, I don't know how to tell you this, but your father was not a nice man, and everyone else knows it.'

'He did what he thought was best,' Young Hector said, smiling tightly. 'Granted, it didn't always work out for the best, but his intentions were good, Marylka.'

He was so damned polite, so desperate not to offend, that she wanted to make him express something, show some honest emotion. She wanted to hurt him, just to see if she could, if anyone could.

'Oh, God, Grandfather! Why are you *still* lying? He's long dead, Mum's –' She stopped. The words 'Mum's dead too,' had almost escaped her lips, but she'd caught them in time and forced them safely into the background again. 'I mean,' she said carefully, keeping control, 'after all that's happened, don't you think it's time we were honest? We're all that's left of this family, after all.'

'Well, that's what I wanted to talk to you about,' said Young Hector, gratefully seizing his chance. 'We are, as you say, all that's left. The problem is where the business goes from here.'

Marylka watched him, thinking to herself 'He's not going to suggest I give up medicine and join the firm, is he? Oh, please, don't let him ask that! I don't want to lift one of his precious framed photos and hit him with it. I couldn't face another funeral, though that would solve half the problem, there'd only be one of us left then.'

'*And*, Grandfather?' she asked calmly. 'I mean, are you asking for my opinion?'

He nodded.

'Sell the whole bloody thing.'

'Please don't swear, Marylka!' Young Hector said almost pleadingly.

She ignored him. 'Give the business away if you like, go and enjoy whatever's left of your life. Stop being a Davidson, be normal for once. Leave this God-forsaken monument to a greedy old man, lock the doors and don't look back. How's that?'

'Pretty much what I was expecting,' he laughed quietly. 'But it's not very practical, is it?'

'I thought it sounded very practical. Why? What have you in mind? And do be careful how you answer that, I'm a nasty bitch when I'm roused, as you well know.'

'I was thinking that I should look after the business for now,' he said. 'Until things become clearer.'

'You mean until a marriage can be arranged between me and some rich creep, someone very like Old Hector. Someone who will agree to take over the reins, keeping the Davidson name, naturally, for a small extra consideration. Subject to contracts being signed, of course.'

'Well, what I was about to say was until you do marry. Things change, Marylka, priorities change. Who knows how you'll feel six months from now?'

'Well, you can forget that little fantasy,' she said firmly. 'There is no possibility in the universe that I will ever marry, Grandfather, and I have no wish to ever have children. The line stops here, the Highland faerie woman was right.'

'The Highland faerie woman?'

'We are bad at marriage in this family, and I don't see any sense in it anyway. I know you don't understand this, but brazen hussies like me don't see marriage as desirable or inevitable these days, in fact we can conduct our lives without a man to hold our little hands. Mum had that position forced on her, but it's one I've chosen.'

Young Hector said nothing; he was a man who found honesty difficult to handle, never mind downright unpleasantness, but she was aware of feeling slightly out of control and she couldn't stop. She looked at him in silence for a moment. 'Grandfather, haven't you ever wondered what the real world is like? Haven't you ever wanted to do something on your own, to get out of that horrible old man's shadow?'

Young Hector leaned forward on his desk and fiddled with a pen. 'I did get out once, you know,' he said quietly.

She sensed him almost looking round, making sure he wasn't being overheard by the rogues' gallery of father and son pictures.

'Really?'

'Yes, it was during the war. 1940; I was twenty years old.' He smiled at the memory. 'I enlisted without my father knowing. He had pulled all sorts of strings to keep me out of the forces up till then, I was supposed to be keeping the business afloat, engaged in essential duties at home, all that sort of nonsense. He thought I was off on a jaunt, didn't find out I had enlisted for weeks, and by that time not even he could get me out. And do you know something? I loved it! All that killing, all that fear, and I'd have done it for nothing.' He laughed quietly, uncertainly. 'It was the first time I'd been away from him, and it was wonderful!'

'And this is the first time I've heard this,' Marylka said. 'Now why would Old Hector miss the chance of presenting you as a war hero?'

'I think the old man avoided referring to it because it was the one thing I'd done out of his control. He liked being in control.'

'Really?' she drawled sarcastically. 'You do surprise me.'

'And I wasn't playing a leading part, that always stuck in his craw, I think. I was just one of many, and a very junior one at that. He couldn't have a Davidson not leading from the front, so he ignored the entire thing. A George Cross would've merited a photo call, but *not* a General Service Medal if you see what I mean. I came back five years later and it was as if I'd been on holiday as far as he was concerned.'

'Did Mum know you had served in the war?'

Young Hector nodded. 'She must've known I went to war, most men did, and I'm sure Bloody Mary would've told her!'

He smiled gently at his father's old insult. 'But I certainly never discussed any of the details with her.'

'Why did you never tell your own daughter about your one big rebellion?'

He shrugged. 'It never really came up,' he said vaguely. 'We didn't really know each other very well. I didn't see much of her when she was growing up.'

'So what did you do when you were a dashing young warrior then?'

'I was in the Royal Navy, on convoy duty in the North Atlantic, avoiding U-boats. I've never experienced anything like that fear, waiting minute by minute to be hit. We were escorting Merchant Navy ships. A great many of their crews came from the Western Isles and were already working at sea when war broke out, then suddenly they were under fire.' He watched his hands playing with the fountain pen. 'We were supposed to be protecting them, but they knew more about life at sea than any of us, pretty often they saved our bacon.' He laughed self-consciously. 'They were the real heroes, not us.'

Marylka looked around the office at the model boats, and paintings of boats, that she had seen many times in her life. She'd always dismissed them as 'Young Hector's toys', but they had taken on a whole new significance now, they were Young Hector's proof that for one brief, shining moment, he had been his own man.

'You lived on adrenalin all the time,' he continued. 'It was terrifying, but exhilarating too in a strange way. When the war was over everyone cried with joy. I cried too, but out of sorrow. Those were the happiest years of my life, but I knew that the end would come. If I was still alive I knew I had to go back to the firm, back under my father's authority.'

For some reason the knowledge that he had once had the guts to escape, only to voluntarily go back again into his comfortable prison, made her almost despise him. 'For God's sake!' she said angrily. 'You'd think there was something noble about running stores and buying property! It's just a way of making money, you know, it's not a vocation imposed on the Davidsons by some deity, or even a demanding nation! It was possible to abdicate, Grandfather, to refuse the throne! You'd survived the war, you could've gone off and done something with your life after that!'

'I would've been too scared, Marylka,' he said quietly. 'I've always had to be told what to do. That's why the navy suited me so well, I wasn't out there leading from the front, making decisions, I was part of a chain of command. I failed at everything else I touched.'

'What did you touch exactly?'

'I failed as my father's son for a start, and I failed at being married. What was it he said at the time? "You can't even keep a woman."'

'A bit rich coming from him, don't you think?'

Young Hector ignored the jibe at his father. 'I failed at running the business on my own too. Your mother was very good, you know, she'd always give me an update before every meeting, and put me in the top chair as though I ran everything, but I wasn't given her gifts I'm afraid. I failed as a father too. I got upset at the funeral because I suddenly thought to myself "What have I done to deserve this?" and the answer was that I was a failure, and no good comes to failures. Helen had all the luck, Auntie Mary was there for her. I always envied your mother having her, you know. The old man let Mary have her because she was a girl, and there was so much love between them, Mary, Millie and Helen. I'd see her coming back from one of their adventures, her eyes gleaming, smiling, excited, and I'd envy her so.'

'That is one helluva admission, Grandfather,' Marylka replied. 'How could you envy your own daughter? Why weren't you just happy for her that she had escaped? I honestly don't understand. You were her father, but you gave up all responsibility for her. Old Hector "allowed" Mary to take her over for God's sake! You allowed him to take over everything and everyone!

And when he died you could've sold the business, for her sake if not your own.'

'But she was good at business!' he protested. 'That was her great gift!'

'She had very little choice, did she? You were so bloody bad at it she had to do something! Her gift was her soft heart, it made her give you more consideration than you deserved! She wanted to study art, did you know that?'

'She never said anything!' Hector stared across the great gulf of the desk between them in surprise.

'Doesn't that say it all then? You didn't know. You were her father, and you didn't know!'

Young Hector stared miserably at some point behind her head, unable to maintain eye contact. 'I told you that, didn't I?' He looked sadly past his angry granddaughter. 'I told you I failed at everything, didn't I?'

'Well, then, you only have to be yourself, Grandfather, that's my advice. You don't have to sell the business, just run it in your own special way and it will fall about your ears anyway. Problem solved!' Marylka got up and headed for the door. 'Look, I'm too angry to talk to you any more, Grandfather, I'm sorry,' she said. 'There's so much more I'd like to say, but I know my mother wouldn't want me to say it, so I won't. But don't bother even trying to run this place. On second thoughts, blow the damn place up instead!'

Walking along the corridor between Young Hector's office and Helen's, Marylka was blinded by tears. She hadn't cried properly once since Helen's death, and she was angry that she'd allowed herself to be sucked into doing so now. What was wrong with her? Why wasn't she coping with this? People did it every day, she sent them off to cope with it, and they did, didn't they? So why wasn't she? He was such a stupid man, Young Hector, such a lily-livered, useless, spineless creature! Her mother had always said he was a victim, that he needed to be protected and looked after. But that was just her sentimental streak showing;

Helen excused everyone. And she had always said Old Hector was driven by fear, well his son had certainly inherited that, though he wasn't driven as much as paralysed by it. She remembered Helen saying he had nothing in common with his father, and she'd thought that herself, but they'd both been wrong. Maybe in some odd way fear and arrogance were two sides of the same coin, because though her grandfather hadn't inherited the old gargoyle's ugliness and desperate greed, he certainly had his vanity. Everything was viewed from his standpoint alone, there was no other; in his own way Young Hector was as self-centred as his father had been. Even the war was to continue for his benefit, no matter how many of those nice sailors from the Western Isles were killed, presumably! And his tears at Helen's funeral had been for *himself*, not for his daughter, she realized. 'He had to take the starring role there too!' she thought furiously. The man had missed his true vocation, he should have been an actor. His entire life had been spent giving an Oscar-winning performance of a tragic victim!

She hesitated outside her mother's office before deciding that she couldn't face it. She turned and went down in the lift instead. On Level Seven of the Mitchell Lane car park she sat in her car, trying to get control again. This really would not do. She had two months to go in her medical residency, she couldn't afford to fall apart. She'd already done surgery and obstetrics, after this she would be free, and if instead of taking a job she wanted to go off somewhere and howl at the moon, then fine. Meantime, though, she had to hold herself together. She picked up the phone.

'Annie? It's me. Look, I know you want me to go through the things in the office, but I can't just now.'

'It's OK, Marylka, take your time. There's no urgency, no one else will be going in there, you know.'

'Yes, I know, but I still feel so stupid!'

'Och, lass, don't be so hard on yourself!' Annie said kindly.

'Please, Annie, don't be nice, I'm feeling slightly fragile at the moment.'

'Look, you wouldn't be your mother's daughter if you felt any other way.'

'Annie –' She couldn't continue, so she pressed the button, ending the conversation abruptly before she broke down completely. Then she sat in the car for what seemed hours, trying to calm herself, before driving down to the kiosk at the exit. She'd only been parked for just over an hour and they wanted £3.80. Her mother had been right about this place, it was sheer, daylight robbery!

17

On the drive back to the hospital she gradually cooled down, and began to feel ashamed of herself for losing her temper with her grandfather. He was an old man, an old weak man, but there were worse faults than being weak, surely? There was being cruel for a start. She blushed crimson at the thought. She parked the car and headed for the porters' desk inside.

'Anything happening?' she asked.

'Aye, well, no' really for you Doctor Kowalski,' replied one of the porters. 'It's for the surgeons. There's been some sorta explosion at wanna the yards.'

'Is it serious?'

He shrugged. 'They've sent wanna the surgical housemen, the wan on Casualty duty, Doctor Buchan. So you can imagine what the backlog will be by the time the poor sod gets back.'

Just then a huge commotion was heard in the distance, coming closer until it burst through the swing doors leading from the ambulance bay, and in came Andy and Mad Mick, pushing a trolley with a patient on top. It was hard to say which caught the eye first, the fact that the patient was inexplicably wearing a white coat, or that Andy, who was pushing the trolley from behind, appeared to be aiming kicks and oaths at Mad Mick who was at the front, with the result that the trolley zig-zagged madly from side to side.

'Ye canny keep your trap shut, can ye? Ya, ya *bam* ye!' Andy screeched, aiming another ineffective blow at Mad Mick. 'Ye just havtae put your oar in, daen't ye?' With that he stopped pushing the trolley, ran to the front, grabbed Mad Mick and pinned him to the wall, as the trolley with the white-coated casualty on board went sideways out of control.

'Bastards!' shouted the patient, sitting up and clutching a bloody dressing to the back of his head with one hand, while the other tried to fend off an inevitable coming together with the wall, upon which Andy was pinning Mad Mick. At the moment of impact he fell off the trolley and lay on the floor, moaning. 'Bastards!' he said again feebly.

Four porters ran to the scene, two trying to pull Andy and Mad Mick apart, while the others went to the aid of the patient, who Marylka recognized as Alan Buchan, the surgical houseman who had been sent to the incident. But why was he lying on the trolley, or rather, at that particular moment, on the floor? The casualty being a medic at least explained why the performance was being played out without any of the concern a bona fide patient had a right to expect. It was a little-known fact that medics got less professional care when ill than the general public; familiarity breeds contempt and so they were treated as colleagues, not patients. Whatever had caused the current little tiff between Andy and Mad Mick, a civilian, an ordinary punter, wouldn't have witnessed such a scene, the fisticuffs would have taken place off stage. But any medic, however flat on his back, was family, and therefore would be expected to understand.

'What happened?' Marylka asked, but Alan Buchan lay down again on the trolley and groaned in reply, adding only a further 'Bastards!' by way of clarification.

'Whit happened? Whit happened?' shouted Andy, abruptly abandoning his attempt to choke his partner to death. 'Ah'll tell ye whit happened! This – this *arse*!' He jabbed a finger viciously towards Mad Mick, who was calmly re-adjusting his green overall and smoothing his hair back into place. '*He* happened!' Overcome by the memory Andy launched himself once again at Mad Mick, who stood against the wall calmly polishing his glasses, shaking his head in exasperation, and appealed without any real urgency, 'Will somebody get a grip o' him before he does hissel' a mischief? Look at the state o' him!'

As the porters hauled Andy off his partner again, the abandoned patient moaned in the background. 'And will somebody get me a sick bowl, I'm going to be –'. And there and then he was.

While he was still retching, Marylka had a look at the wound under the dressing he was holding on to his head, and found a gaping hole in his scalp. 'It'll need stitches,' she said.

'Oh, God! Not stitches!' Medics, hypochondriacs all, made very bad patients.

'But you'd better get it X-rayed as well.' She looked over towards the porters' desk and shouted 'Get his Senior House Officer down here!' But as all the porters were attending to Andy and Mad Mick, she crossed to the phone and paged the SHO herself. The SHO was reluctant to become involved and she had to convince him that he really should take charge of the situation, the casualty was after all his houseman. 'But I'm not his mother!' he responded crabbily. Meantime Andy was calming down enough to explain what had caused the problem.

'There was an explosion in a shed, a gas cylinder they thought, an' they didnae know if anybody had been in there at the time. Coulda been somethin' or nothin'. So in we goes, me, the boy here,' he indicated with his head towards Alan Buchan, and raising his voice to a bellow he shouted, 'an' that *bam* there!' Mad Mick was holding his glasses up to the light, peering short-sightedly for missed smudges, without a care in the world. 'Anyway, Ah'm tryin' tae keep things kinda calm, knowin' the boy here hasnae been tae many big wans, an' the *bam* there, he picks up an auld boot that's lyin' around an' says, "Well, Ah've found a boot wi' a coupla toes in it, see if youse boys canny find the other wan!"'

'Ah was only tryin' tae lighten the mood!' Mad Mick contributed to the narration. 'That eedjit takes everythin' too serious, everybody knows whit he's like. Ah was just releasin' the tension, injectin' a bit o' humour intae the situation!'

'Some'dy should inject a bit o' cyanide intae *you*!' shouted

Andy, getting up and attempting to vault four people to get at his partner again.

'So how did wee Doctor Buchan here get hurt, well?' a porter asked, trying to cover a chuckle.

'Well the boy was that nervous tae start wi', and the *bam* sayin' that, the boy passes oot an' hits his heid on somethin' oan the way doon. Oot like a light he goes, and know whit the *bam* says then?'

All around smirking heads shook as one. 'He says –' Andy stopped to compose himself before starting again. 'He says "Christ, these boys are nae help at a'. Jist think if this had been a major incident. Ye're right, Andy, we havtae dae everythin' oorselves a' the time!"'

'It's true!' Mad Mick responded. 'Christ, ye're aye sayin' that! Ah was agreein' wi' ye!'

'Shut it, you!' Andy yelled back. 'It's *you* that's nae help! We had nae casualties frae the incident except the wan *you* caused by bein' a smartarse! He's only a boy, ye know!'

'Well whit's a' the fuss aboot then? Wan doctor wi' a wee nick on the napper isnae much tae write hame aboot,' said Mad Mick dismissively from the other side of a human buffer or two.

'There *coulda* been casualties!' Andy screamed back, his face bright red and the veins in his neck standing out.

'Calm down, Andy!' Marylka said, but Andy was beyond hearing her.

'An' how were we tae deal wi' the casualties if there were any, seein' as you'd laid oot the doctor?'

'But Andy!' Mick replied with a heavy, patient sigh. 'Ye said it yersel', there *wurnae* any casualties!'

'Except the doctor!' Andy shouted back. 'Except that poor bloody boy!'

'Aye, well, you didnae help!' Mad Mick responded. 'You wur nae help at a'.'

'How d'ye make that oot?' Andy demanded incredulously.

'Well, Christ, ye spent a good fifteen minutes wrestlin' wi' me as though it was ma fault, while the poor bugger there lay bleedin' like a stuck pig!'

There was an almighty bellow as Andy made a supreme effort to get at Mad Mick, and the porters tried to stop him.

'Look, Mick,' Marylka said, 'bugger off somewhere, take a break.'

'Right y'are, Darling!' Mad Mick said, replacing his glasses and bending to kiss her hand with a lascivious wink.

'Ye see whit Ah mean?' Andy yelled in a kind of furious wonder. 'Nothin' gets through! He takes nothin' seriously! *Bam!* Ye're a *bam*, ye know that, daen't ye?'

'Aye, so ye say. Put a sock in it,' Mad Mick retorted. 'That temper o' yours is gonny kill ye wanna these days, Andy.'

'But no afore Ah've killed *you*!' he shouted, as Mad Mick wandered down the corridor in the opposite direction, whistling as he went. 'Ah'll make bloody sure o' that! Ah'll get you before Ah go!'

Marylka was still trying to restore some order. 'And the rest of you, carry Andy off to the canteen and pack him with ice till he calms down. Meantime, will somebody page the SHO again and get "the poor bloody boy" here down to X-ray?'

Once the day's theatrical turn and its leading actors had been dealt with, there remained the problem of how the surgical houseman would deal with his unfortunate experience. Marylka used what was left of her day off to join him in the housemen's Common Room to discuss the situation.

'How's the head, Alan?'

'Bloody sore,' he replied with feeling. 'There should be special rules for us, we shouldn't have to have stitches.'

'Yes, an interesting theory, but how do you feel in general?'

'You mean about Morecambe and Wise?'

Marylka nodded. 'Are you thinking of putting in a complaint?'

'Yeah, that'll be right!' he replied. 'And for the rest of my life every paramedic will be out to get me! There won't be one ambulance that doesn't try to run me over whenever I put a foot outside any hospital, here or abroad! I'm still thinking it through though, there must be some way of getting back at them. As it is I'm going to have to live for the rest of my career with the tale of how I keeled over at the thought of two imaginary toes in a boot!'

'Well, yes, this is true Alan,' she replied, 'but I think More-cambe and Wise could be persuaded to protect your dignity in exchange for a bit of goodwill. They didn't really mean you any harm after all.'

'Meaning?'

'Well, if you put this, um, unfortunate incident firmly behind you without looking back, I suspect they could be relied on to swear blind that you fell, that you tripped rather than keeled over.'

'But everybody heard!'

'But everybody is used to Andy and Mick's floor shows, and Andy and Mick can be very good liars if it's in their interests.'

The houseman thought for a moment, aware that he was caught between a rock and a hard place. 'OK, deal,' he said. 'What choice do I have? But why are you so interested in protecting those two clowns? They'd be bloody lethal in an emergency.'

'Well they're not,' Marylka grinned. 'I did my surgery here too and they're terrific when they need to be. And besides, Andy once did me a favour.'

'Oh, yes?' smiled the houseman. 'This sounds more interest-ing. The lady doctor and the paramedic, eh? Tell Daddy all!'

'You'll be sorry you asked.'

'Try me!'

'He drove the hearse at my mother's funeral, and he was very kind to me on the worst day of my life,' she said simply.

'You're right,' said Alan Buchan. 'I am sorry, and you fight dirty. OK, you've got a deal, but as a favour to you, not to them. Tell them that!'

★   ★   ★

Next day, as receiving houseman, she was called to an ambulance to see a body that had been found in the Botanic Gardens. All she had to do was pronounce the body dead and it would be removed to the city mortuary. It was a stupid procedure; the paramedics were every bit as qualified to determine death as any doctor, especially when, as in this case, the ex-person she was looking at had very obviously died a good couple of days ago. Sometimes they were dragged out of the nearby River Kelvin after months in the water, and barely resembled a human being, never mind one that had an outside chance of being alive. Even so, they had to be certified by a doctor.

In the bad cases the paramedics always stayed beside the houseman to whose lot the grisly task had fallen, out of self-interest they said, because they hated cleaning up their wagons after nauseous medics. In reality though, the paramedics knew how ill-prepared for medical life most housemen were. Having gone straight from school to university, then into the protective hospital environment, they very often had little real experience, yet they were expected to perform as if they had. Once Marylka's first three cases from 8 a.m. on a nice, bright, sunny day, had been to certify three dead children. It had just happened that way, a rotten run of luck, each one unconnected and ranging in age from three weeks to eighteen months. Three little bodies, all with previous bruises to prove that this was but the final act of brutality. The father who had inflicted the bruises on the third little corpse was sitting in the corner of the ambulance crying as she pronounced death. She had wanted to ask him why he'd done it, she had wanted to beat him till he screamed, and go on beating him till he couldn't scream anymore, like the child whose pathetic, already stiffening body lay before them. The paramedic had kept up a cheerful, detached conversation throughout the entire ordeal, though. She couldn't remember everything he talked about, but she knew it was all banal stuff. Something about the film *Braveheart*, and the scene where the Scots lifted their kilts and mooned at the English, all relayed in a quiet, everyday voice, as though they were having a coffee together instead of what they were really doing. He wasn't to know it of course, but she would never be able to look at any part of Mel Gibson's anatomy again without remembering the face of that child, and she would never forget the reassuring sound of the paramedic's voice, as he helped her through it, out of his ambulance, and back into what passed for normal life. It had been the worst day of her life so far, until that nice policewoman with the plastered finger had brought her one that was even worse.

'Drugs, d'ye think, Doctor?'

She looked up at Andy. 'Well spotted, Sherlock,' she replied, examining the tracks on the dead boy's arms. There was a golden age, so she had heard, when no one had to wear surgical gloves to examine patients, but being a modern-day medic she found this hard to believe. Even in the sixties, so it was said, there was nothing in Scotland worse than the occasional Mandrax overdose, and the odd, sensational cannabis find, and that from some high-flyer just back from London who wanted to impress the hicks. But these old medics, she thought, they'd tell you any myth and expect you to swallow it as gospel. 'I think we can say without any real fear of being sued, that this is indeed a drugs-related ex-person, Andy, and younger than me by the looks of him.'

Andy covered the boy with a sheet then followed her out of the ambulance. 'Can ah have a word, Doctor?'

'As long as it's not the kind of word you had with Mad Mick yesterday, Andy.'

Andy looked puzzled, then his face lit up with understanding. 'Oh aye, that!' he said. 'Och, that was nothin'!'

'Poor old Alan Buchan didn't quite see it like that, but he's not pressing charges. You heard that, did you?'

'Aye, aye,' said Andy, 'he told Mick an' Mick told him tae keep takin' the tablets. Imagine him takin' that so seriously!' He laughed as though the world was indeed a funny old place. 'Naw, the thing is, ye know that other matter?' He said 'other matter' as though speaking in code.

Now it was Marylka's turn to look puzzled.

'The, um, the Maryhill matter.' Another coded reference.

She realized he was talking about Helen's funeral. 'Oh, yes, *that* matter,' she smiled wryly.

'Aye, well,' said Andy, looking around to ensure that neither foreign agents nor Mad Mick were eavesdropping. 'Thing is, some character gave me a whacka money.'

'Oh?'

'Aye. Said it was frae some character called Young Hector.'

'That's my beloved grandfather, Andy, nearly eighty years old and still lets people call him Young Hector. Embarrassing, isn't it?'

'It's a bit odd, Ah'll gie ye that,' Andy mused. 'But the thing is, the whacka money was £500! Whit should Ah dae wi' it?'

'Whatever the hell you like, Andy. He won't miss it. He'd only have spent it on a pair of socks or five cigars anyway.'

'Ye think Ah should keep it, then?'

'Of course you should keep it! He's got enough socks, and smoking kills, you know. He's only a lad with the rest of his life in front of him!'

'Should Ah write tae him an' say thanks d'ye think?'

'I wouldn't bother, Andy. He won't miss it, he's got a few bob about him, as I'm sure you've been advised by Mad Mick.'

'Aye, but £500 is £500. He'll no' miss that will he no'?'

'Won't even notice it's gone, believe me.'

Andy stopped walking, massaging his chin thoughtfully between his thumb and first finger. 'Eh, as a mattera interest, Ah suppose you've had a few proposals already then?'

Marylka laughed. 'A few!' she said. 'Mick's proposal was first in fact.'

'Was it a decent wan?'

She nodded again. 'Daft, but definitely decent-ish.'

'Christ, it must be love then!' He walked off again laughing, then he called after her. 'An' see that Doctor Buchan? Tell him Ah'm no' best pleased that he thinks he's daein' us a favour by the way. Tell him if it'd been him that laid intae Mick Ah'd have been a damned sight merr understandin'. Ah widnae thinka landin' him in it.' He waited till he was halfway through the doors. 'If the toes had been in the other boot, so tae speak!' Then he disappeared from sight, but she could still hear him laughing at his witticism, as the doors swung back and forth in his wake.

18

Marylka walked into the Common Room. She was tired, and normally the only thing on her mind was how to get enough sleep, but these days and nights, sleep eluded her no matter how much she needed it. Sometimes she would drop off from sheer exhaustion, only to wake after an hour or so with a sudden feeling of terror, her heart pounding, her legs preparing to run from some unspecified danger. Then she would remember what that terror was, and sleep was ruled out thereafter.

Slumped in the couch in front of the TV was Mark Galbraith, the houseman who had covered for her when the terror had first descended upon her. He was on his own again, something that always surprised her; she had never seen him taking part in any of the crazy discussions the Common Room resounded with, playing pool, or going out for a pint with one of the others. Despite being well liked, everybody's friend, a chap who would do anyone a favour, Mark was always on his own.

'What're you doing here?' she asked. 'We normally only see you as a blur. How come you're sitting there all still and unmoving for once?'

He put a finger to his mouth. 'Shh, they'll hear you! I'm having a lull,' he grinned. 'Not a voice raised in anger for some reason. I must've done something right for once, wish I could remember what it was!'

'So why don't you get out of here for a break, or catch up on some sleep?'

'Why don't you?'

Marylka shrugged. 'Sometimes you're just too tired for even that.'

'Ditto. A bit of mindless TV staring never hurt anyone. After a while you reach higher levels of tolerance y'know, I can sit through Rolf Harris now without even blinking.'

She sat in the armchair opposite him, rather than the couch beside him; it was one of Mark's eccentricities that he didn't like people to come too close to him, so how he managed with patients was always a mystery.

'How's Crusher?'

'Ah, the unforgettable Beryl!' he grinned. 'Still sharp as a tack. Brush against her and it's death by a thousand cuts!' He smiled. 'Actually,' he said, 'she's been very good to me, almost like a mother.'

'Dear God!'

'Yeah, strange isn't it? Keeps asking if I'm all right, do I need anything, why don't I eat or sleep. She really can be quite nice, believe it or not!'

'I think I'll go for "not".' Marylka laughed.

There was a silence, then trying to make conversation she asked, 'Have you got a job lined up?'

'No. You?'

'No. We've both left it a bit late, haven't we?'

'Well, I'm waiting for the voices on high to tell me what to do, I daren't make a move until I know how they feel.'

'Yes, I've had a couple of offers from the Gods, or at least enquiries. "Have you any plans, Doctor? Ever thought of Geriatrics?" That kind of thing, so that you know the job's so bad they can't get anyone else and they're having to scrape the bottom of the barrel!'

Mark still stared at the TV screen.

'Do you remember saying there was some gossip you'd tell me about later?'

He looked blank.

'When my – when I came back to work.'

Suddenly he remembered. 'Oh, that! Hasn't anyone else told you?'

'Not unless I missed it.'

'Well, it was Bruce again,' he said heavily. Mark didn't much like Bruce, the pathologist from Australia, a wild, red-headed maniac who had been christened something else that no one could remember any longer. At first someone had called him Bluey on account of his red hair, then Cobber, but both seemed a trifle too obvious, so he had been re-named Bruce, on the grounds that all Aussies were, or should be, called Bruce. The ethical argument against being obvious had been abandoned by that time.

No one had ever seen anything like him, even though pathologists were strange people to begin with. Something happened to those who entered the dead-end wing of medicine. Either they became more eccentric than they had been to seek employment in Pathology in the first place, or they became old before their time. There was that nice Peter Barr, gorgeously handsome, bright and cheerful, always up to his ears in fun, drove an open-topped vintage car full of girls and spent his entire time partying. He took a six-month stint in Pathology and never left, though those who knew him as the life and soul of every party hardly recognized the timid, humourless creature in the horn-rimmed spectacles if they happened upon him, scurrying along the corridors. They would point him out to those who had never known him, as a means of warning them off a career in Pathology. 'You see that weird bloke?' they'd say. 'He was once a normal human being. He went to Pathology and look what happened to him.'

But Bruce was something else again, he was almost manic, though as no one knew him before he went into Pathology, there was no actual proof that he had ever been anything else. At every party he did the maddest things, though he was well past the age of a houseman. There was that time he had got into the board room, with its rogues' gallery along the walls of past worthies that no one could remember or identify, and that shiny, rather expensive long table in the middle of the floor, below three evenly spaced chandeliers. Armed with a squeezy bottle of acetone and wearing rugby boots, Bruce had swung from chandelier to chandelier, spraying the worthies' portraits with the acetone as he swung. If he failed to make the next chandelier, which he did often, he would land on his rugby boot-clad feet on the table, then go back to the beginning and start all over again. For some reason it was important to Bruce that the three chandeliers should be done in one go. The others had only just managed to kidnap him and spirit him away before he was discovered by 'them', and all the while he shouted the most profane oaths anyone could ever recall hearing, which, considering they were all rugby players, was saying something.

After that came his musical interlude, when he broke into the Chief Executive's spacious suite in the middle of the night and stole her beloved piano, which he then rode down three flights of stairs, yelling 'Hi-o Silver!' At the bottom he slammed into a wall, which caused him no pain whatever, though the piano was somewhat more bruised. But his worst episode to date was undoubtedly the arm one, everyone was agreed on that. From the arm episode onwards there was a shift in opinion about Bruce, he went from being outrageous fun to being slightly suspect mentally. At another party he had taken a great, not to say uncontrollable, shine to an Intensive, a Fourth Year medical student, who was doing her locum for one of the housemen. When the girl pulled back the covers of her bed the following night, she found to her horror a severed arm lying between the sheets and immediately screamed the place down. To show his affection for the unfortunate girl, a besotted pathologist's equivalent of a dozen red roses, Bruce had removed the arm from a cadaver being used by First Year medical students to study anatomy, and left it in her bed as a love token. The others had covered that one up by less than the skin of their teeth.

★　　★　　★

'Bruce?' Marylka asked. 'What's he done now?'

'Well,' said Mark, 'it was at a party.'

'Naturally.'

'Seems that the Chief Exec's his latest passion. So he went missing at the party and was discovered on the roof, five storeys up, on the tiles in more ways than one, running a pair of bright red knickers with "SEX" stamped across them, up the flagpole.'

'What's that to do with the Chief Exec?'

'They were her knickers according to Bruce. How he came by them no one really wants to know.'

'Bright red knickers?' Marylka asked. 'The Chief Exec?'

'Yeah, what a thought. Makes you shudder, doesn't it?'

'So did he get away with it?'

'It had been raining,' Mark said, 'the tiles were wet, and he began to slip. So everyone available formed themselves into a human chain, one holding on to the one in front's ankles, and then the next one, till they reached the daft sod, tied a college scarf around him and pulled him in. It was one of those black, red, yellow and white efforts, belonged to one of the Cardiology Techs, and the label on it said "ECG Dolly". That's all the fuzz found, now they're going crazy trying to find a tech called Dolly apparently.'

'They're all called Dolly!' Marylka laughed. 'It's a group description!'

'Yeah, but they don't know that and no one's telling them. The techs all deny being there, they say this Dolly probably came from another hospital, so the field of investigation is spreading nicely and taking a long time to get nowhere.'

'And what about the knickers?'

'They were still there next day, caused no end of a fuss, dignity of the hospital at stake, all that guff. Interrogations all round, threats of mass dismissal if the culprit wasn't given up, all that sort of thing. The Fire Service eventually had to come and haul the knickers down, hardly a straight face among them. They treated it as a training exercise, but they still said they'd send a bill to the hospital.'

'And what about Bruce?'

'Clean as a whistle. Can't remember a thing about it, so he says. I think there are strong suspicions, bound to be with Bruce's record, but so far no one's talking and the board can't prove a thing.'

'So Bruce survives to appal another day,' Marylka smiled.

'Yes, Marylka, but it's not right, is it? I mean, I know he's only let loose on dead people, but one of these days he could meet some live patients and the mad sod could do anything. Have you ever noticed the way he looks at you? It's like he's putting the evil eye on you, or maybe he just hates me.'

'Why on earth would he hate you, Mark?'

'Well, he always looks at me in a threatening kind of way!'

Marylka started laughing, but Mark was warming to his theme. 'I bet if we checked up with Australia we'd find he'd escaped from some looney bin over there before he came here.' He shook his head disapprovingly. 'I think he's insane, I really do.'

'Oh, come on, he's not as bad as that! He's just – '

'What?' Mark asked.

'Well, a bit daft I suppose.'

'I think he's crossed the line,' Mark stated firmly, 'and you can't let mad people loose on unsuspecting patients. One of these days he'll have to be carted off, I'd put money on it.'

Marylka watched him. Mark, who desperately needed some light-hearted fun, disapproved so much of Bruce, who could do with some sober behaviour. It was an odd world. She could probably do with some fun herself come to that. The day before she had finally gone to her mother's office and cleared it out, a task she had been dreading. Annie, her mother's secretary, looked suddenly old, as though somehow she too was in the past. For the first time she realized that Annie must be in her sixties, a spinster lady, she thought with a slight smile, with black – it must be dyed! – permed hair, sensible cardigan, and her eccentric trademark of bright red lipstick and nails. Marylka watched her quietly as she went through some papers, probably for the hundredth time, and realized that Annie was as nervous as she was herself. This was an ordeal for both of them. She knew Annie had decided to retire when the office was finally cleared out, and she felt guilty as she understood for the first time that she had prolonged the ordeal for Annie by putting this off for so long. She closed the door behind her and looked around. There was something strange about going into a place where the occupant had left with every intention of returning. It felt like an intrusion. It was that *Mary Celeste* thing she supposed, the disturbing way everything lay around, as though Helen had popped out for a minute and would return at any second. The smell of her perfume was everywhere, it was called 'Sublime'.

'Do you know why she first bought that?' Marylka asked Annie softly.

Annie shook her head.

'It was because of Para Handy. You know, the captain of the *Vital Spark* puffer. We were going through Fraser's one day and she spotted the bottle and couldn't stop laughing – you know that way she did?'

Annie nodded. 'She just fell apart,' she laughed quietly. 'You'd see these pictures of her in the papers looking so serious and responsible and that morning something silly had set her laughing so much that she'd had to re-apply her make-up three times! Remember "the wee loast ginger dug"?'

Marylka laughed and nodded, crossing her arms in front of her around her waist, and wandering about the room.

'Sometimes just passing the spot on the stairs outside where it had happened would set her off,' Annie remembered. 'She'd come through the door creased with laughter, saying "The wee loast ginger dug, Annie!" and she was gone for the rest of the morning.'

'Well, "Sublime" was like that,' Marylka laughed gently. 'When he liked something Para Handy used to say it was "Chust sublime!", so she had to have it regardless of what it smelt like.

And every time she bought a new bottle she'd start giggling again, God knows what the sales assistants thought!'

There was less in the office than she had expected. Old Hector's roll-top desk sat suppurating in the corner as usual; she'd see that it went for firewood as soon as possible. 'But it's a beautiful piece!' Helen used to say whenever Marylka tried to get her to dispose of it. 'Yeah, but if you sold it you'd be passing all that nastiness on to some other, possibly innocent, soul!' Marylka would reply. '*Burn* it, Mum!' Looking around now there weren't as many personal effects as she'd feared. Some photos of Marylka in her Bearsden Academy uniform, marking another triumph over Old Hector. As befitted the great man's grand-daughter, Helen had been sent to the upper-crust Laurel Bank, but Helen had sent her daughter to a non-fee-paying school. She had given her own name as Helen Kowalski, and her occu-pation as office manager, and though someone, everyone prob-ably, at Bearsden must've recognized her as Helen Davidson, they certainly had the good grace, not to say good sense, never to mention it.

'Why do you think there's so little here?' Marylka asked Annie. Annie was silent for a moment. 'I wondered about that too,' she said. 'I think the reason was that she didn't really want to be here. She always saw the business as something she had to do *for now*, she never intended making it her life. It was as if she planned to do something else once she'd got the business on its feet, but Young Hector was hopeless, as you know, so tomorrow just never came. I've had the feeling for a while now that there was something else she wanted to do when she had time, though.'

'Any idea what?'

Annie shrugged and shook her head. 'She never mentioned a word, I just had a feeling, you know. I could've been totally wrong about it, though.'

'No,' Marylka said quietly. 'I picked something up too. Kind of restless, preoccupied. There was something, but I don't know what either. I did ask, but I wish now I'd asked her more. But as you say, Young Hector is such a lame brain, maybe she never was going to get the time and she knew it.' She paced over to the window and looked down absently on the traffic below. 'You know I had words with Young Hector?'

'I should think the whole of St Vincent Place knows that!' Annie replied tartly.

'He deserved it, useless man! I told him to sell the business or blow it all up.'

'Oh, Marylka, he'll never do that! It's the ghost of his father, poor man, and you can't blame him for being what he is!'

'I can if I want!' They both started laughing. 'Annie, as far as you know, did he ever have another woman, apart from my grandmother?'

'Not as long as I can remember. I wouldn't bet on before her either, come to that, despite his father trying to make out he was a helluva stud,' Annie replied. 'And I've been around since Old Hector's day. Your mother reckoned he was just discreet.'

Marylka laughed. 'I once asked her if she thought he might be gay. Did she tell you that?'

'Marylka! You did not!' Annie gasped. 'What did she say?'

'Well, I only got as far as "You don't think he's . . ." and she exploded! I said the fact that she'd guessed what I was about to say proved that it had crossed her mind too, and she went ten different shades of red and blustered a bit. I got the "discreet" defence too, but as I said to her, why couldn't he have been just as discreet with a bloke? Besides, everybody in business knows everything about everyone else, there's no such thing as discreet, and he was an excessively pretty young man, wasn't he?'

Annie was sitting in the chair she used to sit in when taking dictation from Helen, or exchanging gossip. 'Want to know what I really think?' she said.

'Yes, go on.'

'Well, given the dog's abuse Old Hector gave him all his life, I'm just surprised that he was able to do it with anyone. I think your mother might well have been the result of Young Hector's first and last attempt.'

'Or better still, maybe she's not a Davidson at all!' gasped Marylka delightedly. 'God, I wish we'd mentioned either possibility to her!' Marylka giggled. 'She'd have disappeared in a puff of smoke! It's a thought, though, isn't it? Maybe she'd have found impotence easier to accept than him being gay when you think about it!'

When they stopped laughing Marylka returned to pacing about the office. 'You know,' she said, 'when I first walked in and caught a whiff of her perfume, it was as if she was still around. But there's really no sense of her here, is there?'

'I know what you mean,' Annie replied with a sigh. 'Maybe it's because, as I said, she wasn't here, not in any real sense, she saw herself as just passing through.'

Marylka had put this task off as long as she could because she couldn't face the pain she thought would be waiting for her in this room, but it had turned into a non-event. Then she sat in Helen's chair and pulled out the desk drawers one by one. They were all empty, Annie had already seen to whatever they had contained, but as she reached for the top right-hand drawer, Annie got up to go.

'I'd take my time over that one if I were you,' she said.

Marylka hesitated, her hand on the drawer, looking at Annie.

'And it's the last thing you have to do, so I'll leave you to it.' Annie smiled and walked to the door. 'Come out whenever you're ready. Take your time.'

She was paralysed with fear. She didn't know what to do. Should she open the drawer or leave it closed? Was it some sort of Pandora's Box? How bad could it be? She looked at the clock on the wall. 'I'll wait for two minutes and then open it,' she thought, but when that two minutes had passed she renewed the promise, then another two slipped past. 'This is ridiculous!'

she thought furiously, and pulled the drawer open. Inside was a small, pink, beehive-shaped box made of a hard plastic material, with a strand of blue wool still hanging from it, and neatly folded beside it, a pair of delicate black lace gloves. As she lifted the gloves a tiny plastic hospital tag fell out. 'Baby Kowalski, F, 7lb 2ozs. 17/6/73. Queen Mother's Hospital.' 'Auntie Mary, Millie and me!' she thought. The lack of personal effects about the office had lulled her into a false sense of security. But now the pain was physical, like a sudden blow deep within her chest, and her mind was full of her own voice silently screaming. 'Oh God! Oh God! Oh God!' it wailed, as she sat at the desk, clutching the box, the gloves, and the name tag that had been put around her own ankle when she was born. It summed up all the love her mother had ever known, and it hurt so badly that she thought she would never gather up the strength to move again for the rest of her life. She sat there so long that she lost track of time, her mind whizzing with memories then totally blank, then she forced herself to take several deep, even, calming breaths. She looked again at the most important items in her mother's life, not one of them worth anything much in financial terms. 'So money can't buy you love after all.' She smiled sadly. Slowly she opened the door and found herself in the outer office, aware of Annie watching her almost from the corner of her eye. 'Thanks, Annie,' she said, without looking directly at her, then she passed through into the corridor and down into the street, Helen's most treasured possessions still in her hand.

She had expected it to be terrible, then it had seemed easy, but just as she was feeling relieved the whole thing had become unbearable. Time was a great healer, so it was said, but when did it start? She remembered Helen's time-machine fixation and smiled. Maybe she had the right idea after all. If only she could be transported to another time, another place, somewhere she could sleep and leave this pain behind her till she felt strong enough to work her way through it. If only.

19

Sitting in the Common Room, half-listening to Mark giving chapter and verse on why Bruce should be deported, she wondered what she should do next. Her eighteen-month housemanship would be over in a few weeks, then she would be a fully-fledged doctor. Once her only concern in life had been to reach this stage. For the first time since she entered Medical School seven long years before, she would have the power to make her own career decisions, to decide what to do, where to go next. But somehow it no longer seemed to matter. She had decided long ago that she wanted to be a medic, not a surgeon; even if the surgeons welcomed females into their little private club, she didn't want to join. They were a weird lot. What was that saying? 'Surgeons can't cope with conscious patients, medics can't cope with the scalpel, and psychiatrists can't cope,' that was it. Well she liked her patients awake, and she had never met a psychiatrist she would let near a dog, not even a 'wee loast ginger dug' come to that, so a medic she would be. She should have fixed up a job as a Senior House Officer long ago from the offers she had had, but since Helen's death she had hit this patch of being unable to finish anything or make decisions. Her work was suffering too, she knew that, nothing she hadn't managed to retrieve, forgotten blood samples, mislaid test results of various kinds, and however worthless and unnecessary everyone knew them to be, they still had to be done. She had called in so many favours from the multitude of departments in the hospital that she would never be able to pay them back, and though she'd survived, she could feel things slipping away from her. She felt out of control and she knew she needed help, but who was there to turn to?

The medical profession was still notoriously unsympathetic to anyone who let their emotions show; it made them not altogether sound, and that was her main problem – her emotions were spilling over into every part of her life, and it just wasn't like her. Admit that, though, and her career could well be blighted before it took off.

Then she remembered Ali Mackay, the self-confessed heretic who had given that odd lecture on bereavement during her last year as a student. He was a consultant in another medical unit within the hospital; she'd seen him around, but she had never talked to him. Sometimes he would catch her eye and smile quietly to himself, wondering what she had been told, because he knew what his colleagues said about him and it amused him. They were all very fond of Ali, and he was an admirable consultant physician, but by also being a psychotherapist he dabbled in black magic as far as they were concerned, and it was better to be cautious. 'Never sit beside Ali in the canteen,' they'd warn. 'He'll ask you what you dreamt about last night and then analyse you.' And because they believed it, that's what Ali did, but if you really looked you could see that he was laughing quietly to himself as he did so.

She decided not to think about her next move, just to make it, but when the switchboard paged him his secretary answered. Dr MacKay was out of the hospital at the moment, she said, but she would leave a message asking him to contact Dr Kowalski on his return. As she replaced the phone her own pager sounded, and it didn't exactly make her day when she discovered Rob Burns on the other end of the phone. He was another one she'd been putting off for weeks, and his annoyance showed in his extremely understanding tone.

'Marylka, I know you're busy,' he said. She could almost see him struggling to keep the fixed grin on his face as he said it. He'd probably practised it in front of a mirror to be sure he got it just right. 'But I really do need to talk to you.'

'Rob, whatever it is, can't it wait? My mother's estate can't possibly be wound up yet, so what is there to talk about?'

There was a pause. 'I would rather have done this face to face, Marylka, but if the only way of achieving that is to tell you in advance, well . . .' He paused again. 'Your father is in the country and wants to see you.'

Marylka could think of nothing to say.

'You see? That's why I wanted to tell you this in person, I didn't want you upset when there was no one around to be with you,' Rob said.

'I'm not upset, Rob,' she lied. 'I was just trying to work out what the hell he wants, and why you referred to him as my father.'

'Because he is, and we need to deal with this situation.'

'"We", Rob?'

'Of course, "we". He must be after something, and I am the family solicitor.'

'Look, I can get some time off tomorrow afternoon. Ask him to be at your office at 2 p.m. No negotiation, he either makes it then or he can sod off.'

'Fine. And there's something else we can talk about afterwards, something Helen should have dealt with, but as you know, putting things off runs in the family. Now I'm afraid it's down to you.'

'What's it about?'

'It's nothing to do with Helen herself, it's to do with old Mrs Ferrier.'

'Auntie Mary?'

'Well, at least I've got your attention at last! See you tomorrow at 2 p.m. I'll be the one who doesn't call you Daughter.'

Everything in her entire life had been easy-going, there had never been a problem, a difficulty that couldn't be worked out and smoothed over. Then suddenly this brick wall had appeared from a clear blue sky. Sometimes she found herself looking back to the days leading up to Helen's death and trying to work out if there had been any clues. Life couldn't possibly change so drastically without warning, it didn't make any sense, but as far as she could see, that was exactly what had happened. She felt like a boxer who wasn't quite being knocked out, but was stumbling from one blow to another, taking counts of eight each time and fearing that one more punch would render him unconscious. There seemed no time to recover from each blow before the next one hit home, like meeting the father she didn't know, and didn't want to know. Why was fate dealing this out to her? When would it ever end, and would she still be on her feet when it did?

She got Mark Galbraith to cover for her and felt guilty about it, but there wasn't time to persuade anyone else, and Mark never refused any request. When she arrived at Rob's office in St Vincent Street, not quite as exclusive as the Davidson HQ in St Vincent Place, he seemed more nervous about her father than she did.

'Are you all right?' he asked.

'Fine, Rob. For God's sake, will you relax!'

'Do you want me to stay?'

'Makes no difference to me. Do you want to stay?'

'I rather think I should, I am your solicitor after all. You are OK about this?'

'Rob, would you like me to get you a glass of water? Wheel Mr Kowalski in. One of my colleagues is covering for me and I don't want to impose on him for any longer than strictly necessary.'

Rob left the room then returned with Jan Kowalski. He was a tall, slim man, dark hair gone grey, brown eyes. High cheekbones too. One up for Helen. He had a coat folded over his arm and was fiddling with one of the buttons. She stood at the window, the traffic noises muted slightly by the double glazing. She said nothing as he entered and didn't ask him to sit down.

'Hello, Marylka,' he said quietly.

'What do you want, Mr Kowalski?' she asked in reply.

'You're angry with me, I can understand that,' he smiled nervously.

'You flatter yourself, Mr Kowalski,' she said evenly. 'Anger would indicate some sort of emotion, and I assure you I don't feel either way about you. You are a stranger, after all.'

'I'm your father.'

'An accident of biology,' she said. 'My mother could've lain down in the street with any passing male for that. In fact these days the materials come in a test tube, then all you need is a syringe. You don't have to go near a man or a doctor, it's called DIY fertilization. You can even buy it through the Internet.' She sensed Rob grimacing. 'I'm doing OK, then!' she thought. 'So once again, Mr Kowalski, what is it you want?'

'I read about your mother.'

'Surely not for the first time. She made the papers fairly often, yet you never felt the urge to make contact before.'

Jan Kowalski looked at her in silence, then he said, 'You look like my mother, did you know that?'

'And if that's true, it is merely a genetic accident, Mr Kowalski, nothing more. She is no more family to me than you are.'

'I just wondered.' He stopped. 'I just wondered how you were coping.'

'A little late in the day for that surely? You gave up any right to wonder many years ago.'

'That's a little harsh.'

'The truth often is. And if you're thinking of trying to lay claim to any part of my mother's estate, I'll tell you here and now that I'd waste the lot on legal fees before I'd let you sniff a penny. You can have that in writing if you wish. You got your pay-off when you left for Australia.'

'You have no idea what it was like,' he said. 'Her grandfather was such a powerful man, there were pressures.'

'Mr Kowalski, let me make my feelings very clear to you, because I really don't want there to be any misunderstandings. Whatever difficulties you had with your wife were for the two of you to sort out. But you had a child, and you not only deserted that child, but you accepted a golden handshake for doing it. That puts you in a very rare category as far as I'm concerned. If I had a child, Mr Kowalski, no one, and nothing on this earth, would keep me from her. There isn't enough power, pressure or money in the universe to make me run out on her.' She was amazed at how strong and cool she sounded; she only hoped it was coming across to him the way it sounded to her.

Jan Kowalski was watching her, looking pained, and suddenly much smaller than when he had come into the room.

'You're not my father, Mr Kowalski, you only fathered me, and that too was a private matter between you and my mother. I had no part in whatever contract you had with her.'

Jan Kowalski turned towards the door. 'I didn't come here for money, I just wanted to see you,' he said.

'And all the years since you last saw me, my mother stopped you, did she? She was such an ogre that you only feel safe now that she's not here?'

'No . . . I didn't mean that. I . . . You have brothers and a sister in Australia now, I wanted you to know that.'

'No I don't. You have fathered other children perhaps, but they have nothing to do with me nor I with them. Please listen carefully, Mr Kowalski,' she continued calmly. 'I do not wish to see you or hear from you ever again. Is that clear? If you try to contact me again in any way I will take out an interdict to stop you. You are an Australian citizen now, I believe, so presumably you could be deported if the Scottish Courts so ordered, and I would not hesitate to ask them. I don't think that would look too good to your employers, and if there's one thing you have always done, it's to look after the cash side of things. Have I made myself clear?'

Jan Kowalski left without a word and closed the door quietly behind him.

'Phew!' Rob said, his eyes wide. 'My God, you really told him, didn't you?'

Marylka chuckled. 'Good, wasn't I?'

'Maybe you were a bit hard on him, don't you think?'

'No. He came here for his reasons, not for mine. I wanted him to know that I have no obligations to him, and no intention of letting him use me to salve whatever guilt he may be feeling.'

'And you're really OK?'

'Rob, I feel better than I have for months! I didn't get a chance to tell my mother how I felt about her before she died, but I got the chance to tell him. I feel as though a weight has dropped off my shoulders!'

'He looked as if it'd landed on *his* shoulders!'

'I was dreading seeing him, but I'm glad I did now, I feel *wonderful*! Bring on Captain Ferrier too while I'm in the mood for dealing with disappearing males! Auntie Mary and Millie have some unfinished business with him I could attend to! And talking about Auntie Mary, what's this great mystery you wanted to discuss?'

'What? Oh, that!' Rob was obviously still in shock. 'Oh, let's not bother about that today, I feel as though I could do with a lie down in a cool darkened room after your dramatic perform-ance! You don't have time just now, let me know when you have more than a couple of hours and we'll go over it then.'

'But I'm curious! C'mon, spill the beans!'

'It's nothing much really,' he said. 'Old Mrs Ferrier left a letter for your mother asking her to carry out certain tasks. I nagged Helen about it a bit, and on the day of the accident she left a message saying she would discuss it with you and get back to me. Of course she didn't. It'll take time that you don't have to go over it in detail, but that's the gist of it. Now trot back to the hospital, and ring me when you've got time. OK?'

Leaving Rob's office the sun seemed to be shining for the first time in a long, long time. She felt in control again, she had handled the great reunion better than she had hoped. Maybe that was a sign she was getting on top of things again. She went back to the hospital, if not elated, then at least at some sort of peace; she had won this round, maybe the fight was at last turning her way. As she went past the reception desk one of the porters called out to her.

'Doctor, Ah've been asked tae tell ye tae report tae Sister Woods as soon as ye came back.'

'Eek! Crusher Woods? You must be joking!'

'No,' he said sadly, 'somethin's happened, y'see.'

'Well? Don't stop there, spit it out!'

He looked around and leaned forward. 'Don't say Ah told ye,' he whispered, 'but it's Doctor Galbraith. He's gone tae the looney bin.'

For a moment her mind tried to make sense of this information. Did he mean Mark had been called to the nearest Psychiatric Unit? Perhaps there was a medical emergency, some psychiatric patient with a heart attack. Or maybe his interest in the demented Bruce's mental aberrations had sparked off a latent interest. Was Mark considering becoming a psychiatrist and had he gone for an interview? It wasn't after all the kind of information that anyone would advertise, maybe he had tried to keep it to himself till the last minute so that the inevitable giggling would be kept to a minimum. But in that case why had he agreed to cover for her? She opened her mouth, but the porter put his hand up, 'Better go up an' see Crusher,' he said diplomatically.

She knocked on Sister Woods's door and was commanded to enter. Dave Morgan, Mark's Senior House Officer was with her, both of them looking shell shocked. Beryl Woods ordered her to sit down, poured coffee out of a jug into a cup, and handed it to Marylka.

'You'll need this, lass,' she said kindly It seemed that not long after Marylka had left the hospital to deal with her father, Mark had wandered down the drive and on to Dumbarton Road. There he proceeded to take out his stethoscope and examine bemused passers-by, saying that 'the voices' had ordered him to do so. One of the ambulances on its way into the hospital had been stuck at traffic lights long enough to see what was happening, and thinking the young doctor was drunk, a reasonable assumption, the paramedics had tried to get him into the back of the vehicle. Mark, intent on doing the bidding of 'the voices', broke free, ran to the bridge over the River Kelvin, and attempted to jump in, once again obeying orders apparently. The paramedics had caught him and rushed him to the hospital, where Mark became even more agitated and ran screaming through the corridors. When he was finally caught it was clear that he was hallucinating and a psychiatrist was called, anathema to every medic present. Mark was then sedated and removed to the nearest Psychiatric Unit.

'You know what these bastard psychiatrists are like,' said Dave Morgan, 'won't commit themselves, though God knows somebody should, but it looks like Mark has schizophrenia.' The words hung in the air like lumps of lead. No one said anything at first, because there didn't seem much to say.

'I blame myself,' Beryl Woods said.

'And so you should, Crusher!' replied Dave. 'You've driven many of us insane over the years, and you meant it every time. Let this be a lesson to you!'

Beryl glanced at him icily and shook her head. 'And why you haven't been carted off remains a mystery!' she muttered. 'I knew there was something wrong with that boy,' she continued, shaking her head. 'Housemen are always half-witted idiots, but there was something about him I couldn't put my finger on, there was a worry lurking in the back of my mind. I should've said something.'

'I know what you mean,' Dave Morgan replied with a sigh. 'I'd love to let you take all the blame Beryl, God knows we'd all like to see you penitent, but I think everybody had some concern about the boy.'

'He always talked about "the voices",' Marylka said miserably. '"The voices" were always shouting at him, telling him how useless he was, that he had to do better. I thought he meant the consultants, everyone did. We all told him that we got yelled at too, that he shouldn't let it get to him.'

They all sat in shocked silence. 'And he didn't like people too near him,' she said, suddenly putting symptoms together. 'Mark was always alone, he isolated himself. You'd all be in a crowd and you'd look at Mark and he'd be alone.'

'I noticed that!' the SHO said, as though the scales had only just fallen from his eyes too. 'I said to somebody not long ago that I'd bet anything that lad was a repressed virgin, either that or he was anally retentive.'

Sister Woods and Marylka exchanged looks of disgust. 'It's the schoolboy mentality,' Beryl said. 'They never quite get over it no matter what age they are. He'll be telling us knock-knock jokes in a minute.'

Marylka tried to laugh, but it stuck in her throat. 'What do we do now?'

'I'm glad you asked that!' said the SHO brightly. 'First of all, here's your bloody pager back again, and second, we'll need some sort of help covering for Mark.'

'Well, surely they'll sort out a locum?' Marylka asked.

'A locum for a loco?' grinned Dave Morgan.

Marylka and Beryl sighed heavily, but still, there was something comforting in his gung-ho approach; sick as it was, it was a positive, moving-on strategy.

'Don't be silly, girl!' he continued. 'Do you think the Trust is made of money? Can't buy BMWs for the pen-pushers *and* provide locums for deranged housemen, be reasonable! No, I'll cover, because I'm a saint and because I'm the next lowest piece of crap, but will you help out? It's only for the next two weeks, then the next slave takes over, another one for Beryl to drive bonkers!'

Marylka nodded. 'He covered for me often enough. Poor Mark. What will happen to him now, d'you think?'

'Well, we've been talking about that,' Morgan replied. 'One of the consultants recalls a registrar going doolally a few years back. Seems if they recover well enough they can go into research, but they're never allowed near patients again. Mind you, makes you wonder about the research they do too, doesn't it?'

'You're telling me you don't wonder already?' Beryl asked. 'Most of it's totally worthless as it is! They've been setting the results first and fitting the research around it for years, the whole thing's a sham!'

'Now, Sister Woods!' chided the SHO with mock seriousness. 'That is a very harsh thing to say! Kindly do not make accusations you cannot prove, or at least that I *hope* you can't prove!'

'The really bizarre thing is that Mark's been loudly advocating for ages that Bruce from Pathology should be committed, kept going on about him not being crazy, but seriously insane and a danger to patients. How ironic is that?' Marylka mused.

'Maybe the Wish Genie is getting things back to front these days,' said the SHO brightly.

'The *what*?' Beryl asked.

'Y'know, like the Tooth Fairy, only it's the Wish Genie. Maybe it gets the wisher instead of whoever is being wished upon!' He stood up and announced, 'Oh, Wish Genie, do not dally-dilly. Give my consultant a great big willy!'

From the chair beside him came Beryl's voice in weary response.

'Wish Genie, listen, and don't you be silly. His consultant's got an SHO who *is* a great big willy!'

In the Common Room that evening the mood was subdued, as the housemen and assorted friends sat in groups discussing Mark's illness. With Marylka were Bruce from Pathology, Fiona the ECG Dolly and Alan Buchan, the houseman scarred for life by Andy and Mad Mick.

'I feel really bad,' said Alan. 'I mean he never refused to take your pager, didn't even seem to mind. I never asked anyone else to cover for me, always Mark.'

'We all did that,' said Marylka, 'but what does it say about the staff of this place that no one spotted he was so ill?'

'Oh, be fair,' said Bruce glumly. 'We're normal people, not psychiatrists.'

'Funnily enough, that's not what Mark thought,' said Marylka. 'He always reckoned if anyone got carted off, it would be you, Bruce.'

Bruce was sitting on the arm of an armchair, his arms folded, when he heard this. 'Me?' he screeched. 'Why the hell would he think that?'

'Because you're crazy, you stupid bastard!' said Alan.

'I am not!' Bruce retorted. 'I just like having a laugh, that's all!'

'Well, take this as a warnin',' said Fiona the ECG Dolly savagely. 'There's a fine line between actin' mad an' bein' mad, an' you've crossed it a helluva lotta times! Just remember we're all bein' victimized over your last episode up on that bloody roof!'

'Was that *your* scarf?' Marylka asked, suddenly putting two and two together.

'I know not,' said Fiona, in an ultra polite voice, 'to what you are referring. What scarf? I know of no scarf, and anyway, I take the Fifth.'

'Mark always said you looked at him funny too,' Alan said to Bruce, who was now thoroughly under siege.

'I didn't!' said the hapless pathologist. 'I look at everybody the same!'

'*In*sane,' muttered Fiona, 'no' "the same". It's all your fault, come to think about it, you drove poor old Mark over the edge, you Aussie nutter!'

'It was probably part of his symptoms, he was paranoid, poor guy,' Bruce offered pathetically.

'You seem,' said Alan Buchan suspiciously, 'to know a lot about it. Mark reckoned you'd escaped from a funny farm in Australia, maybe he was right after all!'

'Oh, gimme a break!' Bruce pleaded.

'Any more saunters across wet roofs in the dark an' you'll get a break, several in fact!' Fiona spat at him. 'Ah wrecked a pair of tights in the rescue, remember, an' broke two fingernails!' She held up two fingers for his inspection. 'An' you can take that as a comment as well!' she said, then looking around she gave a delicate little cough before continuing in her ultra polite voice. 'At least, I would have ripped my tights and ruined two specially cultivated nails had I been there, which I wasn't, whenever whatever it was, got done.' She looked across at Bruce. 'An' Ah won't forget it, you looney! You're next for the men in white coats after what you did to poor Mark!'

Bruce gave in and accepted the unanimous nomination as scapegoat, his denials subsiding as he slipped to the floor, his head sinking mournfully on to his chest. 'It's not my fault,' he said glumly. 'You're taking it out on me just because I'm a stranger in a foreign land!'

'It's because you're *strange*,' Alan Buchan grinned. 'You're a mad bloody Aussie, that's reason enough to persecute you!'

'Anyhow, there is of course one way to atone, Brucie boy,' Fiona smiled sweetly at him. 'The drinks are on you at the Rubaiyat Ah believe?'

They discussed Mark's tragedy, the humour becoming blacker as they held a wake for the person they used to know, the Mark who had now gone, fixing his place in their lives. The black humour was a means of self-preservation, they were mentally and emotionally putting him in the past so that they could move on with life. Marylka suddenly realized that her problem in coping with her mother's death was very likely because that process had been missed out. But who was there to talk to? Her mind searched for something else to think about.

'Any news of Danny Morrison, the one-man Engelbert appreciation society?' she asked Fiona.

Fiona rolled her eyes. 'Aye, Ah saw him at out-patients the other day. When he left us the surgeons had a go at him, did a triple bypass.' She stopped for a moment then asked, 'Do you really want to hear this? Are things no' depressin' enough?'

'Why? What's happened? Didn't the surgery work?'

'Oh, aye, it worked OK, an' he's finished with Engelbert

for ever, reckons it was the singin' that caused his cardiac arrest for some reason.'

'Well, given his bloody awful voice that's got to be progress, surely?'

'No' really,' Fiona sighed. 'Now he's found God. We never saved his life that day he says, an' yet Ah clearly remember tyin' that clown Spencer up in cables so he couldn't get near him. No, God saved him apparently. He offered up a wee prayer before he lay on the couch, then he sang "The Lord's My Shepherd" as Ah did the ECG. His voice is as bad as ever, Ah'll give him that, no divine intervention there. When he left he told me he'd remember me in his prayers. It took all my self-control not to scud him across the back of the head as he went out the door.' She sighed again. 'Sometimes you wonder if you did the right thing. Ah mean, Big Morrison came out of the womb brain dead, he was the perfect candidate for no resuscitation. Sometimes you'd be better lettin' them go when they arrest, Ah swear. Let's be honest, he was a big bam, but is it worse to go with the dignity of a bam, or to live as he is now, as a complete numpty?' She sighed again, then her description of the newly saved Danny Morrison fresh in her mind, she dug her toe into Bruce's rear. 'Right, Brucie,' she said, 'on your feet. Ah feel the need of a tincture or three, an' Ah hear the siren call of the Rubaiyat!'

20

Life on an island moves slowly; progress comes later to far-flung areas, and the sea isolates more effectively than any single-track road to the remotest mainland village. That, Betty knew, was one of the attractions for outsiders, though she never could understand their romantic view of Eilean Òg. Tourists waxed lyrical about the timelessness, the peace and quiet, the slower pace of life, but then they didn't see the place in winter, when the mountain peaks reached out and caught the passing clouds so that the rain fell for weeks at a time. Eilean Òg didn't have much snow, and what fell thawed as it hit the ground because of the sea air. Mostly it rained. In summer it was warm rain, in winter cold, that was the only difference.

The arrival of the ferry was a big event during the winter months, mainly because nothing much else happened. There would be an intense flurry of activity, with provisions being unloaded, the post being taken off, and sometimes relatives arriving for a visit. Depending on the tide you would see them running either up or down the gangway to get off, their faces full of excitement and happiness, but within a few days they would be trying hard to cover up the boredom. Moving to the mainland changed native islanders in ways they didn't really want to admit; they became accustomed to their new way of life, to having facilities that would never come to the island – to more of everything. But still they clung to the idea of their island home, remembering their time there as more than it had been or was. Once they arrived 'home', though, and all their news had been divulged and discussed, the limitations of insular island life would set in, and they would secretly realize that their horizons had widened and they could never return permanently. They couldn't disguise that look in their eyes, though, the guilt at wishing they could jump on a bus or a train and go back to what was now their home, but knowing they were trapped for however long the visit had been planned to last.

Others, those whose connections with the island were a generation or more removed, couldn't admit their disillusionment even to themselves. For some reason they saw the island as Brigadoon, and were unable to accept that their fantasy wasn't real without their entire lives collapsing around them. They reminded Betty of religious converts, more loyal than those who belonged to the place, and unable to hear a word against it. Eilean Òg was Valhalla and Utopia rolled into one, and they were more zealous in defence of the island than those who had been born, raised and continued – condemned in Betty's case – to live there. 'My grandfather lived here,' they would proclaim proudly, pointing with brimming eyes to some decrepit steading, 'and one day I'm going to live here again.' Hearing these emotional declarations she would smile to herself. Did they ever wonder why their grandfathers had left in the first place, and why, for that matter, they had never gone 'home'? Maybe those old emigrants were shrewder than their folk thought.

And if the next generation, or the one after that, did 'go home', it was most likely to be when they retired, and very soon afterwards, as was the pattern, they would die from a combination of boredom and alienation. There was a small development of private houses built especially for these wannabe islanders, some with obscure family connections, and others who had holidayed there year after year and thought they knew the place. Murdo had watched the houses being built in a neat, identical row. 'Wee boxes!' he had snorted, but soon it came to be known as Death Row. It was said that the local hearse couldn't pass the place, that the driver had to fight to stop the steering wheel turning of its own accord, because it made so many visits there, removing the inhabitants to a better place where they belonged much more than they did on their island 'paradise'.

But change did come of course, even to Eilean Òg, however slowly, the main one in Betty's eyes being the demise of Fearann Ban, where she and Martha had slaved as children. Once it was the biggest, richest, most important farm on the island, and Jim Campbell, the latest member of the clan to have it and the fine living it guaranteed handed to him on a plate, had the status of a laird. Mistress Campbell's errant husband could do whatever he wanted on Eilean Òg, in the eyes of the islanders his every indiscretion was forgiven even before it had been committed. The vastness of White Farm and the wealth it represented gave him a standing that ensured nothing he did was disapproved of, but when he took to the drink seriously the islanders weren't above cashing in.

Jim Campbell had dark, brooding looks, a dark man in more than one way, Betty mused, with a strong gypsy resemblance but less morals. As the drink took an ever stronger grip of him it was inevitable that the running of the farm would suffer over the years, and in time Jim Campbell found it harder to keep good workers. Sometimes he was even forced to do the milking himself, and it was well known that he kept a store of booze beside the milk tank to sustain him. The islanders thought that was funny; he was a terrible man, Jim, they would laugh to each other, what a character. Then came the day when Mistress Campbell was confronted by one of the islanders she knew laughed at her, asking for the cow Jim had traded earlier for a bottle of whisky. Once that first cow had gone other people saw their opportunity, and before long a pattern was established. Jim was accustomed to getting whatever he wanted all of his life, and when one bottle ran out he would do anything, pay any price for another, so the islanders made sure there was always one at hand. He would trade anything, livestock, grain, and equipment, and the more Mistress Campbell accepted the situation – and what else could she do? – the more the islanders benefited, and the less respect and therefore fear they had for her or her husband. She tried restricting Jim's access to cash, but he only sold things rather than swapped them.

Gradually, but almost imperceptibly, the area around the big white farmhouse that had given Fearann Ban its name shrank, as land was exchanged for whisky, or for money to buy whisky. At first it barely showed, because Jim Campbell's forebears had added to the farm throughout their lifetimes. The Campbells were regarded as good businessmen because they had no qualms about cashing in on another's misfortune, and over the years they had bought as much land as they could for as little as possible, turning the place into an estate. But as everyone on Eilean Òg had predicted, Jim's day of reckoning had to come. Eventually it became his habit to drink all day, and if the hotels shut and the owners refused to let him stay inside drinking out of hours, as in time they did when he ran out of ready cash, he would board the ferry and drink at the bar all the way to the mainland, and back across to the island again. On one of those return journeys he fell overboard and sank like a stone beneath the waves, until his body was trawled in the nets of a fishing boat three days later. Thereafter what was left belonged to Mistress Campbell.

Her Ladyship was in total control for the first time in her life, and if the islanders thought she would now halt the demise of what remained of the once showcase farm, they were wrong. She sold the place bit by bit, but with more deliberation and design than her husband had disposed of it. Little parcels of land went, then one whole field at a time. Livestock followed, and tractors, ploughs, harrows, balers, and all the other equipment were auctioned. The sheddings that had housed them were dismantled and sold off like kits, and there were plenty of eager buyers competing for a cheap slice, all locals, all anxious to take advantage of the death knell of Fearann Ban, even if they did disapprove of what was happening. Soon all that was left of a once proud estate was the big white farmhouse that had identified Fearann Ban for many generations. And Mistress Campbell enjoyed every second of its obliteration; for her, revenge was far more enjoyable eaten simmering hot. Eventually she sold the house too, with the stipulation that the new owners, rich outsiders with the usual hopelessly romantic notions of island life, would not keep the name of the house. They were only too happy to call their holiday home 'Seaview', the final, sweet insult as far as Her Ladyship was concerned, thereby destroying all physical evidence that Fearann Ban, a once wealthy working farm, had ever existed.

Mistress Campbell and her three daughters then left Eilean Òg for ever. An estate that had been the pride of the island for centuries had been converted into a large stash of cash that would not be spent on Eilean Òg, and the islanders who had provided Mistress Campbell with her loot hated her for it. She didn't care of course, why should she? They had always despised her anyway, and now she had her revenge on all of them, her husband included. She had him buried in the local cemetery, but far from the lair of his rich family and without a headstone. And in the way of small communities, the islanders proceeded to re-invent Jim Campbell after his death, creating in place of the reprobate that he was, a saintly, good-natured chap, who liked a drink and got up to all sorts of high jinks and capers. They castigated Mistress Campbell; if he drank to excess, they said, then she must have driven him to it, and if he behaved like a tomcat and fathered dark gypsy sons all over the place, well that was her fault too; she must have forced him to seek solace outside the marital bed. Jim was a native of Eilean Òg, he could do no wrong, especially now that he was dead, and it was disgraceful that his final resting place wasn't marked. They didn't care enough, though, particularly not those who had benefited from his drunken bargains or the sale of his ancestral estate, to provide a headstone for him, and as time passed the exact location of his grave became more and more vague.

Sometimes older people would pass Seaview and remember that it had once been Fearann Ban and go over the tale of Her Ladyship, the incomer who had married a decent local lad from a good family, driven him to drink then sold the place from under him. They wouldn't have been surprised, they would hint darkly, if his drunken drowning had in fact been the deliberate last act of a desperately unhappy and mistreated man. It all made Betty smile. She had no reason to feel affection for Mistress Campbell, her memories of those hard days and harsh treatment at Fearann Ban stayed too sharp for that, but often she would think about Mistress Campbell and wonder if perhaps unhappiness affected people in different ways. Who knew what Mistress Campbell would have been like if she had never met Jim Campbell? If she hadn't taken that ill-fated job as Eilean Òg's teacher she would have had another life altogether, but once she was trapped there the prospect of that other life had disappeared in a cloud of misery and booze fumes, and Betty knew all about the longing for another life. She could never quite forgive Mistress Campbell for treating two scared motherless children from Glasgow as she had, but still, good for her that she had escaped, she thought, and done so with some style too. What she would have given for the chance to escape from Eilean Òg with a fistful of cash!

Not that it would happen, she had no thoughts of getting away from the island these days, even when Murdo drove her mad, and without a doubt Murdo had a talent for that, aided and abetted by his alter ego and brother-in-law, Lachie. The two of them had been nursing a few broken bones, bruises and bumps recently, after the island football match. They hadn't a mark on them from the game, but their side had been beaten and had refused to accept it. As tradition dictated, the losers had waited at the top of the hill for the winning team on their way home, and engaged them in battle for possession of the small silver trophy they had legitimately won. Murdo and Lachie had captured the cup at the cost of a broken ankle for Lachie, and several fractured ribs and ten stitches in a head wound for Murdo.

'Whit are ye goin' oan aboot?' Murdo demanded. 'Ye should see the state o' the other side!'

'That doesnae make it right!' Catriona replied. 'Ye're far too auld tae be behavin' like this. Ye've got grandweans, ye're no'

a big daft laddie anymerr Murdo, at least ye shouldnae be! Ah
hope Alibel's giein' Lachie hell aboot it tae!'

'For God's sake whit's the fuss aboot?' Murdo protested. 'It's
been goin' oan for years! Everybody does it, there widnae be
any point of havin' the fitba' if we didnae have the fight efter.
Wimmen, ye don't understand anythin'!'

'Somebody'll be killed wanna these days, Murdo,' Catriona
persisted. 'Who'd look efter Red Rock if it was you?'

'Och, don't be daft!' he laughed, reaching out and ruffling
her hair, a gesture that always infuriated Catriona. She hit his
hand away, which made him gleefully reach out again with his
other hand. Catriona slapped him across the broken ribs, stopping him in his tracks.

'Noo that wasnae nice, Catriona. Ye can be helluva heavy-
handed at times!' he grimaced.

'And thank God she is,' Betty said from the sidelines. 'Naebody else can dae anythin' wi' ye!'

'Oh aye, that's right, gang up oan a man when he's injured.
Ye're a nest o' vipers, that's whit ye are!' Murdo eased himself
painfully into his chair in the porch, his expression suggesting
that he had received his injuries in a cause so noble that he
should be enjoying admiration rather than brickbats from his
nearest and dearest. He sat back, gently massaging his ribs.

'Look at ye!' Betty persisted. 'Was it worth it?'

'Aye, it was nae worth it! We got the cup, didn't we?'

'But ye lost the game!' Catriona reminded him angrily. 'Whit
does the cup matter if ye lost the game?'

'Ah wanted it!' Murdo replied simply, relaxing carefully into
his chair.

That was it, Betty thought, that was exactly it; Murdo wanted
the cup and that was all that mattered. There was no point
trying to make sense of it, especially for him, because Murdo
saw no other reason for anything. What he wanted was all that
counted, just as only his opinion made any sense, and if you
disagreed with him he thought you were curiously misguided.

He was exasperating – an understatement, but no one had yet come up with the right description, though many had tried. But there was affection there too, even as you ranted at him or about him. No matter how angry you were with him he never returned it; regardless of how wrong he thought you were – he *knew* you were – he would shake his head, laugh, and ruffle your hair with his great, rough paw. If only everyone else could get away with slapping his broken ribs as Catriona had, though, but even those who wanted to lay hands on Murdo, and had entirely justifiable reasons to do so, knew better. His family and only family, that was his outlook on life, and Betty knew it. It was lucky that his big, infuriating personality was rooted in a close, affectionate family who controlled his excesses and loved him even when he drove them mad. In other circumstances, she suspected, all that strength and self-belief might well have gone in another direction. Without his family her Murdo could have been a terrible man. She looked at his contented smile as he sat in his chair, his slippers on his feet, newspapers at hand, a glass of amber fluid by his side, and the purloined football trophy close by. She shook her head; what did she mean he *could* have been a terrible man? At that moment he looked up at his mother, grinned, winked, and shouted through the doorway, 'Catriona! Catriona! Whit aboot a wee hot chip in here then? Ah'm an invalid, Ah'm in pain! A wee hot chip's no' much tae ask in the circumstances, noo is it?'

21

There had been a time, she remembered it well, a little less than two weeks before, when Marylka felt that she might die from exhaustion. Now, covering her own wards and the absent Mark's as well, she looked back fondly to those days, and wondered what she had done with all that time she had on her hands only a fortnight ago. Arriving back in her own duty room she found Graham Spencer, the Cardiology Senior Registrar, pacing back and forward in his creaking shoes. You could always tell when he was around by the annoying creaking, and the raised hackles of everyone else in the vicinity. It probably wasn't his fault, but he was the most unprepossessing individual. His bushy straw-coloured hair, flying in all directions at once, looked as though a bomb had been detonated on top of his head, and those prominent teeth that some wag had once famously remarked 'follow you around like the Mona Lisa's eyes'. He emanated hassle and panic and drew unpopularity like a magnet, and gags about him considerably worse than the Mona Lisa one regularly took prominent place in the gossip hotline. When the midwife had slapped him on the day he was born, it was said, it probably had more to do with personal dislike than clearing his lungs of amniotic fluid. And the fact that he was an only child was put down to his mother's sense of guilt after her first effort, and if she wasn't still wearing sackcloth and ashes as a penance to humanity, then she should be.

The object of everyone's ridicule was at that moment pontificating to a less than absorbed Fiona as Marylka entered, and though she couldn't hear what was being said she knew from Spencer's face that she was the subject under discussion.

* * *

'We've just had that Ali MacKay down here looking for you,' Spencer said accusingly.

Drat! She'd forgotten all about the message she'd left with his secretary a hundred light years ago. Even so, she looked blankly at Spencer and shrugged. 'And?' she asked casually.

'Well, I just hope you haven't asked him to see one of *our* patients, that's all!'

'I haven't, Doctor Spencer.'

'Who have you asked him to see?'

'Why do you want to know?' she asked. 'If he's not seeing one of your patients what does it matter?'

He looked aggrieved, as if he had a right to know, and as Marylka knew, every other team regarded it as a matter of principle that Colonel Spencer of the First Foot-in-Mouth should know as little as possible about their affairs, just to annoy him. He suspected this of course, but couldn't risk saying so in case he was accused of being paranoid. His colleagues knew this was what he was thinking, and they deliberately kept him wondering if he was paranoid, or if he was paranoid for wondering in the first place; it was their entire reason for not telling him the most unimportant information. They made sure he knew nothing about meetings he had no actual interest in, but wanted to be able to refuse invitations to, and they didn't tell him about dinners and cocktail parties either, for the sheer pleasure of betting on when he might explode. This would occur after several snubs had built up in his mind, and then he would blow over something trivial and entirely unconnected; only then would money actually change hands in settlement of the various bets laid on the time and place when he might go up. Marylka suspected that this might be one of those times. Over at the pub someone would be a few quid richer tonight, as a direct result of the performance he was putting on at that moment in the duty room.

'You'll do yourself no good in medicine associating with him, you know,' he said. He had a peculiarly heavy step, that at

217

the same time managed to sound like the scurrying of some small, agitated creature. In a noisy, busy hospital with hundreds of people moving around, you could always pick out his footstep.

'Thanks for the advice, Doctor,' Marylka replied, and in the background Fiona laughed. 'I'm so grateful that you're taking such an interest in my future career.'

'There's something wrong with him, you know,' Spencer persisted. 'Once a perfectly good medical houseman went to his unit and Ali got at him. Afterwards he gave up medicine and became a psychiatrist!'

'Shocking!' said Marylka, who actually thought that it was.

'And another thing, don't ever look in his eyes.'

'Why?'

'He can tell what you're thinking by looking in your eyes,' Spencer said. 'Everyone knows that!'

'He can actually read minds?' Marylka asked, sorting through a pile of test results to avoid looking in Spencer's eyes, there being no way that even he wouldn't know exactly what she was thinking at that particular moment.

'Yes, he can!' replied Spencer, and squeaked with his usual heavy-footed scurry out of the duty room. As the door shut behind him he pushed it open and entered the room again. 'I almost forgot what I came to say,' he grinned. 'I've got a consultant's post.'

'Congratulations,' Marylka said unconvincingly. 'Where?'

'Newcastle!' said the beaming Spencer.

'Superb!' Marylka said, this time with considerably more feeling.

After he'd squeaked out for the second time Fiona and Marylka collapsed with a fit of giggles.

'I wondered what had got him hyper today, excitement about the new job, I suppose?'

Fiona nodded. 'Been like that all day,' she said. 'Desperate for someone to throw a party for him or stand him a round, so no one has stepped forward!'

'Poor old Newcastle!' Marylka giggled. 'That's one place crossed off my list of jobs!'

'Ah feel as if all my birthdays an' Christmases have come together,' chuckled Fiona. 'When he first told us in the department, Ah was so delighted that Ah almost grabbed the useless sod an' danced with him!'

Marylka laughed, then changed the subject as casually as she could. 'Oh, by the way, were you here when Ali arrived?'

'Yup. Said to phone his secretary if you still needed him.'

Marylka nodded. 'If I ever get a minute,' she said.

'Any news of Mark?' Fiona asked.

'Not really. Apparently it all takes a helluva time to know how well he'll ever be. There's no one anti-psychotic drug, it's a case of trial and error, and it's very early days seemingly.' Marylka sat down heavily in an ancient armchair by the window. 'They say he's very seriously ill. It's an odd thought that, isn't it? When we describe someone as very seriously ill you can see it, drips, monitors around the bed, physically not well, that kind of thing. Yet Mark didn't really look ill, did he? Not in the way we would mean it. I couldn't work with mental patients, could you?'

'No,' Fiona replied. 'Ah have to see them gettin' better an' leavin' the place, or not, as the case may be – as the case often is! Don't think Ah could face workin' with people with no chance of enough recovery to go back to normal life.'

'Yeah, I know what you mean,' Marylka replied. 'I can't imagine what would make someone want to go into that kind of work, it's so open-ended somehow. Getting them as good a life as they're capable of wouldn't be enough for me, I'm afraid. Mind you, there's something to be said for looking at the emotional side too.'

'Ah, ha!' grinned Fiona. 'So you *have* been got at by Ali! Did I ever tell you my Ali story?'

Marylka shook her head.

'It was this guy, just been admitted to the unit beneath Ali's, with an acute infarction, an' he goes an' arrests. We were makin' a pig's ear of it, shoutin' at each other, gettin' mixed up, an' you know what a well-oiled machine we normally are.' She rolled her eyes sarcastically, then continued. 'An' we couldn't even blame Spencer because he wasn't there. His pager was inexplicably sailing off down the Clyde, somewhere off the Cumbraes at the time: then Ah went to use the phone outside the ward, an' that's when Ah realized what it was. The man's family, his wife an' daughter, were sittin' outside the swing doors, an' they hadn't a clue it was him we were workin' on. We kept havin' to pass them to get bits of equipment, an' that's why we were off our game. He wasn't just a patient, he was that woman's man, an' that lassie's father. He was a human bein' for God's sake!'

'How very perceptive and sensitive of you!' Marylka commented.

'Kindly shut up,' replied Fiona. 'Well, by a stroke of luck Ah looked up an' who's comin' down the stairs but the man himself, our very own Ali, puffin' away on his pipe. You always think he's hummin' to himself, don't you?'

'Get on with it!'

'So I grabbed him and asked him to take the family into the side room, an' he looks at my bare feet an' twigs what's goin' on. Now only Ali could do that. An' he stayed with them, chattin' away till we'd finished, yet the patient had nothin' to do with his unit. Nobody but Ali would've understood why Ah was askin' for the family to be disappeared, an' can you imagine any other consultant takin' that amount of trouble? Doin' what a lowly Dolly asked him to do? Then he just wandered off again to wherever he'd been goin' in the first place, puffin' on the pipe an' hummin'.'

'And what happened to the patient?'

'Och, he died. Trust you to spoil a good story! Anyhow, Ah don't blame you if Ali's got to you, an' he has, hasn't he?'

'Well, not exactly, but I have to say, he's the wisest old bugger I've come across in medicine yet. Not that there's much competition when you think of it, though. I mean, look at them. Bruce, Mark, Spencer, the Prof. You can't say any of that lot is exactly normal, can you?'

'Ah sometimes suspect, Marylka,' said Fiona, 'that you, me an' Ali are the only sane people here!'

'Funny that,' Marylka replied, 'I was thinking the exact same thing!'

When Fiona had gone she lifted the phone and called Ali's secretary to apologize for missing him.

'Doctor MacKay's here,' replied the secretary. 'Would you like to have a word with him?'

Before Marylka could reply she heard his voice over the receiver.

'What can I do for you, Doctor Kowalski?'

She wasn't sure if she heard him puffing on his pipe, or if that was how she always pictured him. 'Um,' was the best response she could manage, then she screwed up her face in embarrassment and fought an impulse to slam the phone down again. She heard Ali chuckling quietly, or did she just imagine he would?

'Would you like to discuss a patient with me perhaps?' he prompted gently.

Marylka took a deep breath, held it, then let it out again very slowly. 'No, Doctor MacKay,' she said at last, 'not a patient. Me.'

'Well there's no reason you can't be a patient too!' he chuckled. 'Would you like to come up for a chat now, or would you rather hyperventilate a little more?'

'I'll come up, thanks.'

His office on the third floor had prints of the Western Highlands on the walls, hardly surprising she supposed, given his name. Ali was a tall man, somewhere around his late fifties perhaps, with thinning white hair, and gentle blue eyes with a permanently amused expression playing through them. He sprawled in an armchair, his arms crossed, one hand holding his pipe, and his long legs spread out in front of him, crossed at the ankles as he watched her calmly. There was a feeling of extreme good nature about him, a benign and friendly air, but even so she wasn't sure how to start the conversation.

'Your secretary's very nice,' she remarked, cringing inwardly at how banal she sounded.

He removed the pipe from his mouth. 'Yes,' he grinned. 'Sit down, Doctor,' he said kindly. 'Is it Doctor or do you have a name?'

'Marylka,' she said.

'What a very pretty name,' he said. 'Polish, too, I suppose?' Marylka nodded.

'OK, Marylka, in your own time.'

She sat silently, trying to marshal her thoughts to present her case. 'I'm having a few problems,' she said eventually, and he nodded. 'It's like my entire life has been suddenly blown off course and things, quite ordinary things, keep coming along and blowing me even further off course. Things I would've dealt with before without any trouble, and it's like I don't know who I am, or where, or what to do about it.'

'Well, you *are* a houseman,' he smiled. 'Isn't that par for the course, or is this worse, d'you think?'

'No, it's worse. Tomorrow is my last day as a houseman and I haven't even got a job lined up. I've just let everything slip by because I don't know where I'm going any longer.'

'I take it that you always have before?'

'Yes. I've always been the logical, down-to-earth member of the family, no nonsense, straight to the heart of the matter, a decision maker. I'm the one who always copes.'

'Well, sometimes we cope because we are expected to, not because we can, or indeed should,' he said thoughtfully. 'Has anything happened recently?'

'Well, you know Mark Galbraith was taken off by the psychiatrists?'

'Yes, I heard about that. Poor boy. Don't see much possibility of him getting out of their clutches I'm afraid.' He puffed on his pipe, waiting. 'Anything more personal?'

'That *was* personal,' Marylka said. 'He was a friend, I'd known him since my first day at Medical School.' She looked up to see that easy smile creasing the corners of his eyes with gentle amusement, and looked away quickly. 'My mother,' she said quietly then cleared her throat. 'My mother,' she started again, 'was killed in a car crash six months ago.' She bit her lower lip but her face still screwed up as great, thick tears suddenly burst out and ran down her cheeks.

'Yes, I'd say that was pretty major personal, Marylka, wouldn't you?' he asked.

She was trying to get control of herself. 'I'm sorry,' she sobbed. 'But this is exactly what I mean! This isn't like me! I'm not sure I know myself any longer, and I *hate* it!'

He leaned forward in his chair towards her, his elbows resting on his knees, his hands clasped in front of him.

'Marylka, don't let anyone fool you that they know themselves!' he said quietly. 'Have you wept for your mother at all? I don't mean leaked, but actually wept?'

She shook her head. 'Not till now, damn it!'

'Yes, well, I tend to have that effect on people!' he chuckled. 'Any family?'

She laughed with a bitterness that surprised her. 'No!' she almost shouted. 'Well, there's my grandfather, but he's pretty useless.'

'And have you talked together about your mother's death?'

She shook her head. 'This is the first time I've actually said she was dead. I always felt that saying it would somehow mean it was true. Stupid, isn't it?'

Ali smiled but said nothing.

'I hardly know my grandfather,' she continued, 'and he hardly knew my mother, his only child. We're not what anyone would describe as a normal family.'

'Ah,' he grinned, 'the fabled normal family! If you ever bump into one do give them my card. You'll easily know them, they'll be riding on a unicorn!' He chuckled as though it was the best joke he'd ever heard, and Marylka laughed, more at his amusement than his joke, then she blew her nose.

'So, what do you want to do?' he asked.

'I thought you would tell me what to do.'

'Oh, no,' he said, shaking his head and tutting theatrically. 'Certainly not!'

'Then what's the good of asking for your help then?'

Ali threw his head back and laughed. 'You know, one of my patients said that she'd handed me a tangled skein of wool, and I'd handed it back to her and told her to untangle it herself. I like that, wish I'd said it!'

He had intended it to amuse her, but his mention of the skein of wool instantly brought Helen's voice into her head, telling the story of Millie, her skeins, and her liking for fancy wool. That led just as instantly to the other memory, of discovering the little Bakelite beehive in Helen's drawer, and Marylka found herself slumping forward, another wave of tears blinding her.

'I'm sorry,' she said again. 'I just can't seem to . . .'

'Not at all, Marylka,' said Ali.

Even as she fought to get control of herself, she was thinking with a kind of awe that he was the only individual she had ever met who was totally at ease and unfazed by raw emotion.

'Look,' he continued gently. 'All this indecision that worries you so is your mind telling you that you need to take time to grieve properly for your loss. And if you won't take that time, your mind will force your body into some sort of crisis. It can be suppressed of course, some unfortunate people manage it most of their lives, but it will leak out, or worse still, burst out some time, with perhaps disastrous results. You've probably seen examples everyday without recognizing them, because medical training teaches you to think in a certain way, and to close your mind to every other avenue. Many of the physical illnesses you see being treated with pills or surgery are the result of suppressed emotion.'

'Really?' She blew her nose again, wondering if she would get as far as putting the tissue away this time before the tears ambushed her again.

'Well, look at ulcerative colitis,' he said conversationally, leaning back in his chair again. His hands were clasped behind his neck as he looked towards the ceiling, his pipe clenched between his teeth. 'We accept that as a psychological condition producing physical symptoms, don't we? Is there a rule book somewhere that says *only* ulcerative colitis has a psychological basis? Emotions, or what we do with them, cause a great many physical illnesses, but our esteemed colleagues keep their minds closed, I'm afraid. I think emotions frighten them, which is why most of them are emotionally constipated, as I'm sure you've noticed.'

She thought back to the one or two cases of ulcerative colitis she had seen, a distressing and debilitating condition causing weeping, raw ulcers all over the colon. If medication failed the only treatment was surgery, and when she was a surgical houseman she had watched a sixteen-year-old girl have a colostomy performed, in an attempt to let the colon rest for a while and hopefully recover. Part of the bowel was brought out of a hole made in the stomach wall, and thereafter the girl had to wear a plastic bag under her clothes to collect faeces. Sometimes a colostomy was in place for six months or a year, but if the condition didn't improve it could be much longer, and having to cope with it often affected the patient's psychological state even more. What they really needed was quality psychotherapy, but what they got was the scalpel, even the surgeons carrying out the procedure admitted as much. It was yet another niggly concern, a part of medicine that made no sense, and even as she assisted the surgeon with the girl's operation, she had a feeling of failure somehow. She told Ali about it.

'It was like cutting off someone's leg when they'd come in with a headache,' she recalled. 'There seemed no sense in it.'

'Ah!' he laughed. 'You've got it! By George you've got it! From henceforth you too shall be known as a weirdo!'

Marylka sat in silence, then she looked up at him. 'You asked what I wanted to do,' she said. 'Well I'd like to go away.' She surprised herself, because till that moment she hadn't known this. 'I'd like to go away somewhere and do nothing.'

Ali nodded. 'Is this a temporary sojourn or a permanent one?'

'Oh, temporary,' she replied. 'I just need some time and space to find myself I think.' Then she laughed.

Ali raised his eyebrows.

'I sound like one of those luvvies, don't I?' she laughed.

' "I vant to be alone!" ' he smiled. 'Well, we're all entitled to a luvvie spell occasionally.'

'Doctor Spencer would burst if he knew I was consulting you,' she said.

'Ah, the good Doctor Spencer!' Ali said with relish. 'Now there's a man who does amuse me! The contortions he gets into trying to avoid making eye contact every time we pass each other!'

'You know about that do you?' she asked. 'That he thinks you can read minds by looking in people's eyes?'

'Oh, a lot of them believe that – and I can!' he said with mock seriousness. 'That's how I know there's nothing there as far as he's concerned! But he is such fun, isn't he?'

'Not if you have to work with him!' Marylka replied. 'You know he's got a consultant's post in Newcastle?'

Ali sat up and wrote on a pad. 'Steer well clear of Newcastle,' he prompted himself word by word. 'Now. Fancy a coffee in the canteen?' he asked, looking up. 'Your shout, of course.'

As they walked towards the canteen together she was going over their conversation.

'Wait a minute!' she said. 'You asked me if anything personal had happened. Are you saying you missed all that fuss in the newspapers, plus all the gossip that must've been going round this place?'

'No. I read every word. Gossip's terribly therapeutic you know! The question wasn't whether I knew something had happened in your life, but whether *you* knew it. Besides,' he said with a grin, 'no one could've missed the awful pong of Old Spice in the air as our esteemed colleagues geared up for romantic encounters with the heiress!'

'Yes,' Marylka laughed, 'they have rather stayed faithful to Old Spice, haven't they? But why do I feel so much better now? After all, nothing actually happened. We just talked.'

'You mean without a scalpel being wielded or a magic pill being administered? Because you had reached the point when you needed to acknowledge your loss out loud, a vent has been opened up,' he replied simply. 'I imagine that you had subconsciously decided to hold on till your housemanship was finished, you'd enough to cope with. Incidentally, you know if you're spotted with me your career will be in ashes, don't you?'

She nodded. 'If Graham Spencer sees us at least I know for certain I won't get a job in Newcastle, and that can't be bad.'

Just then Andy and Mad Mick came through the swing doors, heading towards them.

'Oh, God, no!' she muttered. 'Please, not Mad Mick!' But much to her surprise he took his lead from Andy and passed her with barely a nod of acknowledgement. Then a few paces on he turned and shouted after her. 'Darling! Did I leave my pyjamas at your place last night?'

Beside her Ali chuckled. 'Michael,' he addressed the mad paramedic in a voice heavy with authority, 'since the day you first arrived here, many long years ago, you have pulled that one with every female who has crossed your path!'

'Ah know Doc,' Mick grinned, fixing Ali with his lop-sided leer. 'But as Ah say, if ye've got it, flaunt it. Ye canny hide this much sex appeal anyway. Ah've tried, but what can Ah dae?'

At that Andy grabbed him by the back of his green overall and frog-marched him in the opposite direction, but their voices could still be heard, yelling at each other. 'There it goes again, that bloody big yap o' yours!' Andy shouted. 'Ye canny leave anythin' can ye? There's no' a silence ye don't havtae fill wi' some smartarse remark, is there? An' the lassie's wi' a consultant as well, even if it is just auld Ali!'

At that Ali exchanged looks with Marylka, hers amused, his aggrieved.

'Ach, for God's sake Andy, get a sense o' humour!' Mick replied calmly. 'It made the lassie laugh, didn't it? Did ye no' see her smilin' at me? Ah think Ah'm in there ye know!'

'Shut it!' Andy responded, in the distance but still clearly. 'She was grimacin' ya daft sod, she was aboot tae be sick!'

'Christ, there ye go again wi' that temper o' yours! It'll be the death o' ye wanna these days . . .'

'*You'll* be the death o' me . . .'

Marylka turned to Ali as they reached the swing doors of the canteen. 'If Mick gets any more laid back he'll fracture at least ten vertebrae one of these days,' she sighed.

'I'm not so sure,' he grinned mockingly. 'I looked in his eyes there and I'm not sure I liked what I saw.'

'Well, that's nothing to do with your black magic!' Marylka replied. 'Nobody likes what they see in Mick's eyes, that's why we don't look into them!'

22

The following day was her last as a houseman, and she spent much of it ferrying her belongings between the hospital and her flat in Byres Road. She had lived there all through her student years, but she'd barely seen it in the last eighteen months. Having moved as much of her stuff as she could she went back to Rob Burns's office to 'tie up a few loose ends' as he'd put it, which presumably included attending to the great Auntie Mary mystery. She had no idea what it was about, only that it concerned Auntie Mary and that it had been on her mother's mind for the last three years since the old lady had died.

'There are several things we need to do something about, Marylka.' Rob smiled tightly from behind his desk. He was in his late twenties, tall and slim with light brown hair already beginning to recede, and serious grey eyes. He had always been a serious boy though, he had behaved impeccably and diplomatically throughout his life, which she had worked out long ago was why he was attracted to her. It was because she spoke out, and didn't mind taking the inevitable flak for it. For Rob it was sin one step removed that gave him some kind of buzz. He liked notoriety, but only by association. Looking at him across the desk, she noticed that he was resembling his father more and more, he was a clone rather than a son.

'I'm sorry, but some of it may be distressing. Just say if you want me to stop.'

Poor old Rob, she thought, it couldn't be easy for him to be objective with someone he had grown up with, someone he cared for, or thought he did.

'First of all, it'll take some time for Helen's estate to be wound up, there are various foreign ventures to sort out as well as her estate in this country, but her will is quite clear, everything will go to you. There will be no claim from her half-brothers in South Africa. When your grandmother died twenty years ago Helen refused to take any part of her estate, as you know.'

'I didn't.'

'Well, my father was handling things then, and he took the opportunity to strike a deal. In return for letting her half-brothers have the entire estate of the former Mrs Davidson, they would make no claim on anything owned by the Davidson family.'

'Why didn't she want her mother's booty then?'

Rob shrugged. 'As far as I can understand it, she said she had enough, what would she do with more? Apparently Old Hector was furious, went up like a volcano by all accounts. Blamed Auntie Mary entirely for some reason.'

'I'll bet he did,' Marylka laughed, 'and he was probably right as well! He didn't call her Bloody Mary for nothing!'

'But I always thought she was such a sweet, angelic old lady,' Rob remarked.

'She was,' Marylka replied. 'With claws, and they were always sunk into Old Hector's flesh! But good for my mother turning down all that cash, though. Another little victory over the miserable old teuchter, if I'm not mistaken.'

'Next, there's Helen's ashes,' Rob said, looking down at the paper in his hand, more for support than out of strict necessity she thought. 'The undertaker wants to know if you'd like him to scatter them for you.'

'Only if he wants to join them!' Marylka replied. 'Tell Uriah Heep to keep them somewhere safe, I haven't decided what to do with them yet. The answer will come to me, and he can't be that short of space, can he? If he is they can be kept here, can't they?'

Rob looked at her aghast and she laughed. 'You're not squeamish are you, Rob?' she asked. 'My mother did you no harm in life, why would she cause you trouble from the urn?'

He was uncomfortable, so he tried to retreat behind official solicitor speech, with limited success. 'There won't be any problem,' he said. 'Uriah, um, the undertaker will keep them till such time as you request them to be handed over.'

He turned to another piece of paper. 'Now the house in Bearsden,' he said. 'What do you want to do with it?'

'Nothing.'

'Well, it's yours. Do you want to move into it?'

'NO!' She couldn't understand why he had thought such a thing.

'You grew up there,' he said uncertainly. 'I naturally assumed . . .'

She looked directly into his eyes. 'I have my own flat now, Rob, and besides, there's now one essential element missing from the Bearsden house I grew up in.'

Rob looked at her blankly.

'My mother, Rob,' she said softly. She almost felt him squirming and smiled inwardly. Why did she get such enjoyment from discomfiting poor old Rob? She'd been doing it to him all his life and he still hadn't worked out how to deal with it. 'And he was concerned that *I'd* be distressed!' she thought.

'So do you want to put it on the market?'

'No, Rob, just leave it alone.' She sighed. 'It's not taking up any room is it?' she asked, and then regretted it. Rob was not good with abstract thought; if it wasn't down in black and white before him he had difficulty seeing it at all. He had always been the same. 'Rob,' she explained, 'I don't know anything at the moment and that's the truth. I don't know what I want to do, where I'm going or anything else. Do you understand?'

'It's just that it's standing empty,' he said quietly. 'It's not a good thing for a property to stand empty.'

'Well, use whatever security measures you want. Good God, we must have the resources to handle that, surely? But *don't* do anything else. OK?'

'I've already arranged security,' he said.

Of course; he would have. 'I'm going to take some time off to think, Rob, I've decided to go off somewhere by myself for a while, I don't know how long. So much has happened recently, I need time to draw breath. So all I want you to do till I get back is nothing, really.'

He looked alarmed, frightened almost, and she sent up a silent prayer that he wasn't about to declare his heartfelt devotion.

'Is there anything else we need to deal with now?' she asked briskly.

Rob looked even more uncomfortable. 'Well, I've prepared the side room for you,' he said, getting up. 'You remember I told you there was something your mother was going to discuss with you about Mrs Ferrier?'

Marylka nodded.

'I think it might take some time, there's quite a lot of reading and your mother found it all a bit bewildering. And . . .'

'And what, Rob?'

'The police left Helen's personal effects here . . . from the car . . . Do you feel like going through them?'

It was another sledgehammer blow; she had forgotten all about asking the nice young policewoman to deliver Helen's things here. It seemed like another lifetime, another nightmare ago, and now it had come to get her.

'Yes, that's fine,' she lied brightly. 'No problem. I was expecting to go through her things today.' And inside her head the voice screamed again 'Oh, God! Oh, God! Oh, God!'

Rob showed her into the side room, where a tray of coffee and a plate of Marks and Spencer sandwiches, neatly re-cut into dainty triangles, sat waiting in the centre of a large table. Behind the tray was a chair, and in front of the chair, on the edge of the table, was a buff file tied with pink tape. And Helen's black leather bag. She closed her eyes. 'I know I'm an idiot,' she thought, 'but maybe she's just forgotten to pick it up, and when I open my eyes again she'll dash in and grab it.' But when she opened her eyes the bag still lay poignantly in front of her. It was the big one Helen carted everywhere, the one Marylka teased her was like a coal sack. She had all sorts of smaller, stylish bags, but she always went back to this one, said it held more. And that was the trouble; it held so much that she could never find anything. Marylka remembered watching the routine search many times. The fumbling about blindly in every nook and cranny within the bag, the furrowed brow with the usual mutterings, 'That's odd! I'm *sure* it's in here!', the oaths, 'Damn the thing to Hell! Why can you never find *anything* when you need it?' The reason was that the bag did indeed hold everything, but all together in one big mass within the bowels of the bag; nothing had its own allotted place. It always ended the same: after wasting time trying to locate whatever was lost, Helen would unceremoniously dump the entire contents out and sort through them. Then, once she had retrieved what she was looking for, she'd say triumphantly 'There it is! Didn't I say it was in there?' Any suggestion that she would've found it easier in a smaller bag, and as a bonus would avoid the danger of slipping a disc from the weight of the black one, was met with a puzzled 'But it's a great bag! It holds everything!' It was like going round in circles, there was no way of getting any sense either through to Helen, or out of her, where the black leather coal sack was concerned.

And now it lay before her looking pathetically, heart-breakingly personal, with creases and folds put there by Helen's hands, shiny from the way it lay against her left hip. Marylka felt almost afraid to put her hand into it; it was like the fear of deep water, or of going into a cave, but she couldn't say why. Eventually she did what Helen always did and tipped the contents out on to the table, then she sat staring at them, waiting for something to happen. It was all so familiar. She smiled as she focused on the same ancient make-up bag. Helen had changed her allegiance to Elizabeth Arden, she noticed. All the old stuff had been cleared out, and new, almost untouched tubes and containers put in the same tatty old bag. The assistant at the Elizabeth Arden counter must've given her a spiel, or a free gift if she bought two of something. Helen was a wizard businesswoman, but she was a pushover for anything claiming to make her look younger – not that she was *old*, you understand – or the offer of a 'free gift'. She had this childlike delight in being given something, and you just couldn't persuade her that nothing was ever free, that was too logical an argument for Helen to hear. A bottle of Jean Patou's 'Sublime' perfume made her look away and take a deep breath. Various magazine cuttings about hair colourants, a notepad. Helen was always making lists to remind herself of things, then losing them or forgetting to read them, but still when you reminded her about something in particular she would say 'Of course I'll remember! I've put it on the list, haven't I?' Earrings, lots of earrings, mostly single; she was forever losing one earring, but insisted on keeping the other one in case the partner turned up. It never did. And gloves, six gloves, all single again, waiting in hopes of reunion. An unopened packet of Christmas cards; God knew how many years they'd been in there, and pens, lots and lots of pens. She could never find a pen. 'Where do all my pens go?' she'd demand, as though there was a universal conspiracy to deprive her of pens, when in fact they were all here, secreted inside the coal sack. Her purse, an ancient red leather Stratton that, like the make-up bag, had seen better days; her various cards were inside, some change, and a picture of Marylka in her graduation gown and cap, pulling a cross-eyed face. The purse bulged with receipts, probably going back years, she thought. Helen always insisted on keeping receipts because 'you never know when you'll need them.' Her keys, on a dolphin key-ring for the house, and a fire engine one for the car; Helen and her thing about firemen. The dreaded mobile phone. The Christmas before she died Marylka had offered to buy Helen an electronic personal organizer to replace her pile of notepads, and she had delivered her diatribe against mobiles in response. 'What in Hell has an organizer to do with mobile phones?' Marylka demanded.

'It's all the same thing!' Helen replied. 'All these electronic things organizing us, watching us, tying us up in knots!'

'And I suppose they're to blame for the weather too?'

'I wouldn't be surprised!' Helen retorted. 'All this *stuff*, and no –'

'Oh, God, please don't say it! "And no time machine"!'

'Exactly!'

Marylka remembered telling Ali MacKay she was the logical one of the family. When you recalled some of Helen's conversations you had to say there was little competition!

She took two silk scarves from the bag's contents and folded them, removed several opened tubes of polo mints and bars of chocolate-covered marzipan – Helen adored marzipan but swore blind she never ate it because it was fattening. Marylka smiled, she probably believed she never ate it too. There were three opened packets of tissues; she'd lose one in the bag and buy another, and another. The coal sack was full of duplicated stuff; no wonder it was so heavy. Mixed in with all the other bits and pieces were various scraps of paper; proof once again of Helen's inability to throw anything away. There was something scribbled on an empty envelope. She smoothed it out on the table in front of her and read 'Flowers for Millie too'. She sat staring at it, stunned. A few weeks after her mother's death she'd taken flowers to the crypt for Auntie Mary, and for no particular reason she had decided Millie should have her own flowers in future. She and Helen had never discussed this, yet they had thought of the very same thing. She tried to smile. Helen would've narrowed her eyes and pronounced it 'Spooky!' There were no coincidences in Helen's opinion, only occurrences that were 'Spooky!' Helen didn't believe in the paranormal but she wanted to, and Marylka had wasted hours at a time giving rational explanations to the many odd little stories her mother had heard. Helen would nod in agreement, accepting the logic of Marylka's argument, then without exception, she would narrow her eyes and say 'Still though. Spooky!'

And right at the bottom of the pile were the tapes retrieved from the car, all in their plastic boxes; she must've just had a clear-out, she could never find the tape she wanted because she was forever putting them back in the wrong boxes, if at all. Not that she ever admitted it; that too was part of some universal conspiracy against Helen. They must have been put at the top of the bag by the police and ended up on the bottom when Marylka tipped the contents out on to the table. There was one without a box. She picked it up and looked at it. It was partly played; she must have been listening to it when she crashed. It was a Goons tape. She didn't have to play it to know what was on it; Helen had been listening to the 'Ying Tong' song before she died, singing it too, she'd bet. The memory of all those daft journeys with Helen belting out 'Ying Tong Tiddle-i-Po' almost made her cry out with the silliness and the pain of it. 'Damn Spike Milligan!' she thought, then she recalled it. No, bless him instead for making Helen laugh so much. Had he but known, in his own way Spike Milligan was 'a wee loast ginger dug' when you thought about it.

Carefully and neatly she replaced everything in Helen's bag; it was amazing how much easier it was to handle when everything wasn't just thrown into it, not that Helen would ever have accepted that. There was no sign of that last shopping trip, though. According to Annie she had left the office early, before three o'clock, to do some shopping, and the car park had her paying her ransom and leaving at around 6 p.m. But there were no packages and no receipts for that day. No matter what she bought she would have kept the receipts, she knew that. Maybe she just hadn't found anything she fancied, but that wasn't like Helen either; anything was, in her philosophy, better than nothing if she felt like shopping. She couldn't imagine her wandering about the shops for three hours without buying something. Maybe she'd spent the time with some wickedly handsome gigolo in an afternoon of wild abandon. 'Oh, God, yes!' she thought with a smile. 'Please let it have been the gigolo! And let her have run naked into the street afterwards, a red rose clenched between her teeth!' Then as an afterthought she said to herself 'Don't be silly, Marylka! That last bit has entered the realms of fantasy. Leave it at the gigolo!'

She poured herself a coffee and went to the window to drink it, watching the traffic. Her mind was totally empty and calm, not a thought in there, and she'd have bet anything it would've been a jumble of emotions. But she ached all over. She must've been tensing every muscle in her body while going through the coal sack. She did some extravagant stretches, finished her coffee and went back to the table. She untied the pink tape and and opened the buff legal file marked 'Mrs Mary Ferrier'. She took out a thick bundle of papers, and as she did so some old photos fell out. One was of a young woman with a high-necked blouse and a skirt with a bustle. She had seen it before, it was her great-great-grandmother, Elizabeth Davidson, the mother of Auntie Mary and Old Hector. She had seen this picture in Auntie Mary's house in Duke Street, but the other two she had never come across. There was a fuzzy picture of another young woman in a nurse's uniform, taken with a group of wounded soldiers, all staring solemnly at the camera as people seemed to do in those days. Turning the picture over she saw the words 'My sister Lizzie with men from the First War. George Mac-Donald middle row, third from the left. 1917.' Looking again at the photo Marylka saw that George MacDonald was looking at Lizzie. She knew Lizzie had been a nurse in France during the First World War, Auntie Mary often told the story of the sister she loved so much who had died young. Helen and Marylka had assumed she had died as a result of some illness she had caught there. Then there was a head-and-shoulders portrait of a young man in the uniform of one of the Highland regiments, a kilt, a plaid covering one shoulder of his tunic and a glengarry on his head, bearing a regimental badge. He was a handsome young man, with a slightly embarrassed smile and what Helen would have called kind eyes. He also had a moustache; she wondered what her mother would've made of that. Because of the infamous, mustachioed Captain Ferrier who had run out on Auntie Mary and Millie, everyone with a moustache was suspect to Helen. Marylka smiled at the memory, her eyes very quickly welling with tears. On the back was written

'Private George MacDonald of the Argyll and Sutherland High-landers. 1917.' She poured out more coffee and turned to the bundle of letters that she had removed from the envelope, some obviously older than others. She decided to read the newest one, dated two years before Auntie Mary's death.

'My Dear Helen,' the old lady had written by hand. 'If you are reading this then I must be lying not far from that miserable old teuchter your grandfather. You always knew there were things I knew about him, and I once told you that one day I would tell you what they were, and I never did. First because this story is so awful that I couldn't have got through it without crying, and second because he was, after all, your grandfather, and I don't think I wanted to see your face as you found out what he was really like. You have always had a tender heart, Helen, you never see anything but good in anyone, even in those who don't deserve it, like your grandfather. You're like my mother in that, and our Lizzie. Still, I should've told you, I'm an old coward, I know.

'I'm writing this because after we put him in the crypt it made me realize that I can't have much time left myself. I'm getting on now, the old legs aren't what they were and neither are the eyes, and I haven't the energy I once had when we were doing our walks. So I need you to put this right for the family, and for me, because I've felt so guilty about it all these years. There's no one else can do it, Helen, you know that your father is as he is. It's not really his fault, he was a nice laddie when he was young, he just couldn't stand up to his father. I want you to know, Helen, that you have been my greatest joy all these years, if Millie had been all right I would have wanted her to be just like you. I love you like a daughter and Millie loved you too. She couldn't show it, poor thing, but you made life so much better for her, and for me, because you loved her, and she knew that as I did. And that lassie of yours is a credit to you, you've done a fine job of bringing her up in this terrible family. She's a real nippy sweetie, but nippy sweeties always have soft centres, and her heart's in the right place. Whatever problems you think she has will be solved in time, so don't go worrying about her and all the things you wish she'd had. Marylka is a credit to us both, you and me, and there never was a better double act!'

At that the nippy sweetie stopped reading, got up and walked about the room blinking her eyes for a while, to stop her soft centre from turning to liquid, so that she could see what else Mary had written.

'You will find some letters and photos that I've left for you, but I have to tell you the story, and it gives me no joy. To think that I have the same blood as a man who could do such an awful thing to his own kin. I told you many times of my sister Lizzie and what a fine lassie she was. When she died, Hector said she had been buried abroad, and I didn't know the true circumstances until I found some of the papers you now have. They were in that roll-top desk in your grand-father's office, where he kept all the family documents. I was noseying about when he wasn't there, looking for that photo of my mother to have it made bigger and framed. I must've touched something in the desk and there was a click, then a wee door fell open. I put my hand in and found what you now have.'

Marylka read on enthralled. It seemed that Lizzie Davidson was going to marry a soldier she had nursed at the front, George MacDonald. 'You'll see from their letters to each other that they were truly in love. Now isn't that something in our family?' Mary had written. The young soldier had been badly hurt in the last days of the Battle of the Somme in November 1916, and Lizzie had nursed him in the field hospital. He was sent back to the trenches a year later, still suffering from the after-effects of his injuries and from shell-shock. When he heard gunfire again he panicked and ran away, and when he was captured he was charged with desertion and cowardice, convicted by court martial and shot at dawn by firing squad. Young George had died without knowing that Lizzie was pregnant.

It seemed that Lizzie had written to Old Hector for help, but he had married Christine and thought he was going up in the world, so he turned his back on his sister. She came back to Glasgow and went to live in the Gorbals in a hovel, and there she had her child, a girl she called Elizabeth. Some time afterwards she wrote again to Hector, telling him that she was in poor health and had a child to care for, and he apparently responded by telling her not to contact anyone in the family again.

'I blame myself for so much,' Mary wrote. 'Before she died he'd told me Lizzie was still working abroad and there was no way of getting in touch with her, and with the war and everything I was used to not hearing regularly anyway. But deep down I think I knew there was something wrong, I should've made more of a nuisance of myself.' Marylka smiled. Old Hector wouldn't have believed that was possible. 'Lizzie died of TB when the child was two years old, and she was taken into care by Glasgow Corporation. The Corporation sent all Lizzie's effects to Hector and asked if he would provide for the child. When he refused she was sent to people on an island called Eilean Òg.'

Mary, it seemed, had tried off and on to find out more about Lizzie's child, but sometimes she wondered if she should let sleeping dogs lie; what if the child was happy and contented with her new family? 'What kind of family did we have to offer her anyhow?' she asked.

'Oh, Auntie Mary,' Marylka murmured, 'you had Millie to take care of, and you had my mother. Things weren't easy for you either.'

'I tried to find her, but as time passed it became more difficult. All I know is that she was with another lassie and one of them came back to Glasgow later and died. She had lived on this island since she was a wee thing, then when she was sixteen, they sent her back to Glasgow. She didn't know the place and she wasn't used to traffic. She got off a bus and tried to cross the road behind it, and was knocked down and killed by another coming in the opposite direction. I don't know whether it was Lizzie's lassie or the other one, and to tell the truth I think it would've broken my heart to find out it was Lizzie's. Maybe that's why I didn't try harder, but God forgive me, I should have. I've thought back on this so many times, and I think Hector wanted to be found out. What other reason could there be for him keeping those letters after Lizzie died, except for them to be discovered? I think he wanted them found and for him to be forgiven. Well, I told him he would never be forgiven. Before he died he said "Tell Mary I'm sorry," and you asked what he had meant. I think this is what he meant, and as I said to you, he never will be forgiven, because what he did was a wicked, wicked thing. I faced him with it all those years ago and he had nothing to say, he just sat at that desk of his, staring at me, while I told him he'd go to his grave with it on his conscience, and he did. He did get a tiny punishment, though nothing like he deserved. He wanted a title more than anything else in the world, and one that would be handed on too. He was a terrible man. Most people want their family to have health and happiness, Hector was quite content that his family was unhappy, as long as they could be called Sir, or Lord. But I put an end to that. I told him if he ever tried to buy some fancy title that I'd let the papers know what he had done, and I would have, too. Even if I only found out once he'd got his title, he knew I'd still have let the world know, and his reputation would've been destroyed.'

Marylka punched the air with delight. 'Let's hear it for the nasty old lady!' she laughed.

'I was the only one in the family who didn't let Old Hector have the whole business when my father died,' Mary continued. 'I didn't think it would make him any better a man to have everything he wanted. I had intended my money to keep Millie decently, to make sure she'd be well cared for once I'd gone, but that wasn't to be, and you don't need it Helen, and neither does Marylka. So I want it all to go to Lizzie's lassie, wherever she is. Tell her I'm not trying to buy forgiveness for what Hector did in the name of our family, there can be no forgiveness for that, but because it's her right to have what would have been her mother's. And tell her what a fine woman her mother was.'

'And she wasn't the only one,' Marylka said quietly. 'You were quite a woman yourself, Bloody Mary.'

'Every Armistice Day I lay some poppies for young George at the lions in George Square,' Mary's letter continued. 'It's little enough I know, but it's all I've ever been able to do for the poor laddie. Tell his lassie that he wasn't forgotten.'

She sat thinking in silence for a few minutes. When Helen recounted the tales of her childhood walks with Auntie Mary and Millie, she would laugh and say that the old lady would never let her sit on the lions like the other children. 'I don't know why she felt so strongly about it,' she'd say. 'As far as I know, we had no family killed in either War. It was one of my great ambitions to get chased off a lion by the keeper! I felt so deprived!' 'Well, Auntie Mary was of her time, I suppose,' Marylka would reply. 'People who had lived through the wars would've had different feelings about the memorial, more respect.' But the old lady had had a special reason, a personal reason she had kept to herself for decades, until she wrote her letter to Helen. And her mother had apparently done nothing about this, for what reason she didn't know, but she had intended discussing it with her the night she died. If she had, Marylka was in no doubt about what she would have advised. She would've told Helen she had to find Lizzie's child if she was still alive, and even if she wasn't, she had to find any family she might have on that island. It didn't matter if they thought it would be better to leave well enough, or even bad enough, alone, it was what Auntie Mary wanted, and they owed it to her. They also owed it to Auntie Lizzie and to 'Lizzie's lassie'. She collected all the papers together, put them back in the file, picked up Helen's bag and walked along the corridor to Rob's office, where his secretary told her he was tied up with clients.

'Just as well, really,' Marylka remarked. 'Tell him I've taken all these papers home,' she said, 'and ask him to find me a lease on a house on an island called Eilean Òg. Six months minimum. And something decent, I've no intention of roughing it in a but and ben, no matter how quaint it is. And another thing,' she said as she turned to leave. 'Tell him I don't want any messages on my machine when I get home of the "Are you mad? Have you thought this through? Let's talk about it" variety. For once I just want him to do what I've asked. OK?'

23

When Rob phoned it was to say he'd got her a six-month lease on Eilean Òg starting in three weeks. The property was called Honeysuckle Cottage.

'Yuk!'

'What do you mean, "Yuk"?' he asked.

'Well, it's so twee, isn't it? It's like Meadow View or Primrose Lea. Yuk!'

'Maybe it has honeysuckle growing outside the door,' Rob ventured.

'Exactly!' she replied.

'Marylka, you're so cynical! It's probably a charming place.'

'Oh, you romantic fool, Rob!' she said. 'Charming – yuk!'

'Well, anyway,' he sighed, 'it is a very good property, completely modernized, all mod cons.'

'Does it have a proper toilet?'

'Of course it has! Why wouldn't it?'

'Because it's out there, up there, on an island, in teuchter land.'

'They have toilets in teuchter land.'

'They'd better,' she said. 'I refuse to wield a shovel every time I –'

'Marylka, take my word for it, the cottage *will* have a toilet!'

It was so easy to wind Rob up that it very quickly became boring, she thought. 'Listen, Rob,' she said. 'The stuff in the file, how much of it do you know?'

'Bits and pieces. My father helped Mrs Ferrier gather together the details about Private MacDonald. He had to call in a few favours on the old boys' network, but a lot of it she pieced together herself. She looked like your average little old lady, but she was a wily old biddy, and very smart too.'

'*All* the women in my family are very smart!'

He ignored the interruption. 'I haven't read the letters, though, the ones between Lizzie and Private MacDonald, and the others between Lizzie and Old Hector, or the stuff after Lizzie's death. I only know that they exist, but I know the gist of the story, because your mother discussed it with me briefly.'

'Why didn't she do anything about it in all this time? She's had three years and done nothing.'

'I don't know, Marylka. I kept chasing her about it because I needed to get the thing resolved. She seemed very taken aback by it all. It was one of those things she intended getting round to, but, well, time ran out, I suppose.' There was a pause, then Rob said, 'Am I allowed to say something? Suggest a private detective might be easier on you, on all concerned for that matter? Perhaps express an opinion about this venture?'

'Now, Rob, I have always supported freedom of speech, as you know,'

'Good. Well –'

'I hadn't finished. I have always supported freedom of speech, *and* freedom of action.'

'Meaning what?'

'Meaning you're free to say what you like and I'm free to do what I like. Which in this instance means putting the receiver down if you start exercising your right to freedom of speech.'

'Fine. I understand. It's shut up, Rob. But this is very sensitive, you'll have to be very careful how you set about it, Marylka.'

'Yes,' she said seriously. 'I thought perhaps I'd get one of those vans with the massive sound systems and enormous, mega loudspeakers. Then I'd get on the mike and yell "If there are any Davidson bastards out there among you sheep-shaggers, kindly come and kneel before me." That should do, don't you think?'

'Yes, point taken,' he sighed. Then he continued in a soft

voice that instinctively made her want to hold the receiver away from her ear. 'But do take care of yourself. Don't go falling for some big, hairy, tartan-clad macho man and staying there.'

'Oh, what a pity!' she said brightly. 'That was the second part of the plan. 'Bye!'

One of these days she was going to have to face the problem of Rob, but not now; Rob would have to keep. Meantime she had to find out as much information about George MacDonald and Lizzie as she could, which entailed spending evenings reading their intimate letters to each other. And it almost broke her cynical heart, there was no other way to put it, reading their thoughts and hopes for the future and knowing how it had ended for them. It felt wrong too, eavesdropping on the feelings of these two young people, yet it seemed strange too that their voices had been silent for over eighty years. It was almost like a bright, beautiful flower opening up in your hand, petal by petal, one that had lain dormant throughout the decades. You could see the brilliant colour, smell the perfume, in every word they wrote, and as you read there was this silly, illogical hope that somehow the passage of time would enable you to change the ending, knowing all the while that there was no escape, that the blossom would be cruelly cut down very soon. 'Careful, Marylka,' she chided herself. 'It'll be poetry next!' Then she suddenly looked up and laughed out loud. What she had really been wishing for, she realized, was a time machine!

Lizzie first met her George in November 1916. He was brought into the field hospital from the Somme more dead than alive, with serious head injuries caused by shell-blast, and bullet wounds to his left arm and body. He came from Scamadale, thirteen miles south of Oban in Argyll, and as she came to know Lizzie and George, their voices grew louder in her mind, till she could almost hear the conversations they hadn't put down in writing. That would've been the initial bond, she thought, Lizzie's parents coming from Argyll too. No doubt a friendly smile and the kindness of someone, especially someone from home, was a welcome support as George recovered from his wounds. She imagined Lizzie telling him of her family's flight to Glasgow and the new life that seemed to be shaping up for them there, but she would also have told him of her mother's homesickness, and the stories she had grown up hearing about the Davidsons' real home in Argyll. Maybe it was the thing that had kept George from giving in, so far from home, so long fighting in the trenches, and now so severely injured. Marylka looked again at their photos. It was funny how different photos looked when you knew the people in them. The shy-looking George seemed to return her gaze in a familiar way now, there was a friendly expression in his eyes that she hadn't noticed the first time she had looked at it. He had become real to her now, he was family, even if he did have a moustache.

His family were farmers, another bond with Lizzie, and he was one of four brothers and two sisters. Leaving their sisters and younger brother at home to help their parents work the farm, George and the other MacDonald boys had joined the local regiment, the Argyll and Sutherland Highlanders. They had volunteered on the outbreak of what was called the Great War for Civilization, in August 1914. George was eighteen years old at the time, and like so many lads of that blighted generation, his emotions had been whipped up by a frenzied jingoism about King and Country. Undoubtedly he, like all the rest, saw it as a huge adventure. They would all be home by Christmas and they would be heroes. No one would die. They would march home together to cheers and applause, after saving their loved ones, their homes and their country from the Hun. And, again like the rest of them, George was just a lad, he had no way of knowing it was all a lie, that as the years passed hundreds, thousands more of them would end up buried where they fell in unmarked graves that in time would be lost and forgotten. After eighty years those long-forgotten boys were still being dug up in the fields by French farmers working the land, the skeletons of bright, brave, deceived young lads just like George. Others would lie for ever under line after line of identical white headstones, in Belgian and French cemeteries, in their last ghastly military formation.

Both of George's soldier brothers were already dead by the middle of 1916, when the Battle of the Somme began. At 7.28 a.m. on the 1st of July the whistle sounded, sending more than 60,000 British infantry soldiers to do battle for a fourteen-mile strip of land in North East France, between Serre and Maricourt. They had been told that earlier artillery bombardment had already severely weakened the German defences, and that all they had to do was advance and mop up. They climbed out of their trenches in the morning mist, carrying full packs, gas masks, rifles and bayonets, these once eager boys. By that time they had already been fighting in the mud and horror for two years, malnourished, their health affected by the illnesses that regularly swept the trenches. They carried everything they had on their backs because they were advancing, they weren't coming back; a cruel prophecy.

But the Germans, far from being in a weakened state, had an exceptionally fine underground bunker system, with telephones, electricity and water supplies. Their trenches were well-constructed, and so far underground that the artillery bombardment hadn't touched them. So young George, the farmer's only remaining soldier son from Scamadale in Argyll, was sent in formation across No Man's Land to glory, with all the other sons, husbands and fathers, to be systematically mown down by German fire. Wave after wave of them walked straight into the waiting guns, and as one wave fell, another was sent to replace it. They desperately clambered over the bodies piling up on the battlefield, trying to shelter from the incessant hail of bullets and shells behind the corpses of their friends and comrades. Then another wave to replace them, and another. By the end of the first day more than 20,000 men lay dead, with nearly 40,000 injured. By the end of the battle, in November 1916, when George's luck ran out, there were 250,000 British, 195,000 French and 650,000 German dead over five months. A win, according to the generals, victory for 'our' side. Or so the generals said, from their safe vantage points, miles behind the front line.

Marylka opened the buff file again and took out all the photos, searching for the snap of Lizzie with the injured soldiers. The date on the back was May 1917, and from the expressions on their faces the experiences of the men were plain to see. Looking at it before she thought it had the expressionless quality of all old photographs. The serious faces were said to be caused by the length of time it took to expose the film, even the most determinedly fixed grin dissolved eventually. But looking again there was more than that. These men had all been able to walk when this photo was being taken, they would have known that shortly they'd be sent back to the trenches to do it all again, with the strong possibility that next time they might not reach the comparative luxury of a hospital. You could see the fear in those faces when you understood the significance of the photo session. And there, half-kneeling in the middle row, was George MacDonald, his head turned to the right, towards where Lizzie stood at the edge of the group, her incredibly sweet face looking directly at the camera.

The sights she must have seen, the things she must've done, Marylka thought. Surviving in medicine was a challenge in modern times, it hardened you, or rather you hardened yourself to cope. The aristocratic, handsome face of her grandfather, Young Hector, contorted with distaste whenever she swore, yet the language she used in front of him was considerably watered down from normal hospital language. It was part of how you got through some of the things you had to do, that and the black, black humour. The trick was coming out the other end without the darkness of it having taken a grip of your soul, in remembering that it was only a coping device and not letting it become part of who you were. And her world of modern medicine was so different from Lizzie's. In the field hospitals on the Western Front, amputations were regularly performed because there was no time, equipment or staff to do anything else. Often there was no anaesthetic available, and the men had to be held down, screaming, while their injured limbs were hacked off. The injuries Lizzie dealt with every day were in fact gross mutilations of young, healthy bodies. And there was no means of controlling the constant waves of infection, and debilitating, energy-sapping illnesses, like measles and dysentery, affected the nurses and doctors as well as the patients. They fought gangrene with more amputations, all the while knowing they were patching these boys up just to send them out to be shot or blasted to hell again. Yet Lizzie looked sweet, calm and composed; despite it all Lizzie coped and was still human enough to fall in love with George MacDonald from Scamadale, and for him to fall in love with her. Auntie Mary was right, she must have been some woman this Lizzie.

By the beginning of September 1917, nine months after he almost died at the Somme, one doctor recommended that George should return to active service. Another disagreed, but the first held a higher military rank so his opinion took precedence. George was sent to the Ypres Salient, but as soon as he heard gunfire at close range once again his disturbed reactions were noticed by those around him. Physically he had been put back together, scarred but in one piece, but mentally he was suffering from what at the time they called 'nerves'. He could no longer walk in a straight line when the guns sounded, sometimes he shook uncontrollably, and he couldn't sleep. In his letters to Lizzie he recounted all of this in a matter-of-fact manner, and remarked that he thought he wasn't quite well yet, but he would be. Lizzie replied that he should ask his commanding officer for a few days' rest, but when the officer passed the request on, the medical officer refused it without even seeing George. He took the view that the soldier had already had nine months off and had been passed fit by a senior MO. The doctor was probably concerned about his own position; being seen as soft on malingerers would do his career no good whatever. And no doubt he was also mindful of the opinion expressed by Colonel Myers, Army Consultant Neurologist, that a man was either insane and destined for the madhouse, or fully responsible for his actions. So if he wasn't insane when he deserted, he should be shot. There was no room for mitigating factors, mistakes, or grey areas; anyone on his feet was fit for battle, and those who refused to go over the top, or couldn't, should be executed as an example to all the others. After the executions of five soldiers, one officer wrote that 4000 of his men were either mentally or physically unfit to be still fighting. Any of them could do what the five executed soldiers had done, he said, and that was what the military hierarchy decided to prevent, by killing those who did. The logic seemed to be that seeing one mentally disturbed boy shot dead would somehow stop others from developing mental illness.

The letters between George and Lizzie in those months were full of plans for the future, when they would go home to the farm in Scamadale as man and wife, of the children they would have and raise there, of how good life would be again, once the war was over. The concerns about George's health were still there, reflecting more Lizzie's anxiety than his; all his attention was on getting through the present in order to get to the future. What he was clearly suffering from was a form of war neurosis or shell-shock, caused by a combination of fear, the sounds of the conflict, and the sight of the dead and mutilated lying around, day after day and over a period of years. The men of the Great War for Civilization were only boys, boys with shredded nerves after years of barbarity and suffering had been inflicted upon them.

The reports said that Pte George MacDonald had absconded from his platoon in Houthulst Forest in the Ypres Salient on October 1917, but it was clear that one day he had simply walked away from the fighting, leaving behind his rifle and everything except what he stood in. There was no mention of any specific trigger, or if the accumulation of horrors had built up to climax on that particular day, but whatever the flashpoint, George had had enough. He was found two days later and captured without any resistance. He didn't speak when spoken to and had an expression of total blankness. He was, said another soldier, 'Not of this world. Like someone already dead.' At his court martial for desertion he had no legal representation, only a 'prisoner's friend', a padre who had never seen him before but found the shooting of sick men deplorable. The kindly padre drew attention to the differing views on George's fitness for duty by the two doctors, to his behaviour since returning to the front, when it was noticed that he was 'unstrung, less alert and nervous', and to the fact that he had fought bravely since 1914 and was a good soldier. And George, probably at the prompting of his new friend the padre, submitted to the court martial a letter outlining the difficulties he had faced that had led to his desertion. The hope was that some compassion would be shown to the last of the three soldier brothers from Scamadale.

'Dear Sir,' it began. 'I have been a good and loyal soldier for His Majesty since 1914. Two of my brothers have died in the war and I have still done my duty. I was injured at the Somme, but I survived and for that I am grateful to God, because so many of my friends did not. I was sent back to fight again some weeks ago, and with respect to the doctors, Sir, I do not think they knew I was still ill. It is the sound of gunfire I cannot bear, Sir, I find that I cannot stand still or upright, though I do try my hardest. And I shake so much that I truly feel I am a danger to my comrades. When I hold my rifle I shake so much that I cannot say when or in which direction it will fire. I have never been in trouble with my officers for any reason before, and I promise that after this I will do my best to be the good and true soldier I was before the Somme. When the war is over, Sir, I intend to marry a young lady who is a nurse and lead a good life. I humbly beg the forgiveness of His Majesty and of my regiment.' The letter was signed 'Yours faithfully, George MacDonald.' But George was sentenced to death anyway. At the age of twenty-two he would be shot by firing squad on the morning of 28 December 1917.

As dawn approached, the firing squad marched out, placed

their rifles on the ground and walked away. Out of sight of the men, an officer replaced two bullets with blanks. Then he mixed the rifles up, called the firing squad back to their positions and ordered them to pick up their weapons. In this way, it was hoped each man could believe he had not fired the fatal shot. A military policeman sent to escort George from his cell asked him if he wanted to be blindfolded with a reversed gas mask, but he refused. He had written letters, one to his mother, the other to Lizzie, all he asked was that these letters should be delivered. When the padre who had tried to save him gave this undertaking, George thanked him, shook hands with a smile, and said goodbye. Once outside he was strapped to a chair, and a piece of yellow cloth was pinned over his heart as a target for the rifles. His last bewildered words, before the firing squad of ten men was ordered to fire, were 'What will my mother say?'

Firing squad duty was not popular, some officers refused to provide men, and there were mutinies among squads. Often those forced into firing squads deliberately fired high rather than shoot comrades. It was a human reaction of disgust and distress over killing comrades, often from the same regiment. No power on earth could tell them that they weren't committing murder, they knew perfectly well that they were. They were ordinary men, no different from the unfortunate victim in their rifle sights; common sense and decency were part of their way of life, and killing fellow soldiers for being sick was clearly murder in their eyes. But aiming high did not greatly help the condemned man, and in George's case as in many others, he was not killed outright. The officer commanding the firing squad then had to walk forward and shoot him at close range.

Some 306 British soldiers were executed during the 1914–18 War, 35 of them Scots; Field Marshal Douglas Haig signed every execution warrant put before him without the slightest query. Officers who suffered the same symptoms as George MacDonald were sent to Craiglockhart Hospital in Edinburgh, and treated as well as anyone was able to treat their conditions at the time. Privates were shot at dawn. The officers who sat in judgement at courts martial were drawn from the upper classes, while the sick boys they sentenced to death were working class, invariably referred to as 'useless', 'incorrigible' or 'wasters'. At the court martial of Private Peter Black from Newport-on-Tay, the presiding officer sentencing him to death was moved to remark that his regiment, the Black Watch, consisted of 'the scum of Dundee'. Other soldiers, though, made their own protests over executions. When nineteen-year-old Royal Scots Private, Evan Fraser of Glasgow, was shot at dawn on 27 April 1915, a cross was put on his grave giving only his name. His comrades were so enraged by this additional insult that they pulled the cross down and replaced it with another, adding his regiment, rank, number and date of death. Instead of 'Shot', they put 'Murdered'. With the new cross erected they mounted a guard of honour around the grave, until they were once again called into battle. These were men who knew what shellfire was like, who spent every day for years waiting to die, men who knew a sick boy from a malingering coward.

Sometimes the families of the executed were simply told that they had been shot, others were told the true circumstances, and for many grieving families was added the ignominy of their dead boys' names being left out of official lists of war dead, and omitted from monuments. In Newport-on-Tay the opposition to Peter Black's name being added to the town's war memorial was led by the widows of officers who, like their husbands, inevitably came from upper-class backgrounds. But soldiers who had served with the boy stood outside the local hall while a meeting was held inside, promising that if his name wasn't included there would be no monument. Some gathered together stores of gelignite and detonators, intending to blow up the proposed monument, rather than let it stand without his name. In the end they won, but for Peter Black and all the others shot at dawn, there was to be no pardon, far less exoneration, only belated recognition that they had lived and died, killed by their own side.

In 1998 the government, as successive governments had done

before them, expressed 'regrets' over the 'victims' shot at dawn and suggested that their names should be put on war memorials and in books of remembrance, but there would be no pardon. It stated that less was known in those days about the mental and emotional effects of war, though enough was obviously known about the illness as it affected officers to save them from the firing squads. It was thought that a few of those executed had been guilty of crimes, the Forces Minister commented, crimes committed by men living in inhuman and depraved conditions, but even so, the majority must not be pardoned because of the supposed guilt of a few.

So an establishment that had routinely re-written history for its own protection over many generations lacked the courage to add a footnote in this case; clearly not all cowards wear khaki. The French, who executed around 700 of their own men during that war, universally pardoned them in the 1930s, recognizing that the rules of natural justice, as well as military justice, had been violated. But as far as Britain was concerned, the execution of sick boys broke no law of the time, and 'regret' was as far as it was prepared to go.

For Marylka all of this came as a shock. She was cynical about most things, but she had never heard about this issue before. Few had, because the records had been withheld from the public for nearly eighty years. Learning about it now, thanks to Bloody Mary's determination, outraged her sense of justice. She found it impossible to believe that anything so clearly wrong, so inhuman and unfair, could have happened. The First World War was within living memory, there were still, she knew, old soldiers making annual pilgrimages to the battlefields, though every year fewer and fewer. Among them could be one or two who had known George, that's what made the tragedy real, and not just a piece of fiction. The need to know gripped her, and the more she found out the more information she needed. She scoured the shelves of Glasgow's Mitchell Library for information, each piece leading to more books, and read long into several nights, often re-reading the same thing, because most of it was too horrific to take in at first. Auntie Mary had brought Helen up to understand how hard life was for people who had no money, those called the working class, or the lower orders, by those who had, and Helen had passed that knowledge on to Marylka. Her work as a doctor in Glasgow brought her into close contact with those very people, and she had thought she understood just how high the cards were stacked against them. Now she felt sore and sick with shame. Yes, she had an inkling that their lives were a struggle, and she had seen a lot of suffering, but now she realized there was a difference between seeing suffering and experiencing it, as they had. She had prided herself on being aware of class prejudice, of judging people as people, but now she understood how patronizingly limited her knowledge had been.

She walked around her flat in the early hours, trying to get rid of the awful feeling inside, the anger, the pity of it all, the complete impotence. She felt very close to George MacDonald, his shy young face haunted her sleep, but there was nothing she could do to help him. She wondered how it could be possible to feel so strongly for someone who had lived and died so many years before she was born, before her mother had been born. And she thought of Old Hector and his brothers, and remembered something her mother had once said about their reaction to the poverty they had encountered in Glasgow. Their instinct was to escape, to get away from it, whereas Auntie Mary and Lizzie wanted others to be aware of it, so that something would be done. Was the male instinct simply the one dictated by nature, she wondered, to save their own, whereas women were programmed to mother? No, that wouldn't do. Women too saved their own first, mothers had died protecting their children, yet the women of her family felt for others in a way the men didn't. Lizzie was Old Hector's own, so was her child, and he had cast them off. He saved himself and only himself. The family empire was *his* empire, and the truth was that he didn't care whom he sacrificed to keep it afloat and extend it, and in various ways he had sacrificed all of them as surely as he had Lizzie and her child.

If she found this woman, 'Lizzie's lassie', or any family she might have left behind, how was she to face them? How was she to look them in the eye and admit to who she was? For the first time she began to understand something of Auntie Mary's dilemma, and of Helen's too perhaps. Maybe this was part of why the search hadn't been seriously undertaken, shame at having to own up. But it would have to be done all the same. If there was one thing she was sure of, it was that it would have to be done.

There was one letter left, the last one George had written to Lizzie hours before his execution. She couldn't read it. She was drained already, she couldn't face the boy's last word to his love. And besides, it was really none of her business. That letter belonged to George and Lizzie's daughter. She slipped it back into the folder of photos and letters and placed them inside the buff legal file. But there was something lodged in the corner. She emptied the contents of the file on to the table in front of her, put her hand into the corner and brought out a black velvet pouch. Inside was a small, oval, gold brooch. It had a safety chain and pin and its delicate gold filigree edging was inlaid with four tiny diamonds of black enamel. On one side there was the head and shoulders portrait of George MacDonald that Marylka had come to know so well, and on the other a photo of Lizzie. An inscription was engraved around the rim of George's portrait, inside the filigree. 'In memory of Pte George Mac-Donald. 28 XII 1917'. It was a mourning brooch, and as she put it gently back into the velvet pouch she felt a piece of paper inside. She recognized the writing immediately, it was already seared into her mind. It simply said 'For our daughter Elizabeth'.

24

Before leaving for Eilean Òg Marylka had to collect the last of her stuff from the hospital. In her place there was now a new whipping boy, an innocent, bright-eyed lad who would shortly be robbed of all enthusiasm for his chosen profession. It was a bit like policemen looking younger every day; she looked at the new houseman and wondered if his mother knew he was out. There was a tale that once a newly qualified doctor had taken up his post as houseman, and by the end of the first six months the colour of his eyes had changed from brown and interesting, to washed-out grey. She had no idea if this tale was true or even possible, but it should be.

'So you're the paragon of virtue and efficiency, are you?' the new houseman asked.

'Says who?'

'Professor Stein,' he replied. 'I'm only three weeks in the job, and according to him he can see already that I have no chance of measuring up to the last houseman, who was wonderful, marvellous, and dedicated.'

'Yeah, sure,' Marylka said. 'On my first morning he screamed at me in the middle of the ward round. "For God's sake give up medicine now, you useless girl. Go and have babies, it's all you're fit for. That way you can at least save the profession from being brought into disrepute." I'd tell you it got better, but it didn't. When I did my surgical housemanship upstairs the chief greeted me with the words "You don't intend actually *being* a surgeon do you, girl? Because if you do I'll tell you now that your first step will be to have a hysterectomy."'

He laughed.

'You can laugh!' she retorted. 'At least you don't have the disability of being female, but they'll get you some other way. Just remember I told you this, and in times of stress repeat to yourself the mantra of every houseman since the dawn of time: "I won't let the bastards grind me down!"'

Some of her stuff had been left with Crusher Woods, the Sister from Mark's ward. She knocked and went into Beryl's office.

'It's you, Marylka,' Beryl greeted her with a smile. Changed days indeed. 'I've just been toying with whether to rip this up and throw it away.' Beryl handed her a small card. 'I've carried it with me everywhere while Graham Spencer's been around, but if he really has gone to Newcastle . . .'

The card read 'Please do not attempt to resuscitate, and leave all my organs intact,' and Beryl's signature was underneath.

Marylka laughed. 'You carried this because of Spencer?'

'Damn sure I did!' Beryl replied. 'Would you have wanted him rummaging around inside you? What if you'd survived despite his usual efforts, think of the state you could be in!' She took the card back and looked at it again before replacing it in her side pocket. 'I'll hang on to it for a while longer,' she decided. 'You never know, maybe Newcastle will send him back once they discover how bogus his references are, and ask for a refund.' She sat down and looked up at Marylka. 'So, what are you going to do now, then?'

'I'm going over to Eilean Òg for a break,' she smiled. 'I'll decide what I want to do after that. I just came for my stuff and to say toodle-pip.'

As Marylka left Beryl hugged her. 'Thanks for taking on Mark's patients with such good grace,' she said. 'Especially when things weren't too good for yourself. You're a good sort, Marylka. I hope you'll come back here one day.' Then in true Beryl style she said 'Now off with you!' and propelled her out the door.

*   *   *

Marylka found Fiona queuing up in the canteen, a tray of food in her hands.

'You'll never guess what?' Marylka said. 'But Crusher's just hugged me!'

'Thou art one of the chosen then,' Fiona replied. 'Beryl's a friend for life if she likes you.'

'Yeah, but I never really thought she did!'

'Why? Because she once bawled you out?'

'You heard about that did you?' Marylka asked sourly.

'But, of course! Beryl chews people up at least three times a day, but she's fair. Grovel a bit after bein' bashed an' she'll forgive you – but only if she thinks you're worth it. Beryl's no' the worst ogre in this place.'

Then Marylka told her she was going off to Eilean Òg for a while.

'I've got family over there,' she said blandly.

'What? Islands are full of grass an' stuff!' Fiona said, aghast. 'An' are you sayin' you've got teuchter blood, when we've treated you like a regular human bein' all this time?'

'Yeah, well, you can't get your money back now!' Marylka replied. 'But fear not, I shall return.'

'Have you got a job fixed up, then?'

Marylka shook her head. 'No, but I *do* know that I won't be staying in the land of the heather.'

'Don't be so sure, you could end up severely affected by the tangle o' the isles an' never come back.' Tray in hand she attempted an impromptu and very bad highland fling, for some reason shouting 'Hooch!' at regular intervals, until Marylka persuaded her to sit down instead.

'So anything happening?'

'Nothin',' muttered the thwarted dancer. 'Dead dull everywhere.'

'Talking of the dead,' Marylka said. 'Any news of Bruce? The last thing I remember after Mark was carted off, he was turning over a new leaf.'

'Oh, you could say he did that,' Fiona replied with a sigh. 'He discovered concern for his fellow creatures. Some chancer conned research money out of one of the drug companies, an' asked the silly sod to help him in exchange for his name on the paper. Just the thing thought our Bruce, respectability beckonin', serious recognition on the horizon, all that crap. So along he goes, with a few purloined bits an' pieces from post mortems that the owners were no longer usin', on account of their bein' dead.' She looked up at Marylka. 'Did you ever visit the Animal House? The one where the research animals are kept?'

Marylka shook her head again, breaking a bit off Fiona's Danish pastry. Fiona slapped her hand and continued.

'Well *don't!*' she said. 'It's a terrible place! The ECG Dollies were once asked by a Cardiology Registrar to feed some bunnies for him while he was on holiday, he'd infected them with somethin' God-awful, so naturally he didn't want them to die before he got back to kill them. He took us up to the Animal House to see them, an' that was his mistake. We never talked to him again except to hurl abuse at him. All the animals up there have been given somethin' as part of some experiment or other, an' it's just no' right! We were greetin' for days.'

'The ECG Dollies in tears eh?' Marylka remarked. 'Any pictures?'

'D'you want to hear this story or no'?' Fiona demanded.

'Sorry. Go on.'

'Well Bruce goes up with his bits an' pieces, or rather, other people's, an' that night we had a party to celebrate Spencer goin' to Newcastle.'

'Was Spencer at the party?'

'Of course no'! Now stop interruptin'! We'd been callin' Bruce all sorts of swines an' unfeelin' buggers for agreein' to the research deal, an' once he started drinkin' he started thinkin' as well. An' as you know as well as any of us, that's a dangerous combination as far as Bruce is concerned. The next thing we know, he's gone up to the Animal House an' let every animal in the place go. They're a' runnin' all over the place, dogs in Dumbarton Road, bunnies up Byres Road, cats through Church Street, rats, an' guinea pigs, an' hamsters, scurryin' in every direction at dead of night. An' because they've all got some induced disease or other we had to catch them of course. Well nobody outside knew this, they just saw these looneys in white coats grabbin' cats an' dogs an' anythin' that moved, an' they decided we were kidnappin' their pets to do experiments on them.'

Marylka by this time was laughing too much to eat the Danish pastry.

'It's a'right for you, ya teuchter ye!' Fiona accused her. 'But there's no' one shop in the vicinity will sell us anythin'. We've been boycotted. Can't get as much as a paper or a bar of chocolate.'

'Not even a Kit Kat I suppose!' Marylka giggled.

'This is *serious*, you!' Fiona said severely. 'They won't even serve us in the pubs! We're banned from the Rubaiyat!'

'And how's Bruce?'

'Sent to Coventry. But he's no' doin' the research project after all. Apart from that,' she said with a sigh, 'there's nothin' happenin'. Life's dead dull. You're missin' nothin at all.'

The journey to Eilean Òg took four hours. Not enough time to have a sleep and too much time to sit around doing nothing. Instead she went over all the papers she had brought with her in the original file, plus another with details and photos of the rest of the family. But now that she was resolved on doing this thing she was having doubts. What if she couldn't find 'Lizzie's lassie', what if she was dead and her family, if she had any, had moved elsewhere? Did she carry on the search across the entire country, the entire world come to that? What if they were on the island but didn't want to know anything about this? She went over it in her mind throughout the four hours, convincing herself entirely of one scenario, only to re-convince herself of the opposite one ten minutes later. As the ferry drew into the pier, an announcement came over the loudspeaker asking car drivers to return to the lower deck to collect their cars, and as she did so she took a deep breath and decided that she had no choice. As she had been saying for weeks now, this thing *had* to be done, and if she got a rough welcome, or none at all, well, she'd just have to deal with that if and when it happened. If the worst they could do was tell her to get lost, she thought, that might even be preferable to having to tell perfect strangers, perhaps perfectly happy strangers at that, of the family they came from, God help them. Her family, God help her.

25

If the journey had taken any longer Marylka might well have jumped overboard from sheer boredom. Four hours on a ferry, where even the cafeteria staff had to ask if you had tea or coffee, was more than flesh and blood could stand. She had never been on an island before, and at first sight it looked just as she had suspected, grass, sea, and not a lot else. She had no idea where Honeysuckle Cottage was either, so as soon as she drove off the ferry ramp, trying to quash an impulse to start singing loudly at the joy of being on dry land again, she parked the car and looked around for someone to ask. There were postmen scurrying around, taking bags of mail from a metal container that had emerged from the boat, and throwing them into post office vans. She stopped a postman and asked for directions.

'Honeysuckle?' he said. 'That's on Neil's run. See that big fella over there wi' his back tae ye? That's Neil. He'll show ye the road to Honeysuckle Cottage.'

She walked to where the big chap was standing. 'Excuse me,' she said, 'are you Neil? One of your colleagues said you'd be the best person to direct me to Honeysuckle Cottage.'

He turned to face her. 'Honeysuckle Cottage?' he repeated, in the soft accent of the Western Isles.

'My God, what a gorgeous voice!' she thought. 'What a gorgeous man! Gorgeous is the only word that will do for him. Wonder if I can take him home as a souvenir?' He was tall, with dark hair tinged red, and his eyes were so blue and direct that she was sure he must be reading her mind, and that might be embarrassing. 'I wonder if they're all like this?' she thought. 'In which case the females are wise to keep the information to themselves.' She imagined herself updating Fiona's opinion of islands and teuchters by sending a snap of this chap.

'So you're the lady who's rented Honeysuckle for the next six months?' he continued. 'We were wondering who it was.'

'I see the bush telegraph is in fine working order,' she replied, adding a silent instruction to herself to stop smiling at him quite so much.

'Och, there's not much we don't hear about the day before it happens!' He smiled.

The way he said 'Och' was decidedly thrilling.

'I'm going past the road leading to Honeysuckle,' he said. 'If you want to hang on a minute till I load the mail into the bus you can follow me along the road if you like.'

Inside she gave a little giggle. The thought crossed her mind that she'd be delighted to load this particular male herself, or indeed follow him, whichever he preferred. 'Behave yourself!' she muttered, watching him walk – no, stride away towards the red post bus. 'Remember what Rob said about big, hairy, tartan-clad, macho men! On the other hand, Rob who?'

As she followed in the tyre tracks of Adonis the Postie, she began to appreciate that there was a single, winding road around the island, mainly without pavements. They passed through a village that had about six shops, and just outside the post bus stopped. Adonis got out and came back to her car.

'That wee track on your left leads directly up to Honeysuckle Cottage,' he smiled.

'All his own teeth too,' she thought, 'or somewhere on this forsaken lump of rock there is a very good cosmetic dentist.'

'Fine,' she smiled back. 'Thanks for your help.'

Honeysuckle Cottage was in fact two whitewashed cottages knocked into one and extended upwards. It had probably been a traditional couple of houses at one time, and it had that look about it, as though it had been tightened up somehow, an excessively neat and tidy look. Someone had tried hard to keep the cottage outwardly as it was, but the double-glazing and the capped chimneys showed that a certain modernization had been undertaken. It stood on its own in an elevated position, as the estate agents would say, with a clear view out to sea. It was early September but there was already a slight nip in the air, so she imagined the double glazing and central heating were necessities on cold, windy nights, at least for a city-dweller.

Inside, the place was a dream. It had been completely gutted and rebuilt using copious amounts of wood, resembling the best of Swedish open-plan interior design so beloved of the glossies. It was light and airy, with extra windows installed to add to the feeling of space. Obviously no expense had been spared, and the kitchen alone easily merited a design award. The wood here, like everywhere else in the cottage, was a deep gold, and the design and renovations had been thoughtfully worked out. It wasn't like the average holiday home, where it didn't matter how inefficient and inconvenient the layout was, because no one spent long enough in serious residence to become irritated by it. Everything was just where you would expect it to be in your own home, and there were two bathrooms of such sumptuous proportions that she knew she could throw away that shovel. Rob had done well, she'd have to give him that. She wouldn't use three bedrooms, but still, there surely couldn't be too many places on Eilean Òg like this.

Next day Adonis called in his post bus with a card from Rob. 'Remember,' it said, 'what I said about the wildlife. Hope all is satisfactory.'

'Is there anything you need?' he asked.

She decided to remain on the right side of good taste. 'Well actually, if you have a minute maybe you could point me in the right direction,' she said, leading the way into the cottage.

He looked around. 'It's quite a place, this,' he said. 'It's owned by a stockbroker, I think? His great-grandfather came from Eilean Òg, and he had this mad idea of doing it up and spending time here, but his wife hates the place and threatened divorce. The last I heard he was having to sell it, even though he didn't want to. It's a wee bit over the top with the wood maybe. You'd be scared to do any real living in it in case you did some damage. Not a place for bringing up children.'

What a nice introduction to a question she'd been wanting to ask.

'So you have children then?'

'Me? Hell, no! I'm not even married! My father thinks I'm gay!'

She hadn't thought of that. Just how did she ask that one? 'Well each to his own I suppose,' she smiled.

'Och, not that I am,' he grinned. 'My father tends to see things in a kinda black and white way, can't understand why I haven't settled down and produced a brood of grandchildren to carry on the family name for him.'

Marylka had been wondering more what was wrong with the female population in these parts. The rest of the males must be even more gorgeous than him if he hadn't been snared long before this.

'I suppose you'll be one of those writers?' He laughed softly, his eyes crinkling, and he looked so appetizing that Marylka thought she might have to bite him.

'Do you have a lot of writers here then?'

'Och,' he said.

'God, there he goes with that soft "Och" again! Does the man have no idea how his voice melts muscular control?'

'We get them here all the time,' he continued. 'They start out looking sad and interesting. Then they either go mad with the isolation and all the rain we get, and disappear one day, or else they turn native, and before you know it, they're permanently drunk and putting on a local accent! Still, maybe it gets their creative juices running or something.'

'Yes, indeedy!' she thought, 'The "something" part, I think!'

'Well I'm not a writer,' she smiled calmly. 'I'm here to try to find someone. You're a local, I take it? Maybe you can help. I'm looking for someone who was sent here from Glasgow many years ago, some time in the 1920s. They were called boarded-out children.'

'Really?' he said quietly. 'Well everyone knows everyone else here. What's the name?'

'Elizabeth Davidson,' she replied. 'She was a relative of mine, but I've only just found out about her, and I'd like to find her.'

For a moment he stared at her, saying nothing. Either he was so bewitched by her personality and beauty, she hoped, or else he hadn't a clue. She couldn't decide which, as the silence continued, because his face remained lovely, but impassive.

'Tell you what,' he said eventually, 'there's a teacher in the local school who has an interest in the boarded-outs. Maybe he can help. Jump into the bus and I'll drop you off at the school and pick you up on the way back. Save you taking your own car.'

'That would be great,' Marylka replied. 'By the way, my name's Marylka.'

'I'm Neil Craig,' he replied. 'Do you mind if I use your phone? I'm sure it'll be OK, but I'll call Will at the school first to make sure.'

'Yes, fine. On you go.'

He crossed to the phone and dialled a number. 'Aye, Will, it's Neil here. I'm at Honeysuckle Cottage. I've got a lady standing here beside me who's looking for a boarded-out called Elizabeth Davidson. Aye, Will, that's right. I thought you'd be the person to speak to, but I felt it was better to ring first. OK if I drop her off on my run and pick her up on the way back? Aye, well, if you're sure it would be no trouble.' He replaced the receiver. 'You're in luck.' He smiled at Marylka. 'Will says he's got time now, and he'll run you back afterwards as well if that's OK. And I can vouch for him, he's no mad rapist or anything.'

*   *   *

What terribly nice people, she thought, to put themselves out so readily for a complete stranger. On the drive in the post bus Adonis said very little, but it was a noisy vehicle and his voice was soft, so he probably knew conversation would be a struggle. At the school he jumped out and led her into the head teacher's room.

'This is Will, the man I told you about,' he said, introducing her to a tall man in his late fifties. His hair was nearly white now, but you could tell by his eyebrows, and also by the acres of freckles on his pale skin, that once he had been a very red head. 'Will, Marylka,' Neil continued. 'I'll leave her in your hands, and I'll maybe see you later, Will?'

Will nodded absently. 'Aye, aye Neil. I'll see you later.'

As they sat down she was aware of Will examining her across the desk. He seemed slightly edgy and uncomfortable, but he treated her politely enough. Well, she was a stranger here after all.

'So,' he said. 'Can I ask you what your interest is in this Elizabeth Davidson? Just curiosity, you understand, I had no idea anyone else knew about the boarded-outs.'

'I didn't until recently,' she replied. 'A great-aunt of my mother's died a few years ago, and she left some information about this woman, who would have been her niece. I'm following it up because I was asked to. Neil said you had taken an interest in the boarded-outs and you might know where she could be.'

'Aye, well,' he smiled tightly. 'The story of the boarded-outs is part of the island's history, not a glorious part, but I think it's important the children know about it.' He looked around his study, his fingers drumming on the desk in front of him. 'So you know the woman's background then?'

Marylka nodded.

'Well,' said the teacher slowly, 'I have an idea who she might be, but I'm not too sure. Would you mind if I checked this out and got back to you? I'm sorry to rush you, but I have a class to take. Wee schools like this don't have a lot of teachers, I'm afraid.'

'Please forgive me,' Marylka said, standing up. 'I didn't expect you to drop everything for me. It's very good of you to help me at all. I'm glad you were able to see me.'

On the drive back to Honeysuckle Cottage, she wondered why Neil had taken her all the way to the school, when she could have had exactly the same conversation with the teacher by phone. 'Maybe Adonis just wanted my company!' She smiled to herself. As she got out at Honeysuckle, Will shook hands and said he would be in touch, but not to hold out too much hope, he might be on the wrong track altogether. He was polite and friendly, but there was a reserve she couldn't quite put her finger on. She shrugged, reminding herself once again that she was a total stranger here, what did she expect? The red carpet from everyone she met? Besides, he was older than she was, a different generation and an entire culture apart. He was hardly likely to be as near to her wavelength as Adonis.

When Will Craig left Marylka that Monday morning, it wasn't to return to his school to take a class, but to track down his nephew Neil on the post run. Neil's phone call had been the biggest shock of his life and he had no idea how to handle the situation. It had just been an ordinary morning at school, then Neil had dropped this bomb. Here was this young girl turning up out of the blue looking for his own mother, who he knew had wondered about where she came from all her life. But his mother was now over eighty, was there much to be gained from opening up wounds that she might never recover from? The lassie's motives might well be as pure and honest as they seemed to be, but there came a time when the child became the parent, and for Will Craig that time had come with his father's death. His mother was fit and healthy, but since his father's death she'd lost some of her resilience. It was natural, he knew that, but it still meant he had to be sure there was something to gain from putting the girl in touch with her.

Neil was on the other side of the island, sitting by the shore eating a sandwich.

'Well?' he asked, looking up as Will approached.

'Well, indeed!' Will said. 'That was a bit of a shocker, Neil!'

'Ye're tellin' me! When she mentioned Gran's name Ah was so stunned Ah couldnae think of anythin' tae say. The lassie must've thought Ah was daft. All Ah could think of doin' was takin' her tae you.' Now that he was no longer talking to a stranger he had dropped back into his normal speech.

'What a bloody fright I got when you told me on the phone too!'

'Aye, Ah know, Ah heard ye. Ah'm sorry about that. But Ah couldnae think of any way to break it gently, and Ah didnae want her to know who Ah was till we'd decided what to do. So what did ye tell the lassie, then?'

'I panicked, I just got rid of her. I said I might be able to help and I'd get back to her. All I could think of was stalling for time till we had decided what to do. I'm sure she noticed something, God knows what she must think of us. Mad teuchters I shouldn't wonder.'

'So what *do* we do?' Neil asked.

'Christ, Neil, you keep coming up with the questions I want to ask and I don't have any answers! What *can* we do?'

They looked at each other silently, then stared out at the sea.

'Look at us!' Will said, suddenly getting up and marching about the shingle, his feet making crunching noises and his hands stuck deep into his trouser pockets. 'We're sitting here like a couple of ancient bloody mariners consulting the wisdom of the deep! We've got to do something, come to some sort of decision.'

'Well Ah don't think we have a choice,' Neil said quietly. 'This isnae really our decision to make, it's Gran's. The way Ah see it, it's more a question of how we do it, rather than if.'

Will nodded. 'I know, I know. But she's getting on, Neil. Old people feel shock much more. She was a damned sight younger when my Da died and she hasn't been the same since then. D'you really think all that stuff about being a boarded-out still bothers her now?'

'Ah think it does, Will, really Ah do,' Neil replied. 'She hasnae said much about it for a long time, but as ye know, she's still bitter about her time here. Ah think that means she hasnae forgotten, Ah think she'd still want tae know whatever this lassie knows.'

'Aye, well, maybe. I don't know, Neil, that's the truth of it. I just don't know.'

'Look, think how we'll feel once Gran goes if we havnae given her the chance to know who she is. An' then it'll be too late, won't it?'

Will wandered about the shore in silence. 'Aye, you're right, Neil, I know you're right. I just don't want her upset, that's all. Maybe we should talk to the lassie again, tell her who we are, explain about my mother's age and that, ask her for more details.'

'About three o'clock at Honeysuckle Cottage?'

Will nodded, then the two of them headed for their vehicles and drove off in different directions.

Marylka was surprised to find Neil and Will on her doorstep so quickly and invited the little delegation inside.

'The thing is,' said Will with a nervous smile, 'we haven't been quite open with you.'

She looked from Will's worried frown to Neil's beautiful, slow smile and back again.

'The thing is,' he said again, 'that Neil and I are related, to each other, and to Elizabeth Davidson.'

Marylka was stunned, but the only comment she could come up with was 'Oh?'

'Yes,' said Will, squirming about in his chair. 'My name's Will Craig, I'm Neil's uncle, and Elizabeth – Betty – Davidson, is my mother.'

She looked at Neil. 'And your grandmother?'

Neil nodded.

Which meant, of course, that she was related to Adonis. Not closely, but still family. Was it fair, she wondered, was it bloody fair? Then she realized that Adonis had led her a merry dance, the two of them had, and she felt a little aggrieved.

'Well you kept that close to your chest earlier!' she remarked. 'So the telephone call, that was in some secret code was it, to let you know some monster had turned up? I don't bite or anything, you know!'

Will looked as though he'd like to turn and run out.

'Is that what they call being a teuchter?' she demanded of Neil. 'That's your famous Highland welcome, treating the silly tourist from the mainland like your enemy, making me feel completely stupid, Mr Craig?'

Neil smiled a slow, amused smile, looking her right in the eye, making her feel like a prima donna.

'I'm sorry,' Will said, looking increasingly uncomfortable. 'We both are.' He looked at Neil, who looked anything but. 'Please understand that we weren't trying to mislead you, though obviously we did,' Will continued anxiously. 'But my mother's over eighty now, she's a widow, and naturally we're a little protective of her.'

'But I'm not going to do anything to her, Mr Craig,' Marylka returned, a little more tightly than she would've wished.

'I know that's not your intention, I know that. But you must understand what a shock it was for Neil and me to hear you ask after my mother. We have to be as sure as we can be that she isn't going to be upset by what you have to tell her.'

'Sleeping dogs, Mr Craig?' she asked quietly. 'I do know what you mean, it was a consideration for – for someone on my side of the family too. So what do we do? I don't want to upset the old lady either.'

'Well, for a start you don't call her "the old lady",' said Neil with his slow grin. 'Not if you want to keep your gizzard that is!'

'A bit like that, is she?' Marylka laughed. 'I like her already!'

'She was eighty last March,' Will smiled, 'but she's fit and spry. But still, she's my mother.'

'It runs in the family,' Marylka said. 'Her uncle, Old Hector, died at a hundred, her Auntie Mary at ninety-five, and my grandfather, her cousin, is seventy-eight yet he looks about sixty.'

'Look, Marylka,' Will said. 'Could you give us the gist of this story now, and then we'll talk to my mother and find out how she feels about knowing more?'

'I don't see why not,' she replied. 'After all, this is your information too. We're all related, all family when it comes down to it.'

She gave them a shortened version of the history. Of Old Hector the businessman and his unstoppable ambitions, of Lizzie and George. George, she said simply, had died in the Great War. She explained about Auntie Mary's letter to Helen, then the three of them sat in silence. The two men were obviously stunned. While they were in that state she told them about the still thriving family business, but she made no mention of Auntie Mary's will, and her wish to leave all her money to 'Lizzie's lassie', or any family she had had. As they sat listening, she went over Auntie Mary's discovery of Lizzie's fate, and Old Hector's rejection of both her and her orphaned child.

'He must've been a very hard man,' Neil murmured.

'No,' Marylka replied with feeling. 'He was a bastard in the truest sense of the word. How do you think it feels to be related to someone like that?'

'But you can't help that any more than Gran can!' he said softly.

'I know, but still.' She explained how she had become involved in the search for Elizabeth Davidson only weeks before, after her own mother had been killed in an accident.

'Och, lass,' Neil said. 'I'm sorry!'

His words, and more so the gentleness of them, felt as though barbs had found their way to the softest part of her soul, and it was all she could do to keep control. They sat without speaking for what seemed like eternity. 'I have photos and everything,' she told them, 'things Betty should have. But I think she should see them first, and if she decides she doesn't want to, then the rest of the family can have them if they want.'

Slowly Will and Neil explained what had happened to Betty, how she had no idea who she was or where she came from, but she had married Alec Craig, who had come over with her on the boat, and they'd been happy at Red Rock. They'd had two sons and a daughter, and then four grandsons, two grand-daughters and a flock of great-grandchildren. Marylka suddenly laughed and they stared at her. 'I'm sorry, but I was just thinking what Old Hector would've done to lay hands on a few male offspring, and all the time there was Lizzie's lassie producing clans of them! Oh, God, wherever he is now, he has to be told about that!'

The last of the light was going as Will and Neil Craig left Honeysuckle Cottage, both still looking as stunned as Marylka by the day's events and discoveries. They had promised to speak to Betty then get back to her with some decision, but they were having trouble taking it all in themselves. 'And they don't know the half of it yet,' Marylka thought, thinking about the details, about Lizzie being a nurse on the Western Front during the First World War, and George being shot at dawn, murdered for being sick, and dying without knowing Lizzie was carrying his child. Reading their letters and learning about it all had ripped her apart, what would it do to an old lady, even a feisty old lady, of eighty? Will and Neil were right to be cautious, to be protective of her, but they had no real idea yet of how much there was to be cautious and protective about.

She began to wonder if she had done the right thing coming here, stirring up emotions that showed every sign of having settled down over the years. Why was she threatening Betty Craig's peace of mind? Was it simply a means of getting back at Old Hector, spreading the word about what a dishonest, dishonourable old swine he was? She had come here with such noble intentions, to carry out Auntie Mary's last wish, to give an old woman information about her background, but that night in the luxury of Honeysuckle Cottage she tossed and turned in bed, trying to decide if she had really been using all that to settle some long-standing scores against Old Hector. And Young Hector too, because he would have to be told about the Craig arm of the family, and of his esteemed father's treachery, if Betty chose to accept Mary's bequest. And was it possible, probable even, that she was also using Betty Craig to stave off the time when she would have to face Helen's death and come to terms with being alone?

She had decided now; it had been an ill-advised, selfish, indulgent, fool's errand. She should have listened to Rob after all, but no, Marylka Kowalski pushed ahead with everything, she never stopped to consider the true implications when she wanted to do something. She was too headstrong for her own and everyone else's good. The Craigs were innocent people, for God's sake, they didn't need her or any of the Davidson misery in their lives, but she had been so hell-bent on dragging it in anyway. Bloody Mary? You could make that Bloody Marylka with more justification. Well tomorrow she'd see Neil Craig and tell him to forget the whole thing. Then she'd go back to Glasgow, put the situation with all its legal ramifications into Rob's capable hands, find herself a job, and get on with her life. In a few months' time all this would be but a distant nightmare, a salutary lesson in thinking first next time. She imagined herself back at the hospital some time in the future, or more likely, propping up the bar in the Rubaiyat, saying to Fiona over a noggin or three 'Did I ever tell you about my gorgeous teuchter third cousin?' In time that's all this misguided jaunt would mean to her.

Four a.m. She was going home on the next ferry. As soon as she'd made the decision she felt better, and immediately she jumped up and packed the little she had unpacked. And it wasn't so bad really when you thought about it: arrive on Sunday, leave as soon as possible on Tuesday. By sheer good luck she'd met the Craigs as soon as she drove off the boat, they could almost have been waiting for her, so she hadn't wasted much time. It would've been awful to have sat on this island for months before she got to where she now was. And now that she had decided to go she wanted to leave immediately. If only she didn't have to wait for the next boat, if only she could get into the car and drive off this very second and never see this place again. If they wouldn't take an unbooked car on the next boat she would leave it behind rather than wait here any longer. Anyone could have it, as long as she could board the ferry and sail off in the opposite direction. Yes. Tomorrow she'd leave Eilean Òg, tomorrow she'd go home and start growing up.

26

Will and Neil Craig had agonized over how to tell Betty about the girl, before deciding it would be better to talk to her without Murdo being present, because Murdo would take over. He couldn't help it, it was how he was. Will looked at his watch. It was just after 4 p.m. and Murdo would be at work on the farm; even so, if he saw them approaching he'd down tools and join them. Neil volunteered to call home and find out if his father was in the vicinity, and if he was, they would postpone their visit.

'We're in luck,' he grinned when he climbed back into Will's car. 'He's at the north end lookin' at a sheepdog pup, won't be back till after six. Add on time tae talk an' time for a dram, an' we're maybe lookin' at eight o'clock.'

Betty was in her own home beside Red Rock farmhouse. When she saw them coming in together she thought something was wrong.

'It's no' Murdo is it?' she asked fearfully.

'No, Gran, we didnae bring him,' Neil smiled.

'Ah thought . . .'

'There's nothin' wrong. But anyway, you know fine that if the grim reaper came for my Da he'd talk the poor creature to death!'

Betty laughed. 'Aye, well, that's true.' She sat down beside the fire and looked from Will to Neil. 'So what is it then?'

The two men exchanged looks.

'Right,' Betty said briskly. 'We've a' had a good look at each other. Now out wi' it.'

Will and Neil smiled. 'Gran, you know you've always talked about no' knowin' where ye came frae?'

Betty nodded gravely.

'How would ye feel if somebody was able tae tell ye?'

'Ah'd say it was eighty years too late.'

'So ye wouldnae want to know?' Neil persisted.

'This somebody,' Betty said after a while. 'Does he know everything? Who my mother was, my faither?'

'It's a lassie, Gran, but aye.'

All they could hear was the ticking of the clock as Betty thought.

'Would you like us to tell you the bit we know, Mother?' Will asked. 'And then you can see what you think?'

'Aye,' she said quietly. 'An' then Ah can see.'

So, gently they told her what they knew, that her father had died in the Great War before he and her mother could marry. 'I'm sure that happened to many women during the war, Mother,' Will said, and she nodded. Then they told her of her uncle, Old Hector, who had been an ambitious businessman, and of how he turned his back on his sister Lizzie when she was pregnant. Once again the ticking of the clock seemed to grow louder in the silence.

'The lassie who's come has a lot of papers, Gran,' Neil said. 'She has photos of a' the family, an' letters, but she hasnae told us everythin', she wants tae tell you hersel'. Your mother had a younger sister. She died a few years back an' left a letter askin' for you to be found, an' this lassie is the wan that's come lookin' for ye.'

'What's she like?' Betty asked.

Will and Neil looked at each other again. 'She seems nice, Mother,' Will replied.

'She didnae havtae do this, Gran,' Neil said softly. 'Ah don't think she finds it easy. Her own mother died in a car crash recently, she seems awfy raw about that yet.'

Betty smiled. 'So ye're sayin', Neil, that Ah should listen tae the lassie?' she asked.

'Naw, Gran, that's for you to say. Ah'm only tellin' ye what Ah think frae what Ah've seen o' her. If ye decide no' tae see her Ah'm sure she'll accept that an' go away an' no' bother ye again.'

'What dae you think, Will?' she asked her son.

'The same Ah suppose. But if you send her away you'll never know, will you, Mother? This is the only chance you'll ever have.'

She saw them away, promising that she'd let them know as soon as she'd thought it over, then she sat down again and tried to do that. All her life she'd wanted to know. All through the good, happy years with Alec, it had been there in the back of her mind, and she'd felt guilty about it. And in the years since he'd gone, she'd sat here alone by the fire wondering if there was some way she could find out. She'd stare into the flames and try to force herself to think back, to put a face to the feeling she remembered before she came to Eilean Òg, the safe, warm feeling she thought was a woman. She'd learned her mother's name from her birth certificate all those years ago, and assumed she'd been called after her. It said her father was 'unknown', but he wasn't. Her father was George, a soldier from the first war. George and Lizzie, and both had died, one before she was born the other after, and so she'd come here to Eilean Òg. Was there anything else she needed to know then? As for Lizzie's brother, well, what more was there to learn there? Bastard weans were something to be ashamed of in his day, he most likely did what any respectable man would've. Not kind maybe, but typical of the times. He was dead now too, so whoever this lassie was she couldn't have much more to tell her. Besides, it was too late to go back over all that now, she was too old.

She heard the sound of Murdo's van pulling in and noticed for the first time that it had grown dark. Past eight o'clock and not a light on. He'd be at the door in a minute, bursting in, telling her everything that had happened during the day, asking her what she'd done and telling her how to do it better, and tonight she didn't feel like it. But if she asked Catriona to keep him away it would be more reason for him to come in. He was unstoppable, Murdo, nothing for it but to brace herself and get it over with, let on nothing's wrong so that he'd go back into his own house and leave her alone. Sixty years since she'd had him, and she was still thinking up ways to get some peace from him, she thought, shaking her head and smiling.

And right on time, there he was. He'd been to see a pup. After Glen had been kicked by a cow and had to be put down, he said he'd never have another dog. They were just a damned nuisance, he said, he'd do better without a dog. And it was true that Glen led the life of Riley, being carted about in the back of the van and refusing to work as he got older. She'd heard Murdo shouting at him, the entire island heard Murdo shouting at Glen. 'What kinda workin' dog are ye?' he'd yell. 'Well ye're *no*' a workin' dog, ye're a car dog, ye dae nothin'!' And Glen would look back at him mournfully, black affronted that his master should behave in this common, vulgar way. 'Well that's it! If ye won't work ye won't get fed! No' another bite! An' nae merr hurls in the back o' the van either, ye'll get oot an' walk as if ye were a dog frae noo on!' And with that he'd hold the door of the van open, Glen would jump in and settle down, and off they'd go together. It was a scene that was repeated over and over again, but Glen knew his function was as Murdo's pal, he knew he wasn't really intended to work. Oh, the odd cursory round-up of the chickens in the yard to show he could do it if he felt like it, but nothing more. Glen would lie in the shade, waiting for Murdo to finish whatever he was doing, then they would come home side by side, discussing the events of the day.

Murdo liked animals, that was the truth of it, they accepted you unconditionally and didn't mind if you were a bit undiplomatic, they didn't go in the huff with you just because you'd hurt their feelings. He liked the companionship of animals, that was what it amounted to, not that he would ever admit it, of course. No, there had to be a genuine reason for having an animal; the horses were economically more viable than a tractor, and Glen had been needed to gather in the sheep or the hill beasts. But putting him down happened to coincide with not needing him so much, so there wouldn't be another dog. Then, as time passed and he missed having a dog about, he discovered that he needed one after all, and to prove the point he had to have a sheepdog, a dog to work on the farm, not just any old mongrel with four legs and a tail. Red Rock was a working farm after all, not a zoo, Red Rock carried no passengers or pets, though everyone knew perfectly well the farm van would carry the next dog as it had Glen.

'Ah like wanna the litter fine,' he was saying, marching up and down Betty's sitting room. 'But ach, Ah don't know. Ah mean, is there work for another dog?' He took his beret off and scratched his head. 'Ah was thinkin' if Ah got this wee pup Ah'd call him Glen.' He shrugged. 'It's as good a name as any, an' Ah canny be bothered thinkin' up another wan. It won't know the difference anyway, will it? So,' he said in the same breath, turning to look at her, 'what's up?'

'What's up, Murdo?' Betty asked from her armchair. 'Well the game, the moon, the price o' dogmeat. Is that what ye mean?'

'Ye've no' said a word,' he said. 'What's up, then?'

'Murdo, son, Ah've been tryin' tae get a word in since the day ye were born. Ah don't bother noo, Ah just wait for ye tae pause for breath then Ah leap in. Nothin's up!'

'Aye well, if ye're sure. Ye don't want tae come in by an' have a wee hot chip?'

'Murdo, just go hame, it's late. But ask oor Neil tae come in, will ye?'

'Whit for?'

'Because Ah want tae see him, Murdo! There's a message Ah want him to get me in the mornin'.'

'Ah could get it.'

'Aye, Murdo, unless ye meet somebody on the road, or in the village, then we won't see ye till yon time!'

'Aye, well, ye canny just ignore folk, can ye?' he grinned, running his hand through his thick, steel-grey hair.

'Well *you* canny Murdo,' she replied tartly. 'Now go away hame, son. An' Ah'm tired, so send Neil in, an' that doesnae mean come wi' him!'

She had decided. She didn't want to see this lassie. She'd tell Neil to thank her civilly for the information she'd given him and Will, but to say she was quite happy and had no need of any more details. That was it. Best not stir things up. But Neil wasn't happy.

'Gran, Ah don't think ye've thought it over long enough,' he said. 'See, what ye've got tae consider is that this isnae just about you, is it? It's about all o' us. This lassie isnae just family tae you, but tae ma Da, God help her, an' tae Will an' Alibel, an' me an' a' the rest o' us.'

'But Neil, son, a' this is in the past!'

Neil looked at her thoughtfully. 'Know what it is, Gran?' he asked quietly. 'Ye're scared.'

'Scared? Why on earth would Ah be scared?'

'Ah don't know. Maybe you're scared that ye'll be hurt by what ye find out. Or maybe you're scared it'll make ye angry.'

'Don't be daft!'

'That's what Ah think, Gran,' Neil stated simply. 'Look, Ah canny see the lassie till the mornin' anyhow, think about it a bit longer. If ye still want tae send her away then, that's what we'll do.'

He was far shrewder than he seemed, that boy. He liked to give the impression that he sailed through life doing nothing in particular, with not a thought in his head. Not that she had ever thought that of course, she'd always known that he was a deep one pretending not to be, because it gave him the chance to live life as he wanted to. But he was probably right about her being scared. She couldn't explain why, but there was something holding her back. It was like when you'd set your heart on something, a dress, say, and you'd saved and saved every penny, constantly checking that nobody else had bought it, that it was still there. Then the day came when you had the money, and suddenly you started wondering if you really needed the dress, if you even wanted it, and if you bought it, how often would you wear it? It was in your grasp, all you had to do was reach out for it, then you realized that you hadn't wanted it all along. Its real value had been as a dream, as a diversion to amuse you and take your mind off the mundane routine of life. So you bought the weans something instead and went home just as happy.

So all that night in her bed at Red Rock, Betty Craig tossed and turned and got not a wink of sleep, while down the road a bit Marylka Kowalski did the same in Honeysuckle Cottage, neither one aware of the fears and worries of the other, far less that they were exactly the same. By morning they had both changed their minds many times over. 'Ah'll see the lassie,' Betty told Neil. It was the dress thing that had decided her. 'You bought the weans something instead,' she had remembered, and she would do this for them too. Neil was right, it was as much about their family history as hers; they had a right to know, even if she no longer wanted to.

When Neil arrived at Honeysuckle Cottage with the news though, he found Marylka packed and about to go.

'I've been thinking it over,' she said. 'You and your uncle were right, I don't think re-opening old wounds would be in your grandmother's interests. I shouldn't have come here, I should've left well enough alone.'

He studied her face for a moment. Another scared woman.

'Why are you afraid?' he asked quietly.

'Afraid? I'm not afraid! Why would I be afraid?' She hoped her voice didn't sound as shrill to him as it did to her.

'I don't know, but you are.'

They stared at each other.

'What have we got now?' she asked sarcastically. 'The psychologist postman?'

'And why are you angry at me?'

She ran her eye over his left jaw; a punch landed right on the cheekbone would leave him with a spectacular shiner for weeks.

'You *are* angry,' he said. 'You look as though you'd like to hit me.'

Marylka walked back into the cottage, playing for time, her back to him. 'Christ, sensitive, instinctive *and* gorgeous, but I wish he'd just disappear,' she thought. 'Look,' she said, turning to face him again and smiling as sweetly as she knew how. 'I've made up my mind. It's for the best, really.'

'That's not your decision to make,' he replied. 'We talked to Gran and she wants to speak to you. And this is about *my* family as well as yours. We're related.'

She lifted a suitcase and carried it to the door as though that would settle the matter, but he stepped forward and took it from her. 'Sit down,' he said firmly, and for no reason that she understood, she did as she was told.

'Neil, you don't understand,' she said wearily.

'So tell me.'

'It's all so hard!' she said. 'The story isn't as simple as I told you. You probably don't know about the Davidsons, but the family business isn't a corner shop, it's an enormous empire. Old Hector was a famous man.'

'I know that. Do you really think we don't read the newspapers up here? I know exactly who you are too.'

She looked up at him sharply. 'So what was all that old baloney about being a writer then?'

'Och, I'm a teuchter!' he grinned. 'We're expected to be either daft or devious, sometimes it's handy!'

'Twisted swine! So you read it all when my mother died?'

'Aye, but I don't think anyone else has put two and two together yet. You're a doctor, aren't you?'

She nodded. 'I suppose you know my shoe size as well!'

'Now you're being daft!'

'Maybe I am, but you don't know the worst of the story.

Neil, it's so awful that I'm not sure your grandmother will be able to take it.'

'A bit patronizing, don't you think? You haven't even met her, you don't know what she can take and what she can't.'

Marylka looked out of the window and far across the bay. 'OK. Here's one bit. Her father wasn't just killed in the war, he was shot as a deserter.' She turned to look at him. 'How do you think any woman in her eighties would take that? First of all she finds the father she never knew, she discovers he died in battle, then that he was a coward executed by his own side. He wasn't a coward of course,' she continued angrily, 'he was sick. He'd been badly injured at the Somme and was shell-shocked, but officially he was a coward.'

'You sound as upset as you think she'll be.'

'Well I know him now,' she smiled. 'There are letters between him and Lizzie. Reading them would . . . would . . .'

'Bring a tear to a glass eye?'

'Yes,' she laughed quietly. 'They'd do that all right. Lizzie was a nurse on the Western Front, she looked after him when he was injured. They were planning to get married, and when he was shot he didn't know she was pregnant. It's all horrific stuff, I felt bad enough, but how do you think she will feel? It's all so much more personal to her. Then there are the letters Lizzie wrote to her brother asking for help, which she didn't get.'

'Well,' he said after a while, 'you still have to tell her. You have no choice, Marylka.'

She sighed. He was right, she knew that, but all her instincts still told her to flee, not to get any more involved. 'Will you drive, then?' she asked.

'We'll go now,' he replied. He was obviously scared that if he let her out of his sight she might try to swim to the mainland, a well-founded fear as it happened.

'The thing is, we don't want my father to be about, and he's away today.'

'Why?' She imagined a huge, terrifying monster of a man.

'Well my father's a bit of a, um, he's a pest, I suppose! His name's Murdo, short for Murder, you'll understand why later. We'll keep him out of this as long as possible. It's best, take my word for it.'

On the way to Red Rock Neil gave her a running commentary on the scenery, but she wasn't listening. Her stomach was churning and her head ached from lack of sleep; it felt like old times at the Western, and how she wished she was back there. The farmhouse was a traditional, whitewashed, west coast house, with the doors and window surrounds painted a bright red; it was quite picturesque in its way. Betty's house was built on to the side of the main house like a granny flat, and inside she sat by the fireside. Marylka was amazed at the Davidson resemblance. Betty was more robust than Auntie Mary, but she too was under five feet tall, and had the same snow-white hair and blue eyes. As they shook hands she noticed the frightened expression in her eyes, and wondered if Betty was looking into hers and thinking the same.

'Do you want me to go, Gran?' Neil asked.
'No, stay,' she replied, looking at the files under Marylka's arm.
Marylka followed her gaze. 'It might be better if we sat at the table,' she said, 'There's a lot to get through.'
They got up and moved towards the table by the window.
Betty stopped. 'Where's your Da, Neil?'
'It's OK, Gran, he won't be back till late.'
Betty nodded, pulled out a chair and sat down.
Marylka wondered again just what Neil's father was like. 'What do I call you?' she asked. 'Mrs Craig?'
'We're family, lass,' Betty smiled tightly. 'Call me Betty.'
'Well, Betty,' she said, affecting her authoritative doctor's voice, 'a lot of what I have to tell you isn't pleasant. I'm sorry.'
Betty smiled across the table at her. 'Go on, then.'
And so she recounted the story of the Davidsons' emigration

from Oban to Glasgow, of the successful business and the sheer bloody-minded determination of Old Hector. She described Auntie Mary and Millie, Lizzie and the others, and explained that Christine had been a trophy Old Hector had awarded himself. After that came Young Hector, her mother, and herself. They were rich, she said, very rich, but an unhappy lot. If it hadn't been for Auntie Mary, Helen wouldn't have had any life at all, and neither would they now be sitting here.

'Old Hector called her "Bloody Mary" because she thwarted as many of his plans as she could. She discovered what he'd done to Lizzie and she made him pay for the rest of his life. He wanted a knighthood, but he never got it because she said she would expose the way he had treated his sister and her baby.'

Betty smiled; she liked Bloody Mary. Then just as suddenly her eyes welled up. She never knew Bloody Mary, and she never would.

Marylka stopped. 'Do you want me to go on?' she asked. Betty nodded. She brought out a thick pile of family photos.

'This Old Hector sounds a terrible man,' Betty said.

'He was,' Marylka replied. 'My mother always said he was so scared by the poverty he grew up in, that he spent his life getting richer just to get away from it. My mother saw good in everyone, though, even where there wasn't any. Old Hector stood on anyone to get on, his own family included.' She said sadly: 'Old Hector was a tyrant. He wanted everything done his way, he ruled the entire family.' To her surprise Betty and Neil looked at each other and started laughing.

'What is it?'

'Oh, nothing, lass,' Betty replied. 'It's just that we know someone exactly like that!' And the two of them laughed again.

Marylka found a photo of Old Hector and pushed it across the table.

'Oh, my God!' Betty said, showing the photo to Neil. 'Even the same hair, look!'

Neil put his arm around his grandmother and they shook with laughter again. 'Was he tall?' Neil asked.

'No, he wasn't. But my mother said he behaved as if he was. Even years later other people thought he'd been a big man because he yelled at them and ordered them about. He had a big personality and a big voice to go with it.'

Another burst of laughter.

'What?' Marylka asked, bemused. 'What is it?'

'You'll find out!' Neil said, and he and Betty chuckled to each other.

She passed over photos of the rest of the family, then the ones of Lizzie with the soldiers and the portrait of George MacDonald in uniform.

'This is your father,' she said.

Betty drew a sharp breath. 'It's you, Neil!' she said. She held the photo out to Neil then passed it back to Marylka. 'Look, lass,' she said. 'Take away the moustache and it's Neil to the life!'

Marylka looked at George's fresh young face again. Betty was right. When she first saw Neil there was something familiar about him, but now she recognized more than a passing resemblance between George and his great-grandson, not as much as Betty had seen, but still, she was pleased for the old woman, and for herself. She'd become very fond of George since she first 'met' him, of all the characters within this family drama it was George she had felt most for and about. She told the story of Lizzie's meeting with George, of his injuries, and how he'd been sent back into battle when he was still sick. Then very slowly she went over the circumstances of his death. It was the hardest thing she had ever done, worse, she decided than telling relatives that someone had died an hour ago, and she wasn't surprised when Betty lowered her head and wept silently. 'Whatever you do, don't feel any shame about that, Betty,' she said gently. 'He wasn't a coward, he was a boy who'd volunteered and fought in the trenches for three years already. His brothers were dead, he'd nearly died himself, and he was sick. If he'd have been an officer he'd have been sent to a special hospital and treated, but because he was only a private he was ordered to be shot instead. The army should feel ashamed, not George, and not us.'

Betty's head stayed down and Marylka looked at Neil, silently asking him what to do.

'Let's take a break, Gran,' he smiled. 'I'll make a cuppa tea.'

'Betty,' Marylka said gently. 'There are letters here between George and Lizzie. I'll leave them with you to read when you're alone. They're very sad, but they're beautiful too. You should read them in your own time.'

She thought about George's last letter on the morning of his execution, and the mourning brooch in its velvet pouch with the little note from Lizzie, and decided to keep them till later, till all of this had had a chance to sink in. It would be too much for the old woman, she decided, too cruel, and the honest truth was that she didn't think she could bear too much more herself. She decided to keep Auntie Mary's letter to Helen too. These things had kept all these years, she thought, they would keep a while longer.

27

As they left Red Rock Marylka felt drained. It had been a hard couple of hours, and yet at the outset of this adventure she had such high hopes, she had expected to bring some sort of joy to Betty. She was beginning to appreciate why Old Hector had called his sister 'Bloody Mary' too, she thought wryly. This was a beauty, an absolute corker to leave for someone else to carry out. And there was a slight insight into at least one of the reasons why Helen hadn't dealt with it, and Marylka was glad for her mother's sake that she hadn't. Helen had, as Auntie Mary said, a tender heart; this amount of emotion would have devastated her. Just as well really it had fallen to the nippy sweetie to do, she thought with a mocking smile, the nippy sweetie handling it as well as she was.

As she and Neil went through the door at Honeysuckle she asked him anxiously how he'd thought it had gone.

'As well as could be expected, Doctor,' he grinned.

'Oh, yes, very witty.'

'It did, though,' he said. 'What did you think would happen?'

'I didn't know. This isn't an area where I have any expertise. Cut your finger and I'll stitch it up, have a heart attack and I'll tell you what to do. But this . . .' She shrugged her shoulders. 'Will she be OK?'

'She's a tough old bird,' Neil said. 'And I'll keep an eye on her, don't worry. Look, I'd better go down to the school and bring Will up to date.'

'No, don't go. Phone him from here. There's more to come and I don't know how or when to tell Betty.'

*   *   *

While he spoke to his uncle on the phone she fished out Auntie Mary's letter. Apart from George's final letter and the brooch, she'd left everything else with Betty, who had promised to contact her through Neil when she wanted to talk again. But Auntie Mary's letter hadn't just asked for 'Lizzie's lassie' to be found, she wanted all her money to go to her as well, and Marylka had calculated that Betty had enough to think about for the moment. When Neil came off the phone he sat down on the sofa and she handed him the letter.

He started reading, and she watched the different expressions playing across his face. Occasionally he would look up at her and make a comment before going back to the letter. Eventually he finished, laid the pages down, and looked at her.

'That's the bit then? The money?'

'That's the bit. Seems to me that your family has managed pretty well without it. I just wonder whether Auntie Mary is doing you any favours.'

'So how much are we talking about? A few thousand?'

Marylka said nothing.

'Tens of thousands?'

'Keep going upwards,' she said. 'I haven't asked, but it's fairly safe to assume that we're talking into seven figures.'

'Dear God!' he said, his eyes wide. Then he started chuckling and Marylka raised her eyebrows. 'I was just thinking,' he laughed. 'You see, my Gran has always been a great one for the equality of man, she's the reddest thing about Red Rock. I wondered what it would do to her to be related to a rich family, but now I'm wondering how she'll take it once she discovers she's rich herself, a rich Red!'

When he'd gone she went over the day's events in her mind. It was a habit from her days as a houseman. You went to bed every night, if you were lucky, every second or third if you were average, and you'd go over everything you'd done, in case you'd missed something that would get you screamed at in the morning. It was better to know where the landmines were well in advance, then at least you had a chance of jumping clear of the consultants' tempers. Normally she could come up with a balanced view of how things had gone, but she was lost on this one. She couldn't tell if she'd done Betty Craig some enormous harm or not, and still her instinct was to leave quickly and never return.

She decided to keep her bags packed, just taking from them what she needed, re-packing what she didn't, and she found herself fantasizing about how and when she could escape from Eilean Òg. She wanted to go immediately this task was done, and if there was no ferry sailing due she'd hire a boat to take her home rather than stay on the island. If it came to it she'd hire a helicopter, anything except stay here longer than she had to. She wanted back to her life very badly.

And at Red Rock Betty's emotions were just as jangled and uncertain. Over the next two days she read and re-read everything Marylka had left, sometimes with Neil or Will to talk things over with, more often on her own. She found the letters between her parents almost unbearably poignant. There was so much she recognized from herself and Alec that she couldn't help identifying with the doomed young lovers who had been her parents. There was the Oban connection too, where the boat went to, where they had stayed on their surprise wedding trip. And the farming connection; they had always wondered at Murdo's love of the land and his easy way with the animals. She thought back with a kind of wonder to the day she and Alec had ended up married, and how they had walked past the Davidson office in St Vincent Place without knowing it. She remembered Alec buying tobacco for Old Murdo Young, then they had stopped to look up at the tall, elegant buildings, one of red sandstone between two of white stone. They had wondered what kind of grand people were in there, and all the time it was her own family. It was all very hard to take in.

Then she'd go back to Lizzie and George – Alibel would be so proud to discover her grandmother had been a nurse too. There were moments of elation, tempered by others of grief and anger at the sheer injustice of everything that had happened. It made you so angry that you wanted to do something, but there was nothing to be done, it was all over. At times she wished this lassie had never turned up, it was all so painful, and at others she almost hungered to hear more. Then Neil had brought her George's last letter to Lizzie. It was tragic. She ached to reach back through the years and put her arms around them.

'Dearest Lizzie,' it began. 'I know you have tried to get help for me, but please don't blame yourself, nothing could've saved me. They had already decided to make an example of me and maybe they were right to do so. But I can truthfully say, as God is my witness, that I can't remember leaving my post. I remember nothing until they found me and took me back to my unit. Even then I thought I had been walking not far away and got lost, but they said I'd run away. I hope you will always believe that I did not mean to be a coward and bring shame on you and on my family in Scamadale, and if I have, I beg that you will forgive me. You gave me the happiest months of my life, Lizzie, and if the Good Lord gave me the chance to save myself now, but took away the time we had together as the price, I would refuse. I am sorry I cannot give you everything I promised, and that we will never have the children we planned. I hope some day that you will find a good man to care for you as much as you deserve, but that somewhere in your heart you will remember the boy from Scamadale who loved you so much. May God protect you for ever. Your loving and devoted George.'

The lassie had thought she might have felt ashamed that George had been shot as a coward, but she didn't. She'd often seen pictures of the Great War and said she didn't know how anyone could have survived those experiences, and them that did must've been scarred for life afterwards. And there were those young laddies from the second war buried in the local cemetery, and Alec's brother Will. It was the pity of it that caused her tears. It had been there all her life, the inhumanity of those who thought the lives of others were expendable.

And how sad it was to hear of Martha dying all those years ago, yet no one from Glasgow Corporation had even thought of getting in touch with anyone on the island. When she'd been made to leave at sixteen and never got in touch again, they'd thought it was her choice. Many boarded-outs did the same if they moved on. They wanted to put their years of misery behind them and get on with their lives, and so it was understandable that they cut off all contact, all reminders of that part of their lives. But to think of the poor lassie being knocked down and killed like that, almost as soon as she'd arrived in Glasgow, and not a soul to mourn her. And what life had she had? A poor wee mite alone in the world, sent to slave for the Campbells at White Farm, without a scrap of love or happiness all of her short existence. Oh, let them talk to her of their God now if they dared, just let them!

In the days that followed that first meeting Marylka heard nothing directly from Betty, but Neil assured her she was doing all right. He had taken time off from his numerous jobs around the island to be Marylka's companion, and was highly amused that the islanders had decided he was romancing the rich lassie at Honeysuckle Cottage.

'They're saying we're carrying on!' he laughed. 'Isn't it great?'

'Oh, absolutely superb,' Marylka returned. 'I'm so glad you're getting so much enjoyment out of this. It's an ill wind as they say. By the way, won't you lose all your jobs spending all this time "carrying on" with me?'

'Och, my grandmother's a rich woman you know, she'll bung me a few bob to keep the wolf from the door! And you're not short of cash either come to that, I can be a kept man. Aye, I like that. I'm being kept by a rich floozy from the big city, that's the next bit of gossip that'll start! They're very good on islands at knowing everything, even if they have to make most of it up!'

'How do they know I'm rich?'

'Well you must be, stands to reason. You're in Honeysuckle Cottage, and that costs the earth to rent. Everyone knows that.'

'I see,' she replied, glad the entire island didn't know the exact details. 'And what about your lobsters? Aren't they missing your attentions?'

'Now you're being daft again!' he said. 'I always attend to my lobsters, you don't pay enough for my services to be a serious rival to them!'

They laughed. 'All those years studying medicine and I can't beat a lobster!' Marylka said.

'The gossip is doing me no end of good with my Da though,' he grinned. 'He keeps winking at me. He was scared I was homosexual, now he thinks I'm one helluva man, so he does. Any day now he thinks he'll have me married with a whole crowd of weans!'

'And why aren't you already?' Marylka asked. 'You're more or less presentable, cousin, you must have had your chances. No special girl, no secret love child?'

'No,' he replied firmly. 'And there won't be until I know what I'm doing and where I'm going.'

'That sounds profound!'

'Just practical,' he replied, the conversation turning as serious as his expression. 'On islands people tend to get together young, I think it's the boredom that does it.' He smiled a quick smile. 'I've known too many weans born by accident, and left to grow up as best they can without fathers. Maybe it was what happened to Gran and Grandpa that made me take more notice, but I don't think you should take things like that for granted.'

And while they waited for Betty to absorb all the information Marylka had given her, he told her of his grandmother's experiences as a boarded-out, about her slavery at White Farm, the way the islanders looked down on the boarded-outs, and the lack of love throughout her childhood. She had never forgiven the islanders for how they had treated her, and all the other children before and after her too, children with tragic back-grounds like Betty's. She wasn't an islander, she always made a point of saying that, neither did she want to be one of them. But she had been delivered here like a parcel and there was nowhere else for her to go. Well that was something that might have changed now, Marylka thought.

'So do you think she's wrong for feeling so bitter towards the islanders?' Marylka asked.

'Of course not!' he replied. 'Her feelings for Eilean Òg are based on her experiences, you can't tell someone their experiences are wrong, can you? But I was born at a different time and in different circumstances. What I'm saying is that her experiences aren't mine. This is where I was born. I don't like how my grandparents were treated, but I belong here.'

'And you wouldn't leave?'

He shook his head. 'Oh, I'd like to travel a bit. I love the sea. I'd love to sail around the world, but I couldn't live in a city, I'd always come back here,' he replied. 'What about you? Would you ever leave the city?'

'Never!' she said. 'I'm not a country type, never could be, would never want to be. I'm like you, I belong where I was born.'

'So are you missing the city now?'

'Yes, I am. Can't see the attraction of this place at all. It rains too much, and I keep looking for the towns and the cities, and there aren't any, there's just grass. Does that offend you?' she asked.

'Of course it doesn't offend me! What do you think I am, a big wean? It means we'll only ever see each other in passing though, and that's a shame.'

'Why?'

'Because we get on I suppose.'

Once he'd gone she thought about how different their lives were, and their outlooks. She had grown up cocooned by the

Davidson name and the Davidson fortune, but she had never really been aware of it. Helen made a point of keeping life as near to other people's as she could, though Marylka hadn't realized that for many years. There were no luxurious holidays in exotic locations, partly perhaps because Helen had hated her enforced visits to South Africa when she was a child, and no extravagant, expensive presents either. Marylka got no more pocket money than her school pals, and her uniform had been the one set by the school, so she hadn't felt any different from the others. The business was regarded as Helen's work, not as a family fortune, and she left it at the office when she came home. That was all because of Auntie Mary's influence, of course, because the old lady had instilled her values into Helen, and as Helen always said, no amount of money could make things right for Millie, could it? So it wasn't the cure-all everyone thought it was.

But there were differences of course, though again Marylka hadn't been aware of them as a child. There was no anxiety about paying bills, no fears about the future, and that must have an effect on people. Often she had known patients suffering from serious illnesses, who only thought about when they could get back to work, because if they didn't their families would suffer. It did no good to remind them that their families would suffer more without them, because that wasn't the point. The point was that the rent had to be paid, and the electricity. She had never admitted it to anyone, but until she got her own flat she had no idea that you had to pay for gas and electricity; she knew they'd laugh if they knew. But because bills hadn't been a problem for her family they were never discussed, they were simply dealt with, so how was she to know?

The flat had been a luxury, she knew that. It was only when her mother bought it for her that she understood she came from a wealthy family, before that she thought she was the same as everyone else. And all the time the Craigs were on this island, working for every penny, worrying about the harvest or the prices at the markets. Though Red Rock wasn't a big, rich farm, they were better off than many, as Neil readily conceded, but still their lives depended on things often outwith their control, and on constantly working to bring in money to get by on. That was a concept that wasn't natural to her, she had never been aware of real need in her life. Even now, Neil stayed with his family because much of the housing on the island had been bought by outsiders, to be used as holiday homes for a few weeks a year. People from the mainland, often from England, paid hugely inflated prices for property, outbidding local people who lived and worked on the island and had families there. 'They're called White Settlers,' Neil grinned. 'Or Ferry Loupers! But the truth is that most of us were, a generation or so ago, some whether they chose to be or not.'

It was a week before Betty felt up to talking to Marylka again, but it was an easy, companionable time, and she managed to fight the urge to leave. Neil decided to bring Betty to Honeysuckle Cottage, because his father was eagerly awaiting Marylka's arrival at Red Rock, to announce what he was convinced would be impending nuptials. Murdo would, he said, 'descend', if he spotted her at Betty's home. When she saw Betty again Marylka wondered why she'd been so worried; the woman was obviously a Davidson to her fingertips, she was indestructible. They sat by the window and went through the social niceties of coffee, biscuits and stilted small talk.

'Well now, lass,' Betty said. 'There are things I want to ask, if that's all right with you.'

'Of course.'

'Do you know where my mother and father are buried?'

'Yes, I do. There's one more letter for you to read from Auntie Mary.'

'Bloody Mary?' Betty smiled.

'That's right!' Marylka laughed. 'Lizzie was buried in a small cemetery in Glasgow without any markings, but Mary found it and had a headstone put up. George was buried in a village in France.'

'Have you been there?'

Marylka shook her head.

'I'd like to go.'

'Fine, that can be arranged,' Marylka replied. 'And you must have family around Oban too. Your father had a younger brother and two sisters. I'm sure we'll be able to find someone.'

'Well, that's fine, then. Neil here can take me.'

Marylka looked at Neil. Should she mention the money now? He looked away, laughing quietly to himself. 'Well, you're a lot of help!' she thought.

'There's more Betty, there's something I have to tell you.'

'You'll love this, Gran!' Neil chuckled.

'Shut up, you!' Marylka said. 'It's about Auntie Mary's letter, the one she left for my mother asking her to find you. You see there was a lot of money, and she wanted you and your family to have it.'

Betty looked from Marylka to Neil.

'A *lot* of money!' Neil laughed.

Marylka drew him a look of annoyance.

'He's right, Betty, though he could be a bit more serious about it. You'll have to see the family solicitor to find out how much, but it will be a lot.'

Betty looked at them blankly.

'Well,' Neil laughed. 'How does it feel to be a traitor to the cause, *Mistress Campbell*, you rich bitch!'

'I've been thinking,' Marylka said, ignoring the interruption. 'You could come across to the mainland when you're ready. There's no one in my family home in Bearsden, I've had my own flat for a long time. You can use the house as a base if you want.'

Still Betty said nothing.

'Well, say something!' Neil said.

'When's the next boat?' she asked.

The news that he wasn't about to marry off his only son did not go down well with Murdo Craig. When the purpose of

Marylka's arrival was explained to him he was forced to have a few blasts of Vino Collapso to cheer himself up. The end of his mother's search for her roots gave him no pleasure, and Auntie Mary's legacy made no impact either. Murdo was of the mind set that you only needed as much money as you needed, and once you had that anything more had no value. A family do was organized anyhow, to welcome Marylka and introduce her to the rest of the clan. As she entered Red Rock Murdo's first words were 'Where's your man?'

'What man?'

'So ye've no man then? You're no' wanna they lesbians are ye?'

Marylka noticed that unlike the rest of the Craigs, Murdo spoke to her in his own dialect. This was a man who made no concessions, she sensed, and much to her shock and horror he even looked like Old Hector.

'No, I'm not a lesbian!' Marylka replied, and a voice inside her head said 'I can't beleive I'm actually answering that question!'

'Well, then,' Murdo continued, 'ye can marry this son 'o mine if ye like. He's no' married either.'

'Well she canny do that Da,' Neil said. 'Whit would Tarquin say?'

'Who's Tarquin?' Marylka asked.

'That's his boyfriend,' Murdo replied.

She spun round and looked at Neil. 'Wha . . . ?'

'Forget it,' he smiled, waving his hand dismissively. 'I'll explain later.'

'They tell me you're a doctor,' Murdo said. 'Ah do a wee bit doctorin' masel'.'

'That's novel,' Marylka thought. 'A medical farmer. Interesting.'

'Would ye like a wee taste o' my home brew?' Murdo asked her.

'*Murdo!*' Catriona warned from behind him. 'Ye're no giein' the lassie any Vino Collapso! Behave yersel'!'

'Och, don't say she doesnae drink!' he shouted. 'Christ, a

lesbian an' TT as well. Does she have her ain teeth d'ye think?'

Marylka had no idea what her teeth had to do with anything, but Murdo quickly cleared up the confusion.

'Naebody's natural anymerr,' he complained. 'The world's a queer place.' He looked at Neil. 'Especially where Tarquin's concerned.'

'Who the hell's Tarquin?' she asked, exasperated.

'I told you,' Neil replied. 'Don't ask.'

Murdo was already in full flood in another direction, though. 'So ye've got a lotta money Ah hear,' he said conversationally. 'How much have ye got exactly?'

He was quite unlike anyone she'd met in her life. She wasn't sure whether he was deliberately rude or simply being himself.

'How much have *you* got?' she shot back at him.

Everyone laughed, Murdo too, but he didn't reply. She had a sense of scoring a point. Neil put his arm around her shoulder.

'I did say you'd find out about my Da, didn't I?' he grinned, and Marylka nodded. 'Well, here he is. It doesn't get much better I'm afraid.'

And as she listened to Neil she could also hear Murdo speaking in the background – did the man have any other way except yelling? – and the others saying 'Wheesht!' and trying to shut him up.

'Look at that!' he was saying. 'He's got his arm around her an' she's lettin' him! Looks tae me as though he's got further than that tae! Whit? Whit?' he was demanding, his face a picture of innocence and purity. 'Whit have Ah said noo? Ah'm just sayin' she's used tae him touchin' her! Where's the harm in that?'

'*Murdo!*' Catriona shouted back, and beside Marylka Neil laughed and shook his head.

'Has anyone ever thought of punching him?' she asked.

'Lots of people,' Neil said. 'All through his life. He just laughs. He offends everybody, yet I've never known him take offence himself. I don't think there's anything can be done about him.'

'Well there's a few drugs we could try. Cyanide to start with.'

'And do you think we've not tried that already?' muttered Betty watching Catriona trying to reason some politeness into her big son.

'And belladonna, and arsenic. The bugger's immune to everything, take it from me!'

She liked them all, the whole, noisy rabble of them. Her mother had always regretted that there were no good men in Marylka's life, every one was either a despot or a coward, in some cases possibly both. Helen worried that it had put her off men for life, and it had made her more wary, she had to admit that. But there were good men in her life now, a wealth of them, and though they'd appeared too late for Helen to know them, she already felt confident enough with them to want Betty's family around in the future. Will was a quiet but decent man, with a pleasant wife and three children. His son, Sandy, like his uncle Murdo, was a natural farmer. He worked with Murdo, though no one knew how he managed it, and it was agreed that one day he'd take over Red Rock with Neil's best wishes, and while he did whatever he ended up doing with his life. By that time Murdo and Catriona should have moved into Betty's house, but as everyone said, that way lay insanity. There was no way that Murdo could live so close by without interfering in how Sandy was doing everything. Alibel was a younger version of Betty, and her husband Lachie was obviously devoted to her, and to the entire Craig family, though as Alibel herself had been known to say, no one would ever know for sure if he'd only married her to gain Murdo as a brother-in-law. As Alibel left to return to her own home that day, though, Marylka was aghast at what she thought was yet another of Murdo's natural gaffes.

'How much have ye had tae drink?' he demanded of his sister.

'Hardly a drop!' she replied, looking flustered. 'Now you be quiet, Murdo! Lachie, make him behave!'

'Where's her bag?' Murdo shouted to the assembled company. 'Don't let her oota here before we have a look!'

The bag was located and turned out without any ceremony by Murdo.

'Right,' he said looking around, 'does anybody see anythin' here that belongs tae them?'

In the background Alibel was protesting loudly, but he took no notice, even when no one claimed anything from the pile of contents he was roughly shoving back into her bag.

'Right, Catriona, take her through the kitchen an' don't let her oota yer sight! Lachie, you hold her arms tae her sides till she's strapped into the car!'

'What on earth's going on?' Marylka whispered to Neil, as Alibel was marched through the kitchen and out of the house, with Murdo giving loud instructions all the way.

'Och well, Alibel has a condition,' he grinned. 'She suffers from alcoholic kleptomania. When she as much as sniffs booze she kinda takes things that don't belong to her.'

'Things?'

'Aye. Anything really. I've lost count over the years, let's see now. Somebody's washing, the plug for the bath, empty milk bottles, hats, coats, the odd chicken, alive or dead. That sort of thing. The last time she had a sherry here she took Da's dinner out of the oven and he's had a job forgetting it, that's why he's making a fuss.'

'But I saw him pouring her a drink earlier.'

'Aye, well, that's the thing about my Da, he likes to exploit other people's weaknesses. He's an evil big bugger really! What you have to do is stand up to him or ignore him, and Alibel being his wee sister, she's never quite managed either.'

Later, she gave him the velvet pouch containing the mourning brooch with Lizzie and George's photos and the note from Lizzie. She had intended giving it to Betty earlier at the house, but there were too many people there.

★　　★　　★

'Give it to her when she's alone,' she told him, 'and stand by for tears.'

'Och, that's not fair!' he said. 'George's letter was bad enough. Why can you not do it yourself?'

'Because, Neil, I'm leaving first thing in the morning.'

'Oh,' he said quietly. 'I see.'

28

She had been home in Glasgow for four days and Marylka still couldn't stop pinching herself. At she waited on the pier on Eilean Òg, she had been so anxious to get on the boat for the return journey that she could barely sit still in the car. 'Something's bound to go wrong,' she thought. 'The damn thing will sink before my eyes and I'll be trapped here for weeks. Or my booking's gone missing and they won't let me on.' In which case, she decided, she'd abandon the car, run on to the ferry, lock herself in the first toilet she could find and refuse to come out till she saw Oban.

As the boat finally berthed at Oban, she had an irrational moment of panic that a huge hand would reach down out of the sky, pick her up and take her back to Eilean Òg. She made up her mind to self-combust if that happened. Arriving back in Glasgow she greeted every landmark. 'Hello, Great Western Road!' she yelled cheerfully. 'How ya doin', Botanic Gardens? Hi there, you gorgeous BBC studios!' Once inside her flat in Byres Road again, she walked around touching everything. Two weeks she'd been away, and she'd planned to stay away for six months! 'I'd have *died*!' she thought, happily filling her own kettle, in her own kitchen, in her own abode. She'd handed the keys of Honeysuckle Cottage to Neil and suggested he could make use of the remaining five and a half months of the lease. 'It's time you got away from your parents,' she told him, 'especially Murder!' He'd liked the cottage from the moment he'd stepped inside, and soon she was pretty sure he'd have the wherewithal to buy it. It could be his own little niche, somewhere to come back to in between adventures on the high seas.

He had taken up so much of her affections that it was funny to think that a few weeks ago she hadn't even heard of him, far less met him. They 'got on', as he'd said, and Betty had noticed it too.

'You two make a very handsome couple!' she'd told Marylka quietly. 'And I'm not just saying that because it would please Murdo!'

'Oh, stop matchmaking!' Marylka had replied. 'We hardly know each other! But I must confess that he's the most man I've ever met, Betty. And I mean Neil, not Murdo! But there's no chance. I couldn't live on this or any other island without going insane, and he couldn't live in a city.'

'Och, lassie! All men can be made to change their minds!' Betty replied.

'And do I strike you as the kind of female who'd take the kind of male whose mind can be changed?'

Betty said nothing, but reached out and touched her hand with an understanding smile.

Today she had a meeting with Ali MacKay at the hospital; she'd arranged it the minute she came back home. She had done a lot of thinking during her time on Eilean Òg and she wanted to discuss her ideas with him. After that she would see Rob to report back and then, well then she'd see.

Ali was sitting in his study, the pipe in its usual position.

'I've always meant to ask you,' she said. 'Is there anything in that pipe?'

'Of course not!' he replied. 'Not *now*. There is sometimes. Very rarely, actually. Well, yes. But only sometimes. And what a silly question, Doctor! Don't you know that smoking's bad for you?' he demanded, then chuckled to himself. 'I use it as a prop, if you must know, because it gives me a certain authority, don't you think? A certain patrician air! Now what have you been up to since we last met?'

She told him of Eilean Òg and the family she had discovered there, and the heights and depths of emotions they had scaled together.

'Sounds as though you've gone through a wider and deeper gamut of feelings than at any time in your life. Would that be right?' he smiled.

'Yes, it would. And I don't know how to put this, but it's somehow helped put my mother's death into some sort of perspective, into an order. It's like a piece of mosaic, not a particularly brightly coloured one, but you need dark ones in the picture too, don't you?'

Ali nodded. 'Ah, the rich mosaic of life!' he said, looking inscrutable. 'So much prettier than a tapestry, I always think, and it's very poetic too!'

'Yes, I have noticed that tendency of late, and it worries me! And I've been thinking. I want to stay in medicine, but I'd like to look closer at the emotional side of things. Is there any chance that I could work alongside you? I know I'll have to wait till there's a Senior House Officer vacancy, but I'll do something else till your present chap trots off. All I want to know is whether you think it's a goer?'

'Oh, I say!' he said delightedly. 'I've turned you, haven't I? Ha ha ha! They'll stop looking in your eyes soon!'

'As long as they stop pouring on the Old Spice,' she laughed. 'Well? What do you think?'

'I think you may well be in luck,' he said, removing his empty pipe from his mouth. 'And you have that fine chap Graham Spencer – ah, God bless Newcastle! – to thank for it.'

'Now that's downright unnatural!' Marylka grimaced. 'What's he ever done to deserve thanks?'

'It's called the Pecking Order Syndrome,' he said with mock seriousness. 'With Spencer's departure to minister to those lucky, lucky Geordies, the post of Senior Registrar in Cardiology became vacant, allowing Dr Paton, the Cardiology Registrar, to move up. Our SHO has applied for his job and looks set to get it, and if he does, that will leave his post up for grabs. I can't promise anything, but I would advise you very strongly to apply.'

'You're a genius!' she laughed delightedly.

'Well, if you say so,' he grinned. 'Personally I think I've only reached semi-genius level.'

'Y'know, Spencer tried to warn me off associating with you last time I saw him, said you'd turned a perfectly normal houseman into a psychiatrist. But even a semi-genius wouldn't do such a thing, would he?'

'Well, he had the story half-right,' Ali replied, smiling at her expression, 'which is more than he managed for his patients!' He lay back in his chair. 'For some reason, the boy was already determined to become a psychiatrist; he came to this unit because I was here. Which proves, of course, that he hadn't completely gone to the dark side!' He laughed quietly. 'He still became a psychiatrist, but I like to think I let some light in there all the same. I'd imagine – or maybe I just hope – that he's not as quick as his colleagues to dope people to the eyeballs, or to prescribe ECT.' He snorted derisively. 'ECT! The watch is broken, therefore I'll jump on it and it will work,' he said, shaking his head. 'How can you administer treatment when you don't know how it works? Anyway, unusually for him, our dear friend Spencer was partially correct. I didn't turn the boy, so much as interfere with his worst intentions, but the myth took hold and I got the full blame.' He sighed. 'It's a hard life even for semi-geniuses, young Doctor Kowalski. It's not all rich mosaics, y'know!'

As she left his study she looked back. 'Incidentally, I'm a bit curious. Who do you talk to when things get bad?'

'Oh, I talk to the dog,' he replied.

'The *dog?*'

'Yes. I call him in and put my problems to him, and he solves them.'

'Really?' Marylka raised her eyebrows.

'Nothing's stumped him yet. He just lies there on the rug, listening, then he gets up and leaves when I've finished talking, and takes all my problems with him. Don't know what I'd do without him. He's marvellous.'

'So how does that actually work then?'

'How should I know?' he asked. 'You never question a *real* genius at work!'

'You're nothing but an old quack really, aren't you?' she asked.

'So I've been told!' the distinguished consultant replied thoughtfully. 'But then, to be sure I'd have to ask the dog . . .'

After seeing Ali she phoned Fiona and arranged to pick her up later for lunch. First of all she had to see Rob to bring him up to date with the great quest. Betty and some of the family would be coming over to the mainland in a week or so to stay at Helen's house, so that Betty could meet Rob to sort out the legal niceties of Auntie Mary's will. As she went over her adventures he sat across his desk listening to her like the diligent solicitor he was, nodding and looking serious. Once it was all explained she waited for him to talk.

'So, no big, hairy, tartan-clad, macho man then?' he asked.

'That's all you have to say?' she demanded.

'Well it's been on my mind,' he said apologetically. 'In fact I was tempted to drop everything and come over, but that would've been irresponsible.'

'As well as impromptu, on the spur of the moment, spontaneous, and possibly fatal to your constitution as a result, Rob,' she thought.

'Well, the only attractive man I met was my cousin Neil, and I think he'll want to stay at Honeysuckle Cottage, so could you get on to this stockbroker chap and beat him down to something affordable please?'

'How did you know the owner was a stockbroker?' he asked.

'Everyone on Eilean Òg knows that. His great-grandfather came from the place, he restored the cottage and doesn't want to sell but has to.'

'We went to school together actually,' Rob said. 'His wife hates the place and refuses to go back.'

'I have a certain sympathy with his wife,' Marylka replied.

'The island life not your cup of tea then?'

'Not even a sip.'

'That's good,' he said as though he was addressing a judge, 'because I want to talk to you about something.'

'Oh God! Here it comes!' she thought.

'Marylka, you and I have known each other almost all our lives, and you must know how I feel about you,' he said stiffly.

She looked at the floor-to-ceiling bookcases behind him, the books standing in serried ranks. Somewhere in there must be the very one he cribbed this speech from. He should throw it out.

'Rob,' she said, 'please stop. This won't work, honestly.'

He looked hurt.

'And don't look like that. Rob, you're very good at logic, you should be able to see what I'm saying. You like me because your father has always thought we would make a neat match. I'm sure he and both Hectors have discussed it over the years, especially recently, then you could take over at the helm of the Davidson empire. And you like the mad things I do and say, things that you would never dare. Am I right?'

'Well I do rather admire your ability to be naughty occasionally,' he grinned sheepishly.

'Yes, as long as it's at a distance,' she explained. 'If we got together we'd destroy each other. No, that's not true,' she grinned, 'I'd destroy you. Imagine it, Rob. You've just been made President of the Law Society, or the Bar Ping Pong Team, and you're wearing your official robes or whatever, so they take a picture for the archives. And when it comes out, your good lady wife is standing beside you pulling a crossed-eyed face and sticking her teeth out.'

She rifled about in her bag and brought out the photo Helen had carried in her purse, inside the black coal sack, the photo of herself in her academic robes on graduation day. 'Look,' she said, handing it over. 'That face.'

Rob studied the photo, his brow slightly furrowed. 'But you won't always want to pull silly faces at the wrong moment, Marylka,' he laughed. 'We all have to grow up!'

'Ah, but Rob, that's the point, two points actually,' she sighed. 'First of all I *will* always do those things, that's *me*, and second, what you see as the wrong moment, I see as the right moment. We're too different, Rob, we always will be. I'm funny as long as I don't have any connection to you. If I did, then I'd be embarrassing. Do you see what I mean?'

Going down in the lift after her chat with Rob she thought she probably had matured; not long ago she'd have simply told him to 'Bog off', and left it at that. She took a deep breath. Today she would clear up loose ends, attend to all those things that had been hanging untidily around her life. Young Hector was next. She had been wrestling with the dilemma of whether to tell him the whole story of his horrible old father's worst deed, the worst one that had come to light so far, anyhow. He was seventy-eight years old, was it fair to drop this in an old man's mind? 'Rubbish!' she thought, 'He's like all the rest of the clan, tough as old boots!' But was she doing it for the right reasons, or was she taking revenge on him, making him the scapegoat for her feelings about the Davidsons? But even if there was an element of that, he could hardly not be informed when an entire missing arm of the family suddenly appeared, especially as they'd be in her mother's house. The tale could be censored of course, the most painful details could be left out, leaving his devotion to Old Hector intact. 'No,' she thought, 'that isn't an option.' After all, the one who had faced most pain had been Betty Craig, and she had taken it on the chin. Young Hector wasn't much of a man, she knew, but he would have to be enough to do the same.

At the St Vincent Place office, she stopped off first to talk to Annie, her mother's secretary. It would be the last time she would ever look inside the inner room where her mother had worked, the last time she would ever see that roll-top desk that had played such a part in Old Hector's act of betrayal. He had harmed everyone, not just Lizzie and her lassie, but the entire family; they had all been marked by the shame of it, they always would be, and that damn desk sat there, like a monument to it.

Her mother's room looked so empty. It was a strange thing to think, because it was no longer in use and so obviously was empty. First of all Helen had gone, and then she and Annie between them had removed all traces of her ever being there, so of course it would be empty. But there wasn't even the slightest whiff of her perfume any longer; Helen had *completely* gone. A vase of fresh flowers sat on her desk, a token of affection from Annie seven months on. But soon Annie would leave too and there would be no link left with Helen, no one to leave flowers.

She told Annie of her discovery of the Davidson islanders, and smiled at the 'Oohs', 'Aahs', and 'Fancy thats!' in response to the tale.

'And Helen knew?' Annie asked in surprise.

'She knew what Old Hector had done,' Marylka told her. 'She hadn't tried to do anything about it, though.'

'There was something,' Annie said. 'Remember I said that? There was something on her mind, but I thought she was trying to summon up the courage to quit, and go and do all those things she wanted to do.'

'So now I'm going to tell Young Hector.'

'Oh, Marylka! Do you think you should? He's an old man now, what good would it do?'

'Annie, everyone has protected him all his life, apart from his ghastly old father, that is. Mum took on the business for him, she did all the work and still gave him star billing as though he was in charge. Even when she died I wasn't going to let him see her in case it upset him. At all costs everybody had to protect Young Hector. Well this time he'll have to face up to the facts. He's going to have to meet these people – his family.

I can hardly tell him I found the whole damn lot under a gooseberry bush, can I?'

Annie nodded. She looked convinced, but Marylka suspected she could put together the opposite argument and convince her of that too. They had all been brainwashed into treating her grandfather with kid gloves for far too many years, but even when you knew that it wasn't easy to go against that.

'Do you want me to buzz him and say you want to see him then?'

'Yes, Annie, that's a good idea,' she replied. 'But there's something I've been wondering about, maybe you can help. Remember the day Mum died?'

Annie bit her lip. 'You know, it's silly, but I still have trouble with that,' she smiled weakly. 'The notion of just saying she's dead. It makes it so final somehow. Daft, isn't it?'

'I know, Annie, you almost feel like a traitor for going forward. I was looking at a photo of her the other day, and for some reason it suddenly felt like looking at a photo of someone from the past, someone who was dead. D'you know what I mean? It wasn't just a photo of Mum, but of how she *used* to look. When she was alive.'

They sat silently thinking their thoughts, then Marylka pulled herself together.

'Well, enough of the morbid stuff!' she said brightly. 'On that last day she left before three o'clock to go shopping, didn't she? Yet she hadn't bought anything and she still left the car park at six o'clock.'

'That's what she said she was doing,' Annie smiled, 'but I happen to know that she didn't!'

'Come on, then, out with it! Don't just sit there looking smug!'

'Well, one of the office juniors saw her in Ingram Street just after four,' Annie said. 'The girl had gone to get tickets from the Ramshorn Theatre, and she saw Helen.'

'What was she doing?'

'Just walking, the girl said. Looked perfectly happy just walking and looking about.'

'Oh, well, bang goes the gigolo theory,' Marylka thought. 'Pity!'

But of course, Ingram Street. It was all there. Wee Harry, the Fruit Market, the horses she'd been scared to pass as a child because of their eyes, the Foulis brothers under the pavement, the fire station – God! Helen's thing about firemen! And the Ramshorn Kirk, their church. All those walks with Auntie Mary and Millie. She'd been retracing her childhood footsteps. She'd spent her last hours on earth reviving memories of the happiest times of her childhood with Bloody Mary!

Young Hector looked terrified as she walked in and sat down opposite him. Last time she'd been here she'd shouted at him and all but called him a creep and a lousy father. No, she *had* called him a lousy father, come to think of it. He must be sitting there wondering what little harangue would be forthcoming today. She smiled, trying to set him at ease. 'That's it, Marylka,' she thought. 'Lull him into a false sense of security, why don't you!' 'Grandfather, you know how you've always wondered why Old Hector didn't get a knighthood? Well, I've something to tell you,' she began, and as the story unfolded his expression didn't alter. 'And now they'll be coming to stay at Mum's house to sort out the legal details with Rob, so you're bound to meet them,' she finished.

He sat looking at her but said nothing.

'One of the family was in the Merchant Navy during the war, he was killed on convoy duty,' she said, reminding him of his Royal Navy days in an attempt to get some reaction, but he only stared wordlessly at her. She tried again. 'Would you like to read the papers and letters?' she asked.

He looked stunned.

'Look, I'll leave you to digest this,' she said quietly. 'Give me a ring if you want to talk.' She got up and walked to the door.

'The old bastard!' she heard him say behind her.

'What, Grandfather?'

'That miserable, contemptible, old bastard!'

Marylka had never heard him swear in her entire life. If she as much as said 'Damn' in his presence he'd wrinkled up his well-bred nose and ask her not to use such language. 'Pardon, Grandfather?' she asked.

Young Hector got up from his desk, and moved towards the rogues' gallery of framed photos of himself with his father that filled the walls and almost every surface. With one sweep of his arm he knocked the prized collection on to the floor, and there was a loud crashing noise as the glass broke into shards. Marylka watched, mesmerized, as her aristocratic, beautifully suited, debonair grandfather proceeded to jump up and down on the shattered remains in his hand-stitched shoes.

'All my life he force-fed me with stuff about upholding family honour and not letting him down. The filthy, two-faced, double-dealing, manipulative bastard!'

Marylka stood at the door trying to stifle great waves of choking laughter.

'Bloody Mary the old bastard called her! Bloody Mary! She was the only honourable member of the family! She should be called *Saint* Mary!'

'Oh no, Grandfather,' Marylka giggled. She was fighting an urge to join him in his war dance, but this was his show, he deserved his moment of rage, she thought. 'She liked being called Bloody Mary, it proved that she was winning!'

She stood at the door watching him, wondering still at how graceful he was as he cursed and rampaged about his office, throwing furious punches at anything connected with Old Hector. He was a picture of perfectly controlled rage, there was nothing common or vulgar about him even as he wreaked mayhem on his office. 'Another dream realized!' she thought merrily, as Young Hector continued to trash his office. She opened the door to find his secretary standing outside, her eyes wide, her face almost pale with fear.

'I think you could maybe get some big containers,' she told her. 'Something strong, something that will take broken glass, and take them into Young Hector's office. But not for a while.' She started to move towards the outside door. 'Oh,' she said as an afterthought, 'what does Young Hector drink?'

'Apart from champagne?' his secretary asked.

'Naturally!' Marylka thought. 'Yes, apart from champagne.'

'Brandy, sometimes.'

'Well, wait till ten minutes of silence have passed, then take him in a glass and a bottle, but be ready to duck just in case! Then I'd just stand back. There could be rather a lot of very rude Navy songs coming from in there! And don't call the police unless he actually comes through the wall!'

In the corridor between Young Hector's office and Helen's, Annie was watching anxiously. 'What's happening?' she whispered to Marylka.

Marylka put her arms about Annie and held on to her, still shaking with laughter. 'I think it's what the experts call "closure",' she chuckled. 'And whatever you do, don't risk walking along the pavement under his window for a while!'

Once outside she collected her car from Mitchell Lane '£5.20! Scandalous!' – and drove round the never-ending one-way-street system that served as traffic control in Glasgow. Past George Square, its gardens now almost all covered over with bright red asphalt, of all things. Helen would've been outraged, she would've regarded it as the desecration of an old friend, and who could blame her? By destroying the Square the Council had probably saved one gardener's wage, giving them that much more to spend on civic bean feasts. Turn right past the City Chambers, then second left into Ingram Street. She drove along slowly, imagining her mother walking here on that slushy, wet day last February. At the end, just past what used to be the fire station, she turned left into High Street, on to Castle Street, then right at the Royal Infirmary, towards the entrance to the Necropolis. Getting out of the car she walked to the family crypt, and standing outside she addressed Old Hector.

'Listen, you horrible, nasty old man! I've got a few things to tell you. Bloody Mary has had the last laugh. We all know what you did to Lizzie and to her lassie. I've found her and her family, and they're going to get all that lovely cash Mary left them, cash *you* made for the business. How's that for revenge, then? Your son's down in St Vincent Place calling you all sorts of bastards, ripping up your photos and getting drunk, and your empire's about to fold because there's no one to take it over. The Highland faerie woman was right, she got you in the end. Oh, and another thing. Lizzie's lassie had two sons, think about that, *sons*, and now she's got grandsons and great-grandsons, and every one is a decent man.' She stopped for a moment, thinking of Murdo. A picture of him popped into her mind; he was smiling his infuriating smile, the beret he wore for work sitting at a rakish angle on his head. How did she describe Murdo? 'One of them's a bit like you,' she said, 'a bit weird, but a good man for all that. He's a tyrant, but he has feelings, he loves his family and they love him.' That would have to do; she would defy anyone to encapsulate the undiluted essence, the wonder that was Murdo. 'If you'd been half the man he is, Lizzie's family could be keeping your rotten business going, but more importantly, they'd have been part of this family. Well, you lost a lot of good years for us, but they're part of the family now, the best part. So how does it feel to lose you miserable old teuchter?'

She was probably just imagining it, but she could have sworn she heard someone inside the crypt laughing quietly, and a delicate, ladylike voice in her head saying, 'Well done, nippy sweetie!'

*　　*　　*

She was late arriving back at the hospital to pick Fiona up for lunch, so she wasn't surprised when she wasn't waiting outside. But when she went inside to look for her she found reception deserted, and everyone, including Fiona, in the examination room. The place was so crowded with people that it looked like a major accident, in which case she decided to get as far away from the proceedings as possible, leaving them all to it. Then she noticed that everyone was laughing and decided it must be some sort of orgy. Fiona appeared, caught her arm and dragged her inside.

'You've got to see this!' she laughed. 'Mad Mick's been stabbed!'

'So why are you laughing, you weird person?' Marylka demanded.

'Come in, come in!' Fiona replied.

Inside the examination room Andy was telling all and sundry what had happened, and there wasn't a dry eye in the house. Meanwhile Mad Mick lay on an examination couch being ignored and shouting objections. It seemed that the two paramedics had been called to attend to a fracas between two drug addicts over some dodgy heroin. Mick and Andy had succeeded in getting one into the ambulance, leaving him lying on the left side of the vehicle, before retrieving the second one. While Andy was attending to the various cuts and bruises of the first one, Mad Mick had put the other one on the right side, but he was still annoyed apparently, and on seeing his fellow druggie he had lunged at him with a knife, only Andy was between them with his back to the knife. Mad Mick had caught the movement out of the corner of his eye, and to save his partner he'd dived between the knife and Andy, taking the blow himself.

'An' that's when it got really daft!' Andy said. 'The guy got Mick in the right shoulder, an' Mick was that angry he nutted him! Ah turned roond tae see Mick wi' him on the deck, gettin' laid tae him, an' could Ah prise the daft bugger aff?'

In the background Mad Mick was loudly demanding treatment, so while everyone else was enjoying Andy's tale, Marylka wandered over to lift the dressing on Mad Mick's shoulder and examine the wound. The mad one looked up and stopped mid-yell.

'Oh, hello, Darling!' he said switching instantly from plaintive wail to his playboy voice. 'Ah thought ye'd run oot on me. Couldnae resist the sex appeal, eh?' His nearly crossed eyes leered at her, affecting a wink through the cracked glass in his specs.

'Shut up, Mick,' she said in reply.

'Have you set the wedding date yet, Darling?' he continued. 'Ah've seen this nice wee Merc Ah'd be willing to accept as your giftie to the groom, Darling!'

'Shut up Mick,' Marylka said again. The wound wasn't serious, so she replaced the dressing and turned back to Andy for the rest of the story.

'Ye're no' just gonny leave me here tae bleed tae death are ye?' Mick screeched.

'Ssh!' Marylka said. 'Andy's talking! Anyhow, it's only a scratch, a couple stitches or twelve and a tetanus shot and you'll be fine.'

'Fine? Fine?' Mad Mick demanded. 'My arm's hangin' by a sliver here! Ah could get a job as that bloody wan-armed guy the Fugitive fella chases on the telly!'

'So what're you complaining about? Did pretty well for the first one. He got to work with David Janssen and Harrison Ford, didn't he?'

'Well, that's helluva nice, intit?' Mad Mick demanded. 'Ye come back then run away again, leavin' yer ain beloved bleedin' tae death here, *and* you show callous disregard an' a'! This will cost ye, y'know! Ah'll sue, Darling!'

Back at Andy's laugh-in Marylka tuned in again.

'He wasnae annoyed at bein' stabbed,' Andy was saying. 'He was doin' his nut because he thought the druggie was tryin' tae kill *me*! Took two cops an' me tae drag him off, he'd completely lost the heid, roarin' like a bull an' screamin' blue murder!'

'Will somebody dae somethin'?' Mad Mick demanded from behind the assembled company. 'Get me a priest!'

'Ye're no' a Catholic!' Andy replied. 'Whit d'ye want a priest for? Anythin' for effect!'

'Ah am *so* a bloody Catholic!' Mick yelled.

'Ye canny be a Catholic, Ah'd have known that!' Andy said. 'Ye're at it ya mad bugger!'

'Ah am *not* at it!' Mad Mick retorted. 'Whit dae ye want? Four verses o' "Faith of Our Fathers"?'

'Ah wouldnae advise it, ya evil swine ye!' Andy replied. 'A' these years Ah've been drivin' ye aboot an' you've been drivin' me crazy, an' ye never tellt me ye were a Catholic afore!' Andy shouted at him.

'Noo whit the hell would Ah tell you that for? It's nae bloody business o' yours is it?' Mad Mick shouted back. Then he looked at Marylka again. 'I would however be prepared to dump the Pope for you, Darling!' the playboy said, smiling horrifically at her.

'The name Michael didn't perhaps give you a clue then, Andy?' Marylka asked quietly.

'Naw, it didnae!' he responded. 'These days there's perfectly nice, normal people ca'ed Tim names, ye canny always judge by that!' He turned again to the prone figure of Mad Mick. 'Well,' he continued, deeply wounded by his partner's deception, 'ye picked yer time tae let me in on that secret by the way! A' these years Ah've been discussing Rangers strategy wi' ye, thinkin', *sure* ye wur wanna us, an' you've probably been phonin' up Parkheid oan the quiet an' tellin' them every move! Well, frae noo oan Ah'll be singing "The Sash" at the start o' every shift, see how ye like that!'

'You dare!' Mad Mick yelled back.

'Whit's up, Michael?' Andy wheedled. 'Ah'm only tryin' tae inject a bitta humour intae the situation, just livenin' things up like! In fact Ah'll gie ye a few choruses right noo!' He opened his mouth and began to sing, dancing about in front of Mad

Mick's bed of pain. 'Oh the sash my father used to wear —'

'Just you bloody dare, ya, ya *Animal* ye!' Mick responded, sitting up and shaking his fist so hard he almost fell on to the floor.

'Noo, noo Michael!' Andy said soothingly. 'Ye must learn tae control that temper! It's like Ah've always said, it'll be the death o' ye wanna these days. Christ!' he said, rubbing his hands together as he turned to address his audience once again. 'But Ah've waited *years* tae be able tae say that tae him!'

'Oh,' Marylka thought happily, 'it's so *good* to be home again!'

29

The plan had to stay on hold till the right conditions came along. She needed a dry day with a gentle breeze, not a howling gale, or even a slight wind, and it had finally come in late September. She called Rob, Annie and Young Hector, and Betty, Will and Neil, who were staying at Helen's house, and told them where to meet her. Rob arrived first. Just once it would be nice to see Rob dash in very late, looking as though he had slept in or grabbed the first clothes he could find, but it would never happen, she knew that.

'Are you sure about this?' he asked disapprovingly.
'Yes,' she replied.
'It seems very silly to me,' he opined.
'I'm sure it does, Rob.'
Annie was next. 'Hello there, Rabbie, son,' she greeted Rob. 'Written any good poems lately?'
He smiled meanly in reply.
'Miserable sod!' she muttered to Marylka.

Betty, Will and Neil arrived in a taxi just after Young Hector. She was amazed to see that Neil was wearing a suit and tie, but he still looked gorgeous.

Annie nudged Marylka. 'Now *that*,' she said with heavy emphasis, 'is what I call a stoatir! If I were a few years younger,' she patted her jet-black hair with her scarlet painted nails and nodded to Neil, who smiled back at her. 'To hell with the age difference!' Annie said. 'I've always wanted a toyboy!'

'Rob *hates* him!' Marylka whispered.

'Well, are you surprised?' Annie whispered back. 'Look at the difference between them. Chalk and, well. My God, he's good enough to eat!'

Marylka joined Betty and her family. 'So what's with the suit then?' she asked Neil.

He looked embarrassed and ran a finger around his shirt collar.

'Och, it's Gran!' he replied. 'Nothing will convince her that everybody in Glasgow doesn't wear their Sunday best all the time! How people wear these things at all beats me, I feel like a trussed chicken!'

She looked around. 'No Murder?' she asked Neil.

'No Murder,' he grinned. 'My Da doesn't much like the mainland, he says it's "just a big noise", ironic as that seems! He and Lachie once went across on the boat, and when it reached Oban they got off. Da said "Right, Lachie, that's us been, nobody can ever accuse us of not trying the mainland." Then they turned round and got back on the boat again for the return journey.'

'It's not that I'm disappointed,' she laughed, 'though I did wonder what he and Rob would make of each other!'

'Och,' said Neil, glancing at Rob dismissively, 'Da would have that one in therapy for months if their paths ever crossed!'

And even stranger than Neil in a suit was the sight of Young Hector wearing slacks and a sweatshirt. Admittedly it was an Armani sweatshirt, but a sweatshirt all the same, and for Young Hector even designer casual meant serious dressing down. She hugged Betty as Uriah Heep pulled up last of all, handed the urn to Marylka and made a swift getaway. You could see by his expression that he did not approve of these goings-on, or maybe he was still smarting from his previous encounters with Marylka over Helen's funeral.

She arranged the family, both official and unofficial, to stand in front of the Fruit Market Theatre, then crossed the road to the Ramshorn, which would for ever be the Firemen's Church. She went inside and began climbing. As the steeple rose the spiral staircase inside grew narrower. On the first level, where the four clocks faced in different directions, there were tiny windows behind the workings, and on the next were downward-facing slats covered with wire mesh to keep the pigeons and starlings out. She looked up and was delighted to see the bell still hanging in the roof. The rumour that the bell had gone had been a great sadness to Helen, the Ramshorn bell had been part of her childhood memories. 'Look, Mum!' she said to the urn clutched in her hands. 'The bell *is* still here!' Finally, with her shoulders touching the sides, she reached a hatch on the next level, leading on to a small, flat roof. Marylka climbed through. There was a shallow balustrade at the edge, but it didn't look as though it would prevent you from falling if you slipped. She looked down; the ground was about a hundred feet below, she reckoned, lucky she had never suffered from vertigo. Slowly and carefully she opened the urn and gently emptied Helen's ashes on to the flat roof, then she reached into her pocket, brought out a bottle of Helen's favourite 'Sublime' perfume and sprayed into the air in a wide arc. Helen never went anywhere without her perfume, so why should she this time? 'This is it, Mum,' she said quietly. 'But it's not exactly goodbye, because you'll always be here. Here's lookin' at you, kid, as Humph the Dumph would say!' She smiled, remembering Helen's tight lipped reaction to her parodies of Humphrey Bogart. Leaving Helen's ashes on the roof of the Ramshorn she eased through the hatch, back down the spiral staircase, and ran across the road to where the others were waiting.

It was the perfect ending. The gentle breeze would carry Helen to every nook and cranny along Ingram Street, over the cobbles, past the fire station, and up High Street and Castle Street to the Calton. She could visit Auntie Mary and Millie in the crypt across the road anytime she wanted to, borne on the softest wind to all the places she loved for evermore. It was the nearest thing to a time machine Marylka could give her, and somewhere along the route she might even renew her acquaintance with a certain 'wee loast ginger dug'. As Helen departed into the sky over Glasgow, it had crossed Marylka's mind to ask the assembled company to join her in a few identical verses and choruses of the Goons' famous anthem, but she decided that might just be gilding the lily, so instead she sang it to herself. She put her arm around Betty's waist as they watched Helen taking to the air, and on the other side Neil draped his arm around her shoulders. Rob stood watching a little apart from the others, the words 'big, hairy, tartan-clad, macho man' clearly written in his expression.

'Rob,' she said, 'I was thinking. About Auntie Mary and Millie . . .'

'No, Marylka!' he said firmly. 'We are *not* going down that road! Do you know how difficult and time-consuming an application to exhume is? Leave them where they are!'

'It was just a thought,' she said, smiling again at how easy it still was to wind him up.

'Besides,' smiled Young Hector, 'I think it's better to leave Bloody Mary lying there beside him, as an everlasting thorn in the miserable old teuchter's flesh. Don't you?'

'Ying Tong Tiddle-i-Po. Amen!' said Marylka.

In the Cheapside fire of 1960, the walls of the bonded warehouse collapsed onto the firemen fighting the blaze, killing nineteen. These photos show what was left of one fire engine.

The morning after the Cheapside fire, and the horror on the faces of the people in this photo is clear to see. Glasgow has always held its firemen in great affection, and those who were alive in 1960 still have vivid memories of Cheapside. Particularly striking is the obvious shock and distress of the young fireman in the foreground.

A view of the Old Fruit Market in 1955, taken from Candleriggs and looking towards St David's church, known in Glasgow as the Ramshorn Kirk, in Ingram Street. With the Central Fire Station a few hundred yards further along Ingram Street, it was also known as the 'Firemen's Church', and it was the focus of the funeral services for the men killed in the Cheapside blaze.

1964 and horses and carts were still in use in the Old Fruit Market. The horses often slipped and fell on the cobbled streets, or bolted in the bustle, and local children would sit around in the expectation of entertainment and the fruit scattered from the cart.

SOURCES

Convoy, John Winton (Michael Joseph)
The Merchant Seaman's War, Tony Lane (Bluecoat Press)
For the Sake of Example, Anthony Babington (Leo Cooper, 1993)
Shot at Dawn, Julian Putkowski & Julian Sykes (Leo Cooper, 1998)
'Shot at Dawn', BBC Reporting Scotland
'Air Fasdadh' (trans. 'Domestic Servants'), Media nan Eilean for BBC
  Eorpa

Meg Henderson

The Holy City

'*The Holy City* is a novel about growing up in the close-knit blue-collar community of Clydeside from the Twenties through to the present day, as seen through the eyes of Marion Katie MacLeod. Meg Henderson has pieced together an enormous jigsaw of memories to create a vision reminiscent of a Stanley Spencer painting. The overall effect is of being at your auntie's, of listening to an enthusiastic storyteller, of the fascination of taking a microscope to seemingly ordinary lives, seemingly mundane situations and bringing them into dramatic focus.'   *Scotland on Sunday*

'An enchanting tale of a remarkable woman from Clydebank, whose sometimes heartbreaking, sometimes hilarious but always mesmerising memories of the wartime blitz on her beloved town stay sharp half a century later, giving her the strength and the courage to meet everything that life throws at her.'   *Scotsman*

'This marvellous debut is packed with characters whose grittiness and passion transcends poverty and tragedy.'   *Options*

'A hugely absorbing story. Henderson brings the horror and pain of these wartime experiences vividly to life with vigorous humour, common-sense wisdom and vitality.'   *Observer*

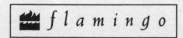 *flamingo*

Katharine McMahon

Footsteps

The women in Helena Mayrick's family have always led secretive and tragic lives. For generations they lived on the crumbling Suffolk coast which both nurtured and haunted them. When Helena's comfortable marriage is devastated by her husband's violent death, it seems that she, too, is locked into the cycle.

Helena is invited to research a book on her grandfather, H. Donaldson, the celebrated Edwardian photographer. At first, she is reluctant to immerse herself in family history, particularly as Donaldson's relationship with her grandmother, Ruth, is shrouded in mystery and turmoil. But gradually, as the story of enigmatic Ruth and the elusive, passionate Donaldson unfolds, Helena finds that the past, like the present, was shaped by cruel dilemmas and the demands of love . . .

'This well-shaped and lovingly-crafted novel of domestic drama and emotion offers satisfying rewards. The theme of *Footsteps* – that of the effects of misplaced, frequently repressed love and passion on succeeding generations of women – is put together with intelligence and feeling, a grasp of narrative pace and an empathy for the weather-buffetted Suffolk coast where it is set. The author's touch is appealingly fresh and she succeeds in suggesting the complexity, waywardness and inexplicable patches that constitute life. A good read.'   ELIZABETH BUCHAN, *The Times*

'Irreducibly delicate and tough-minded.'
BRIAN MORTON, *TES*

flamingo

Gretta Mulrooney

Araby

'Tenderly funny and genuinely moving. I loved it.'

FIONA MORROW, *Time Out*

'On hearing of Kitty Keenan's admittance to hospital, her grown-up son Rory returns to Ireland to comfort his father and await the diagnosis . . . Rory's narrative, charting the steady decline of her health, is interspersed with a series of flashbacks through which Kitty emerges larger than life. For Rory, these snapshots of the past are part of a process of unpicking the odd tangle of love and petty grievances that characterise familial relationships. Mulrooney's ability to make sense of the contradictions in clear, precise prose is the most remarkable achievement of the novel. A beautifully observed study of reconciliation, *Araby* makes astute points about conflict and shifting values between generations.'

JAMES EVE, *The Times*

'Kitty is a magnificent diva of discontent: contradictory, ludicrous, sharp-witted, thick-skinned, the sort of character best enjoyed from a distance . . . The narrative of her decline and death is worked with frequent flashbacks to Kitty's heyday, and her enthusiasm for Catholicism, medicament, hobbies and quarrelling . . . What is admirable about Mulrooney's writing is the way she manages to keep the tone buoyant, while alluding to many heartbreaking strands of family history. For both Kitty and Rory, this is a story of gallant survival.'

RUTH PAVEY, *Independent*

flamingo

Meera Syal

Anita and Me

'A marvellous crash course in Asian/Brummie culture. Funny, moving and packed full of wonderful surprises.'

Like every nine-year-old girl, Meena can't wait to grow up and break free from her parents. But, as the daughter of the only Punjabi family in the mining village of Tollington, her fight for independence is different from most.

Meena wants fishfingers and chips, not just chapati and dhal; she wants an English Christmas, not the interminable Punjabi festivities she has to attend with her embarrassing Aunties and dreadful cousins, Pinky and Baby – but more than anything, more than mini-skirts, make-up and the freedom to watch *Opportunity Knocks*, Meena wants to roam the backyards of working-class Tollington with the feisty Anita Rutter and her gang . . .

With great warmth and brilliantly observed dialogue, Meera Syal creates a superb cast of characters, from the wise and devious old Nanima to the curious Mr Worrall, stranded in his front room since the war. Written with extraordinary grace and charm, and just a hint of wistfulness, *Anita and Me* is a unique vision of a British childhood in the Sixties, a childhood caught between two cultures, each on the brink of enormous change.

'A wonderful book – very funny and very moving. *Tom Sawyer* meets *Cider With Rosie* en route to India via Wolverhampton. Treat yourself.'

flamingo

Isabel Allende

Paula

'Allende's best work to date . . . she has everything it takes:
the ear, the eye, the mind, the heart, the all-encompassing
humanity.' *New York Times*

In December 1991, Isabel Allende's daughter Paula became
gravely ill and fell into a coma.

'Allende's writing is so vivid we smell the countryside, hear
the sounds, see the bright birds, smell and even taste the soft
fruit. Moving through Paula's last days, we enter that world,
and share it, gladly, sadly, gratefully, and ultimately changed
by the very reading of it.' JULIA NEUBERGER, *The Times*

'This is a tender, moving and vivid record of a mother's
agony at the bedside of her daughter. *Paula* begins as a long
letter as a way of giving her back the life that is ebbing away
. . . the result is a mesmerising story. In flawlessly rich prose
Allende shares with us her most intimate feelings. An
emotionally charged, spellbinding memoir.'
GABRIELLA DE FERRARI, *Washington Post*

'Allende brings us the natural storytelling power so evident
in her novels to this courageous testament. She shares her
personal tragedy with a warmth and passion that make *Paula*
exceptional.' CLARE BRISTOW, *Sunday Express*

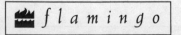 *flamingo*